KT-873-272

The Christmas Party

Carole Matthews

sphere

SPHERE

First published in Great Britain in 2014 by Sphere

Copyright © Carole Matthews 2014

The moral right of the author has been asserted.

*All characters and events in this publication, other than those
clearly in the public domain, are fictitious and any resemblance
to real persons, living or dead, is purely coincidental.*

All rights reserved.
No part of this publication may be reproduced, stored in a
retrieval system, or transmitted, in any form or by any means, without
the prior permission in writing of the publisher, nor be otherwise circulated
in any form of binding or cover other than that in which it is published
and without a similar condition including this condition being
imposed on the subsequent purchaser.

A CIP catalogue record for this book
is available from the British Library.

' ISBN 978-0-7515-5217-1

Typeset in Sabon by M Rules
Printed and bound in Great Britain by
Clays Ltd, St Ives plc

Papers used by Sphere are from well-managed forests
and other responsible sources.

MIX
Paper from
responsible sources
FSC® C104740

Sphere
An imprint of
Little, Brown Book Group
100 Victoria Embankment
London EC4Y 0DY

An Hachette UK Company
www.hachette.co.uk

www.littlebrown.co.uk

Merry Christmas!

Thanks for choosing to delve into my novel, *The Christmas Party*, which is amazingly my 25th book. That's worth a celebration! I hope you're feeling suitably festive or, if you're not quite there yet, that this story gets you in the party mood.

Now I'm an author, I work mainly alone. Although I do share an office with my partner, Lovely Kev. When it comes to our office Christmas parties, they're quite sedate affairs. We go to a very posh restaurant – the same one every year – with one other couple. We have a very convivial time with canapés and *amuse bouches* served. We may drink a little too much but no one snogs someone inappropriate in the stationery cupboard and we don't even have a photocopier! But I remember a time when I did work in proper offices for large companies and I've also served my time as a corporate wife. Back in the day, I went to some very raucous Christmas parties – some that involved not only red faces the next day, but disciplinary action and resignations. Oh dear. So I've drawn on my considerable experience to bring you a riotous tale of the office Christmas party.

If you do go to a Christmas party this year, I hope that you have a fabulous time and have only wonderful memories of it. With every good wish for the festive season!

Love, Carole ☺ xx

Also by Carole Matthews

Let's Meet on Platform 8
A Whiff of Scandal
More to Life than This
For Better, For Worse
A Minor Indiscretion
A Compromising Position
The Sweetest Taboo
With or Without You
You Drive Me Crazy
Welcome to the Real World
The Chocolate Lovers' Club
The Chocolate Lovers' Diet
It's a Kind of Magic
All You Need is Love
The Difference a Day Makes
That Loving Feeling
It's Now or Never
The Only Way is Up
Wrapped up in You
Summer Daydreams
With Love at Christmas
A Cottage by the Sea
Calling Mrs Christmas
A Place to Call Home

To my dear friend Bern,
for fun and inspiration.

The Day of the Christmas Party

Chapter One

'You need to have eyes in the back of your head with that one, Louise Young. You mark my words.' Karen from Customer Accounts gives me a meaningful look and inclines her head towards my dear boss's office. 'There was a scandal involving his last personal assistant, you know.'

I didn't.

She leans forward and checks that no one's listening. Quite unlikely when there are only the two of us here.

'There was talk all over the office about *an affair*.' The last bit is whispered, feigning discretion while she clearly relishes sharing the gossip. 'She was a nice girl too. By all accounts.'

I'm sure she was.

'Everyone called her Knicker-Dropper Debbie after what happened.'

'Wow.'

'Oh, yeah.' Karen flicks the tinsel she's wearing as a feather boa and examines her nails. Her reputation as the office oracle is a source of great pride to her. I only met her a few weeks ago, when she kindly helped me with a query about one of Tyler's clients, but I already feel as if she's been a good friend to me. She's been showing me the ropes at Fossil Oil and I'm glad of her insights. There's nothing she doesn't know.

So I'm also hoping that Karen is my best bet in relieving my current plight. It's fair to say that I'm experiencing certain difficulties at Fossil Oil, and up to now I've been trying to handle them by myself, but I can't hold it in any longer. Anyway, I've finally taken my courage in both hands and spilled the beans, confiding my woes to Karen. She doesn't look surprised at all, which worries me even more.

Deep breath. Here goes. I hate to admit it but my boss, Tyler Benson, takes every opportunity to touch, grope or brush against me. I've never encountered anything like this before and I'm at a loss. I just don't know how to deal with it. He's my boss, my senior here. I should be looking up to him, learning from him. He should be mentoring me, teaching me. I shouldn't spend my days running round my desk to keep away from him like I'm in a Benny Hill comedy. It's got to stop and I'm hoping that Karen, as she clearly knows the score here at Fossil Oil, might have some bright ideas.

Besides, who else can I tell? I'm the new girl and I don't feel I can go running straight to Human Resources the minute something goes wrong. What would that look like? They might think I'm too weak to manage my job. I'm a responsible grown-up and have to show that I can stand up to Tyler and sort this out myself. But, believe me, I think I've done all I can to communicate to him that I'd rather he kept his distance and didn't paw me. However, it seems to be like water off a duck's back to Tyler. Which is tricky, because on the one hand I love my new job and really need to maintain a good relationship with him. But on the other hand I don't want things to carry on like this.

'You need to tread carefully with Tyler,' Karen warns. 'He's such a slimy toad, everyone knows that, yet he can do no wrong in this place.'

'Why?'

'Brilliant salesman. That's all this company is bothered

about.' Karen deals with the tea she's brought from the vending machine for us both, stirring this way and that with a plastic spoon in a ponderous manner. 'I can't stand him, but you can't deny that he knows how to play the corporate game.'

I think I realised that on day one.

'When it all blew up, poor Debbie was the one who was squeezed out, not Golden Balls.' Tea dispensed, Karen continues to play with her tinsel adornment. 'You don't want that.'

I most certainly don't.

Karen and I had a tea-break date to meet up in the staff canteen but at my request she's come to my office instead. If I don't use this short time to put up some Christmas decorations in here, there won't be any at all. Tomorrow is Christmas Eve and I need to get a move on or I'll miss the boat completely. There are some fabulous, outsize baubles hanging in the main atrium of the building, but the rest of the place is bare. I'd hate it if I didn't mark Christmas at all in my own office. How miserable would that be?

'I don't know why you're bothering,' Karen says, nodding towards my stash of decorations as I blow up yet another balloon.

I pinch the top closed and take a breather. 'It's Christmas. I want it to look pretty.'

Karen waves a hand at my decorations. 'Christmas a-go-go.'

'Likey?'

'Lovey. They're too good for this place.'

They're actually mostly bits and bobs that I brought from home. Mum and Dad have boxes and boxes of the stuff in the loft, lovingly gathered over the years. They are the king and queen of Christmas junk and they didn't mind me pinching a few bits to liven this place up. I think Mum was quite relieved that I was taking some of it off her hands. Our loft must be like the Tardis. She's accumulated so much Christmas stuff over the

3

years, there's barely room for the humans once she gets it all out. Still, I have to say that they don't look too bad at all.

'It'll be nice,' I assure Karen.

My friend shrugs her indifference to my attempts to be festive. I've not been here at the Fossil Oil Corporation for very long – just a few months – and now Karen has taken me under her wing, and for that I'm very grateful. This is a massive, fast-moving, glamorous company and I so want to get everything right.

'Tyler Benson is *far* too important for them to lose him, Louise. It's the likes of us – the oppressed masses – who get the boot when things go pear-shaped.'

I sigh. 'How very depressing.'

'Better to keep your tits covered and your gob shut and hold him at arm's length for as long as you possibly can. He might get bored and leave you alone.'

'But he'll only do it to someone else. It's sexual harassment or something. He shouldn't be allowed to get away with it.'

She shrugs again. 'You can try to fight it if you want to, but don't say I didn't warn you when they're handing you your P45.'

'That's something I can't risk. This is the first decent job that I've had since Mia was born.'

'She's four now?'

I nod. 'Not long before she's five.'

Karen looks at the picture I have on my desk. 'Pretty like her mum.'

Mia is a pretty girl, and I don't think I'm saying that just because I'm her mum. She's got my brown hair and deep blue eyes, my creamy colouring. A chip off the old block, but with a sprinkle of extra cuteness. There's very little of her father in her, which I'm always thankful for. Mia is definitely her mother's daughter. My heart warms just to think of her and I miss her

4

every minute of the day when I'm away from her. 'She started school in September, which freed me up to rush back to the big bad world of work.' And, by some divine miracle, I've bagged myself a really great job.

'What did you do before you had her?'

'I was behind the counter in a bank. Being a cashier wasn't the best job in the world. You've seen those uniforms. But I didn't mind it. The hours were OK, the pay all right, and there were even prospects for advancement. At least, there were when I started.'

'So why leave?'

'By the time I was due to return from maternity leave, my branch had been closed, and they wanted me to go over to Bedford, which would have meant travelling miles to work every day – a good hour each way in rush hour. With a new baby, I didn't think I could manage that.'

'Bummer.'

'Tell me about it.'

I've bought a pretty Christmas tree for the office, which stands on top of the low filing cabinet as if it were tailored for the space. It's the only thing I've splashed out on. It was cheap and cheerful in Home Bargains but it glows with different colours and there's a sweet star on the top. I bought one for Mia too, in pink, for her bedroom. I abandon the balloons for the moment and climb on to my desk to pin another pretty gold-coloured garland into the corner.

'I was struggling enough just trying to get through the day at home,' I tell Karen as I drive my drawing pin home, hoping it holds. 'I had no idea how much work a baby was until I had Mia.' I smile at my own naïvety.

'Why do you think I haven't got any kids?' Karen shudders at the thought.

'The bank couldn't – or wouldn't – offer me part-time hours

5

either, which, apart from the inevitable drop in money, might have helped a bit.'

If I'm honest, my life was a total mess then. Looking back, I think I had a touch of the baby blues, but you never really want to acknowledge that, do you? So I was trying to soldier on when I just felt exhausted and overwhelmed by it all.

I jump down, cross the office trailing the garland in my wake and, using a chair as a ladder, fix it diagonally across the ceiling. Maybe I should have got my mum to come in for an hour after work to do this. That would have been a plan. She'd have been in her element and I'd love to show off my posh office to her. She's been so supportive while I've been out of work and I want to make her proud of me. I want her to see that I'm getting my act back together.

'Was there a *Mr* Young on the scene?' Karen asks. 'Couldn't he have helped?'

'Mia was a good baby, but Steve and I were going through a really difficult time. We'd never had the easiest of relationships, and after Mia was born he just got worse and worse.' I shrug, as if the pain isn't still there when I talk about this. 'Mum and Dad were trying to help, but they were having to tiptoe round Steve too as he didn't like them in our house too much. He said that they invaded our privacy. They fuss, my parents, but they have hearts of gold. Steve could never see that side of them: they just irritated him beyond belief.'

'Sounds like a twat.'

'Yeah.' I can't disagree with her succinct assessment. I still wonder now what I saw in him. He was a bad boy and I should have run a mile in the opposite direction when we first met.

To shift the image, I turn my attention back to the balloons, tying them into bunches with elastic bands. I'd like to say that there's some sort of colour scheme, but there isn't. This is a party pack of assorted colours, so I'm having to take pot luck and lump it. Besides, when it comes to Christmas, colour co-ordination is vastly overrated.

'With all that going on, I really don't know if I could have coped with the stresses and strains of modern-day banking anyway,' I confess. My confidence in myself was at an all-time low. If anyone had snapped at me, there would have been tears. 'There are hardly any front-line staff left now, just rows of cash machines and lots of grumpy customers who, quite rightly, complain that there aren't any staff. I didn't have the strength to face going back to that, so I gave in my notice, hoping I'd find another job quickly. Turns out I was way too optimistic. I hadn't bargained on how hard the recession had made it to move around in the job market.'

'It's tough out there,' Karen agrees. 'My sister's been out of work for ages, and she went to university and everything.'

That's another reason why I feel so lucky to have got this position. How many kids have gone through university, only to find themselves doing menial jobs on minimum wage? Or, worse, not employed at all.

'So where's Mia's dad now? I assume you're not together any more.'

Shaking my head, I pin the balloons so that they blossom out from the corners. 'He walked out on me and Mia while all that was going on and we haven't seen hide nor hair of him since. Last I heard, he was running a bar in Spain, ducking and diving, which would suit Steve down to the ground.'

Good riddance too. He was so controlling that, when he went, it was the first time in years that I felt I could breathe freely without asking anyone's permission.

'You could give me a hand instead of sitting there on your bum,' I say to Karen.

'Nah. Christmas is not my bag. Can't stand it. You're making a great job of it. Knock yourself out.'

The only problem – and it was quite a major one – was that he stopped paying his half of the mortgage on our tiny house the day he left.

My debts, of course, started racking up instantly. I wasn't working and was struggling to get another job. Spending all day at home alone with Mia had me slowly tearing my hair out. I tried to manage on my own but it was just so hard. When I contacted the mortgage company to tell them of my situation, they foreclosed on the loan and I had no option but to sell the house.

It went for less than Steve and I had paid for it, so I was instantly in negative equity. Yet it still broke my heart to leave. It was just a tiny, terraced place with a garden the size of a handkerchief, but it was in a good area and it was home. My home. Mine and Mia's. I kept it spick and span as I've inherited the house-proud gene from my mum.

'We had to move back in with my mum and dad,' I tell Karen. 'That was the only downside.'

What could I do? There was no way I could downsize: there's nowhere smaller to go than minuscule. To rent somewhere was even more expensive than the mortgage had been, so that was out of the question too. Eventually, and with much soul-searching, the only option was to go home to Mum and Dad. Thank goodness they were more than willing to take me in. Bless their hearts.

But Karen doesn't need to know all this. Some things are better kept to myself.

'If I had to live with my parents we'd all kill each other within a week,' she chips in.

'To be honest, it was such a relief. Mum and Dad swept in and looked after us both, as I knew they would.'

'They sound great.'

'They are.' Throughout my life, they've just taken everything I throw at them with stoic supportiveness. 'Mum looked after

Mia and I got a job in Boots, mainly stacking shelves. It wasn't great, but it brought some money in.' Not enough to pay off the twenty grand I still owe on the house though. At least my sanity slowly returned. With my parents helping me, I got back on my feet and my confidence started to come back too. 'That was fine for a while. I was doing a job that wasn't very demanding and I could concentrate on giving Mia a good start. With my mum and dad's financial support, I could spend more time with her, but I couldn't rely on them for ever. It wasn't fair.'

To be honest, they've never uttered a word of complaint. But I got to a point where I began to believe that I had so much more to offer the world than making sure its favourite brand of toothpaste was always to hand. Not that there's anything wrong with that. I just wanted to find something with a bit of a challenge and with more opportunities to progress.

'So now Mia's at school all day and it's time for you to strike out again,' Karen says.

'Yeah. Just because I'm a single mum, it doesn't mean I'm on the scrapheap. I've got so much to offer, and doing it for my daughter has given me the drive I need. I'd love to have the cash to buy Mia little treats and make her proud of me.'

I want to turn my life around. I want to be someone who's going places. I want to pay off all of my debts. I want to make sure I've got a good, steady income and our own home.

Standing back, I admire my handiwork. 'Do you think I've put enough up?'

'Depends what you're aiming for. You passed the bounds of good taste with those balloons, but you've not yet achieved Santa's-grotto level.'

'Then we need more.' I delve into Mum's boxes. A trio of white glittery reindeer statues that we bought together in Next a few years ago. Perfect.

That's why I feel so very fortunate to have landed this position at Fossil Oil after such a long gap. Despite my parents' assurances that any company would be lucky to have me, I'd been bruised by too many rejections and was terrified that my skills were just too rusty. Yet, despite my worst fears and insecurities, this time round I got a job quite quickly.

'I only had five other interviews before I landed this job.'

'Result!'

'It's been a steep learning curve, but I feel I'm holding my own here.'

'Everyone likes you,' Karen says.

Which is nice to hear.

'The money's good, the job's fantastic. I've no complaints on that score . . .'

'The only problem is that Tyler is very free with his hands and his smutty comments,' she concludes.

'Yes.' I hug the biggest reindeer to me. 'Now I've been given this chance, I want to really make something of myself.' The last few years have been hell. Absolute hell. If it wasn't for the love of my mum and dad and my darling daughter, I don't know how I'd have survived.

It's not been easy though. Who wants to go home to their parents at the age of twenty-nine, a single mum with a daughter in tow? They've been great though. The best. They've never once been judgemental about my poor choice of partner or the debts that are haunting me. And they're the most perfect grandparents anyone could have. They've done nothing but lavish love on Mia. She, in turn, absolutely adores them. I know I'm lucky – incredibly lucky – to have their love and support. But there's no escaping the fact that I'm back in the room I last inhabited when I was eighteen.

That's why there's no way on God's earth I'm going to let some jumped-up little toad like Tyler Benson spoil it for me.

Chapter Two

The Fossil Oil offices are fabulous, befitting a company with money pouring out of its ears. When I first started working here, I felt intimidated just walking through the doors. The central glass-walled atrium is enough to take your breath away. It towers right the way through the building and there's a bit in the middle that's filled with an profusion of exotic plants. Splodgy artwork abounds – though most of it looks as if it has been daubed by Mia. There's a lovely coffee shop in reception just for employees, and glass elevators whisk you up to the offices. Mine's on the third floor, with a fab view over the cityscape of Milton Keynes. It's wonderful. There's a white desk and lime-green filing cabinets and I have it all to myself.

Yet, in truth I'd rather be out in the department with everyone else, where they have open-plan cubicles. Then Tyler Benson would have less opportunity to touch me up.

'Is all this festive bling getting you in the mood for the Christmas party tonight?' Karen asks, eyeing the reindeers suspiciously.

'Yes. Deffo.'

Despite her disdainful glance, I deploy the trio of reindeers in a line along the windowsill and then look out over the city. The vast expanse of sky is heavy with the threat of snow. I wonder, will we have a white Christmas this year? Mia would love it. Last time there was really heavy snow at Christmas she was too small to enjoy it. This year we could be out there building snowmen together. No doubt her indulgent grandad will buy her a little pink plastic sledge – I've seen him eyeing them up in Homebase for weeks. It's sad really, as that should be a job for her own dad; he has no idea what he's missing out on by not having his child in his life.

The offices are stark, though, very minimalist, and didn't feel very Christmassy. I do like to get a bit festive. I'm all for Christmas, despite the extra expense, which everyone could do without. It's even more lovely now that I do it all for Mia to make it special for her. My mum and dad used to go all out for me and my brother at Christmas and I've sort of carried on the tradition.

'I've never been to a posh do like this before,' I confide to Karen. The Christmas party is being held at Wadestone Manor. I had a quick Google of it a few days ago and the place looks amazing. A big stately home in the middle of nowhere. 'I'm not sure what to expect.'

'The party's usually OK. A bit boring. All the top bosses rock up so everyone has to mind their manners. Hopefully they'll all go home early and we can let our hair down. It livens it up if you can cop off with someone in another department,' Karen continues, even though I've only got half an ear on her chatter. 'There's no way I'm going home on my own tonight.'

I roll my eyes at her.

'This year should be a bit better. We've all been nice little employees and made them lots of money so they're putting on a big show for us. There's a free bar too. Yay! It'll make a change getting something back for once.' Karen claps her hands together excitedly. 'Look, I've had my nails done.' She holds them out for me to admire. 'I'm having my hair done later and

I've got a new dress. It's very A-list. I wouldn't look out of place on a red carpet.'

'I haven't got a new dress.' My old faithful LBD will be pulled out of the cupboard and pressed into service once more. 'I'm having my hair done though.' A rare treat.

'You should get an up-do,' she advises, piling her own mass of blonde hair on to her head and striking a pose. 'Sexy.'

I'm not sure that 'sexy' is the look I'm going for. 'Moderately attractive yet definitely unavailable' is my goal, and I hope my hairdresser can do something with me. It might be an ask too far. The last time I bought conditioner it was from Poundland, and I can't even remember when it ran out. Consequently I have the hair of Kate Middleton but without the gloss, bounce or insanely expensive celebrity cut.

'I could give you the name of the woman who does my nails,' Karen offers. 'She's a wonder. She might be able to squeeze you in later.'

I shake my head. 'Can't afford it.'

There's no way I'd ever tell Karen the truth about the parlous state of my bank account. That's my problem and mine alone. The nearest I'm going to get to a manicure is, if I've got five minutes to spare later, I'll see if I can squeeze a bit out of one of the half-dozen used bottles of nail polish that are tucked away at the back of my drawer, supposedly out of Mia's reach. Though I did recently come home to find Gramps sporting neon-pink nails and I'm sure it wasn't because he has a secret side to him and likes to be called Geraldine at weekends. It had Mia's stamp all over it.

To me, the office still seems under-garlanded and so I pull two more out of the box. Perhaps I should put some decorations in Tyler's office as a sign of peace, but then I think he might take it as a sign of something else and decide against it. If anyone could misconstrue festive decorations as foreplay then it

13

would be Tyler Benson. These concertina garlands are taking a bit of untangling and I suspect that's because they've been in the loft since I was in nappies. Maybe longer. But vintage is the new contemporary, right?

Karen doesn't seem to mind that I'm slightly distracted by my task and finally abandons her chair to stand and hand me drawing pins. I've obviously guilted her into being festive.

'I got off with Kelvin Smith from Business Management last year,' she says. 'We had a high old time. Shagged me ragged for weeks. It was bliss. And, then, well . . . ' She twiddles her hair in her fingers. 'You know what it's like.'

I tut my sympathy, even though I haven't a clue what it's like. I can't remember the last time I was shagged ragged – or even dated anyone for more than a couple of nights. I've been resolutely celibate since Steve left.

I stretch up to pin my second tranche of garlands, on tiptoe on my desk. I want them criss-crossing the office, dipping nearly to head height in the middle. To make sure it exceeds all bounds of good taste, I add even more balloons. I must try to get a bit fitter. Clearly, running round after a four-year-old doesn't count as cardiovascular exercise as I'd hoped. I'm out of breath after blowing up a dozen of these babies. They look nice though.

'Retro tat' is Karen's considered verdict.

'I don't think you can be too tacky when it comes to Christmas decorations.'

Karen grimaces. 'If you say so.'

I stand back on my desk, pleased as Punch with my handiwork. Now it's starting to look a lot like Christmas. I wonder if Tyler would object to me playing a few Christmas songs in the office.

Then the man himself, my octopus boss Mr Tyler Benson, sales director of Fossil Oil, sweeps into the office and I feel myself automatically tense.

'Good Christ!' he exclaims. 'What's all this crap? Anyone would think it was Christmas.'

He's a good-looking man, there's no denying it. He's in his early forties, I'd say. Always immaculately groomed. I bet his watch cost more than I earn in six months. He's got closely cropped hair, which may be an attempt to disguise a burgeoning bald spot, and I suspect he really, really hates the sprinkling of grey that graces his temples. His eyes are steely grey like polished pewter and, try as I might, I can see no warmth in them. They are the eyes of a ruthless go-getter, a shark. Eyes that say 'No one will stand in my way.'

'Still, nice view,' he quips and I can see him trying to get a sneaky look up my skirt.

I've taken to dressing like a frump since I've been working here. I'm usually all polo-neck jumpers and loose-fitting trousers, and I'm already regretting my choice of a skirt today. Any clothes that are remotely tight-fitting seem to push Tyler into overdrive. I wore a blouse once that showed a modicum of cleavage – we're not talking Holly Willoughby here, just a smidge – but he drooled over me all day. I couldn't wait to get home and change. Anything that has a hint of lace, even black tights, ankle boots – all of these things start Tyler dribbling. I'm learning fast. I used to have a maths teacher at school who'd go round all the girls, furtively stroking their backs as he pretended to help with a tricky bit of Pythagoras' Theorem while surreptitiously trying to see who was wearing a bra and who wasn't. I think it's scarred me for life. And Tyler Benson just reminds me of him.

One day I'd like to come into work in a bustier, leather mini-skirt, fishnet stockings and dominatrix stilettos. I think Tyler would spontaneously self-combust, and that would be an end to that. All I'd have to do was scrape the goo that remained of him from his desk and continue life gloriously ungroped.

15

Wherever I go, he seems to be right behind me, trying to cop a feel. It's as tedious as it is intimidating. I spent too many years living with a control freak to let the same thing happen to me at work. Yet here I am, dressing not to please myself but to try to avoid Tyler's roving eye. Today's skirt is sensible tweed and down to my knee, but that doesn't stop my boss from ogling.

I pull it down, embarrassed. He gives me a wink before turning to my colleague. 'Hello, Karen. Chatting again? Haven't you got any work to do?'

'I'm discussing future strategy for outstanding accounts with Louise,' she counters effortlessly, and I wish I could be so crisp with Tyler.

'Looks like it,' he says as he heads to his own office.

'Tosser,' Karen mouths and holds up her middle finger to his retreating back.

'You've got Josh Wallace coming to see you,' I say after him. But his door slams shut.

Karen and I both roll our eyes. I bury myself in decorations again. Would one of my mum's singing Santas be too much?

'He married Linda from Lubricants in September.' Karen gives a wistful little puff of breath.

'Josh Wallace?'

'Nooo,' she says, now annoyed by my lack of attention. 'Keep up, Louise. Kelvin Smith.' Karen brushes the end of her tinsel boa across her lips. 'Mind you, I've got my eye on bigger fish. I don't mind telling you, I wouldn't say no to Josh Wallace. He'd better watch himself.'

Josh is Tyler's right-hand man and, as Karen has informed me, one of Fossil Oil's hottest men.

'He's definitely the blue-eyed boy of Fossil. He's single, sexy and going places. Much like my good self.' She polishes her nails on her tinsel. 'If he stays in favour with Tyler – and that's no mean feat – that man is destined for Great Things.'

And, at that very moment, the man we're talking about arrives.

'Hello, ladies,' he says as he breezes in.

'Josh.' Karen flushes and smiles at him in a simpering manner. Her eyelashes go berserk, fluttering like a bat's wings.

I can see why she finds him attractive. Of course I can – I might be celibate but I'm not blind. Josh Wallace has that rugged, rugby-player handsomeness. Big shoulders, bigger thighs. He looks sharp in his grey business suit and crisp white shirt, but that doesn't disguise that underneath it he's all muscle. His hair is fair and is swept back, curling slightly at his collar, totally against the grain of current fashion. His eyes are brown and warm and look compassionate. Certainly in comparison to Tyler Benson's, anyway. He instantly gets extra Brownie points for not trying to peer up my skirt.

'The decorations look great,' he says. 'They should let you loose on the rest of the offices, Louise.'

'Thanks.' I give Karen an I-told-you-so look.

'Hi,' he says, turning to my friend. 'How are you, Karen?'

She pouts slightly. 'I'm lovely thanks, Josh. How are you?'

'Good.'

I climb down from my desk and he turns his attention to me once more. 'I've got a meeting with Tyler.'

'I'll let him know you're here.' I buzz Tyler and inform him.

Josh is always on the road and I haven't really got to know him properly yet. There have been any number of brisk, businesslike phone calls, but we've never had the time to do anything more than exchange polite pleasantries in passing. In the couple of months I've been here, I've done little more than see him whisking in and out of a meeting, or dashing along a corridor. The man seems to be in perpetual motion. This is the first social event I'll have been to, so I haven't seen him at any of the other things that have been organised. To be honest, bowling isn't my bag.

Sometimes, he pops his head round my office door just to say hello and he seems nice enough. Once, in my first week, he brought me a chocolate-chip muffin from the canteen. What's not to love? We've never found time for a proper chat though. In contrast to my boss, I only hear good things about Josh Wallace.

Karen twiddles her hair again as she coyly asks him, 'Are you going to the Christmas party then?'

'Oh, yes.' Josh claps his hands together. 'Big night out. Wouldn't miss it for the world.'

'Perhaps we can find time to have a drink together?' Karen suggests.

'I'd like that,' he says. 'What about you, Louise? Up for a drink at the party?'

'Yes,' I shrug. 'Why not?'

Then Tyler flings open his door and comes to slap his deputy on the back.

'Good to see you, Josh,' Tyler says, all beaming smiles and bonhomie. 'Good to see you.'

Josh glances back at us as he's ushered away. 'See you later, ladies.'

'Wow.' Karen lowers her voice even though they're both now safely closeted in Tyler's office. 'A drink with Josh Wallace on the cards, hey? I haven't even left the building and reckon I've scored.' She pulls her fist to her waist in a hammer motion. 'Get in there, girl! Woo-hoo! He is *so* at the top of my Must Have list. I've had a *mega*-crush on him for yonks.'

I've already come to know that this means about two weeks in Karen's fickle book of office flirtations.

'Fit or what?' She fans herself theatrically. 'I am *so* going to get me some of that at the Christmas party.'

I laugh. 'Really?'

'You just watch me.'

'I don't think I'd ever mix business with pleasure. You know what they say: "Don't get your honey where you get your money."'

She's aghast. 'What miserable bugger said that? There's nothing better than a little work-based affair.'

'What happens when it all goes horribly wrong?' I caution. 'You've got to face them in the office every day. Look what happened to Knicker-Dropper Debbie.'

'She was playing *way* above her pay grade,' Karen counters.

'Don't do anything too reckless.'

'Reckless?' Karen gives me a look. 'Chance would be a fine thing. If I were a betting woman, I'd have a pound on tonight being as dull as ditchwater.'

Chapter Three

Kirsten was going to make an effort this year. A big effort. She swore it to herself. Again. Yet the truth was that she'd attended far too many of these functions to enjoy them any more. But for Tyler's sake she'd do her wifely duty and put on a good show.

She always dreaded corporate functions now, and the office parties were the very worst of the worst. They were usually so stilted: the staff couldn't relax as they felt they should be on their best behaviour with all the bosses around. She could only hope tonight's Christmas party would be a bit more fun and would get her in the festive mood.

She hated Christmas. It never felt like a time of celebration. For her, it marked the end of another year of her life. A life that, no matter what she did, felt as if it no longer belonged to her.

Kirsten sat in front of her dressing-table mirror. Tonight, she'd pin on a smile and be bright and vivacious. It was something that used to come naturally to her, she thought, and she was determined to find that person again before she lost all sight of her.

She'd been at the salon for hours and as a result she was freshly highlighted in honey blonde and her glossy locks hung in loose curls to her shoulders. Her nails had been sculpted too. A whole day had slipped away, never to be seen again, just on making herself pretty. She hoped it was worth it. Perhaps even Tyler would notice. Though, in fairness to him, he'd been very solicitous in recent months. But that made her anxious too. There was usually a reason for Tyler being attentive to her. And it was never an edifying one.

Picking up her blusher brush, she flicked it over her high cheekbones with studied determination.

'Are you nearly ready, darling?' Tyler said as he came in from the adjoining bathroom. He was freshly showered and he rubbed at his damp hair.

She looked at his reflection in her mirror. The white towel, slung low on his hips, accentuated his toned stomach. Despite a surfeit of business lunches and functions like this over the years, he still kept himself in reasonably good shape. He spent hours at the gym. Or, at least, he told her that was where he was going. She did sometimes wonder. He certainly came home from his 'workouts' looking flushed in the face and pleased with himself, but sometimes he smelled just a little too fragrant. Not the wholesome scent of shower gel or soap, but a whisper of another woman's perfume still clinging to him.

He planted a kiss on her shoulder. 'It's quite a drive to Wadestone Manor. We should be on the road soon.'

'Yes, nearly there.' Kirsten slipped in her diamond earrings. An anniversary present. Or was it birthday?

'I do love a Christmas party.' He rubbed his hands together with glee. Tyler was obviously feeling very jolly. 'It'll get us in the festive mood.'

'I want this year to be different,' Kirsten said.

'Different?'

It probably wasn't the best time to raise this, but when was? They never talked to each other any more.

'You know how it is, Tyler. Because of the stupid way Fossil Oil works, we've never been able to put down roots anywhere.

We have no friends, no social life. Which means that, invariably, on Christmas Day it's always just the two of us staring at each other over the dining-room table.'

'I like it quiet.'

'I get so bored. I want us to do things. Together.'

Her husband looked slightly worried by the prospect. 'Like what?'

You'd think after ten years he might know the things she liked. It seemed not. 'I'd like us to curl up in front of the fire, or go for a long walk in the snow.'

'How do you know it will snow?'

'If there is any. We can walk with or without snow. It's fun. Romantic.'

Despite years of her trying to persuade him otherwise, Tyler felt there was no point in a walk unless he was following a little white ball with a golf club in his hand.

She remembered a time – before Tyler – when those small pleasures had been hers. Country pubs, long walks through rustling autumn leaves, romance, contentment. All when she was young, wide-eyed, filled with optimism and spirit. And with no idea what life would throw at her.

'All we do is sit unspeaking, watching terrible television.' Late afternoon, Tyler normally cracked and shut himself away in the study for a few hours, leaving her to the terrible telly until she could no longer stand it. Normally, she couldn't wait for Christmas Day to end. 'I don't want you to work.'

'Last year was a one-off,' he insisted. 'We'd only just arrived back from Paris.'

Ah, yes. A six-month stint in Fossil Oil's French headquarters. Executive Development. They were big on that.

'Before this, in one year alone you've been posted to the USA, Greece, Belgium *and* France.'

'It's excellent experience,' Tyler reminded her.

22

'For you, perhaps,' she countered. 'Less so for me.'

The Executive Development Programme was as exhausting as it was unnecessary, in Kirsten's opinion. Fossil Oil were well known for placing impossible demands on their employees, often relocating them at a moment's notice for no good reason other than the fact that they could. Even families with school-age kids were dragged all over the globe for scant reason. Without children, the Bensons were cannon fodder for the corporate machine.

They'd landed back from Paris the week before Christmas. Her husband, keen to get back up to speed in the UK, had spent most of Christmas Day taking phone calls from other Fossil Oil executives who failed to understand the concept of a work/life balance. Kirsten had locked herself in the hall closet and cried, only emerging an hour later with eyes red-rimmed and raw. Tyler hadn't noticed that either. If Christmas had come round every five years, say, she might have been able to stomach it.

However, this year would be different. That was her solemn vow. This year she'd make an effort. There was no way they could go on like this. Their marriage was teetering on a knife edge and she wanted to do all she could to pull it back from the brink.

'We should be settled back in England for a while this time,' Tyler said, his tone placatory.

'Fingers crossed.' Though, if she was honest, even England didn't feel like home any more. Nowhere did. It was as if she was rootless, floating. It was no way to live. 'It would be nice if you could ease back on your workload, Tyler. It would be good for us to spend some time together. And I don't just mean sitting watching television. We should concentrate on our relation-ship—'

'There's nothing wrong with our relationship.'

'—make some friends, perhaps even establish a role in the

local community. Perhaps even stay long enough to find out if there is one.'

She turned from the mirror and looked up at him. 'I'm forty-two, Tyler. It feels as if I've spent the best years of my life trailing after you as you've scrambled your way up the corporate ladder with Fossil Oil.'

'You've done all right out of it.'

'Maybe I should have stayed at home while you roamed the offices of the world.' Kirsten had trained as a teacher and, at one point, had a nice post in a primary school and quite a promising future. She'd enjoyed her job and been good at it. 'All I've got to show for my career is, somewhere in among all the packing cases that have moved across continents with us, a cardboard box full of the sweetest letters from my pupils.'

'That's nice though.'

She'd loved children then. Adored them. It was their open curiosity and capacity for learning that filled her with enthusiasm. Now she didn't see any children, other than to pass them in the street, from one end of the year to the next. They didn't even broach the subject of having their own family any more. With Tyler it had always been next year when he earned more, next year when he'd reached this or that level, next year when it was quieter at work, next year when they'd stopped travelling. And, of course, next year never came. Then suddenly she'd turned forty and she felt that 'next year' had passed her by. Tyler earned more, reached the next level, got busier and busier and travelled endlessly. But many people in this situation still managed to have children. For Tyler it felt as if Fossil Oil was all the family he needed, but perhaps it wasn't enough for her.

'If it hadn't been for Fossil, I could have done a lot of things. I could have forged myself a successful career. I might have made headteacher. I could have found some friends, had a normal life. Whatever that might be.'

'Hindsight is a wonderful gift, Kirsten. We're still young. Relatively. It's not too late to do those things, if that's what you want.'

'I wanted to be with you.' It was what wives did, wasn't it? Sacrificed themselves on the altar of their husband's career. How very foolish it sounded now. Here she was, a decade later, relying on Tyler for her income, for her life. 'I know no one outside of the beauty salon and the gym. I thought about throwing a party at home this Christmas and then realised that, beyond the employees of Fossil Oil, I don't actually know anyone who I could invite.'

Tyler went to speak.

She held up a hand.

'Don't say we can invite Lance and Melissa. That's exactly what I mean.'

This was the only time they'd actually spent two consecutive Christmases in the same country. The last ten years had been marked by fleeting acquaintances and empty hours. The only people she had long-term relationships with were the women in the Relocations Department at Fossil Oil who engineered her tediously regular home moves.

'We've spent so little time in one place and have always lived in rented homes that it makes me feel like some sort of nomad.'

'Look at this place,' Tyler said, holding out his arms. 'It's stunning. People would cut off both their arms to live somewhere like this.'

'We've had some beautiful homes, of course. I can't deny that. It's always someone else's choice of furniture though, never my own.'

This place *was* amazing: a four-bedroom Georgian townhouse in Hampstead. Handy for both the London office and the M1. It was all chandeliers and original windows in a quiet, leafy street, slap bang in the middle of a conservation area. No one could argue with its pedigree.

'I've reached a stage in my life where having the biggest or shiniest home on the road just isn't enough. Nothing in this house is ours. I don't clean it, don't decorate it, don't plant a single flower in the garden. When we move – as we will – there'll be nothing in it to show that we've ever been here. All I do is stare at the four walls.'

'We can move somewhere else,' Tyler said, frowning. 'If that's what you want.'

'No,' she said. 'That's not what I want at all. You're missing my point entirely.'

'But this is a great place, and you didn't want to live near the office.'

Fossil Oil's latest venture had been to build a shiny new head office in Milton Keynes and the company had now moved, lock, stock and barrel, out of its base in central London, which was deemed too expensive.

Another reason she'd taken to travelling with Tyler was that she hadn't been able to trust him unless he was right under her nose. In her holidays from university she'd worked as an office temp and had endured a number of bosses who were just like Tyler, as libidinous as they were ambitious. Not that her being hot on his heels had ever actually stopped him from playing away. It was just that she had endless hours in which to be suspicious of him. She really should have kept up a job. Or had children. Or both. Perhaps she *should* have worked hard and climbed the greasy pole to the top of her own profession. Or maybe she would have been more content to spend her time at home if it had been somewhere filled with kids of their own. Then again, no doubt Tyler had the dominant genes and all their offspring would have ended up just like him. She'd have had no chance then. One Tyler Benson was more than enough.

'I've promised you I'll take a few days off over the holidays,' Tyler soothed.

After she'd nagged him incessantly. He never usually took time off and always dashed back to the comfort of Fossil Oil as soon as Boxing Day was over. He'd probably go in even earlier if the offices actually opened. But, with the few days at home that he'd promised her, perhaps he was going to try his best this year too.

'We'll talk about these things then.'

'Promise?'

'Cross my heart and hope to die.'

He crossed his bare chest and she lifted her hand to caress the spot.

'I'm going to do my very best, using fair means or foul, to make sure you don't sneak off to the study for a few hours.'

'I'd rather you use fair means.' Her husband traced his thumb over her cheek. 'This Christmas can be fun, Kirsten. If you want it to be.'

The Christmas tree was up, and that wasn't always a given. It depended on her mood or whether their belongings were still in transit from somewhere or another. For a change, she'd bitten the bullet and brought in Christmas planners to do it for her. It was a small and viciously expensive company who had been recommended by the chairman's wife, Melissa Harvey. They'd gone to town on the place and, she had to say, it looked marvellous. Far better than when Kirsten ever did it herself. Even Tyler had commented on the decorations, and Tyler very rarely noticed anything. Though he'd certainly notice the cost when the bill came in.

After much consultation and the presentation of mood boards, the planners had decorated the house in a rather traditional theme in gold and silver. The real tree that they'd put in the living room was absolutely breathtaking when the lights were on. It could be a cold room and this brought a much-needed degree of warmth to it. The scent from the pine needles was heavenly. On a few evenings she'd even come to sit in here, rather than watch the television over the breakfast bar in the kitchen where she often spent her time. Kirsten decided that she'd definitely use them again next year. If, of course, they *were* still in England. And there was the rub. She simply never knew.

'I want to make Christmas a happy time for us.' She wanted to be a person who looked forward to it, embraced it, as she once had many years ago. There'd been too many filled with sadness, emptiness, dwelling on things that might have been rather than appreciating what she had. This year, she'd thrown herself into Christmas shopping and, whereas she normally hated the crowds, she'd quite enjoyed the whirlwind. Both Kensingston High Street and Regent Street looked fabulous in their festive garb, and that had helped. As a result, there was a selection of carefully chosen and beautifully gift-wrapped presents for Tyler under the tree.

'Then let's start tonight.'

She felt herself brighten. 'Do you think we could? At the Christmas party? They're always so dull.'

'We can liven it up. A few drinks, a bit of dancing. Could be just what we need.' He pulled her to her feet and held her tightly, swaying in time to non-existent music. 'It's the most wonderful time of the year,' he sang tunelessly as they danced.

She laughed. Kirsten didn't think Tyler really enjoyed Christmas, any more than she did. It was something to get through rather than to be enjoyed.

'I've had your suit cleaned,' she told him. 'It's hanging in the dressing room.'

'That's why you're my favourite wife,' he teased. Putting his hands gently on her bare shoulders, he kissed her neck. 'Let's have fun tonight.'

It seemed like a long time since they'd had fun together.

Maybe Tyler was right: she should just let her hundred-and-fifty-pound-plus-tip hair down tonight.

'Let's,' she said. Her hand covered his. 'If we both try, it could be like old times.'

'Yes. It will be. Definitely.' Another kiss and he moved away from her.

'Just promise me you won't abandon me the minute you get there and talk about work all night.'

'Of course I won't.' But Tyler was already searching in the drawer for his cufflinks. He found them with a cry of 'Ah-ha!' and disappeared in search of his dinner suit.

Kirsten sat down again and put on her necklace. A thin gold strand with a single one-carat diamond hanging from it. Christmas present from two years ago? Quite possibly. Idly, she wondered what Tyler might have bought her this year. The value of his presents always went up in direct proportion to the amount of bad behaviour that he had to apologise for. Most years it meant something sparkly with diamonds. At the very least, this last twelve months should secure her an extravagant bracelet under the tree.

Tyler came out of the dressing room, in his shirt now and fiddling with his cufflinks. 'Can you fasten these, darling?'

She didn't remember buying him these ones, but had never had the nerve to ask where they'd come from. Some questions you really didn't want answered. He proffered his wrists and she fastened them for him.

He slipped on his jacket and tugged the cuffs into place. 'That's me ready.'

'You look very handsome,' she told him truthfully.

'We'd better get a move on.'

Throughout their marriage, Tyler had very much lived his own life. Half the time, she never knew where he was. There seemed to have been a little less gadding about since he'd been

29

at the office in Milton Keynes, but she wondered how long it would last. Not long, if she was reading the signs right – and she was a past master at that.

'Louise offered to book us a hotel overnight,' he said over his shoulder. 'I thought you'd want to come home, but I left it open. I know you rarely drink at these things, anyway.'

That was true enough. She felt ridiculously superior when everyone else was falling about paralytic, saying the most stupid things, and she was the only one stone-cold sober. Perhaps that was the flaw in her plan. A couple of well-aimed glasses of champagne could cheer her up considerably.

'If we're going to have fun, party-party and all that, then you might fancy a glass or two. Lance has laid on a free bar for the staff. Madness. That will ensure everyone's pissed out of their head within an hour.'

'Including Lance?'

Tyler shrugged. 'As always.'

'I'll see how it goes,' Kirsten said.

'Hotel or cab home, either suits me. Put a few things in a bag. You don't have to drive. Louise can fix something up if you change your mind.'

Tyler talked about his new secretary too often. He dropped her name into the conversation too casually and at every opportunity. That was always a warning sign. The last secretary had been Debbie and he'd done the very same with her. Debbie this, Debbie that and, quite obviously, Debbie the other.

When he spoke of Louise, she imagined her young and beautiful. Louise wouldn't have lines round her eyes or grooves that ran from her nose to her mouth. 'Puppet lines', they called them, and sometimes that was exactly what she felt like. Tyler's puppet. Whatever Tyler wanted her to do, she did.

She was still in her prime. Forty was the new thirty, wasn't it? And yet, some days she felt older than time itself. How old was this Louise? she wondered. Well, she guessed she'd find out soon enough. She'd be there tonight and they'd come face to face for the first time. She'd chosen her favourite dress for the occasion, a white Armani number. It was halter-neck with a plunging neckline and a low back. The material clung to her curves and showed off her toned body. She looked as good as she possibly could. Let's see how this Louise competed with that. At least the hours spent in the gym proved useful sometimes.

This could be her moment to reassert her claim to Tyler. It was time to fight for her man. If only they could both throw off the weight that had insidiously settled on their shoulders and find the people they once used to be, maybe there was hope for them. Perhaps, if she could be the woman he used to love, then he wouldn't look elsewhere. If he could be the man she thought she'd married, then perhaps she could look at him with love in her eyes once more.

Tonight, she was going to try her best to love her husband again and to make him love her back. It was the best reason she could think of for enduring the Christmas party.

Chapter Four

Melissa reached up to fasten the silk bow tie that hung limply and expectantly on Lance's dinner shirt. Her nimble fingers deftly twisted and twiddled it into the desired shape. It was a deed she'd performed for more years than she cared to remember now, and she stood back to admire it. Years of practice had, in this case, made perfect. She patted it into place affectionately.

Lance Harvey checked his reflection in the stridently lit mirror in the hall. Her husband was older than her by eleven years, sixty-six to her fifty-five. Which hadn't seemed so very much at one time, but now she thought the age difference was starting to show.

'What would I do without you, angel?' Lance said as he sucked in his stomach and lifted his chin.

'Oh, I'm sure you'd manage.' She kissed his cheek.

'Never. You're the light of my life.' Her husband glanced at his watch. 'Do we have time for a small bourbon before we leave?'

She shook her head. 'Martin will be here any moment. You can have one in the car.'

He looked content with that idea.

There'd come a time, perhaps soon, when he'd stop working and it would be just the two of them together all day. How would she cope then?

'Has Bud made any more noises about you retiring?'

Lance shook his head. 'No. That's definitely on the back burner for now.'

Bud Harman, who headed everything up in the USA, liked his executives to hang up their corporate hats early, but Lance wasn't buying into that. So far, he'd soundly ignored all hints to that effect. Fossil Oil was his life. It always had been. He'd stick it out until the bitter end, until someone forced him to go.

'Besides, you know me, honey. What would I do if I retired?'

That was the burning question. How *would* Lance fill his days? He knew nothing but work, had no friends, no real interest in anything other than the oil business. He lived and breathed Fossil Oil. But surely there must come a time when he simply couldn't carry on?

'If you do, would you like to stay in England?'

'I haven't thought about it,' her husband admitted.

'It would be nice to have a home that I could truly call our own. Perhaps we could get a little cottage somewhere and settle down?'

Due to Lance's work, Melissa rarely went out of London. He didn't like to have her too far away from him as he often used her as a sounding-board for some new proposal or initiative that had been mooted and which he, increasingly, struggled to understand.

'There are some very beautiful parts of the country – Hampshire, Devon, Cornwall. It would be nice to take some trips.'

Lance laughed. 'Can you see me whiling away my days in a twee little cottage with a thatched roof?'

Melissa too laughed at the very thought. 'No, honey. I can't.'

'There are a few good years left in me yet.'

'I know that, sweetheart.' She smoothed the collar of his dinner jacket. 'We should think about it though. You know how time rushes by. It pays to start making plans. We could retire to Florida, spend our twilight years soaking up the sun. You could even take up golf again if you had the time.'

Lance used to play once, but only because work had required it. Now, like everything else, it was difficult to find the spare hours.

'Do you think we'd see the boys more if we were retired?' he asked.

It was always a difficult subject between them. She was much closer to their sons than Lance was and she felt that, not too far below the surface, he resented that. 'Oh, yes. I'm sure we would. Or we could visit them.'

What she meant was that she could visit them alone. Lance would never bother, even if he was retired. And that was why he wasn't closer to the boys.

His 'Harrumph' was the only answer she needed.

The children were grown-up now, men not boys, both nearing thirty, and they had lives of their own. Rich and interesting lives. It was a great sadness in her life that they rarely saw them.

'Are they coming for Christmas this year?' he asked.

'No, no,' Melissa said. 'But I'm sure they'll Skype us.' It might be Christmas, but the only time she'd have with her children would be a rushed five-minute phone or video call from some distant part of the world.

Drew and Kyle had spent most of their young lives in boarding school. A good one in England, all funded by Fossil Oil. At least it had given them some stability at the time, but she regretted that now. She had tried to keep them at home with her as they followed Lance to his different postings around the globe. It gave Melissa a home life too, a life outside Fossil Oil. She loved doing the school run, waiting for the boys to come home so that she could read with them, play games. It gave an otherwise shallow existence some meaning. But it wasn't ideal for the boys. They had to change schools so often that their education suffered. They'd just start to settle in, make friends with their classmates, there'd be tentative and awkward play-dates or they might start to get invites to birthday parties at burger bars, and then Lance would announce that they were off again. They were always the outsiders and that was never a good feeling. She knew that only too well. It had been a terribly painful decision to leave them behind as she trailed after Lance. And she wondered now how she could have packed them off so young. Boys needed their mother's love. They needed a father who was there for them and Lance had never been. Yet, despite their parents' failings, thankfully they'd turned out to be decent, caring young men.

'They should have come into the oil business with me,' Lance said. 'That's a proper career. They're both layabouts.'

'They're so not,' Melissa chided. 'They just want different things to you. There's nothing wrong with that. They want to be their own people. Money doesn't matter to them.'

'They don't mind taking ours,' Lance grumbled.

Melissa had done her very best to steer them away from the corporate game and it seemed to have worked. She'd never wanted them to grow up to be their father's sons. She and Lance might have all the trappings of wealth, but the truth was they had no life.

The opposite was true of their sons.

'Drew does great work,' she said. 'You know that. You should be proud of what he's achieved.'

'Huh,' Lance said.

Their eldest was in Nepal, working as the manager of a small orphanage. They had thirty children in the home and he sometimes sent her photographs of them, all beautiful smiles and shiny faces. It was a hand-to-mouth existence and, largely without Lance's knowledge, Melissa regularly wired him money.

One day she hoped to visit him, even though he assured her that she'd be horrified by the conditions in which he lived.

Lance snorted. 'At least he's doing better than Kyle.'

It was true that their youngest boy had never really grown up and had a very hippy lifestyle that Lance totally disapproved of. He had piercings everywhere – nose, ears, lips, you name it. He had those big black earrings that made holes in your ears. Lance couldn't even look at them. In the summer he'd work teaching surfing or, last year, with a company that offered bungee jumps off a bridge in South Africa. In the winter he headed to ski resorts in California or Europe and taught snowboarding and worked in bars. One year he'd been a chalet 'girl', and it felt strange to know that her son could bake a great cake whereas, due to usually having staff, she could barely boil an egg.

'He's doing fine,' Melissa insisted. 'He's young yet and he's having fun. How can we begrudge him that?'

She could see Lance's frown deepening and, in an effort to steer him from his favourite subject to complain about, she said, 'How do you like the house decorations this year? Haven't they done a great job?'

Lance looked around him and nodded.

The vast hall in their latest house was decorated beautifully for the festive season. She'd used the same company she'd employed last year and they hadn't disappointed her. She was so pleased that she'd recommended them to Kirsten Benson too.

The tree was over ten feet tall and dressed with traditional baubles in red and gold. The banister of the sweeping stairs had a holly garland weaving through it that went right up to the first floor. All the mirrors were decked with holly arrangements topped with red velvet bows. There was another tree in the living room that was just as sparkling, just as lavish.

'They look great, honey. Good enough to eat.'

'Speaking of which,' Melissa said, 'I've decided to cook

myself this year.' It was some time since she'd made the effort and now, at the last minute, she was wondering if she should have arranged for a chef to come in.

'You don't have to do that.'

'Most of it's being sent pre-prepared from Fortnum's, so there's no need to worry. Whatever we have, it will be edible.'

Cooking was definitely not her forte. Even with a little help from her favourite store, there was still the potential for disaster and a sandwich for Christmas lunch.

'The dining-room table has already been set. That looks pretty too.' It glittered with crystal and golden charger plates – both sourced by the Christmas planners. 'I hired all the crockery and glasses. Our china and crystal is somewhere in a storage facility, it was too much effort to retrieve it.'

If only the boys had come home they might have had a lovely time with the family all together. As it stood, amid all this festive loveliness, she and Lance would be here alone. Lance's career had provided for all this opulence, but it had certainly come at a high price.

'We could have gone to a hotel again,' he said. 'Then you don't have to do anything.'

Frankly, she'd seen enough of hotel rooms in her lifetime. 'That's a lovely idea, but I would just like for us to be in our own place.'

'You're such a home bird,' he said and hugged her tightly. 'Now we'd better get to this Christmas party as we're the star turn. Ready when you are, honey.'

He held up her fur coat for her and she slipped her arms into it. Picking up her diamanté clutch bag, she sighed inside. Yet another Christmas party. She was a veteran of them now. Thirty years a corporate wife had seen to that.

'You look lovely tonight, Mrs Harvey,' Lance said. 'As always.'

'Thank you, sweetheart.' The truth was that it was all smoke and mirrors. Beneath the emerald-green sheath dress she wore, there was shapewear that was nearly cutting her in two. Eating would be a trial too far. Staying a size eight – in British sizes – didn't come easily these days.

The glaring brightness in here was condemningly harsh. If it had been her own home she would have changed it to something more subtle, more flattering. The light showed the fine etching of laughter lines much too clearly. Laughter lines. That was the biggest laugh of all: it wasn't an overdose of jollity that had caused these babies, it was the years slipping by with alarming regularity that had left these blots on her facial landscape. She was like a tree, a gnarled old oak. You could count the summers she had sweltered through and the winters she had weathered by the number of lines on her face. Since she'd turned fifty, she'd embraced the miracle of Botox as you would a lover, in the hope that it would keep her looking younger. But you could only fight it for so long. Once your body hit a certain number, everything drooped, sagged and dried up. It didn't stop her from trying to hold back the sands of time though.

In the ten years since they'd been rudely plucked by Fossil Oil from the cosmopolitan delights of New York, they'd wandered like executive vagabonds through various offices in Europe. Then Lance had been promoted to chairman of Fossil Oil UK and they were posted to London, where the dampness of the summers had merged inextricably with the slightly fuller dampness of the winters. Mind you, at least her skin had enjoyed a brief respite from the penalties of ultraviolet over-indulgence.

They'd now been based here for longer than usual, almost two years. Finally, she was starting to enjoy it. She liked this house well enough and it certainly looked beautiful dressed for Christmas.

'I want to get there early to do the rounds and press some flesh.' Lance glanced out of the window by the door and clapped his hands together. 'Martin's waiting outside with the car.'

'I'm all yours,' she said and he took her arm. Lance closed the front door behind them and, his step still sprightly, they crossed the gravel as he escorted her to the car.

By the fountain in their sweep-round driveway, Martin held open the door of the Bentley for her while she slid into the luxurious warmth of the car. Martin had been with them since they'd been in England, which could be considered long-term. He was a nice man. Loyal. Reliable.

She nodded to him. 'Good evening, Martin.'

'Evening, Mrs Harvey.'

It was a bitterly cold night and snow threatened. A white Christmas was looking likely. That would be nice. All the previous times she'd spent Christmas in England it was, so very often, grey and raining.

Lance got in beside her and the car purred away, heading towards Wadestone Manor. She didn't think she'd been to this venue before, so that was something to look forward to. There was something else to look forward to as well, but that was her secret.

'Will tonight be insufferably boring, honey?' she asked. It was always more taxing when the party was for the whole of Fossil Oil. When it was just the executives you knew where you stood. Introduce even the most junior of staff and, so often, it descended into mayhem. People didn't know how to behave these days.

'Probably, my sweet.' Lancelot Harvey smoothed his fingers through his wavy silver hair. He noticed Melissa scrutinising him and smiled back at her.

'You look very handsome, Lance.' And he did.

She knew that it was a constant marvel and source of pride to Lance that, despite having seen the wrong side of sixty, his hair was no thinner than when he was still a fine young buck, wowing the girls as the rising star on the college football team. Now it was silver-white and it made him look very distinguished. Though he hated it and complained constantly that there was no goddamn colour left in it.

But then both she and Lance knew full well that you could never have everything you wanted in life. Over thirty years of marriage and virtually the same length of service with Fossil Oil had proved that, on more than one occasion. He was so different now from the swaggering young man who'd swept her off her feet with his enthusiasm and ambition. She was still green, just out of college herself, when they met, and they'd married after a whirlwind romance, much to her parents' displeasure. Though they were mightily relieved that she had tied the knot when her first son was born just six months after the wedding. That hadn't stopped her own quest for a fulfilling career though and even with two toddlers she'd been working her way up to be a tax specialist in a respected company. She'd enjoyed it too – the power, the adrenalin buzz of meetings. They'd managed quite well when Lance was a relatively junior sales manager at Fossil and had only travelled inside the USA. He could manage to be at home most weekends and a full-time nanny had taken up the slack in the week for her.

When her husband had been promoted and burst on to the global scene, it had been impossible for her to continue her own career. Another regret. If she wanted to climb the ladder, it would have meant more time away from home, longer hours, later nights, earlier mornings. The boys were already spending too much time with hired help and it was unfair on them.

When he was offered his first overseas posting, a big step up, together they agreed that they'd put everything into Lance's career. She'd give up her job, take the boys out of school, and they'd travel with him. They were so in love, the world was in the palm of their hands and they wanted to embrace it whole-heartedly. It was to be a big adventure. And it was. For a while.

Lance poured himself a neat bourbon from the small cocktail cabinet in the car and took an unhealthy gulp. He smacked his lips in appreciation, even though he'd only just finished a glass in the bedroom while he was getting ready. He was probably most of the way through a bottle or even more by this time of the day.

'Anything for you, honey?'

'No, thank you.' It wasn't that she didn't drink, but it always served her well to be less drunk than Lance. 'Is there anything we need to discuss before we get there? Are you going to talk to Tom Davidson about the refinery proposals tonight? I can run through my ideas again, make sure they're fresh in your mind.'

He patted her knee. 'Not now, sweetheart. Tonight is purely fun. I have a few announcements to make, but that's all.'

'What about?'

'This and that,' he said cagily.

It was unlike him not to discuss the ins and outs of Fossil Oil dealings with her.

'The rest of the business can wait until tomorrow.'

She raised an eyebrow. 'Really?'

He shrugged.

Lance must be mellowing in his old age. That was probably the first time she'd ever heard him say that.

The car hit the edge of the city and headed out into the rolling countryside towards Wadestone Manor, taking the twist-ing bends and the narrow lanes smoothly. Martin was an excellent driver.

The Christmas party was always the highlight of the social calendar for the staff. Whenever there was a free bar provided by Fossil Oil, they usually took as much advantage of it as humanly possible. It was always total chaos and, in years gone by, she'd tried to persuade Lance to leave as early as was deemed polite.

'Tyler and Kirsten will be on our table, that should liven things up a bit,' Lance said.

'Oh, are they?' Melissa feigned surprise. She knew they would be. Of course they would.

'You always enjoy their company.'

'Yes. That'll make the evening more entertaining.'

In the glass that separated them from Martin, Melissa's reflection wore a sceptical expression. Lance patted her hand affectionately. She turned to gaze out of the window at the passing countryside, unable to meet her husband's eye.

The truth was that she enjoyed Tyler Benson's company much more than she should.

Chapter Five

The hairdresser is tipsy. And she's dressed as Snow White. The other stylists in the salon are kitted out as the seven dwarves and it looks as if they've all started on the festive spirit a bit too early. Consequently it takes her an age to put up my hair and I'm nearly frantic by the time she's finished. I show my displeasure by just giving her my usual tip and not something more generous as I normally would at Christmas. Being three sheets to the wind, I don't think she actually notices anyway. I'm only glad that I haven't booked in for a short-back-and-sides. In fact, I should probably count my blessings that I didn't get one.

Now, of course, I'm running late. Back at home and in the privacy of my room, I wriggle into my little black dress, which, sadly, is just that bit tighter than the last time I wore it. When I've managed to zip myself up, I admire my hair in the mirror. It's swept up in a very Audrey Hepburn, *Breakfast at Tiffany's* way and, given the circumstances of its creation, I'm somewhat relieved to say that it looks great.

Mum has lent me her favourite necklace – a triple string of pearls with a pendant in the middle – which adds to the sixties-icon vibe, and I'm wearing pointy black stilettos. It's so long since I dressed up that I'd actually forgotten I could look like this. Miss Holly Golightly would be proud of me.

Goodness knows what Tyler will think of my outfit, but tonight I don't care. I want to look glamorous. You can't go to the Christmas party dressed like a frump. After all, I have Karen from Customer Accounts to compete with. I don't want to be totally overshadowed by her. Hopefully there will be enough people around that Tyler won't be a problem.

'Mummy!' Mia's voice comes from her bedroom. It has just the right level of whine in it to tug at my heartstrings. As well she knows. 'Mummy!'

Grabbing my black patent handbag, I go through to see her. She's sitting up in her little bed, looking beyond adorable in her pink pyjamas with bunny rabbits on them. Her similarly pink Home Bargains Christmas tree sparkles on top of the tallboy.

'You must be a good girl and go to sleep now,' I say. 'Mummy won't be gone for long.'

'Don't go out.' A little tear runs down her cheek and I brush it away with my thumb. 'Stay with me.'

'Don't be a silly-billy,' I chide gently. 'Gramps and Granny will look after you. Promise me that you'll be a good girl, or Santa won't come.'

'He will,' she wails. 'Santa always brings me lots of toys even if I've been really naughty. He loves me.'

I can't help but smile. 'He does, and so do I, but this is my office Christmas party. It's work and I have to go. It's very important for Mummy to be there. I'll tell you all about it in the morning.'

I know why she's being like this. I hardly ever go out without her now and she doesn't want to be left behind. She's also taken to sneaking into my bed in the middle of the night and when I feel her tiny, warm body snuggle in next to mine, I'm not hard-hearted enough to take her back to her own room. It's a rod I've made for my own back.

'I've got a headache,' she complains.

'No, you haven't.' I stroke her hair which frames her perfect, heart-shaped face.

'Lie down next to me,' she says.

'For five minutes.' I try to sound stern but in truth I'd rather be staying at home too. My eyes are heavy and I'm so tired after a long day at work.

I never seem to have enough time with Mia now. Tyler likes to keep me there till all hours, so it's often six-thirty or even later by the time I leave the office. Thanks to my dear parents, when I get home Mia has already eaten her tea and is usually ready for bed. Then I've just got half an hour to read her a bedtime story and the rest of the evening is spent flaking out in front of the television with my folks.

I'm now an expert on *Midsomer Murders* and *Flog It!*, which they record for me every day because, for some inexplicable reason, they've decided I like them. I don't have the heart to tell them otherwise. So I endure watching people being killed by giant cheeses falling on them and others trying to auction off the most terrible tat that has been hiding in their loft since time began, and smile gratefully because my parents are such very, very kind people. Without their constant support, I don't know where Mia and I would be.

My childhood home has been decorated for Christmas since the middle of November. My dad likes to grumble about it, but I know he enjoys it too. Now that they've got Mia here, they're like big kids themselves. Some of the Christmas decorations they have were probably among the first invented.

I remember them getting their current tree when I was Mia's age, so they've certainly had their money's worth out of it. I suspect it came from the long-defunct Woolworths in its heyday. It's looking a bit moth-eaten and ragged now, but even if they won the lottery I don't think they'd replace it. 'Sentimental value', my mother says. Which usually means it's fit for the skip. But once it's all done up in its festive finery – some of the more dubious decorations hand-knitted by Mum – I have to admit that it doesn't look half bad. Mia certainly doesn't seem to notice that it's seen better days. We have to go through a weekly ritual of standing in awe before the tree while Granny tells her where each and every one of the decorations has come from. I'm surprised that my mum even remembers. No, actually, I'm not.

'Lie down, Mummy,' Mia cajoles.

'For two minutes.' I try to sound stern, but Mia knows she's on to a winner.

So I turn off her bedside light and the room is filled with a soft golden glow. I risk damaging my fabulous hairdo and snuggle down next to my daughter. Softly I sing her favourite lullaby, 'Hush Little Baby'. It's the one I've sung to her since she was a baby, the same one my mother used to sing to me at bedtime when I was Mia's age. Slowly, she drifts off.

It seems like seconds later when my dad is gently shaking my arm. I blink my eyes open, not knowing, for a split second, where I am. It appears, however, that I've drooled on the pillow.

'I don't like to disturb you, love, but what time are you going to this party?'

That makes me sit bolt upright and, of course, I wake Mia too. Next to me she rubs her eyes.

'It's nearly half-past seven,' he adds.

'Oh, no.'

'Should I have woken you earlier, love? I didn't realise the time.'

'I've missed the coach,' I tell him, my shoulders sagging.

'Not to worry, Lou-Lou. If you still want to go, I'll run you in the car.'

'You can't do that, Dad.'

'It's no trouble.'

'But it's miles.'

'No, no,' he says. 'Not that far.'

'Don't go!' Mia starts again, and she wraps her arms round my waist, clinging like a limpet.

The temptation is very strong to shrug off my dress and Mum's jewels, ignore the money I've spent on my hairdo, mark it down to experience and just stay here with my deliciously cosy daughter. But then I think it would look bad if I didn't show. I'm sure Tyler Benson would hold it against me and I can't risk doing anything that would cost me this job.

'I *have* to go,' I tell her. To Dad, I say, 'Duty calls.'

Which is why, ten minutes later, with my hair only slightly askew, my dear dad is backing his Ford Focus out of the garage.

'Is Mia warm enough?' Mum says as we stand at the front door waiting for him.

'Yes. She'll be fine.' Of course, my dear child won't stay in bed and insists on coming with us. I've caved in because I'm now in too much of a rush to face a full-on tantrum. She was immediately placated when I agreed that she could come along for the ride. I'm worried that at four years old she knows exactly how to play me. What hope is there for me when she reaches fifteen?

'You should be in your bed, Little Miss Young. Why don't you stay here with Granny? It's cold out here.' Mum rubs at her arms to convey Arctic temperatures. 'Brrr.'

My daughter is immovable. All she does is cling to me more tightly. She's in my arms, wrapped in her fluffy pink dressing gown and bunny slippers. Her favourite teddy, Eric, is coming too and we had to find him a scarf to wear as it's cold. In fact, Mum's right, it is bitterly cold. There are slight flakes of snow blowing in the air – nothing substantial yet, but the threat of more is there. Another reason why my dad shouldn't be getting the car out.

I kiss Mum's cheek. 'See you in the morning. *Don't* wait up.'

'Be careful, Louise,' she says. 'Don't do anything silly.'

I laugh. 'Like what?'

'I don't know.'

'This job is important to me, Mum. Really important.' I haven't told my parents that my boss is a randy old goat. Dad would be marching down to the Fossil Oil offices and demanding to see the person in charge, as he would have done with the headmaster when I was at school. 'I'm not going to do *anything* to jeopardise that.'

Putting Mia in the back of the car in her booster seat, I get in the front next to Dad. I suspect that my darling daughter will force herself to stay awake until we reach Wadestone Manor even though her head is lolling with tiredness. I'm equally sure that she'll be fast asleep the minute Dad turns for home.

Mia loves all the show tunes from the musicals, so we're all singing along to 'These Are a Few of My Favourite Things' when, half an hour later, Dad pulls in at the very grand and imposing gates of Wadestone Manor.

'Oh my word, Lou,' he breathes. 'This is a fancy place.'

It is. And that makes me nervous. 'Are you sure it's the right one, Dad?'

We've only just driven through the gates and already I feel intimidated.

'I think so, love. Better check your invitation.' Dad pulls over to the grass verge of the sweeping driveway.

Hurriedly I get the invitation out of my bag and scan the details. I turn to him and nod. 'This is it.'

'Good job you had your hair done,' says my father, who usually notices nothing.

I'm now wishing I'd gone the whole hog and bought a new dress.

Dad puts the Focus into gear again and we make our way towards the house along a driveway lined by beautiful specimen trees.

'Look, Mia,' I say, pointing into the trees. 'Deer.'

She peers out of the car window. 'Bambi,' she says.

'That's right. Clever girl.'

'What a sight,' Dad says, awestruck.

They bound across the road in front of us, an impressive herd with a stag at the head. Dad proceeds even more carefully. 'You don't want one of those through your windscreen,' he says in a doom-laden voice.

We wind through the trees until ahead of us is the most spectacular fountain, all lit up in the darkness. It's a sea god, surrounded by nymphs and all kinds of mythical creatures.

'Look at that, Mummy!' Mia gapes wide-eyed.

'I wish the neighbours could see this, Lou-Lou, then they'd know my little girl has gone up in the world.'

I think my parents were embarrassed, worried about what the residents of Clonmel Close would think about me coming home, up to the eyeballs in debt, tail between my legs, daughter in tow and one spectacularly failed relationship chalked up. They have something to brag about again, now that I have a fab job and am getting back on my feet.

Dad trundles up to the house, which looms magnificently ahead of us, clearly still uncertain whether we should be here or not. The long, straight gravel drive is flanked by two immense lawns dotted with statues illuminated in the dark. Twinkling lights are strung in the trees around us. Dad's little car feels somewhat dwarfed by it all. The crunching of his tyres sounds loud and vulgar. The house itself looks as if it's been modelled on a French chateau, complete with ornate stonework and pretty towers. Lights blaze out from every window and there are two enormous Christmas trees either side of the wide steps that lead up to the front door. Who could possibly own a place such as this?

'What a place for a party!' is Dad's verdict. 'I've never seen the like.'

Me neither. I'm slightly terrified now. 'Shall I see if you can both come in and have a sneaky peek?'

'No, no.' Dad shakes his head so much that it might fall off. 'I'm in my cardigan. You can't go in a place like that in your cardigan.'

'I want to come in,' Mia chimes.

'Oh, no,' Dad says. 'You stay here with Gramps.'

I think we're both having the same vision, of a place stuffed with eminently breakable and priceless antiques.

'Gramps is right,' I tell Mia. 'I promise I'll take lots of photos.'

'You have a lovely time, Lou-Lou,' he says. I can see his eyes filling up with tears. 'You'll knock them dead looking like that.'

'Dad,' I say. 'You'll start me off.'

'I'll come and pick you up. What time do you want me?'

I laugh. 'I'm not fifteen, Dad. I can get the coach back. The company have laid it on. No need for you to turn out.'

'I don't mind. I'd rather you were safe and sound.'

'It might snow later.'

'I'll leave the car out in case you change your mind.'

'Put it in the garage. And go to bed. I don't want you waiting up for me. I'll be late.'

'How late?' Mia wants to know.

'Will you both stop fussing!' I tell them. 'Now I'm here, I'm going to make sure I enjoy myself.'

'Ring me if you need me to come out,' Dad says, obviously not having listened to a word I've said.

I kiss his cheek. 'I won't ring. I'm a big girl. Don't worry about me.'

He grips the steering wheel. 'You're still my little girl,' he says, voice husky. 'No matter how old you are.'

'Thanks, Dad.' I get out of the car and open Mia's door so that I can kiss her too. 'Be good for Gramps and straight to bed when you get home. No fuss.'

'I love you, Mummy.'

'You can go into my bed, so that you know when I come home.' I hug her tightly. Everything I do, I do for her.

'It'll be over by the time you get in there,' Dad says.

'I'm going. I'm going.' I close the door and wave goodbye to them.

Dad starts the engine and slowly turns away. I take a deep breath and walk up to the fabulous mansion with butterflies in my tummy.

Chapter Six

The Bentley slowed to a stately pace as they wafted through ornate gates at the entrance to the Wadestone estate. In the headlights, Melissa could see startled deer scatter from their path.

'I hope tonight is going to be very special,' Lance intoned. 'I want the staff to have a night that they'll never forget. I've really pushed the boat out, as a goodwill gesture to thank them all for enduring the move to Milton Keynes stoically.'

Or less than stoically in some cases, Melissa thought. Some of them had needed to be dragged up there kicking and screaming. People who were settled in communities with their families had all been uprooted on a whim. She'd advised Lance to fight against it, but he hadn't listened. Once, he used to take her advice unfailingly. Behind every successful man there was an ambitious woman. She was his sounding-board, his counsellor, and always had been. Now she was sure his memory was failing and he seemed to retain very little of what she said – about anything, not just business matters. His concentration was terrible and she worried how he managed in board meetings. The move had gone ahead regardless of the upheaval. Knowing Fossil Oil, this time next year they'd have decided that they really had to be based in

London after all and they'd relocate the same people all over again.

'This party is costing a goddamn arm and a leg,' Lance added. 'I hope the staff appreciate it.'

'I'm sure they will. Everyone enjoys the Christmas party.'

'Some of them too much,' he said sagely as he swigged his drink. 'We don't have to mix too much. You just sit there and look beautiful as you always do. After the meal I'll say a few words of encouragement, rally the troops for the new year. We can bow out gracefully as soon as you're ready.'

'I wouldn't like to think how many of these we've done together over the years, honey.'

'Well, there'll be less of it to contend with pretty soon, angel.' Lance refilled his glass and then there was a meaningful pause before he said, 'I spoke to Bud Harman today.'

Melissa smoothed the tightly fitted skirt of her emerald silk gown over her thighs and raised an eyebrow. There was something in Lance's tone of voice that she didn't quite like. A barely detectable ripple, a quaver, a tightness, certainly a hesitation. 'How so?'

Lance twisted his cufflinks in his sleeves and continued to look straight ahead. 'We're going home. Back to the States.'

Melissa dropped back into her plush leather seat, which let out a squeak in protest. 'Well, there's a turn-up for the books. When was this decided?'

'Today. This morning.' Lance drained his glass. 'I'm going to head up a new project.'

America? Home. She knew it would come at some time, but not just now. Not when she was finally enjoying herself in this rain-soaked country. She was shocked to her core.

'A new project?'

'Hmm.' That cagey tone again.

'That sounds suspiciously like you're being sidelined.'

53

Melissa's face felt as if it had been drained of blood. In the glass it looked paler than it had a moment ago, before Lance's earth-tilting announcement.

'Staff Assessment Criteria and Key Employee Development programme. "SACKED" for short,' he explained.

'*Sacked?* You're kidding me.'

'Oh,' Lance said, frowning. 'I see what you mean.'

'The first thing you have to do, Lance, is get that name changed.'

He shrugged. 'Well, whatever it's called, the programme is a global restructuring of the company. This is a crucial role for me, honey.'

'You mean you're being made chief wielder of the hatchet?' She hadn't meant it to sound so disdainful. Lance would, no doubt, be pleased about this. He was always happy to do whatever was required of him by Fossil Oil. He was a corporate man through and through.

Yet for once a weary look pinched Lance's features. 'It's a chance to get off the corporate merry-go-round for a while, Melissa. Running Fossil Oil is a young man's game now and ... I would only ever admit this to you, but I'm tired. I've been with this company for so long, I've seen everything before and I'm jaded. I need my batteries recharging and this might give me some time to do it.'

Anxiety was fluttering in her chest. She didn't want to be dragged halfway around the world again. Not now. 'What happens when you've finished with this "project"?' Call it what you will, they both knew what it really was. Lance was going to be in charge of a firing squad. 'What happens when your batteries are recharged and surging on full power again? Suppose there isn't a pretty coloured horse left on the corporate merry-go-round for you to ride?'

'We'll cross that bridge when, and if, we come to it. Maybe then it will be time to ease back on the throttle.'

Melissa felt her shoulders slump.

'Perhaps that retirement home in Florida might not be so far away,' Lance offered.

The thought made her blood chill. 'So it's signed, sealed and delivered then?'

'Pretty much. A few i's to dot. A few t's to cross.'

Her husband had an over-casual look fixed to his features and she eyed him suspiciously.

'There has to be a catch, Lance, otherwise you wouldn't sound so edgy. I know you.' There was a pain behind her eyes that hadn't been there previously and, despite the comfort of their chauffeured car, one was now developing in her neck to match. 'When exactly do they want you to start this crucial role?'

Lance cleared his throat; she knew it was a bad sign. It was the sound that said somewhere a nail had been struck firmly on the head. After years of marriage all her husband's annoying little habits were deeply ingrained in her psyche. This was one of them.

'Saturday,' he stated flatly.

'*Saturday?*'

'I've had Veronica book flights. The e-tickets are on my desk in the study.'

'But it's Christmas Eve tomorrow, Lance. Saturday is Christmas Day. Who in God's name moves home on Christmas Day? I've ordered a sixteen-pound turkey from Fortnum and Mason for our Christmas lunch.'

'Maybe we can still eat it before we leave for the airport, sweetie.' Lance looked wounded. 'It's an evening flight.'

'You expect me to pack and be on a flight to New York the day after tomorrow and still have time to cook a turkey? I don't think even that Nigella woman could manage that feat.'

Lance shrugged. 'You know the form, honey. You must be used to it by now.'

That was true enough. She was used to upping sticks at a moment's notice, but this time she wanted to dig her heels in. 'What about I stay here for a few more weeks and then follow you when you're settled?'

If she was here for a little while longer, she might be able to tie up one or two loose ends that she needed to.

'No, no, no. I want you with me, by my side, honey. Where you always are.'

He patted her again and she felt like screaming. He struggled to manage without her now. They both knew that. Even before she had suggested it, she knew Lance would never allow it. Where he went, she had to go too.

'It will be good to get back to New York,' she said. Though in her heart she didn't feel that at all.

'Washington DC,' Lance corrected quietly.

'DC?'

Lance merely nodded in confirmation.

'Why DC, in heaven's name?'

Lance swallowed his bourbon. 'That's where the project is based. If that's what the company wants, who am I to argue?'

'You're the chairman. Can't you do it from here? I thought this new office of yours was supposed to have all the very latest in space technology – satellite link-ups, video conferences, beam-me-up-Scotty machines? They're all terms I've heard bandied about liberally in the last few months. I know you've got them.'

'We've been here for a few years now,' Lance noted. 'That's a lifetime in Fossil Oil terms. Isn't it time we had a move? Don't you feel restless?'

'I like it here.' Melissa could feel herself coming perilously close to tears.

'You hate it here.' Lance charged his glass again. This time when he gestured towards her with the bottle, she nodded.

She downed it too quickly, the fiery liquid burning her throat and threatening to make her cough.

'Every year you complain about the summer, then you complain even more about the winter. You hate the service and the fact they never put enough ice in your drinks. You hate the food. You've never once tried steak-and-kidney pudding.'

'Just because I don't eat steak-and-kidney pudding, Lance, it doesn't mean I haven't grown to love England. In my own way.'

'Not two weeks ago you were so sick of the rain, you said it was like permanently living under a power shower.'

She'd hoped he hadn't remembered that. 'I've bought a new umbrella since then,' she protested feebly.

Lance gave her a wry smile. 'Methinks the lady doth protest too much. You know you'll adore DC! Think of all those Congressmen's wives and committees. All the worthy deeds you can do for the needy in front of the right people. DC is charity-ball seventh heaven. You know how you love a canapé and a good cause.'

It was pointless discussing it, Melissa knew. Fossil Oil had decreed it and that invariably meant it would happen. Unless, of course, Fossil Oil decided otherwise.

In any case, as Lance said, two years in one place had been tantamount to a minor miracle. Before that they had roved Fossil Oil's European holdings – eight weeks in Belgium, eight months in Greece, eighteen months in Paris. In between all that, they'd regularly shuttled back to London for meetings. The list read like an airline timetable. In most places there'd scarcely been enough time for her to establish – well, let's say *connections*, before they'd flitted off again, Lance chasing promotions like eccentric Englishmen chase butterflies.

At least she'd had time in England to enjoy a smattering of *liaisons dangereuses*. However, she'd found that it was true what they said about English lovers: in most cases they had kept their socks firmly on.

The tears threatened again and she bit them down. By some insanity Tyler Benson had become her latest lover. One of Lance's own favoured directors! In Lance's eyes, Tyler could do no wrong. If only he knew. She'd never played so close to home before and she knew it was madness.

She also recognised that, this time, it wasn't just a no-strings fling to fill her empty days.

Tyler was different. His heart would be hard to break. He was ballsy and bright and destined for the top job, not unlike Lance had been thirty or more years ago. He would also be tough to leave.

Over the years, Melissa had made love to many men and had walked away when she tired of them, untouched by the burden of emotion. If she'd been younger and more impressionable, this time she would have said that she was in love. Not to him. Never to him. She felt as if he'd taken a piece of her soul and, if she was honest, there wasn't a lot of it left to spare.

'We'll get a nice place in Georgetown. You'll like that. All those shops.'

'I can't spend all my life shopping, Lance. Maybe I could get a job, a real job, at one of the charities?'

That would make the move away easier; she needed something to occupy her time.

'Why would you do that? It would take you away from me. You know I need you as my wingman.' Lance looked at his wristwatch. It was gold and emblazoned with the company logo – unimaginatively and unsurprisingly, a fossil: the distinct spiral of an ammonite. It was studded with four diamonds, each of them marking some long-forgotten milestone with the company. 'There are going to be a lot of tough decisions to make and I can't do it without you.'

The discussion, it seemed, was over. For now. 'Does anyone else know you're leaving yet?' Melissa asked.

Lance shook his head.

'Not even Tyler?'

'Especially not Tyler. I think he could do very well out of this and I want it to be a surprise for him. I'm lucky, honey. He's been a great right-hand man. Tyler's always got my back.'

She kept her eyes fixed straight ahead.

'I'm just waiting for Bud Harman to fill me in on the final details. There's a new international director on board too, and I need to talk to him.'

'Who?' She hadn't heard anything about this either. 'When did this happen?'

'Last-minute, but we've been trying to poach him for a long time. Now we've got him. Everyone has their price.'

She was sure Tyler knew nothing about this either.

'He's supposed to be coming along tonight,' Lance added. 'I thought it would be a good opportunity for them to meet. I don't want to say anything to Tyler until I know what the full deal is.'

'Are you going to tell the rest of the staff tonight that you're leaving?'

'I don't know.' Lance sucked on his teeth to show his indecision. 'It might put a downer on things. I've got such a good team at Fossil Oil. They've got tremendous respect for me and are so dedicated too. I think they'll be sad to see me go and it could well spoil the party mood if I announce my imminent departure now.'

'Well, as you think fit.' If he delayed, at least it would give Melissa some breathing space. She needed to speak to Tyler before there were any shock announcements. And a day's grace might not seem like much, but it would at least give her time to think and make contingency plans.

Lance didn't need to know, but she was looking forward to this party more than she ever had before. And for all the wrong reasons. It had been more than a week since she'd last seen Tyler, when they'd spent a hurried and torrid few hours together in a hotel in Bayswater, and it felt like a lifetime. She hoped that tonight they'd manage to snatch some time alone. Tyler Benson was a fantastic lover and one she couldn't let go of lightly. He was young, energetic, eager. His body when he held her was firm, hard. The sex was fantastic but, though she didn't want to acknowledge it, it meant more than that. Much more. Even now, sitting next to her husband in his lavish company car, she wanted to feel the hands of his young pretender on her. If she closed her eyes, she could replay every second of their last tryst in her mind. He'd pushed her to the bed, his mouth hot on hers, kissing her with a passion that had been missing in her marriage for many a long year. She could picture him hitching her skirt, his skilful, tantalising tongue finding places that made her gasp with pleasure.

'All right, honey?' Lance asked.

Melissa, mouth dry, forced her eyes open and licked her lips. She was getting all hot and bothered just thinking of Tyler and there was only so much you could blame on the menopause.

'Yes, of course.'

'Here we are,' Lance said as Martin pulled up outside a spectacular mansion. 'Are you ready to face the troops, honey?'

She nodded, unsure of her voice. The truth was that with every fibre of her being, she yearned for Tyler's touch. Melissa didn't think she'd ever truly yearned before. Now she was going to have to leave him, and the thought was unbearable.

Chapter Seven

'Who the hell is paying for all this?' Tyler Benson complained. 'That's what I'd like to know.' He was keen to make sure he took all the credit for it, and equally keen to make sure that none of it came off his budget. 'Look at it.'

'It's beautiful,' Kirsten breathed.

It was certainly the most spectacular venue yet for the office party. Normally they'd use one of the chain hotels in the area near the London office, something perfectly functional but pretty bland. Anything else had been deemed ridiculously expensive for a staff knees-up. Clearly the budget had gone out of the window this time. Wadestone Manor was stunning, and Tyler had seen some pretty impressive places in his time. This surpassed them all.

'It looks like a French chateau.' Tyler gazed around. 'This is the sort of place I'd like to live in. If only I'd been born into a banking dynasty or been the child of a publishing magnate.'

Instead, his dad had been a lowly electrician, his mum a school dinner lady. No chance of owning a chateau there. Though they had once owned a static caravan down on the coast. They'd thought that was the height of decadent luxury. His dad would have fainted if he'd still been around to see all this.

'It does seem more lavish than the usual Christmas party,' Kirsten noted.

'Tonight's supposed to be a no-expenses-spared thank-you to all the staff for relocating from London up to the wilds of Milton Keynes. Lance's idea. There was a lot of grumbling about it at the time, but then people grumble about everything. It seems to have worked out OK.'

Lance's personal assistant, Veronica, had co-ordinated the whole thing and whichever company she'd drafted in to pull it together had done an amazing job. Even Tyler, who was a take-it-or-leave-it kind of man when it came to Christmas, couldn't fail to be impressed.

Every public room in this substantial stately home had been decorated with ornate Christmas trees – they were virtually the size of the ones in Trafalgar Square. God only knew what they'd cost. There was an enormous marquee on the back where dinner would be served. Someone had gone to town on that too. It was billowing with white fabric like a ship in full sail, and there were so many Christmas trees that it looked like a bloody winter wonderland or something. Afterwards there was entertainment. A casino was set up in one room and there was the obligatory band and a disco. Who knew what other delights awaited them before the evening ended.

'It reminds me of our wedding,' Tyler said. Kirsten had gone all out for that too.

'I think our wedding was a little more tasteful than this,' she said, nose wrinkled.

What a day that had been. Everyone said it was the wedding of the year. Kirsten was happy, excited. Sadly, it was probably the last time he'd seen her like that.

He looked at his wife. She was still very beautiful, no doubt. He liked having her on his arm. Heads turned when she walked into the room. Usually other men's. He was proud of that. After all, he'd coveted her when she was on someone else's arm. And who wouldn't want a wife who looked like Kirsten? He'd already clocked the wives of his colleagues and they were mostly dumpy women squashed into dresses that were too tight and too young for them. Kirsten was class.

It was just a shame that he never felt as if she was on his side now. Her sideways glances at him were always disapproving, her mouth tightly pursed. She didn't seem to know how to have fun any more. He couldn't remember when she'd last thrown back her head and laughed out loud. In the early days, when they were first together, they'd laughed a lot. Hadn't they? When had that all started to go wrong? Kirsten had everything she ever wanted and more. Now she'd told him that they needed to work on their relationship, and that was something that men – him at the top of the list – avoided at all costs.

'The rest of the coaches must have arrived.' Tyler nodded towards the main door, where the Fossil Oil staff were arriving in droves. Transport had been laid on to take them from the offices out to the Wadestone estate. It was clear that they were, even at this early stage in the proceedings, all high on festive and other kinds of spirits.

This anteroom where they were being served welcoming champagne and canapés was exquisite, full of towering marble pillars and ornate gilt mirrors.

'Oh yes.' Tyler took a canapé from a passing tray. 'I can definitely see myself living somewhere like this.' One day, when *he* was the one officially running Fossil Oil. 'Look lively,' he said to Kirsten. 'Lance and Melissa are here.'

'Deep joy,' she muttered. 'Is he sober?'

Tyler sighed. 'It's early yet. I can only hope so.'

He also wished, fervently, that the evening wouldn't be too tricky. He was playing with fire there, that was for sure. How on earth had he got himself embroiled in an affair with Melissa

Harvey? It had seemed like a good idea at the time; now he thought it might have been an uncustomary lack of judgement.

A waiter breezed past him carrying a tray of champagne and he grabbed two glasses. He passed one to Kirsten.

'I'm driving tonight,' she reminded him.

'Don't. Let's stay over,' he cajoled. 'Or get a cab.'

'I don't know. I like to be in my own bed.'

'Then have just one.' He pressed the glass into her hand. 'A little one. By the time you've eaten a turkey dinner, there'll be no trace of it. It'll loosen you up.'

'I'm not sure if I want to be loose.'

'We were going to have fun, dance, kick up our heels, remember?'

She smiled at him. 'So we were.' Without further protest she took the glass and gulped at the fizz.

He wanted Kirsten relaxed and mellow – preferably quite drunk – not on guard all night. Plus it would be nice to stay over in a hotel, make love in a four-poster bed. It had been too long since they'd done that. He snaked his arm round his wife's waist and squeezed her tightly.

He downed his champagne in seconds. It was good stuff, and again he felt his paternal instinct towards his budget take a hit. This was *so* not coming across his desk.

Lance and Melissa were making their way through the exuberant crowds, coming in their direction. The chairman was shaking hands and slapping backs as he came; Melissa trailed in his wake, a smile that was just short of sincere pinned on her pretty face. Tyler's dearest hope was that Lance might, for once, stay sober for this evening – that had a snowball in hell's chance – but he had no intention of being so himself. He was going to get through this night on a sublime mix of divine benevolence and strong drink.

Eventually, Lance and Melissa reached them.

'Tyler, my man!' Lance reached out and held his arm and his elbow in a vice-like grip. He shook his hand until Tyler's fingers throbbed.

For someone who abused his body so much, Lance was a strong, fit man. He could drink everyone under the table – and had done so many times at conferences – and still be as fresh as a daisy the next morning. For a man of his age, his recuperative powers were truly astonishing.

Next to him, Melissa was embracing Kirsten. The ladies air-kissed and he heard them exchange a friendly greeting. That was all fine. Now all he had to do was make sure that he kept them as far apart as possible for the rest of the evening.

Lance turned his attention to Kirsten. She smiled warmly and kissed Lance's booze-flushed cheek.

'Hello, Lance, it's lovely to see you again. You're looking very well.'

'That's what I like!' he boomed. 'A nice bit of flattery from a pretty young thing. It makes my heart glad, even though you don't mean a word of it.' He winked at Kirsten.

Quickly Tyler grabbed two more glasses of champagne and handed them to Lance and Melissa. With only a moment's hesitation, he took another one for himself.

'Cheers,' he said and they all clinked glasses. Melissa brushed her body against his arm and smiled at him.

This was no good for his heart. Even for him, a man who always liked to follow his impulses, hooking up with Melissa Harvey was a step too far. There was a phrase that he should have heeded about not doing doo-doo on your own doorstep. He'd remembered it far too late, but there'd been something afoot at Fossil Oil that he wasn't party to and he didn't like it. Tyler had always prided himself on keeping his finger on the pulse. It seemed only sensible to have an intimate informant on the inside track, and Melissa had proved very useful in converting her pillow talk with Lance into pillow talk with him. If he was honest, it was easier to have a conversation about the business with Melissa than it was with Lance. She was one sharp cookie, and anyone who went to Fossil Oil board meetings knew that nothing was ever passed until Lance had taken it home and run it by Melissa. She'd have done a better job as chairman than her husband did. That's why initially he'd hooked up with her, but now he was in this up to his neck and didn't know what to do.

She was a player, Melissa, and he was too. They had a lot in common. And, for a time, it had been mutually beneficial. It wasn't just about the sex – though there was a confidence in an older woman that he admired – they also both enjoyed the cut and thrust of Fossil Oil and he could talk to her about his doubts and fears in a way that he never could with Kirsten. His wife saw Fossil as the enemy and didn't want to hear anything about it.

Now, however, Melissa had become clingy. She demanded to see him more and more. She phoned him at inopportune moments. More than once he'd had to duck into the bathroom and run the shower while he spoke to her so that Kirsten wouldn't hear.

There was no doubt they'd had some fun together, but now it had to end. Melissa just didn't seem to understand that. He'd tried not returning her calls, wriggling out of her constant pleas to see him. She was older than him and much wiser: you'd think she'd know the score. He loved Kirsten, of course he did. This was something else entirely. Something very separate to his marriage.

'Hello, Tyler,' she said. 'How lovely to see you.'

Her eyes held his for longer than was sensible and he hoped no one had noticed. Kirsten in particular. He and Melissa had to have a talk tonight. He wanted this to be a clean break where they remained good friends and, more importantly, she didn't feel the need to confess all to Lance.

Lance's PA appeared. Veronica was a competent woman as well, far too dedicated to Lance and completely impervious to Tyler's charms. Not that he hadn't given it a good go. Yet, whatever he did, there was no way that she'd part with any useful inside information for him.

'Do come and have your photographs taken,' she urged and ushered them towards an area of the reception room where a studio set of a winter wonderland had been created, with a backdrop of a snowy scene complete with twinkling stars and Christmas trees laden with fake snow. The floor was covered with fake snow an inch deep.

They were shown past the waiting junior staff and Veronica slotted them into place at the head of the queue until the photographer was ready for them.

First, Lance and Melissa stepped forward. Both grinned obligingly for the camera, staged faces that they were used to showing to the world. Then he and Kirsten joined them. Kirsten stood next to Lance while he went to Melissa's side. Fake snow engulfed his shoes. Melissa slipped her arm around him and he felt her fingers forage beneath his dinner jacket to caress his bottom. Not good. Not good at all. He needed to stop this *now*. Before Melissa thought it could go any further. But how?

He glanced at Kirsten, whose smile was frozen in place. Lance's arm was round her and he wondered if the chairman was doing the same to his wife. Old goat.

Then, as they were all beaming cheesily for the camera, he saw Louise arrive and it wasn't the flashgun going off that had his eyes popping out of his head. She looked unbelievably delicious. How could he not have spotted this before? It wasn't that he hadn't noticed she was quite fanciable at the office – but not in this way. Now that she was scrubbed up, she was an absolute stunner. She was wearing some demure black dress, but looked as sexy as hell. Her hair was swept up, showing off her long, slender neck. His mouth had suddenly gone dry. He viewed it as a perk of the job to have an affair with his assistant, which had got him into trouble more than once. After the last incident, he'd sworn off office relationships. He'd let Human Resources pick his new assistant and this one was bright all right. Louise was as sharp as a tack. He was only surprised that she wasn't further up the ladder already. He'd only made a few half-hearted attempts to flirt with her, but she was having none of it. Not that it had bothered him. There was always someone willing if he felt the urge.

But tonight he was seeing her in a different light. Louise looked truly ravishing and he decided that whatever it took he needed to get to know her better.

Chapter Eight

I stand frozen to the spot on the verge of the reception room. This house is completely awe-inspiring. I've never been inside a place like this before and it's almost overwhelming. I wish now that I'd caught the coach with the others. At least then I would have been able to come in with Karen rather than make an entrance all by myself which is so daunting.

Scanning the room, I look for a friendly face, but see no one I know. I haven't been at Fossil Oil long enough to make friends properly and sometimes I feel that, as Tyler Benson's personal assistant, some of the staff actively avoid me.

Everyone's in a good mood already and the room is bubbling with excited conversation. Waiters hurry by with trays of champagne, but I can't catch anyone's eye.

I know I can't stand here all night like a lemon and, just as I'm bracing myself to join the fray, I feel a hand touch my arm and I whirl round.

It's Josh Wallace and I'm sure my face must be the picture of relief.

He leans in to say, 'Hello, Louise. This is a magnificent venue, isn't it?'

'Gorgeous. I feel a bit like a fish out of water though.'

'Never.' His eyes take me in from head to toe, but not in a

creepy way like Tyler. 'You look like you suit this place down to the ground.'

I feel myself flush when I answer, 'Thank you.'

'Can I get you a drink?'

'That would be lovely.'

Josh stops the first waiter who waltzes by. There must be a knack to it, one that I haven't yet got.

He hands over a glass of fizz.

'To a great evening.' He clinks his glass against mine.

'I'll second that.' I notice that my hand is shaking as I drink. 'You're a veteran of these parties?'

He nods. 'Oh, yes. I've been to one or two in my time.'

'I feel like a complete novice. I haven't worked in a long time and when I did, the Christmas parties certainly weren't as lavish as this. If we were lucky, we used to nip down to Wetherspoon's for a burger and a pint with a few party poppers.'

He laughs. 'This is a cut above, even for Fossil. But the company's had a good year. Despite the economic downturn, the money's been rolling in. My own sales have been through the roof too.' He shrugs those square shoulders which are flattered by his dinner suit. 'It's nice that the employees see some of the benefits.'

As I've only just joined I feel that I haven't actually done any of the hard work, but I'm sure I'll earn my money next year. From what I've seen so far, Tyler Benson will certainly want his pound of flesh.

'How is it, working for Tyler?' he asks, reading my mind.

'I'm still getting used to it.'

A knowing smile. 'Very diplomatic. You'll go far.'

I return the smile. 'I hope so.'

I want this job to be a stepping-stone. I'm grateful to have gone from stacking shelves to personal assistant, but I'd like to think that I could work my way up at Fossil Oil. At the interview, the human-resources manager said that there'd be opportunities for advancement. I've just got to keep my nose clean and do a good job.

Then Karen appears. She's breathless and giggly already. Her cheeks are flushed bright pink and they match her outfit.

'Hello,' she shouts at us even though we're standing just in front of her.

She lurches forward and comes perilously close to spilling out of the top of her strapless dress.

Her head swivels away from me. 'Hi, Josh.'

I smile: her voice is very simpering, even for Karen. Her fingers twiddle her hair and she licks her lips enticingly and plants a rather slobbery kiss on Josh's cheek, at which he looks slightly shocked.

'They're taking photos over there.' She waves her arm in a random direction. 'Come and get one done.'

With a theatrical wink back at me, she grabs Josh by the hand and drags him away. He gives her a benign smile and gestures with his head that I should follow. Not knowing what else to do, I duly fall in step. We wind our way through the crowd until we reach the photographer. There's a short queue and we join it.

There are two topless 'firemen' models on hand to have their photographs taken with the single ladies – and some of the gay men. They're causing quite a stir and are doing great business posing for photographs on the over-the-top Christmassy set. I daren't let my mother see a picture of this backdrop or, I tell you, she'll be recreating it in our living room.

When we reach the head of the queue, Karen pulls at my arm. 'You and me with the firemen,' she says.

'No, no, no.' I sound like my father. I tug from her grasp. 'I'll sit this one out, if you don't mind. You go ahead and fill your boots.'

The last thing I want is for Tyler Benson to see me in a photo with either of these two hunks. I don't want him to think that I'm available or looking for some fun. Because I'm *definitely* not.

'Spoilsport,' Karen says, but she's still grinning when she totters forward in the fake snow and on to the wintry set.

Immediately the firemen hoist her into their arms and hold her aloft between them. She squeals with delight, posing and pouting for the camera.

They put her down and she weaves her way back to us, now completely giddy. 'That was amazing!' She jiggles her boobs back into her dress. 'You don't know what you're missing. Your turn.'

I hold up a hand. I can't go up there on my own while people are watching. Even if the firemen are out of the picture. 'No. It's not for me. Honestly.'

'Do it! Do it!' she urges.

'Have your photograph taken with me,' Josh says. 'It's not often I have the chance to be snapped with the most beautiful woman in the room. We should have something to remember this party by. I think it will be a very special night.'

I shrug my acceptance. This I can manage, and I'm glad he's stepped in to rescue me from Karen's excesses. 'OK.'

So he takes me by the hand and leads me into the little slice of winter wonderland. We stand amid the snowy trees, the fake icicles and polystyrene snow. Josh gently slips his hand round my waist and we smile nicely for the camera.

Even in my high heels he's taller than me, and I feel ridiculously protected by this kind gesture. Though, it's fair to say, I can feel Karen's eyes boring into me.

When the photographer has finished we go to make our escape.

'Oh no you don't,' Karen says to Josh. 'You're not getting

away that easily. Now it's my turn.' And, while he smiles apologetically at me, she clamps his hand in hers and whisks him back on to the set so that she too can be photographed with him.

She does full-on pouting and preening, draping herself over Josh while he stands looking a lot more uncomfortable than he did with me.

At the other side of the room a gong sounds and someone announces that dinner is served. The crowd surge forward and I get swallowed up as people jostle towards the front of the queue.

Karen and Josh leave the winter wonderland and are carried forward in the crush towards the marquee where the main party is to be held. I'm hemmed in and can't reach them. I see Josh glance back, but he doesn't see me. Then Karen links her arm into his and he's gone.

Chapter Nine

Kirsten stood alone, self-consciously fiddling with the stem of her glass. She was trying to make this drink last, but the temptation to grab another one from the stream of waiters passing by was almost overwhelming.

Tyler had been waylaid by some sweating old man whose cummerbund had rolled itself to a thin, tight sausage across his stomach. It was a revolting sight to behold. They were head to head, deep in discussion. Lance had also drifted away to talk to other members of staff and was currently doing what he did best, slapping backs and guffawing loudly.

When they were left by themselves, she'd turned to Melissa. 'Thank you for the recommendation of the Christmas planners. They've made a wonderful job of the house.'

'You're more than welcome,' Melissa said, but her eyes travelled the room and Kirsten could tell that she was distracted.

'What are you doing for Christmas?'

'Er . . . ' Melissa said. 'Could you just excuse me? I must visit the powder room.'

'Of course.'

Melissa sashayed away from her and, disappointed, Kirsten watched her go. She had always secretly admired Melissa. She was a woman who seemed to know how to play the corporate game. Usually they got on quite well at these things, although Melissa seemed content to keep her at arm's length. But tonight she didn't seem to be in the mood for small-talk and Kirsten was left alone again. As she so often was.

Most people were now making their way through to the marquee where dinner was being served. This was what she hated about office parties. She never really fitted in. No one at Fossil cared who she was and, the minute they arrived, Tyler got embroiled in work issues and forgot she was there at all.

She looked at her husband across the expanse of hall that separated them. His eyes were roving the remnants of the people heading into dinner and he struggled to keep his attention on the rather agitated man in front of him, who seemed to be telling him some sort of sob story. He would learn, no doubt, that Tyler was not a sob-story type of man.

As she watched more carefully, his restless eyes returned time after time to rest on a pretty young woman on the other side of the room. Though the woman seemed to be blissfully unaware of his attention, Kirsten wasn't.

She glanced at her watch. Hours to go yet. Hours and hours of this. Standing on the sidelines, just waiting. Was it too much to hope that something would liven up this evening? If she wanted to be with Tyler, she'd have to make her way through the throng to get to him. What was she even doing here? she wondered. Tyler would have been so much happier on his own – moving and shaking, schmoozing and scheming. She, in turn, would have been happier left at home with a gin and tonic and a chick flick.

Tyler never wanted to go out at the weekend as he was always too tired. He liked to slump on the sofa with a bottle of wine, nothing more. By nine o'clock he was normally too sozzled for coherent conversation, or fast asleep and snoring. Kirsten had very few friends of her own. There were several casual acquaintances, women who she said a passing hello to at the gym. One or two who she might go for a coffee with, but that was it. There were no close girlfriends who she could call on to go out for a meal or a glass of wine. No wonder she was so ridiculously lonely.

She thought, in the new year, that she might try to get closer to Melissa. She of all women must understand some of the things Kirsten was going through. Fossil Oil ruled her life too. Perhaps, later this evening, she'd ask Melissa if she'd like to go out to lunch with her. Perhaps they could share a glass of wine and a Caesar salad, swap stories about being a corporate wife, laugh and gossip. How she longed to do that again.

Next year would be different. She would grab control of her life back and do things for herself. She'd give Tyler some ultimatums and, hopefully, turn their relationship around. She had so much to be thankful for and she hated feeling so disenfranchised and discontent. It had to stop.

'Hello, Mrs Benson.'

Jolted from her musing, Kirsten turned to the woman standing next to her. It was the one Tyler had been ogling. She was bright-eyed and beautiful. Her hair, piled high in a trendy up-do, was glossy, her skin flawless, her body ripe with the seductive promise of a younger woman. What was she? Late twenties? Certainly the right side of thirty. Much younger than Kirsten, anyway. Just looking at this fresh-faced girl made her feel every one of her forty-two years. How she wished she could be that age again, with the whole of her life before her. What different choices would she make then?

'Hi. I'm Louise,' the girl said, all smiles. 'Tyler's new assistant.'

'Oh.' Kirsten tried not to stare too hard at her. Of course she was. Tyler would never hinder himself with a plain assistant.

'I thought I'd come over and introduce myself.'

She was bubbly, keen to please. Her husband would like that too.

So this was Tyler's new fling. She could see the attraction. Who wouldn't? In comparison to herself the girl was dewy, gleaming, enthusiastic, full of life. Beside her Kirsten felt like a dried-out old husk. Although Louise's outfit clearly wasn't expensive, she looked sophisticated and understated. It made Kirsten feel like a footballer's wife – overdressed and trying too hard.

'I bet you've been to loads of these Fossil Oil dos,' Louise continued.

'Many, many.' Too many. Far, far too many.

The last time she'd caught Tyler having an affair with his assistant – Debbie – it had been because someone had kindly sent her an anonymous letter to inform her of it. It hadn't been a surprise. In fact, she'd half-wondered whether it might have been Debbie herself who sent it, to try to break up their marriage, galvanise Tyler into leaving her or something stupid like that. Perhaps that's what he'd promised to do; Kirsten wouldn't put it past him. Whatever the plan, it had nearly succeeded. She'd been on the verge of walking out. Only a lot of begging from Tyler and a crippling attack of insecurity had made her relent. If she left him, where would she go? She was the wrong side of forty with no job, no money, no home of her own. She was utterly dependent on Tyler. And she hated it.

When it had all blown up Debbie had been unceremoniously sacked. Tyler was too valuable for Fossil Oil to lose. Pretty secretaries, it seemed, were ten a penny. Now, merely a few months down the line, it was clear that Tyler was playing away again. So much for all his heartfelt pledges, his sweet-tongued promises that he'd change his spots. She should have known better.

There are things that men don't notice but women do. With Tyler there were too many late-night showers when he came home, the scent of another woman on his shirts, the shifty phone calls. He deleted every text that he received or sent, a sure sign of someone with something to hide. She wondered how many of the staff here knew about this latest tryst. How many of them were looking at her now over the rims of their champagne flutes with pity? How many were sniggering behind their hands?

There were rumours about Lance too being a womaniser, and his heavy drinking was legendary. Perhaps it was a requirement for all Fossil executives. She looked at Melissa and saw her own future writ large. It wasn't a vision she particularly wanted.

'I'm a novice.' Louise gave an anxious laugh and Kirsten's attention snapped back to her. 'I'm really nervous. My knees haven't stopped knocking yet.'

She should offer her some comfort, a word of advice, but Kirsten could find nothing to give. She had to concentrate to keep a picture of Louise and Tyler entwined together out of her mind. Where did they meet? A hotel? Her house? In the stationery cupboard at work? On the boardroom table? Kirsten wouldn't put it past Tyler. She knew only too well that he liked to take risks.

Kirsten had hoped that this time she might make a friend of Tyler's personal assistant rather than an enemy. Some of the other corporate wives seemed to manage it, but she never had. Perhaps that was because so many of them saw her as a love rival rather than the boss's wife. Sadly, it looked as if it was to be no different this time.

'My daughter, Mia, would love it here,' Louise added. 'She's only four and very impressionable.' The girl gazed round, eyes wide with awe. It looked as if she too was easily impressed. 'Do you have children?' she asked.

'No.' Kirsten never quite knew how to answer that question. 'I don't.'

There was a difficult pause between them.

'Well.' Tyler's assistant was uncertain now. 'No doubt we'll see each other at these things in future.'

'I'm sure we will,' Kirsten said tightly.

It was an awkward moment. Kirsten didn't know what to say to her. It was as if she was looking at herself ten years ago. She wanted to ask this pretty woman if she loved Tyler, she wanted to warn her against him, tell her that his kind of love was selfish, destructive and manipulative. That she would end up like her, insecure, clingy, jealous. Yet her cruel streak wanted Louise to find that out for herself. She should tell her that Tyler would use her for a short while and then let her go, as he'd done with so many before.

Kirsten wasn't one for confrontation though. Now she didn't even question Tyler about his comings and goings. What she didn't know couldn't hurt her, was the theory. And yet it did. Of course it did. Over the years she'd had to batten down her emotions to cope. But it had made her feel dead inside. Empty.

'I'd better go in for dinner,' Louise said, slightly awkward now. 'Are you coming?'

'In a moment.'

Kirsten felt churlish, as if she was the one in the wrong here. She had to admire Louise for her brazen front. The girl seemed to be genuinely trying to be nice, but that didn't make up for the fact that she was sleeping with her husband. She desperately needed a friend, but not a friend like that.

'I'll see you later,' Louise added. 'Hope you have a lovely evening, Mrs Benson.' She hurried away.

That left Kirsten alone again. She gazed at the stragglers of the crowd with a growing lack of interest and watched with dismay as the waiters bearing silver trays of brimming champagne glasses gradually started to disappear. So much for not drinking. Now she really could kill for another glass of fizz, and at this rate it looked like she'd have to.

Chapter Ten

Rushing into the marquee, I'm slightly panicky that I'm late. Wow. That was an excruciating meeting with Tyler's wife. She's one ice-lady. Perhaps living with Tyler has made her into a Stepford Wife. She certainly seemed like one.

I'd hoped that we might strike up a rapport, perhaps even become friends or something. It might make Tyler think twice about touching me up, if I was pally with his wife. Well, it looks like that was a pipe dream. Kirsten Benson is probably the sort of woman who has a huge circle of wealthy women friends. What would she possibly want with the likes of me?

I catch up with the crowd as they scan the table plans. Lance's scarily efficient assistant has drawn them up and I can only hope that I've been nice enough to Veronica in my first few months for her to seat me with someone who won't eat me alive. Maybe I should have bribed her with chocolate treats from the staff canteen in advance.

This place has been done out on a breathtaking scale. The marquee is white, draped with gossamer chiffon that sparkles as the light catches it, making it look like oil on water. Glass icicles hang from the ceiling and there are lavish chandeliers like frozen waterfalls down the centre. The tables have pristine white linen cloths and are decorated with silver candelabra. The chairs are silver and the dance floor is made up of white squares which light up in time to the music. Currently, there's a DJ playing mellow mood music. In the middle of the floor, there's a vast ice sculpture in the shape of the ammonite that is Fossil Oil's beloved logo. Smoky tendrils of dry ice drift across the floor.

In all corners of the marquee there are towering Christmas trees, also white, which are dressed with oversized silver baubles. The whole thing is breathtakingly beautiful.

There's a bar which is serving free booze all night and it seems as if many of the staff have already grown tired of the impressive decorations and are instead availing themselves of the gratis alcohol.

I don't ever want to reach the stage where a free drink is more attractive than something like this, so I stand inside the doorway and take it all in, trying to memorise every bit to tell my daughter. With my mobile phone, I snap a few photos to show Mia in the morning. She'd be in her element in here.

When I've finished taking photographs, I carefully scan the room. Of Josh Wallace there's no sign. He and Karen have disappeared without trace. Karen seems to be setting her plan to take him home with her in action already. Well, good luck to her. I have no need of that kind of thing.

I feel exhausted and yet the night is still young. It was flipping hard work talking to Kirsten Benson, I can tell you. Tyler's wife is stunning to look at, but it was like trying to converse with a lump of stone. Perhaps it's no wonder Tyler's developed a roving eye. Just so long as it stops roving in my direction sometime soon, then everything will be fine between us.

I'm sure I wouldn't be so miserable if I had all that she has. Karen told me that they live in a stonking great house in Hampstead. Hampstead, for heaven's sake! I thought only TV stars lived there. And she doesn't work or anything. Hasn't lifted one of her immaculately manicured fingers in years. She looks like a woman who's used to a life of ease. I bet she has a wardrobe full of cashmere and you can just tell that the dress she's wearing didn't come from Primark like mine. She has flawless skin and is as slender as a reed.

I should be massively jealous. She's living the sort of life I'd like for myself and Mia but, oddly, I feel quite sorry for the woman. Although she's expensively pretty, she also looked very fragile. Brittle. I should imagine that living with Tyler Benson has worn her down over the years. I wonder if she has any idea that her old man has an eye for the ladies.

Then, speak of the devil, my boss appears. He's with Tom Davidson, who runs the refinery at Coryton. He shakes Davidson's hand vigorously and then abruptly turns his back on the man. He heads in my direction and my stomach flips, but not in a good way.

'Hello, hello,' he says as he sidles up to me. 'You're looking particularly gorgeous tonight, my lovely sidekick.'

I paste a smile on my lips. 'Good evening, Tyler.'

My boss doesn't understand the concept of personal space. He stands about two inches away from me and, if it wasn't for the wall behind me, I'd step back. As it is, I'm trapped.

Point to remember for future. Never get stuck against a wall with Tyler Benson. I've already learned not to get in a lift with him on my own if I can possibly avoid it. There's actually a company directive that prohibits male employees from getting into a lift with a woman on her own. Tyler obviously hasn't read it. The man has octopus hands.

His eyes rove over my body, lingering too long at the little cleavage that I'm now regretting showing. He leans in and puts a hand on the wall over my shoulder. Really, any closer and we'd actually be having sex. This despite the fact that our colleagues are all around. Maybe he'd feel differently if he knew I'd told Karen all about him. I try to make myself smaller, much smaller. I don't know whether it's the drink kicking in, but he seems to be even smarmier than usual.

'Fine,' he says. 'Mighty fine. You've hidden your light under a bushel, Lovely Louise. I'll be the envy of Fossil Oil with such a pretty personal assistant.'

He says 'personal' in a sleazebaggy way.

'I'd rather they notice me for my sharp brain and excellent administration skills.'

He shrugs. 'That's a really great necklace.' His fingers caress the pendant that hangs from my mum's pearls.

'Thanks.' I get hold of it and try to move his hand away, but not before he's traced a line down my chest and towards my breasts. Creep.

Can't someone see this and rescue me? He's like this in the office too. Every single time he passes my desk, he tries to brush against me. If he brings me work, he leans so far over me that I'm nearly pressed flat to the desk. I try to do all I can not to get into these situations. I try everything to get him to leave me alone without actually saying to him, 'Back the fuck off!'

If this was some stranger in a nightclub, my inclination would be to knee him in the bollocks. But this is my boss. What can I do? Physically assaulting him would not enhance my promotion prospects.

Tyler angles his hips into mine and I jam my clutch bag between us to try to stop him attempting actual penetration. It reminds me of when I used to go to school discos and the local heartthrob would try to grind his groin into you during the slow dances. I sort of hoped that men got more sophisticated as they got older. It seems not.

My clutch bag is proving quite an effective method of contraception, but I'm feeling very uncomfortable with this situation. His *wife* is in the very next room, for goodness' sake. Has the man got no shame?

Then, just as I'm thinking that I'll have to say something or push him away, Josh Wallace appears.

'Tyler!' He claps him on the back and Tyler straightens up pretty swiftly.

I almost sag with relief.

'Josh. Good to see you.' In truth, he looks as if Josh is the last person on earth that he wants to see.

'I brought a drink for you, Louise.' He holds out a glass of champagne, which gives me the perfect excuse to extricate myself from Tyler's clutches. While Tyler is distracted, I move away from the wall and towards Josh.

'That's very kind. Thank you.'

'I need to talk to you, Tyler,' Josh says. 'When you've got a free moment. But for now, can I whisk this young lady away from you? Dinner's about to start.'

'Is it?' Tyler takes in the rest of the room and realises that the tables are filling.

'Catch you later.' Josh takes my arm and adeptly steers me away.

'We'll have a dance when the disco starts,' Tyler shouts after me.

Not if I can avoid it, I think.

'That was a very timely intervention,' I whisper to Josh when we're out of earshot. 'I can't thank you enough.'

'Tyler's all right,' Josh says. 'He's a bit of a lech, but I think his heart's in the right place.'

'It's not his heart I'm worried about.'

Josh laughs. 'I hope it's OK, but I did a bit of furtive jiggling with Veronica's table plan. She'd put me next to Ken Jones from IT. I don't drink, but I might have been tempted to start. I never understand a single word he says. Everything goes right over my head. I thought I could find much more agreeable company than that and I switched place cards. He's now with the moaning minnies of Alginate Sales and I have you sitting next to me.'

I like the thought that he finds me 'agreeable company'. It sounds so very Jane Austen.

'Where did Karen go?' I scan the room for her, but I can't catch a glimpse, even in that hot-pink dress. 'I thought I might be next to her too.'

'I did a bad thing,' he confesses with a sheepish grin.

I wait to hear what.

'I sort of jiggled her on to another table as well.' He flicks a thumb behind him to indicate where. 'You don't mind?'

'Not at all.' I try to hide my smile. Poor Karen! She'll be heartbroken. 'I'm just glad of a friendly face.'

Josh pulls out my chair for me and gratefully I sit down. When I glance back at Tyler Benson, he's staring straight at me, face as dark as night and frowning.

Chapter Eleven

The light touch of a warm hand making contact with the bare skin of her shoulder made Kirsten jump.

'Hey,' the voice behind her said softly, 'Kirsten Benson, as I live and breathe.'

Spinning round, Kirsten was aware that her mouth was suddenly dry, and it wasn't entirely to do with a dearth of champagne. She'd know that voice anywhere. Even after all this time.

This was like a dream. No, a nightmare. No. Definitely a dream. Her vision went blurry and everyone else receded into the background, fading to nothing as the man in front of her was brought into sharp relief.

His face hadn't aged at all. Not one jot. No grey hairs. No fine lines. Sickeningly, everything was exactly as she remembered it. His dark hair was swept back in the very same style. His fringe, over which he'd never had any control, flopped forward. The jewel-blue eyes still twinkled with laughter when he smiled. It was as if the years had fallen away.

Her heart knew him instantly too. It quickened and tightened as she looked at him. The colour, so carefully applied, drained from her face and it felt as if the ground was disappearing beneath her feet. The urge to reach up and touch him, to make sure that he was real and not just a mirage, gripped her. She clenched her hands into fists to stop herself.

Kirsten cleared her throat to make sure her voice knew that it was required to speak.

'Simon Conway,' she breathed, squeezing the words out of the dustbowl that had previously been her throat. 'Well, well, well.'

He smiled, and a warmth that had been missing for too long flooded through her.

'It's been a long time.' His voice, as it had always been, was as gentle as a lover's caress.

Ten years and six months. That was *exactly* how long. Absolutely nothing that had happened in the intervening years had made her forget. If she was pushed, she could probably even count the days.

She tried to be sparkling, though her palms had grown clammy and damp. 'Wow.' She struggled to steady herself. 'This *is* a surprise. What on earth are you doing here?'

'I'm back in England,' he said nonchalantly.

Was he feeling remotely like she was? He looked as cool as a cucumber. Only the intensity of his gaze gave anything away. He was pleased to see her – more than that – she could tell.

'Really?' Keep it light. Keep it light. 'For a visit, or on a permanent basis?'

'I'm here to stay,' Simon said. 'At least, I hope so.'

'That's nice.'

He cocked his head to one side and gave her an easy smile. 'Is it?'

So he was back. After so long. She thought she might hyperventilate, and wished someone would bring her a chair that she could swoon into, some ice for her forehead. Simon Conway, when she had least expected it, when she thought he was out of her life for good, when she thought she'd never lay eyes on him again, was back.

He was standing there, looking so casual, so assured. Clearly, this wasn't doing to him what it was doing to her. In fact, her heart was now banging so loudly, she was marvelling that she'd managed not to have a heart attack on the spot.

'A delighted and spontaneous kiss for an old friend might be welcome,' he teased.

An old friend? Was that how he saw himself?

Simon proffered his cheek.

The very last thing she wanted to do was get close enough to brush her lips against his skin. Oh, how the memories came flooding back. A tsunami of them. Yet what else could she do? Her traitorous lips tingled in anticipation.

In spite of her reluctance, she leaned towards him and pecked him lightly on the cheek. There was a hint of stubble and it grazed her skin so softly, so exquisitely, that she wanted to press her face against it. She wanted to feel his flesh against her flesh. Kirsten tried to ignore the several essential beats her heart decided to miss, and the familiar spark of electricity that flashed between them. Time might have passed, they might have changed as people, but that raw chemistry was still very much there.

When she pulled away, there was a trace of lipstick left on his smooth, tanned cheek and nothing on God's earth would have persuaded her to revisit that cheek with her thumb to rub it away.

Simon made no comment on the brevity or impact of their contact, but then perhaps he hadn't felt it quite the way she had. However, when she looked into his face again she was sure he seemed distinctly more ruffled than he had a few moments ago.

'You look well,' he said. 'More lovely than ever.'

'Thank you. I only wish it were true.'

His eyes held hers. They were challenging, daring, mischievous. Loving. As they had always been. 'The years have been kind.'

'No,' she said. 'Not really.'

She was aware that Simon's hand was still resting on her skin, on her shoulder. He'd drawn her to him with an assured casualness and, though she so wanted to shrug it off, she couldn't. There had been nights, so very many of them, when she'd longed to feel this touch once more.

He laughed. 'You do look like you've seen a ghost. Is it so much of a shock to see me again?'

'It's possibly the last thing I ever expected,' she admitted candidly. Perhaps he *was* a ghost. A ghost of her past. A ghost of what her future might have been. 'Especially here.'

'Are you pleased?'

Taking a deep breath, she said, 'Delighted.' It didn't even come close to describing how she was feeling. Now she was unable to meet the clarity of his eyes and looked away. She had to keep this under control. If she fell for Simon all over again, then she'd be lost. 'Tyler will be pleased to see you too.'

Simon looked at her as if she should know better. Which she did.

'Where is Tyler?'

'He was over there with a man in a too-tight cummerbund trying to look enthralled, but I can't see him now.' Perhaps he'd gone through to dinner without her. It wouldn't be the first time. When he became engrossed in something to do with work, everything else went out of the window.

'Is he still the same old Tyler?'

'Oh, yes,' she answered. 'Nothing much has changed there.'

Again, his smile lit up his handsome face.

'Men never grow up, do they?' she added.

His voice was husky when he said, 'Some of us do, Kirsten.'

Even the way he said her name sent an illicit thrill through her.

He regarded her levelly. She'd always loved his eyes. At first glance they could seem cold and harsh, like the first light of dawn. But behind them there was always the promise of the sun to come. And she felt like a person who had been starved of the sun for too long. Marriage to Tyler was too often like a long, hard winter. Relentless and grey.

'I've missed seeing you,' he whispered. 'So much. Yet even I didn't realise quite how much until now.'

'Don't, Simon,' she said, shaking her head. What was the point?

He was making her feel like a gauche teenager again. He was so different from Tyler. Physically, emotionally, in so many ways. Taller for a start, and darker. His hair was effortlessly smooth and sleek, like the coat of a well-groomed cat. He was lithe with wider shoulders, slimmer hips, longer legs. Tyler was more straight up and down and although he couldn't quite be classed as stocky, he had a figure that offered no more room for expansion.

Simon had always been the sporty type – rugger, cricket, golf and the odd game of squash with Tyler. Except that Tyler had played him under sufferance because Simon always won. Her husband wasn't naturally sporty; he played some golf and squash, because it was the thing to do if you were a corporate man, to ease relations with similarly minded customers. He went to the gym because it sounded like a good thing to say. In reality, he did just enough that it allowed him to drink like a fish and not yet take on the shape of one.

Simon's personality had always been sunnier, less intense. He used his humour to comfort or gently tease, rather than to cut or score points like Tyler did. At least, he used to be like that. Now that he too was a corporate being through and through, for all she knew he could have grown up to be just like Tyler. Kirsten felt that was a thought worth hanging on to.

'You still haven't answered my question,' she reminded him,

trying to steer the conversation back to safer ground. 'What on earth *are* you doing here?'

His face darkened momentarily. 'Hasn't Tyler said anything?'

'No.' She shook her head. Simon didn't need to know that she and her husband rarely talked about anything of note.

'Ah.' Finally he dropped his hand from her arm and folded his arms across his broad chest.

The imprint of his fingers remained burning on her flesh.

Simon pursed his lips, a frown appearing beneath the floppy fringe. 'Maybe he doesn't know yet either.'

'Know what?' She was trying to ignore the fact that she desperately wanted Simon to touch her again.

'I'm Fossil Oil's newest recruit.'

Kirsten's eyes widened. 'Tell me you're not.'

Simon nodded. ''Fraid so.'

'Next you'll be telling me that you're going to be working for Tyler.' Kirsten gave a perplexed laugh. 'God help you if you are.'

There was an awkward little silence. Even when the two men had been close friends there always was an underlying spike of rivalry between them, despite all the amiable shoulder-thumping that used to go on. Kirsten's face fell. '*Do* tell me you're not.'

Simon checked that no one was around to overhear before answering. 'I'm not exactly going to be working *for* Tyler.'

'No?' she queried. 'What then?'

He raised his eyebrows knowingly and gave an apologetic grimace. 'I'm his new boss. Tyler's going to be working for *me*.'

Kirsten laughed out loud and then clapped her hands to her mouth. 'Gosh, I shouldn't laugh. He'll hate it! You know that.'

Simon smoothed his hand over his hair, lifting his fringe back, only for it to fall again. 'Lance was supposed to make an announcement. Today. In the office.'

'Lance is supposed to do a lot of things that he doesn't. As you'll no doubt soon find out.'

'He knows of my relationship with Tyler. Or my *previous* relationship,' he corrected. 'I thought Lance might have taken him to one side, broken it to him gently.'

'It probably wouldn't occur to Lance to treat Tyler, or anyone, with kid gloves. Your new chairman usually prefers a more baseball-bat type of approach.'

Simon made a *tsk* noise between his teeth. 'I need to speak to Lance.'

'What job is it, Si?' She instantly regretted using the familiar name for him that only a privileged few were allowed to do. It could well be that she no longer fell into that category.

'I think I'd better square it with Tyler first.'

'Don't you trust me to keep a secret?'

'I just think I should be man enough to do my own dirty work.'

'Tyler won't stand for it, you know.'

'He may not have any choice. There are big changes ahead for Fossil Oil. I can say no more than that.'

'Why come back now, Si?' she asked with a tremor in her voice that had appeared unbidden. 'Why Fossil? You could have gone to any other company in the world.'

He looked at her earnestly and lowered his voice, despite the fact that there was no one around. 'I think we need to talk about that later.'

'Why?' Kirsten asked. 'What is there to say?'

His beautiful eyes clouded over and he held her with a searching look. 'Do you really need to ask that?'

They were interrupted by the sound of a clanging gong. 'Ladies and gentlemen!' the liveried master of ceremonies announced. 'Can you please make your way through to the marquee. Dinner is served.'

There were only a few of them left in the reception hall now and Tyler was still nowhere to be seen. Thank heavens. He'd be apoplectic with rage if he saw Simon here.

'We'd better go through.' Simon held his hand under her elbow, and again she felt giddy with the sensation of his skin against hers. He escorted her to the marquee.

'Thank you. And now I'd better join my errant husband,' she said.

Together they looked at the table plan. She would love Simon to be at the top table – preferably next to her. Heaven knew she could do with an ally here tonight. On the other hand, she prayed that someone would have the good sense to seat him somewhere else – preferably as far away from Tyler as humanly possible.

'You're over there,' he said. 'I'm *way* over the other side. Looks like they've tucked the new boy out of the way. For now.'

Simon looked sadly at her and let go of her elbow. 'I really *do* want to talk to you later,' he insisted, the sincerity in his eyes confirming the depth of his intent. '*Alone.*'

Before she could reply, before she could tell him that would be a really terrible idea, he turned from her and walked away. She was vulnerable and she was sure he could tell that. Simon could read people well. But she remembered so very clearly exactly what kind of damage the oh-so-suave Simon Conway could do. It would serve her well to remember that.

Chapter Twelve

Melissa settled Lance next to her. 'Are you OK there, honey?'

'Sure am.' He reached for the nearest wine bottle, not even checking the colour before he filled his glass.

She turned away from Lance, pleased to see that Tyler was sitting on the other side of her. It would be difficult to get any time alone with him tonight, there were so many people around, not least Kirsten, but she could at least talk to him at dinner.

This was the first time she'd come face to face with Tyler's wife since their affair had started, and it pricked her conscience. When Kirsten was out of sight, she was, sadly, very much out of mind. The only person Melissa considered was Tyler. Yet she knew how she'd felt when she was in Kirsten's shoes and it wasn't pleasant at all. Melissa wondered what she would think of her if only she knew. What would she feel about her husband eschewing her bed to sleep with a more mature woman, and his chairman's wife to boot?

The whole of Kirsten's demeanour said that she'd rather be a million miles away from here, and Melissa could sympathise with that. In some ways looking at Kirsten was like seeing a version of her younger self.

Oh, she'd been so in love with Lance at that age, desperately trying to keep his attention when she knew that his eyes were straying. The things she used to do to gain his interest in her would make even the madam of a brothel blush. It hadn't worked. She wondered what lengths Kirsten Benson went to in order to keep her own husband entertained. Tyler might say that they never slept together now, but she knew he wasn't the sort of man who would tolerate a sexless marriage. Tyler Benson was definitely a sex-every-single-night sort of man.

She and Lance hadn't been intimate for years. And even if Lance's eyes roved now, there was nothing he could do to follow it through. An ever-increasing dependency on the demon drink had put paid to whatever prowess he'd once had in the bedroom.

Whatever the reason, the end of their physical relationship had all been a terrible blow to her self-esteem. Her confidence had plummeted. Once she'd taken part in the Miss New York City pageant and come second; that was damn nearly winning it. When their sex life had drawn to a gradual and inevitable close, she was sure that if Lance didn't want her in that way any more, then no other man would. Thankfully, she'd been wrong about that.

Maybe she should have got herself a puppy or a kitten to keep her company, but when they moved about so much it was difficult to take a pet with them. So she'd taken lovers instead. They'd generally been much easier to leave behind.

Yet she'd now become involved with Tyler Benson. It had started at a Fossil corporate event, much like this. Tyler flirted, he couldn't help himself. It was obvious that he was trying to keep the chairman's wife sweet, and why not? They'd chatted about Fossil Oil too and he was bright enough to know that she could be a useful ally. Initially, he seemed surprised how much she knew about the oil business, about Lance's dealings. Perhaps that was part of the attraction too.

A few days later, at his suggestion, they'd met for lunch in a quiet hotel in London. A secluded table. There'd been more flirtation, but she'd also given him the inside track on Lance's thinking about some of the key projects. They did lunch twice more, lingering longer each time. After the third time, they played footsie while they perused the menu, then skipped lunch altogether and Tyler booked a hotel room. That was six months ago and they'd managed to meet up almost weekly. It was the one day out of seven that she most looked forward to. It gave her something to live for.

Tyler made the blood fizz in her veins again. Parts of her that she thought were long dead were vibrant, excited once more. It wasn't that she was quite on the last descent on to the runway of old age, but her landing-gear was certainly lowered. Her auburn hair was kept that colour purely due to chemical intervention. The wrinkles on her forehead and round her eyes and mouth were similarly banished. Her skin benefited from the most expensive anti-ageing cream money could buy.

Tyler had made it clear from the very start what their relationship was about, but that didn't make it any easier. He told her that he loved his wife – very much – that their affair was just for fun. He'd been crystal clear about that.

But, somewhere along the line, it had gone wrong. She'd fallen in love with him. How very foolish was that?

Her lover sat down next to her and, as he pulled his chair in, she slid her hand surreptitiously on to his thigh. Under the tablecloth, he placed his hand on top of hers and turned his hundred-watt smile on her. Suddenly, the world was a better place.

'I'm looking forward to this,' he said.

'Me too.'

'Where the hell have you been, Tyler?' Lance barked.

Tyler beckoned to a waiter who was making a last bolt towards the kitchen and swiped a glass of champagne from his tray. 'I got talking to Davidson about the refinery problems.'

'So you *have* been to hell,' Lance said sympathetically.

'Tell me about it.' Tyler swigged down the fizz.

'We should talk about that later,' she whispered to Tyler. 'I've had some further ideas that might help to keep the costs down. I tried to talk to Lance about them, but he's not listening.'

'He isn't listening to much these days,' Tyler complained.

'We'll put our heads together later if we get a chance.' And, hopefully, more than their heads.

The table was beautifully dressed, with crisp white linen, silver candelabra, shimmering crystal. On each plate there was an ornate silver Christmas cracker.

'Shall we?' Tyler said. He picked up his cracker and offered it to her, their fingers brushing each other's.

Together they tugged and laughed as the contents spilled out on to the table.

'A fortune-telling fish,' Melissa said. 'Just what I always wanted.'

'Your future's going to be very bright,' Tyler said smoothly. 'You don't need a plastic fish to tell you that.'

She must remember that Tyler would be under Kirsten's direct scrutiny tonight and they should be very careful.

Tyler unrolled the green paper crown for her and carefully placed it on her head. 'Very fetching. It matches your dress.'

Melissa was entirely sure that it didn't go with one-carat-diamond earrings, but she was prepared to humour him. 'I don't seem to have a joke.'

'I'll tell you one,' Tyler said. 'What does Father Christmas do when his elves don't meet their sales targets?'

She smiled with good humour. 'I don't know.'

'He gives them the sack.' Then, still laughing at his own joke, he turned away from her and to his wife. 'Kirsten, pull your cracker with me.'

'I don't really want to, Tyler.'

'Pull it, Kirsten,' he urged. 'Please.'

Reluctantly she held it out to him and yanked on it. A small present fell to the table and Kirsten examined it. 'A penknife?'

'The crackers are probably made in Korea or somewhere,' Tyler said. 'Perhaps their health-and-safety standards are a little more lax out there.'

Kirsten gave Tyler a threatening look. 'Could come in useful.'

'I think I'll look after that for you!' he teased, but his accompanying laugh held a nervous edge.

'I'll keep it, thank you.' With a humourless smile, Kirsten slipped it into her handbag.

'Put your paper hat on,' Tyler urged.

'I spent a hundred and fifty pounds getting my hair done.'

'Put it on,' he cajoled. 'It's Christmas. You'll look sweet.'

'I don't want to look "sweet". I'm not putting the hat on. End of.'

With a defiant flourish, Tyler unfolded the crown and jammed it on. It was pink and he looked ridiculous.

'Lovely.' Melissa saw her husband reach for the bottle of wine again and blocked his move with a smooth, well-practised action. 'Lance, honey, would you like to pull your cracker with me?'

'Huh?' Lance looked up from the glass over which he was hunched. Already his rheumy eyes were glazed over with alcohol. He fumbled to find the cracker and handed it to her. Melissa clasped his fingers round it and together they pulled. The present fell on the floor and she didn't bother to retrieve it, but she unfolded his festive hat and put it on for him.

'Don't forget that you should welcome the staff and say grace, honey.'

'Don't fuss, angel,' he slurred.

The more he drank, the more belligerent he became. But the

more he drank, the more chance she had of slipping away unnoticed with Tyler.

'Melissa's right, Lance.' Tyler came to her rescue. 'You'd better make a move. The natives are getting restless.'

Lance lurched to his feet and staggered towards the stage.

'Should I go with him?' Tyler whispered to her, already rising from his seat.

She stilled him with her hand. 'He'll be fine.'

Tyler sat down again.

Lance was now front of stage and took the microphone from the stand.

'Good evening, everyone. I'd like to welcome you all to the Fossil Oil Christmas party,' he said. 'It's been a fantastic year for us all. Profits are up. Business is booming. This evening is to celebrate a new start for our company. There are plans for big changes in the new year, but more of that later. For now, let's offer up a prayer of thanks to our maker.'

While Kirsten was looking away from them and towards the stage, Tyler whispered to Melissa, '"Big changes"?'

She lowered her voice. 'Yes. I need to speak to you about that too.'

'You know about this?' he muttered back.

'Some of it,' she admitted.

Tyler tutted at her in exasperation. She knew he liked her to keep him abreast of all developments. Sometimes it annoyed her that it was *all* he wanted to talk about in bed. But then there were times when they sat together curled in the duvet, finishing a bottle of wine and kicking around some of the problems that Tyler was facing at work, just as she'd done with Lance all these years.

'And he's going to announce it tonight?'

'I don't know. He said not.' But now it sounded like he would. Sometimes when Lance had been drinking he was a loose cannon.

'Why am I the only one not in the loop?' Tyler complained.

'Lance only found out about it today.' So he said. 'As soon as we can get away, I'll tell you all I know,' she promised.

On stage, Lance lowered his head. 'God of goodness, bless our food, keep us in a pleasant mood. Bless the chef and all who serve us, and from indigestion, Lord, preserve us. Amen.'

A mumbled 'Amen' came back from the staff.

Lance made his way down from the stage and, as one, hordes of waitresses who'd been waiting in the wings swarmed in to serve their starter of soup. It was probably all that Melissa would manage to eat. These dinners were always loaded with carbs and none of those had passed her lips since the eighties.

She shook out her napkin, which read *Merry Christmas to One and All*, and spread it across her lap. Her soup was put in front of her and, just as Tyler was about to be served, Lance lurched past and stumbled into the waitress, who cried out. Tyler turned to see what was happening at the same moment that the plate she was carrying was knocked out of her hand, tipping it up so that the soup splashed out of it and splattered all over the front of Tyler's dinner shirt.

He jumped back with a startled cry and Melissa rushed to his aid, frantically dabbing at him with her *Merry Christmas to One and All* napkin. His face was like thunder.

'That bloody husband of yours,' he hissed under his breath. 'He'll be the death of me.'

'It'll be fine, Tyler,' she soothed, keeping her back to Kirsten. 'Trust me. Everything will be fine.'

Chapter Thirteen

Tyler was beginning to wish that he'd come down with some deadly illness. Well, perhaps not deadly, just something debilitating for twenty-four hours. Anything rather than be at this party. He'd hardly touched his soup, mainly because there was more of it on his shirt than in the bowl. Before he could finish the rest, the waitresses came to clear the table for the main course.

The bizarre thing was that he'd been looking forward to this do. He was held in high regard by the staff of Fossil Oil and it was good to show a united front with them. It helped to loosen up relations. Despite what Lance said, this year had been tight for sales, everything was getting harder and he thought it would be good to let his hair down for a couple of hours, get him in the mood for Christmas.

Now he wasn't so sure.

The table they were on was filled with excruciatingly dull people. There was Kelvin Shaw, head of finance. Bore. Shaun Thomson, who ran Alternative Fuels. Nightmare. Then there was Stephanie Lewison, who headed up the research laboratory. Her partner was a woman, which Tyler had suspected all along. No wonder she'd proved resolutely immune to his charms.

This lot certainly weren't going to prove to be a laugh a minute. Which was a shame. He'd hoped that he and Kirsten could have fun tonight, throw themselves into the Christmas spirit – God knew there was enough of it flowing in here – and perhaps start to get back to how they used to be. They hadn't been out together in a long time and, while his wife might have preferred a romantic dinner to the Christmas party, it was a start.

He wanted to give Kirsten a great Christmas this year. In fact, she was demanding it and he felt duty-bound to deliver. All that fuss with Debbie had unsettled her. He'd smoothed it over, obviously, but there was nothing like a few strategically timed diamonds to win over a woman's heart again. It was Christmas Eve tomorrow, so he'd have to find an hour to run out to the shops in the city to buy her something or, preferably, get Louise to do it for him.

He loved Kirsten. He was sure he did. Who wouldn't? She was a beautiful woman. It was just that there was so much else going on in his life.

Take Melissa here. She was stroking her hand up and down his thigh under the table and he really, really wished that she wouldn't. Kirsten was in a very weird mood tonight and it seemed to be getting worse, as if all her senses were on red alert. One wrong move and it could all end badly for him.

Melissa was a mistake. He knew that now. She was an attractive woman, there was no doubt about it. But she was high-maintenance and she was Lance's wife to boot. He shook his head at his own folly. If you played with fire like that, the likelihood was that you were, at the very least, going to get your fingers burned. Now he was quite worried for other parts of his anatomy too.

All he'd wanted was to find out a few of the chairman's secrets from her, and in that regard their affair had been very lucrative, but now the risks were too high. He'd enjoyed talking to her about the business. She'd become the confidante that he'd never had before and that had been a bonus he'd never expected. Yet now she seemed to be falling in love with him, and that could never, ever happen.

He'd told her the score. She knew that, in his own way, he adored Kirsten and that there was no one else for him but his wife. He might have the odd fling, but they didn't matter. He thought Melissa would understand that, play the game. Now Tyler wanted to break it off, but there was an addiction on his part too. It was useful to know all of Lance's thoughts about the business, and on more than one occasion Melissa's insider knowledge had given him the edge in a meeting. That would be hard to give up.

But there was something going on at Fossil Oil that he wasn't party to. Melissa had just confirmed as much. Lance was being very secretive at the moment and that didn't bode well. Tyler was his right-hand man, the wily, youthful Robin to Lance's ageing Batman. He should be all-knowing. If he didn't have a clue what was happening, who'd be there to catch the ball when Lance inevitably dropped it?

There was general chatter at the table, but Tyler was struggling to join in. He was distracted, on edge. Lance was worrying him as well. Even for Lance he was half-cut too early in the evening, and there was a long way to go before bedtime.

'Pass the other bottle of wine, Tyler,' Lance said, across his wife.

He and Melissa exchanged a worried glance.

'Are you sure?' Tyler whispered.

She nodded almost imperceptibly.

Tyler shrugged and reached for the bottle at the other end of the table which hadn't been touched. He passed it down to the chairman, who proceeded to glug it into his glass.

Under the table, Melissa's hand wandered higher up his thigh.

He glanced across at his wife, who was looking particularly stunning tonight. Sometimes Kirsten complained that he didn't notice her. And sometimes she was right. He took her for granted, he knew that. But she was a woman who had everything she wanted. She only had to ask and it was hers. Wasn't that what most women desired? She didn't have to worry her pretty little head about anything. If she needed money, he gave it to her. Everything in the house was done for her. If anything broke, she just picked up the phone and called Fossil Oil's maintenance department and it was sorted. She didn't even need to touch the garden, someone came in to do that. Kirsten's life was a bed of roses.

He grinned across at her and she smiled softly back. That look, he knew, was reserved just for him. Next year would be different, he thought. He'd stop all this messing about. He was getting too old for it and he didn't want to end up like Lance. His new year's resolution would be to get fitter, healthier. He'd give up drinking, actually go to the gym when he said he was there. He'd ditch the other women, Melissa being at the top of the list. It was time to turn over a new leaf. From now on, it would be just him and Kirsten.

Then, across the room, Louise caught his eye. She was sitting next to Josh Wallace, head thrown back in laughter. Clearly, his right-hand man was being very amusing. They could have done with some of his hilarity at this table. His mouth went dry. God, she looked sexy tonight. In the office she was always wrapped up in jumpers and such. The sort of stuff librarians probably wore. It didn't stop her from being attractive, but he'd never known that she could look like this. Her neck was long, slender. Her throat was flushed. There was a brightness, a sparkle in her eyes that he also hadn't noticed in the office. She wasn't just a looker, she was sharp too. A challenge. He liked that.

What he didn't like was how cosy she looked with Josh. Tyler

104

stroked his chin as he watched them. They were on a table with the rest of the sales managers. What a motley crew they were. Lazy bastards every one of them. They'd all rather be lounging in the office, hanging round the secretaries, rather than out there in the harsh world, making deals. Except for Mr Super Sell Himself, of course, the inimitable Josh Wallace. That man could sell ice to Eskimos, and he'd saved Tyler's bacon more than once.

Tyler had seen his potential when he'd first started at Fossil Oil and had taken him under his wing to groom for superstardom. But, recently, there were some days he felt that Josh just wasn't grateful enough. He was getting far too big for his boots. Too many people were noticing just how good he was. The man seemed to believe that he now ran Fossil single-handedly with nothing more for support than an iPad and a top-of-the-range Audi.

Tyler glowered at him. If he hadn't been such a good salesman and brought in so much money for the department, Tyler might have been tempted to sack him, just to take him down a peg or two. Then he'd learn that there was no such word as 'indispensable' in the oil business.

It was only the fact that his sales figures were so strong that protected him. In times of recession every other sales manager's figures were down, yet Josh continued to buck the trend. Thank Christ. If Josh Wallace went, and left him exposed, then it would be Tyler's head above the parapet.

'Tyler?' Kirsten was frowning now. 'You're staring.'

He snapped his attention back to his wife. 'Sorry. Just thinking about something the head of the refinery told me. We've got a few issues there.'

Despite his attempted deflection, Kirsten scanned the room until she settled on where his gaze had been. Her eyes fixed on Louise, who happened to look up at the same time. His assistant smiled in their direction, but Kirsten's features were frozen.

105

'We may have a few here,' she said coolly.

It would serve him well to remember that Kirsten was a jealous woman. A jealous woman with a penknife in her handbag. Tyler shuddered.

Kirsten's expression was grim, but before he could begin an explanation – or even think of one – the main course was served.

So often at these big corporate events, the food was disappointing, yet this looked like the real deal. There was a tranche of succulent white turkey breast, golden roast potatoes and all the trimmings. Now Tyler was ravenous. Apart from a few spoonfuls of the soup, he hadn't eaten since breakfast. Lunch had involved a meeting with the Business Development team and three cups of strong black coffee.

As he contemplated the deliciousness of the dinner in front of him, Lance stood up and lurched forward. 'Is it time for my speech yet?' he said, knocking the table.

Tyler lunged to steady it, but misjudged his movement. His elbow caught the edge of his dinner plate and he catapulted his Christmas dinner, with astonishing precision, right into his own lap.

'Oh my,' Melissa said.

He sat there wishing he was anywhere else. There was a mound of creamed potatoes covering his groin, with a bacon-wrapped sausage sticking out of it which looked quite obscene.

'Oh, Tyler,' Kirsten said, voice heavy with exasperation.

'I was only trying to help,' he protested.

Melissa was the first to galvanise herself into action. She swept up his *Merry Christmas to One and All* napkin and set to mopping his lap, scraping away the potatoes with more enthusiasm than perhaps an uninterested party might have.

'You can't let Lance give this speech,' she whispered to him when she had her back to the table.

106

'How am I going to stop him?' Tyler hissed back as he bent forward to put his ear closer to her mouth.

There was gravy as well as soup on his shirt now. He even found an errant sprout in his suit pocket.

'I need to be alone with you before then.'

'I have no idea how we're going to get away.' He had to be careful. Kirsten seemed to have eyes in the back of her head tonight.

'We have to try. I have something that I need to tell you urgently.'

On a night that was already proving to be testing, that was music to Tyler's ears.

Chapter Fourteen

The very second my soup is put in front of me, my phone rings. I rummage under the table and find it in my handbag. It's Dad.

'Excuse me,' I say to Josh. 'I need to take this. Urgent call.'

'Is there a problem?'

'I hope not.' I rush back out to the anteroom where the drinks reception was held, heart in my mouth. Like every mother who is away from her child, I instantly start to fear the worst. I can feel Tyler Benson watching me as I leave.

As I hit the now-empty room, I head for the winter wonderland display. 'Hi, Dad. What's wrong?' My voice sounds too loud and echoey in the vast space.

'Oh, nothing, love,' he says. 'Just wanted to tell you that we got home safely and to see if you were all right.'

'I'm fine.' I start breathing again. 'Is Mia OK?'

'Fine, love. She's tired. It's way past her bedtime.' Said for Mia's benefit, not mine. 'And Gramps has been teaching you a Christmas carol, hasn't he?'

I take a longing glance at the marquee where my lovely dinner is going cold. The polystyrene snow comes over the top of my shoes and I tuck myself in next to one of the Christmas trees.

'She wants to say goodnight, love.'

'Thanks, Dad. Put her on.'

'Mummy!' she cries as if she hasn't seen me for weeks rather than just an hour or two.

'Hello, sweet pea. Are you being good for Granny and Gramps while Mummy's at her party?'

'No,' she says.

'Then you need to be a good girl.'

Theatrical sigh down the phone. 'Ohhhh Kaaaay.'

'I'll say goodnight and then you go up to bed.'

'I want to sing my song.'

'Now? Can't it wait until Mummy comes home?'

'Shall I stay up specially?'

So cute. So very cute. 'No, sing it now for me. That would be lovely.' I have mentally written off my soup. Hopefully this will be a short song and I can get back in time for the turkey. The waiters are tidying up around me and giving me sideways glances. I go deeper into the Christmas trees.

'OK,' my daughter says. 'Are you listening properly, Mummy?'

'Yes.'

Deep breath. 'Good King Wenser last looked out on the Easter Stephen. When the snow layabout, deep pan crisp pan even.'

I can't help but smile, not just at the twisted lyrics but at the fact that it's sung at full volume and, essentially, all on one note. I hold the phone away from my ear.

Key change. 'Brightly shone the moo that night. Though the frogs were cool. Anna porman came inside, gathering ...' A lengthy pause. 'What was it, Gramps?'

Stage whisper: 'Winter fuel.'

Big finale. 'Winter fuuuuu-uuu-eeel.'

'That was brilliant,' I tell her, and, ridiculously, there's a tear in my eye. Despite the fact that I don't have much hope of my daughter becoming a pop star and keeping me in the style I'd like to be accustomed to. We're such a tight unit that I hate being away from her. 'Did you learn all that tonight?'

'Yes. On the way home.'

'You're so clever.'

'Shall I sing it again?'

'No, no, no,' I say. I'm hoping that at some point I'm going to get back to the strangely welcome attentions of Josh Wallace. I also hope that, in the meantime, Karen hasn't decided to slip into my place. 'You can sing it again tomorrow.'

'Say night-night,' Gramps urges.

'Night-night, Mummy.'

'Night-night, sweet pea. Love you to the moon and back.'

Then Dad comes back on. 'Isn't that grand?'

'Fab.'

'She's such a quick learner. Just like you at that age. How's the party, love?'

'It's fine, Dad. Nice.'

'I can come for you,' he says. 'No trouble. I left the car out.'

'Dad ...'

'I'll be there in a flash. I can come straight after part one of the *Strictly* Christmas special finishes.'

'I think I'm probably going to stay later than that, Dad. Make a night of it.'

'Oh.'

'I'll get the coach home. Don't. Wait. Up.'

'You know your mother worries when you're not in.'

'I'm fine. Really fine. I'm having a great time.'

'Oh. That's good. Watch what you drink. It can creep up on you.'

'Dad, I'm a big girl now. I know all that.'

'People do silly things when they've had a drink.'

'Not me. There's no need to worry. Look, I've got to go, Dad. They're about to serve dinner.'

'Lovely. What are you having?'

'Turkey, Dad. I'm having turkey. Got to go.'

'My favourite,' he says. 'I do like a bit of turkey.'

'Love you,' I say. 'Hanging up now.'

And before my dad can say anything else, I cut off the call. I must get out more often if this is the effect my only night out in living memory has on them. What will they do when Mia and I are set to move out? They might chain us in the basement.

With that thought in mind, and feeling quite glad that my parents' house doesn't actually have a basement, I hurry back to the marquee. Tyler's eyes follow me across the floor again. I feel like sticking my tongue out at him. Instead I mutter, 'Fuckofffuckofffuckoff,' under my breath.

As I feared, when I get back to my table Karen has slid into my seat. She's looking rather settled. She has a proprietorial hand on Josh's arm and is fashioning a tinkling laugh.

Josh looks up as I approach. 'Everything all right?'

'Yes. Fine. My daughter wanted to sing "Good King Wenceslas" to me.'

'That would be urgent.'

'I don't think she understands the concept of me-time. And, like all mothers, I assumed it was a call about an impromptu trip to A&E.'

'But she's OK?'

'Yes, totally.'

'Good.'

He seems genuinely concerned, and that's nice.

'Oh to be bogged down by commitments,' Karen says with added drama. 'Glad I'm free and single.'

'And available,' she forgets to add, but I think both Josh and I get the picture.

Then I stand there a bit like a lemon until the waiters sweep in with the main course. With a barely disguised huff Karen somewhat reluctantly extricates herself from my seat.

'Just keeping it warm for you.'

I bet.

'Catch you later.' She gives a little wave to Josh and what I interpret as a warning glance to me.

I'm putting this down to the fact that she's been drinking to excess and hoping she'll be all sweetness and light in the office tomorrow. Albeit with a monster hangover. Slightly harried, I sit down and let out a sigh.

'I'm afraid your soup's gone cold,' Josh says.

'That's the least of my worries. I'm just glad I'm back in time for the turkey.'

Josh smiles at me. 'Me too.'

Chapter Fifteen

I think I'm becoming paranoid. Every time I look up, Tyler Benson's gaze is fixed on me. Now his wife is doing the same thing. I pretend not to notice and return my attention to Josh, who is proving to be a very attentive dinner companion. Twisting in my chair, I keep my glass in my hand, so that it's blocking their view of my face. What else can I do?

Josh tucks into the lovely Christmas dinner that's been served. 'Don't let it bother you.'

So he's noticed too.

'It's very difficult,' I tell him. 'I don't want to upset Tyler – he's my boss. But I'm not the slightest bit interested in being yet another conquest for him.'

'That's probably what he finds most attractive about you.' Josh spears a sprout and studies it, contemplating whether to eat it or not, before popping it into his mouth with a slight grimace.

'They're good for you.'

He points at my plate, which is barely touched. 'Then you'd better eat yours.'

To be honest, I can hardly eat my dinner, I'm so anxious. I don't want to put a foot wrong this evening. The marquee is filled with Christmas songs while we eat and the mood of the staff is very jovial. Above the chatter, there's a layer of laughter and a contentment that's palpable. This feels like a very aspirational company to work for. People are upbeat, keen to get on, and I so desperately want to be a part of that for many years to come. I can do things with my life in a company like this. If only it wasn't for Tyler Benson.

'Our Tyler loves the thrill of the chase,' Josh says, getting back to our conversation. 'Whether it's a sales contract or a woman, he likes to be the hunter.'

I sigh. 'How very Neanderthal.'

Josh laughs. 'Don't worry about it too much. He's kicking around at the moment because we're at year-end.'

'The devil always finds work for idle hands.'

'He does indeed. Come January, we'll all be flat out and he'll be far too busy to bother you.'

'I hope you're right.'

'I'll look out for you,' he promises.

'Thanks, that's very kind.' It would be nice to know that someone at the office has my back, although I feel as if I'm going to have to learn to fight my own battles with Tyler otherwise he'll keep treating me as a pushover.

'There's something going on at Fossil,' Josh confides. 'I'm not sure what. But I've got the impression that Tyler Benson is going to have his hands full very soon.'

As long as his hands aren't full of my bottom, then I'll be happy.

'How long have you been working for the company?' I ask.

'Eight years now. Some days it feels a lot longer.' He refills both of our glasses. 'I joined them as a salesman when I was a callow youth of twenty-five and not long out of university. I'm gradually working my way up the corporate ladder.'

'Sounds like you've had quite a meteoric rise to me.'

'I'm ambitious, Louise. I want to get to the top.' He lowers his voice. 'I wouldn't say this to just anyone – well, no one really – but Tyler Benson's job has my name on it.'

I do hope so. I'd rather work for Josh Wallace any day of the week. All those late nights might not seem so bad. And then I check myself. I haven't had thoughts like this in years. When Mia's dad left us, I swore that no other man would ever darken my door. My daughter is the focus of my life now. I could count on one hand the amount of dates I've had in the last four years and they were all fairly disastrous. And yet there's something beguiling about Josh's brand of understated charm. Where Tyler Benson is brash, loud, arrogant, Josh is just the opposite. He's considered, he laughs readily but it's not a hideous guffaw and, although he seems a confident man, I can't help but feel that there's an underlying vulnerability. I think he'd be a good boss. Fair. Plus he looks kind of cute in the yellow paper hat that came out of the Christmas cracker that we pulled together. It's on lopsided and it makes him look very boyish. I resist the urge to straighten it.

'What about you?' he asks. 'What did you do before joining Fossil?'

'I was working in Boots, stacking shelves,' I say honestly. No point in trying to make out I'm something I'm not. 'Before that I was in a bank. When Mia was born, she was my priority. She's four now, nearly five, and has started to go to school full-time, so it's time for me to kick-start my career again.' That sounds like I ever had one. 'My mum and dad help me with childcare.'

'Are they babysitting tonight? Or is she with your husband?'

I could pretend, at this moment, that there's still a 'Mr Louise' on the scene. Josh seems to be making a play for me – but not in a creepy way like Tyler. In fact, it's been so long since someone chatted me up, it feels quite nice. Do people still even say 'chat up'? If I told him I was still in a relationship, that would certainly put paid to any 'available' vibe I might be giving out. But for some reason I want to be honest with him. If he is interested in me, then he'd better know up front what the score is. I come with baggage, with a capital B.

'No husband. No partner. No nothing. Just me and Mia. And my parents, of course.' He might as well get the full story. 'They're great. Which is just as well as they've got us both living at home with them now.'

'Ah,' he says. 'That must be tough.'

Yes. No chance of coming back to my pad for a night of passion, Mr Wallace. Process that.

'It works really well. I couldn't manage without their help,' I tell him. 'But I still want to get my own place again. If I can.'

'That's the reason why this job is so important?'

'Got it in one.' I know I should keep this light, impersonal, but Josh is very easy to talk to. 'My ex left me with a lot of debts too. It's going to take a while to clear those.'

'You'll do it,' he says. 'I was in the same boat when my wife and I split. It took time, but I dug myself out of it.'

'How long have you been divorced?' I should have got the low-down on him from Karen. She'll have done her homework. I bet she knows everything there is to know about Josh's personal life.

'We split up twelve months ago. Just before Christmas last year.'

'That must have been awful.'

'It wasn't the best Christmas I've ever spent.' He gives me a wry smile. 'They say it's the most difficult time of year for relationships. Doesn't the divorce rate soar in January?'

'What a depressing thought!'

'Yeah. "Here's your Christmas present, I'm off!"'

'Do you have any children?'

'No,' he says sadly. 'That was never really on the cards. Shame, really.'

'I guess it's for the best. In some ways.'

'Yeah, I suppose so.' He shrugs. 'Still, life goes on, doesn't it? She's happy now. I guess that's all that matters.'

The waitresses engulf us again and take away the plates before returning with Christmas pudding and great platters of mince pies. This is a sumptuous Christmas feast. More wine is brought to the table and glasses of champagne for the toast as, apparently, Lance Harvey is rumoured to be giving a big thank-you address to the staff later on. Must be good news, if we're raising our glasses with decent fizz. I'm only relieved that I'm not having to pay for any of these drinks. If it was left to my budget, I'd have made one glass of wine last all night. As it is, despite promising myself I'd stop at a couple of glasses, I'm drinking far more than I'd intended.

I think of my parents' own, distinctly more modest Christmas celebration, which I look forward to every year. Their ritual hasn't changed since I was a child and now I feel as if I'm passing it all on to Mia. I'm sure we're the only household in Britain who still sit down together and watch the Queen's speech. My dad gets positively delirious if it's followed by a 1970s Bond film. I hope that, one day, I might have a marriage like theirs. One that's unshakeable and grounded in shared simple pleasures.

'What are you doing this year?' I don't know why I'm asking him this.

'Nothing much,' he says. 'I've been so busy at work these last few months, I haven't even thought about it. This is my Christmas dinner.' He stares appreciatively at the brimming bowl of Christmas pudding in front of him. 'It'll probably be egg on toast for Christmas Day. If I remember to get some eggs in. And some bread.'

'Ah, the bachelor lifestyle.'

'It's not all it's cracked up to be,' he says sadly. 'I used to love coming home to Corrine and our little house. Unfortunately, she didn't like me being away so often. That's the cost of climbing higher. Every rung has a sacrifice attached to it.'

'Surely she understood that?'

'There's no doubt Corrine wanted me to get on in life, but I don't think either of us realised the toll it would take on our relationship. I was travelling all over the place. One day in Scotland, the next in Belgium, then back to Kent or somewhere. Sometimes, I didn't even make it home for the weekend. I guess in the end she just got lonely.'

'Did she leave you for someone else?' Then I realise what I've said. 'Sorry, that's none of my business.'

'It's fine.' He gives a laugh and there's no bitterness in it. Perhaps he has moved on. 'She went off with the bloke who used to deliver our organic fruit and veg box.'

I give him a sympathetic look. 'I'm sure there must be a joke in there somewhere.'

'Yeah,' he says. 'I don't blame her. He's a nice bloke. Homely. In a weird way, when she left, it made me more determined to go as far as I could at work. While I haven't got any commitments – romantic or otherwise – I really want to push the envelope. The worst thing is going home to an empty house.'

'I can sympathise with that. When Mia and I lived in our own place, once she'd gone to bed, I was on my own all the time.' I think of the nights I spent just staring at the television, wondering how to break out of the rut we were in. 'It can be lonely.'

'Yeah. Life isn't bad though. I've got so many plans for the future.' He gives me a shy smile. 'I just need to find someone who's happy to come along for the ride.'

At that moment, Karen comes to the table. I'd intended to keep an eye out for her but, to my shame, I'd completely forgotten. Doesn't look like she's faring too badly though. She's currently flanked by the two half-naked firemen and is giggling madly. Her cheeks are flushed and glowing. Her breasts, if possible, seem even more jiggly than they did earlier. I don't know how her dress is managing to contain them.

'Raffle tickets!' she says. 'There are some fab prizes.' She leans against Josh as she waves her book of tickets at us. 'I'm here to relieve you of your cash. A pound a strip.'

I search in my handbag for some money. 'I'll have one.'

One of the firemen holds out his bucket and I toss in my pound. She tears me off a strip of tickets and I note a steely look in her eye as she hands them over. It's clear that she thinks I'm intruding on her territory. I hope she doesn't realise that Josh actually moved her off this table.

'I'll give you a fiver,' Josh says.

'Men have to give a forfeit too,' Karen tells him. 'Hand over your bow tie and, later on, you have to pay a tenner to get it back.'

Josh shrugs his compliance. 'OK.' He goes to undo his bow tie, but can't quite get it. 'I'm all fingers and thumbs. Could you give me a hand, Louise?'

He offers me his throat and my fingers also fumble as I loosen it. As I move closer, I can smell his aftershave, musky and inviting. He has a strong throat, also inviting. I'd like to run my fingertips over the bit that dips just below his collar. Then I realise what I'm thinking and I cough to hide my discomfort, hurrying to undo the tie. 'There you go.'

Josh slides it out from under his shirt collar and undoes the top button. 'That feels better.'

His bow tie goes into the bucket held by the other fireman. There seem to be an awful lot of bow ties in there that all look identical. How will they know which one belongs to whom? I'd be a bit hacked off if I threw in a silk one and got polyester back. But maybe Karen has a foolproof plan.

'Thank you, Josh,' Karen simpers. 'What about a dance later?'

'I'm not much of a dancer,' he says. 'I'll have to turn you down.'

Karen's face doesn't flicker. 'I'll *make* you dance with me, Josh Wallace. Just you wait and see.'

She waltzes away, chin up, chest out, the two beefy firemen in tow.

I turn to Josh. 'I believe her.'

He laughs and there's something in his eyes that warms me down to my toes. 'I had hoped that my dance card was already full this evening.'

Chapter Sixteen

The next thing Kirsten knew was that Tyler was grabbing her by the hand. 'Let's get this party started!' he declared.

'Not yet, Tyler. Let the dance floor fill up a bit.'

'Noooo,' he said. 'We should show these youngsters what we've got.'

Despite her obvious reluctance, he pulled her on to the dance floor with him.

The Christmas dinner was finished and now some of the employees were relaxing back in their seats with coffee while the more exuberant were already up and dancing to the band, who were playing lively covers of current hits. Some of the staff had headed straight to the casino that had been set up for the evening.

While the white floor beneath their feet pulsated with light, Tyler shimmied in front of her. Kirsten didn't really feel like dancing. The small amount of dinner she had managed to eat was sitting like a lead ball in her stomach and there was a headache blooming behind her eyes. The strobe lights were doing little to help. But she'd promised herself that she'd try to be the life and soul of the party tonight, remind Tyler that they could still have fun together. So she duly smiled and shimmied back.

A part of her also wanted to show Simon Conway that she was having a great time. She didn't want him to see her feeling vulnerable and unloved. He was standing out of the disco lights on the far side of the dance floor, but she could feel his eyes on her. It had taken all her concentration throughout dinner not to search him out and see who he was with.

'Look at this.' Her husband glanced down at his soup-stained shirt and the sheen of creamed potatoes adorning the front of his trousers, and tsked. 'I look like a walking menu. Someone will be getting a dry-cleaning bill.'

'It was an accident,' Kirsten soothed. 'Don't let it spoil the evening.' Then she realised that Tyler had yet to see Simon at the party and knew that a bit of spilled food would soon pale into insignificance.

Jerry Oakley from Human Resources – someone Kirsten did know – and his wife, Sheila, were strutting their funky stuff next to her and Tyler. They exchanged pleasantries but it was hard to hear anyone speak above the band. The song was 'YMCA' and they were doing the motions enthusiastically. Jerry was grinning widely and, clearly unused to such exertion, dabbing his sweating forehead with a handkerchief. He looked like he was in a Turkish bath rather than an extravagantly festive marquee.

Lance and Melissa danced on the other side of the Oakleys. She still hadn't managed to have a chat with Melissa. All the fuss at dinner had made it impossible.

She did like Melissa. Or could do, given the chance. Even though she must be in her mid-fifties now, Melissa looked great for her age. Her auburn hair shone and her green eyes sparkled. Her figure was lean and toned, which showed an enthusiasm for the gym, or good-quality shapewear. She hung on Lance's every word and laughed daintily at his silly jokes. She'd been with Lance for years and yet still looked like a woman in love. What was her secret?

Kirsten would like to bet there wasn't the constant bickering in her home that characterised the Benson residence. She regarded Melissa with growing envy. If only she could be more like her. There was a woman who knew how to play the corporate game. She was always at these functions, loyal and steadfast, standing by Lance's side. Melissa never looked as if she'd had to be dragged there screaming and kicking. Perhaps Melissa was a different kind of animal from her and actually enjoyed these things. It would help matters along considerably if she could be more like that. Perhaps later, when the evening quietened down, she could talk to Melissa and ask her how she managed. Maybe they could fix up that lunch date she'd thought about earlier. Lance drank too much, Kirsten knew that. And there were rumours that he had a wandering eye. Though you wouldn't know to look at him as Lance, when he was sober, was so attentive to his wife. Perhaps he'd calmed down as he grew older. Kirsten wondered if Tyler would do the same. She hoped so.

It seemed as if Lance and Melissa had found the key to making a corporate marriage work. A partnership where there was always a third party to be considered above all else: the company. With a bit of advice from Melissa, perhaps there'd be hope for her and Tyler yet.

Breaking into her musings, Tyler said, 'Did I tell you that you look beautiful tonight?'

'No,' she said. 'But thank you.'

He took her hands and they danced for a couple of tunes. The music made her start to relax and she liked Tyler when he was like this. He was laughing, joking, waving to acknowledge various members of staff as they passed – faces she recognised, with names she could never memorise.

If only he could be like this all the time. More often than not, though, he was tight-jawed and stressed. Fossil Oil might have high remuneration packages but you paid for them by letting it drain the life-blood out of you.

Tyler put his head close to hers and murmured, 'I'd better go and have a word or two with Lance. He's giving a speech soon and I'm worried about the amount of booze he's necked. I want to make sure that he's still on the same planet as the rest of us.'

She knew that sometimes it was touch and go with Lance. And she knew that his drinking laid a heavy burden on Tyler's shoulders. The chairman relied heavily on Tyler who, most of the time, practically ran Fossil Oil.

'Where's he off to now?' Tyler looked anxious. Lance was moving from the dance floor, leaving Melissa alone. 'He can't be doing his speech so soon? I'd better catch up with him. Will you be all right if I leave you for a while?'

'Yes,' she said. 'Melissa's by herself now. I want to try to catch a word with her.'

Tyler looked askance. 'With Melissa? What for?'

'Just to be sociable. It's ages since I've seen her.'

'Right,' he said. 'Right.' But he didn't look as if he felt it was right at all. 'I'll be back as soon as I can.'

'Don't disappear for hours, Tyler.'

'I won't. Of course I won't. Shall I take you back to the table?'

'No need.' She shook her head. It was silly to be so anxious about being left by herself. 'I'll be fine.'

Seeming less certain now, Tyler moved away, leaving her on the dance floor. When he reached Lance, he wrapped his arm round the older man's shoulders and steered him away.

But as she headed towards the chairman's wife, Melissa moved away from her and started to dance with another of the executives whose name Kirsten couldn't recall. So much for her planned cosy chat. Maybe it was just as well: Tyler wouldn't want anyone to think there was anything wrong in their relationship, let alone having her confide in Melissa. It was just that sometimes she desperately needed a friend and it would be nice to have one who might just understand.

Oh, well. She'd visit the powder room, find another drink and wait for Tyler to return. Though now that he and Lance had locked horns, that could be some time.

Most of the staff were now up and dancing, piles of handbags accumulated on the floor as the women danced around them. Across the marquee she could see Tyler's assistant, Louise, dancing with one of his managers. She remembered his name, Josh Wallace. He was a nice guy. Eager. Rather like Tyler had been at that age. The girl was laughing, flirting. It was clear that she liked putting herself around. Maybe Tyler would have his hands full with that one. She could only hope it didn't last. They never usually did.

Kirsten turned to leave the dance floor and, as she did, she found Simon Conway standing right in front of her.

'Dance with me,' he said.

Once again the old feelings rushed straight back. It was as if there was a switch thrown as soon as he was in close proximity.

'Simon, I shouldn't.' She turned, anxiously checking that Tyler hadn't seen him. 'You of all people know that.'

His smile was warm, encouraging, and he was clearly brooking no argument. She remembered how very determined he could be. That was one of the things she used to find most attractive about him.

'It's the Christmas party, Kirsten. Dancing with someone inappropriate is obligatory,' he teased.

Simon moved close to her. Unfortunately, at the same moment, the band decided to play a slow tune and, in one smooth move, Simon took her in his arms. She felt herself stiffen and thought about resisting, but realised that she didn't have the strength.

'This is madness.' She pressed a hand against his chest in an attempt to keep some space between them, but that only made matters worse as, beneath her fingers, she felt his heart beating as fast as hers.

Despite not wanting to, she fell so easily into step with him. They swayed in rhythm together and it was as if they hadn't been apart at all. Simon's body was disconcertingly familiar against hers, which was both alarming and comforting at the same time. His face was so close to hers that she could inhale the fresh, sharp scent of his aftershave, which tingled her senses. She could feel his breath against her neck like a welcome summer breeze.

Surreptitiously, Kirsten's eyes drank him in. He looked good in a dinner suit. No, not just good. Perfect. His movements were carried out with a natural and exquisite economy of effort. If they'd been waltzing, he'd be the sort of man who'd sweep you round a ballroom with your feet barely touching the floor. Unless you were married, of course, Kirsten reminded herself sharply. And then, in the presence of Simon Conway, you would want to keep your feet very firmly on the ground.

Thankfully, Tyler was nowhere to be seen: she knew he'd be furious if he saw his wife and his one-time friend in a clinch.

'All I've wanted for a very long time is to take you in my arms again.'

'We can't have this conversation, Simon.'

'We must,' he insisted. 'There were things that should have been said that weren't.'

'It's so long ago,' she countered. 'Everything has changed. We're not the same people any more.'

At one time, over a decade ago, she and Simon had been lovers. Before she married Tyler.

'Do you remember when we first met?'

'Of course I do.'

It was at a party. She couldn't even remember whose now – someone's birthday maybe. Just another night out with friends that she hadn't expected to change the course of her life for ever.

Tyler had been chatting her up, flirting outrageously. She'd found him amusing, if a bit too arrogant for her liking. He'd given her all his lines and she'd let him, not thinking it was something she'd take further than that night. When he'd gone to find a refill for her drink, his friend Simon had moved in and that was it. She'd fallen from a great height for him. Simon was everything she'd ever dreamed of in a man. He was handsome, charming, ridiculously romantic. By the time Tyler returned with her drink, he'd found her otherwise occupied, and she'd spent the rest of the evening with Simon. Despite Tyler's best efforts he hadn't managed to dislodge his friend and she hadn't wanted him to. Simon was effortlessly entertaining and Tyler simply hadn't been able to compete.

'We hardly left each other's side after that night,' Simon said.

It was true. She felt as if she'd found part of her missing self, and within the week they were talking about a future together. It was more than she could ever have hoped for. She only had to look at Simon and her heart lifted.

'Do you remember me filling that dingy rented room you had with red roses while you were out at work?'

She smiled at the memory. 'The scent was incredible. Like heaven.'

It was the morning after they'd first slept together. She didn't dare to ask if he remembered that. He'd loved her slowly, tenderly, deliciously. It was all stored in her mind for ever. There wasn't a single moment of it that she'd forgotten.

Simon had been everything to her. He'd read poetry to her and taught her how to enjoy good wine. She admired his drive, his ambition. They'd had a great social life and a wide circle of friends. And, despite being pipped at the post, Tyler Benson was the closest of them. Back then, he and Simon were more like brothers than friends. Not so now.

'Tell me what you're thinking,' Simon murmured.

Before she could say anything, a hand clapped Simon on the back.

'Welcome on board!' Its owner, a jocular, rotund man, swayed before them. 'Mark Finlay, Finance,' he said by way of introduction.

'Simon Conway.'

'I know. I know.' Mark tapped the side of his nose, indicating discretion, with anything but. 'The word's out, Conway. Heard you're going to give that bastard Benson a run for his money.' He gave a conspiratorial wink.

'Well . . .' Simon began, embarrassed.

'Not before time too,' Mark Finlay chortled. 'We're all behind you. He's a wily bugger though. You'd better mind your back. If anyone can get him to toe the line though, it's you. So a reliable source tells me.' He slapped him again. 'Let's get together over a bottle in the new year.'

'Let's,' Simon agreed with forced enthusiasm.

Mark Finlay lurched away.

Kirsten raised her eyebrows.

'It was the drink talking,' Simon assured her. 'He didn't mean it.'

'Of course he did,' she said flatly.

One slow song segued into another. She knew she should stop this and walk away now, but something held her. There was a huge glitter-ball sparkling above them, showering fragments of light across the dance floor. They fluttered over Simon's face like snowflakes. Dry ice swirled around their feet. Slowly they circled the huge ice sculpture of the ammonite in the centre of the floor. Kirsten felt as if she'd momentarily slipped into another world, as if – however fleetingly – it was just the two of them once more.

'I'm not back to destroy Tyler,' he said softly. 'If that's what you think.'

She stood back from him. 'Then why exactly are you here?'

'Surely you don't need to ask that?'

'I do. Why here? Why now?'

He held her eyes and she blinked away the welling tears. 'There isn't a moment during the last ten years that I haven't bitterly regretted that we split up.'

'I can't do this now, Si.' She looked round, terrified that Tyler would see them. 'This isn't the time or the place.'

'Are you happy with him?'

'That's none of your business. You gave up any rights to know what's going on in my life a long time ago.'

He lifted her chin so that she was forced to look at him. 'Your smile is the saddest one I've ever seen.'

His embrace on her tightened and she pulled away. 'Someone will see.'

'I have to talk to you. We need to find somewhere that we can be alone.'

'We don't, Simon. There's nothing to be said.'

'That's where you're wrong, Kirsten. What I have to say can't wait any longer.'

She shook her head. 'Nothing good can come of this.'

'That's where I beg to differ.'

Finally the song ended and she broke away from him. 'It's been very nice seeing you again, Simon. I hope you'll be happy in your new job. If we see each other at future Fossil Oil functions then I'm sure we'll be very civil to each other.'

Then, for the sake of her own sanity, she fled from the dance floor and the temptation of Simon Conway.

Chapter Seventeen

Melissa was worried now. Lance was due to give his speech, but even she'd never seen him quite so plastered before. She wondered briefly if someone had spiked his drink and then dismissed it as a ridiculous notion. He was a drunk and that was all there was to it.

He was slumped into a chair backstage while front of house it was business as usual. The band played a cheerful Christmas song while Tyler continually hoisted Lance back to an upright position.

Tyler turned to her, his face dark with anxiety. 'He can't go on like this.'

'No,' she agreed. 'Can't you give the speech?'

He stepped away from Lance. Her husband slid towards the floor and they both let him. Tyler lowered his voice: 'Lance said he'd got an important announcement to make. I haven't a clue what it is. Have you?'

'Part of it. I think,' she admitted.

'Then I wish you'd told me.'

'I only found out in the car on the way here, Tyler. I haven't really had time to process it myself. That's why I wanted us to find some time alone together.'

Tyler raked his hair in exasperation. 'It's impossible with all this going on.'

'Melissa!' Lance cried drunkenly. 'Melissa, where are you?'

'I'll get him some coffee,' Tyler said.

'Make it black and strong,' Melissa suggested to Tyler's retreating back. He raised an eyebrow in acknowledgement.

Kneeling down before her husband, she murmured, 'Hey, honey. How are you feeling? Shall I get Martin to bring the car round and you can have a little nap in the back before you give your speech?' She knew that Lance's powers of recuperation were astonishing. An hour's sleep and he'd be as right as rain and ready to open another bottle. 'You can do it later, if you like. No one will mind.'

'I'm fine,' Lance said, rousing briefly from his inebriated state. 'Leave me alone.'

He could normally drink like a fish and still look like he'd touched nothing stronger than lemonade all night. Perhaps his constitution wasn't what it used to be. His liver must be damn near shot to pieces by now with the liquid abuse he'd given it over the years. Not that he ever told her what the quack really said at his compulsory annual medical review – Fossil Oil's sole attempt to show that it was a truly caring company.

If it was anything more intimate or potentially more difficult than discussing which type of breakfast cereal he preferred, Lance's lips usually remained tightly clamped together. According to Lance, the doctor simply confirmed what he knew all along, that he was a miracle of modern science, fit, robust and with the stamina of a man half his age. Not once did the word 'alcoholic' enter the picture.

How had she ever let herself get into this situation? Her father had been a drunk and, having watched her mother struggle single-handedly with the family skeleton that kept weaving its way out of the cupboard waving a bottle, she vowed that she'd never be put in that position herself. Yet here she was, replicating the same old behaviour pattern. She should have left

Lance years ago. She should have just taken the boys and gone, while she had a chance of happiness. But where to? They never stayed anywhere long enough for her to make friends. Not good friends. Not friends you could confide in. Not friends who would help you out in a crisis. There'd been plenty of those over the years and she had handled them all alone.

The glimmer of hope that one day Lance would change had long since gone. This was what she was facing for the rest of her life. Most evenings Lance had to be helped from his car by Martin. He didn't even stay awake long enough to eat dinner with her. She always waited for him and then invariably ended up eating alone. He'd sleep on the sofa until eleven o'clock, when she'd turn off the television. Sometimes, she'd rouse him and take him to bed. Other evenings, when it was clear that he was out for the count, she'd put a throw over him, leave him where he was and go upstairs alone. If he was particularly bad, she'd sleep in the armchair next to him.

Whichever way, he'd still be bright-eyed and bushy-tailed in the morning. It was staggering.

What was she to do? How could she leave Lance now? She was inching nearer to sixty every day. She'd given up a damn good career for Lance. How could she resume it this late in life? Who would want her? She hadn't ever lived entirely alone since her twenties, and she had to admit it was a frightening prospect.

The only things that made it tolerable living with Lance were her affairs. Yet it was getting harder to turn heads. She could Botox up to her eyeballs, but there was no denying that she was no longer a spring chicken. She knew Tyler had only started their fling because he felt she could supply him with information. Of course he had: powerful men all wanted women who were twenty years younger than her. It was only afterwards that it had blossomed into something else.

But it still wasn't enough to sustain her. She had no money in the bank. No life to call her own. And Lance *needed* her. These days he could barely function without her. She'd become his nursemaid, not his wife. How he managed to run Fossil Oil, goodness only knew. It was mostly down to Tyler holding it all together, and her advising Lance in the background. Yet she knew that Tyler had Lance's job in his sights and one day he'd lose patience, turn coat and snatch it for himself.

Moments later, Tyler returned with a pot of coffee and a cup. He squatted down next to her. 'Let's get some of this down him.'

'OK.' She poured some coffee into the cup while Tyler watched hopefully. 'Hey, honey,' she cooed at her husband. 'Why don't you try some of this? Tyler very kindly brought it for you.'

Lance raised red-rimmed eyes to her face. They barely seemed to focus. 'You think I'm drunk, don't you?'

'The thought never crossed my mind, sweetie.'

'I think I might have had one over the eight,' he confessed candidly.

She thought he might have had one over the *eighteen*, and wondered if the news from Bud Harman was troubling him more than he'd admitted.

Melissa held out the cup for him. 'You know you've got to give your speech in a minute.'

'I don't want any coffee,' Lance stated truculently.

Melissa sighed. Why did drunks revert to belligerent behaviour patterns more suited to five-year-olds?

'I think you *do* want some coffee, honey,' she said encouragingly. 'It'll do you good.'

'I can do it myself.' Lance brushed her hand away and in doing so knocked the cup, which sailed out of her hand and hit Tyler mid-flight. The liquid splattered all over his shirt and the cup clattered to the floor.

'I don't believe it.' Tyler glanced down at the brown stain on his shirt and rolled his eyes to heaven. He didn't even try to mop it up.

She looked round for yet another *Merry Christmas to One and All* napkin, but could see none.

'If we can't get him on within the next ten minutes then that's it. The rest of the staff will be too far gone to listen anyway. They're hammering the free bar. This is a total disaster.'

Melissa calmly picked up the coffee pot and the cup again. She brushed the carpet fluff from the rim and poured the thick black liquid into it. 'He'll be fine,' she said. 'Just fine.'

Chapter Eighteen

Tyler helped to support his chairman as he stood. 'Better get this over with, Lance. Time to go on stage.' He glanced at his Fossil Oil Corporation watch and noted that it was getting late in the evening. Already this felt like the longest night of his life. 'No need to labour the point. Just a quick pat on the back for everyone. Rally the troops. Onwards and upwards for next year. Blah, blah. That should do it.'

Lance, bleary-eyed and red-faced, nodded his consent.

The sooner this was over with, the better. Hopefully he could then snatch five minutes alone with Melissa to find out what else she knew about the plans afoot at the company. After that, he'd make sure they were both packed off home. Only then could he return his full attention to his wife.

'Will he be all right?' Melissa whispered to him.

Despite her assurances of a few moments ago, she looked more than a little concerned too.

'I have *no fucking idea*,' he hissed back. 'Just start praying.'

As they went to climb the steps to the back of the stage, Lance stumbled. Tyler put out his hands to catch him. This was worse than he thought. What sort of speech was Lance going to give in this state?

'Look, Lance, why don't I just say a few words?' Tyler

suggested amiably. 'You can sit here and have another coffee.'

'I don't want another coffee,' Lance complained. 'I want some bourbon.' His eyes searched for Melissa. 'Get me a bottle of Jack, honey.'

'We can get all the staff together in the new year. You can fill me in about what's going on,' Tyler continued pointedly. 'We can do a big ta-da then. Why don't I pop on stage instead and say thanks for coming and have a very merry Christmas and a happy new year? That's all I need to do, nothing more. You can toddle off and have another drink.'

'I need to do this *now*,' Lance insisted.

On stage, the band were coming to the end of Slade's 'Merry Xmas Everybody'. The staff were in high spirits, though none of them quite so high as the chairman. They were jumping around, punching the air, clearly celebrating what had been a good year for Fossil Oil. He hated to interrupt their fun, but these things had to be done. It was the Christmas party after all, and it wouldn't hurt to remind them who was paying for this little jolly.

Tyler signalled to the band leader that he wanted to wheel Lance on stage.

'Thank you, guys!' the lead singer shouted out. 'We'll be taking a short break, but we'll be back later with another selection of top chart hits!'

There was rapturous applause and much whistling from the easily pleased crowd as the tinsel-tongued crooner strutted off the stage as if he'd been performing at Wembley Stadium.

With unaccustomed nerves, Tyler took the microphone. 'Good evening, ladies and gentlemen. The chairman of Fossil Oil, Mr Lancelot Harvey, would like to say a few words.'

Tyler led the half-hearted applause while people drifted back to their seats, irritated by the unwelcome interruption to their dancing. Reluctantly, and with a silent prayer for God's mercy, he gave the microphone to Lance.

The chairman stepped forward. He looked for all the world like a has-been cabaret compère – reduced to a squalid life of working men's clubs, introducing unfunny comedians and second-rate magicians whose tricks didn't work. Yet he was the head of a world-class company. How was it that Lance was still running the show instead of him? Tyler wondered idly whether Lance had some dirt on Bud Harman. It had to be something really mucky. There must, at the very least, be photographs of him in a gimp mask. Otherwise, how else would he keep his job?

If Tyler hadn't been on show, he'd have put his head in his hands. He'd never been squeamish before but he certainly didn't have the stomach to watch this. He could only hope that Lance rose to the occasion. God knew, by some divine intervention, he usually managed to.

'Merry Christmas, everybody!' Lance called out.

The staff applauded thunderously. There was whistling and shouts of 'Woo!'

'I hope you've been enjoying tonight's party and all the lovely free drink. I know I have!' Lance laughed jovially.

This was going to be all right, Tyler thought with a rush of relief. He was going to get through it.

'You're the best employees a company could ever have!' The chairman smiled and soaked up the appreciation. 'Fossil Oil has reported a profit of seventeen billion pounds this year.'

A cheer went up and there was rapturous applause.

Before it died down, Lance added, 'And it's all because of you!'

Foot-stamping now! Tyler laughed. Why had he ever worried? This was Lance's forte. Keeping up staff morale was when Lance came into his own. He turned on the charm and everyone melted before it. He had an incredible charisma about him. Tyler could still learn a thing or two from him. Wily old dog!

He glanced back at Melissa and she too looked relieved. She'd joined him at the back of the stage and passed him a glass of champagne. Tyler swigged heartily from it. That had been a close call. Everyone at Fossil knew that Lance liked a drink, it was the worst-kept secret. But no one really knew the extent.

Lance went to toast them before realising that, for once, his hand was missing a glass. A look of momentary confusion crossed his face.

'Here you go, Lance.' Tyler quickly stepped forward and handed him his own drink.

'Is everyone's glass charged?' Lance raised his glass high. 'To Fossil Oil.'

The staff, one and all, echoed his move and called out, 'To Fossil Oil!'

It was quite a moving moment, Tyler thought. This was a great business to be in. Trading conditions were tough and getting tougher all the time. The global economic downturn was no one's idea of fun. But, in his department, they were weathering the storms. Just about. Due in no small measure to his own efforts. He hoped he'd be duly rewarded next year.

'That was great, Lance,' Tyler whispered in his ear. 'Just right.'

'I'm not done yet.' Lance turned a disdainful eye on him and Tyler rocked back.

Lance held up his hand and the staff quietened down.

'However!' he boomed, fully in his stride now. 'That's seven per cent down on last year. Seven per cent.' He looked as if he could scarcely believe it. 'The ravenous exploitation of shale gas, particularly in the USA, has hit revenues hard. So, unfortunately, that means we will have to implement some minor belt-tightening. Like every business, we have to have an eye to economies. We have to be a lean organisation. There must be no waste. No excess.'

Tyler glanced uncomfortably at their surroundings, at the party they'd thrown this evening. *No excess?* They could have just given everyone a free Christmas dinner in the staff canteen. He did a quick calculation. There'd certainly be no change out of a hundred grand for this bash alone.

'Bud Harman, global chief executive president of Fossil Oil, has decreed there will be cutbacks.' Lance shook his head sadly. 'So cutbacks there will be.'

Now there was an uneasy shuffling among the crowd. They didn't like the sound of this any more than Tyler did.

'Bud is implementing a new programme of radical economies, starting with the introduction of SACKED. Staff Assessment Criteria and Key Employee Development.'

The staff had been stunned into silence now and Tyler discreetly covered his eyes with one hand. SACKED? *SACKED?* You couldn't make it up. What the hell was it anyway? He didn't know, but it sounded like it had Bud Harman's mucky fingerprints all over it. He'd had no inkling that this was coming. Nothing at all. Why hadn't Lance told him?

Lance ploughed on, unheeding of the deadly hush that had fallen on the entire room.

'There are currently five hundred and fifty staff alone in our British affiliate at Fossil House. Introducing the SACKED initiative will cut our staff numbers by one hundred.'

There was an audible and horrified gasp from the assembled staff. Not surprisingly. Tyler thought one might have come from him too. He spun round to look at Melissa. Hadn't she had any idea about what was going on? He'd thought she'd be a reliable source of information. But it was clear from her face that she wasn't a party to this.

When he risked glancing at the staff again, most of them seemed to have lapsed into a catatonic trance.

Lance held up his hand and shook his head sympathetically. 'I know that will come as a terrible shock to many of you. Well, to all of you. I found out myself only this morning. But times are hard and we must all share the pain.'

A discontented rumble began as people started to express their disbelief. Tyler, as dumbfounded as everyone else, risked peeping out from between his fingers. He wasn't generally known for his empathy, but it was hard to look at the stricken faces in front of him and not want the ground to open up and swallow him.

'We will be issuing redundancy notices in January. As soon as the office opens again.' Lance, thank heavens, was winding up. 'For the staff who remain, it will be onwards and upwards for the new year. For the rest of you, I wish you all the very best for the future.'

What would it mean for him? Tyler wondered. Surely his own future at Fossil was assured? He needed to talk to Lance, but it was pointless while he was so drunk. He'd never remember what had been said in the morning. His next best bet was Melissa, and now he *definitely* needed to get her on her own as soon as possible.

'All that remains for me to do is to thank you all for coming this evening and to wish you all a very merry Christmas and a happy new year,' Lance concluded joyfully. 'Enjoy the rest of the party. Have a few drinks. Dance. The night is still young!'

Tyler was aghast. Lance's sincerity was truly touching.

Lance replaced the microphone and weaved off the stage.

There was an unearthly quiet, and a sea of white, open-mouthed faces, frozen rigid with shock, stared disbelievingly after their departing chairman.

As he half fell down the steps, Lance made a lurch for the

bourbon bottle that Melissa was now holding. But Tyler was there first and snatched it from his reach.

Lance, unperturbed, rubbed his hands together and smiled. 'I thought that went well.'

On the stage, the lead singer of the band bounded back to the microphone. 'Are we going to party?' he shouted. The band launched into 'I Wish It Could Be Christmas Every Day'.

The staff, as one, turned and bolted as fast as they could for the free bar.

Tyler put the bottle of bourbon to his lips and tipped the burning amber liquid straight down his throat.

Chapter Nineteen

Josh and I finally get to the front of the queue at the bar. 'Champagne, please,' I say when he asks me what I'd like to drink.

With a bit more pushing and shoving, he gets a glass of fizz for me and a Coke for himself. Then we stand and look at each other in a slightly dazed manner, both shocked after the chairman's bombshell.

'Well,' Josh says, perplexed. 'That was a bit of a bolt from the blue.'

'Completely unexpected. I don't think Tyler knew anything about it either, from the look on his face.'

I know he won't be happy about that. My boss likes to think he's got his finger on the pulse.

'I hadn't heard a whisper either. As far as I knew all was well. I thought the announcement was going to be something good for the employees.' Josh shakes his head. 'I can't even get drunk. I couldn't do my job without a car, so I gave up alcohol years ago. But, right this moment, I've never felt more like downing a double brandy.'

'Me too.' If this is going to be my first and possibly last Christmas party with Fossil Oil, I'm going to make sure that I make the most of it. And currently that translates into joining the fray and drinking a lot of free booze. It seems as if most of the staff have come up with the same idea. And who can blame them? Like me, they probably thought their jobs were as safe as could be.

How will they decide who'll go and who'll stay? As one of the last to join the company, will I be the first to be shown the door?

'I'm worried now,' I admit. With having a decent salary, I was starting to make good inroads into my debts. I pay very little to Mum and Dad – at their insistence – so that I can use most of my salary to clear the outstanding mortgage. That could all crumble about my ears. With the sweep of a corporate arm, I could be right back where I started. 'I thought I was going to make my career at Fossil. Who knows what'll happen now?'

'No doubt we'll find out soon enough.'

'How can a rich organisation like Fossil treat its staff so shabbily? It's Christmas, for heaven's sake. Couldn't they have waited until January to tell us? At least then people could have enjoyed Christmas without worrying.'

The festive season will be spoiled by having this axe hanging over our heads. I'm quietly seething inside.

'It's the way of the world now.'

'Well, it isn't right,' I grumble.

The dance floor is full again and the band is playing a raft of wholly inappropriate cheery Christmas songs. They seem to be oblivious, and no one else really seems to mind either.

There's a strange air of abandonment among the staff. At the bar, the drinks are going down at a rate of knots. Normally staid members of staff appear to be exhibiting a wild reckless-ness that there'd been no sign of just a few moments ago.

'If it's any comfort, I'm sure we'll be safe,' Josh says. He has to lean closer for me to be able to hear him as the band is play-ing louder and louder. 'There are a lot more people with their heads on the chopping block ahead of us.'

143

'I don't know if that makes me feel better or worse.' But I do know that my heart is in my boots.

I glance up, in time to see Karen from Customer Accounts jump on to the stage. She wrests the tambourine from one of the backing singers and shimmies across the front of the stage, banging it against her bottom.

'All I want for Christmas is you,' she shouts out. She wiggles her bottom and points to various people in the audience. 'You, you, you!'

If I'm not mistaken, she's already had quite a few of these men.

'You!' The last person her gaze rests on is Josh. She waggles her finger determinedly at him. 'You!'

He shifts uncomfortably, but seconds later Karen is off again, banging away with the tambourine.

'Wow,' I say, nodding towards her.

Josh laughs shyly. 'I guess bad news affects people in different ways.'

The lead singer pulls Karen to him and she shrieks loudly down the microphone. I feel like covering my ears, but it seems impolite. Karen obviously isn't going to let a little thing like looming redundancy spoil her evening.

Good for her. I wish I could say the same. I'm certainly not in the party mood any more. I actually feel like lying on the floor and weeping. Right now, I'd really like to ring my dad and tell him to come and collect me. But, having told him to put the car away and insisting that I could fend for myself, I don't like to drag him out on this cold winter's night. Besides, he'd wonder what was wrong and, if I can, I'll try to put off telling them for as long as possible. They'll be out of their minds with worry for me.

I might be out of a job in the new year but at least we can have a good Christmas. My heart breaks for Mia. I wanted to make her so proud of her mummy. Now it's all up in the air again.

'Chin up,' Josh says. 'There's nothing we can do about it. We just have to wait and see what unfolds.'

'Your sales figures are great,' I remind him. 'The best. I'm certain you won't be on the hit list.'

'And you're Tyler's assistant. He's not going anywhere.'

'You don't know that. He might think about getting out and going to another company.' Like a rat deserting a sinking ship. I'm sure the man has no morals. I wouldn't put it past him. I don't know Tyler Benson all that well, but I already know that whatever happens he'll be sure to put his own interests first.

'I hadn't thought of that,' he admits.

Inside I'm still reeling. 'How can they make that much money – *seventeen billion pounds* – and still be cutting staff?' I can't even imagine what *one* billion pounds must look like.

'Companies are like that now. They want more and more out of each employee. These days I'm doing the work that two sales managers used to do.'

'How will they manage with fewer people then?'

Josh shrugs. 'They just do. But the work gets done in a more slapdash manner. Customer service plummets. They push everyone to breaking point and then the staff that are there are always off sick or cave in with stress.'

'That's a terribly bleak picture.'

'And this is the season that's supposed to be jolly.'

'I thought I could count on this job. I had no idea I'd still be in such an unstable situation.'

'You don't know what will happen yet. We'll all have to wait and see. You never know what difference a day can make.'

'That's true enough. Yesterday, all I had to worry about was a boss who was groping me every five minutes. Now I'm thinking how I'll tell my parents that I might be on the scrapheap again so soon after scrambling up off it.'

Josh frowns. 'What did you say about groping?'

I realise what has inadvertently slipped out. 'Nothing,' I say. 'It doesn't matter.'

'I'm thinking this is more than his usual over-the-top flirting?'

Then I realise that it *does* matter and that I really want to tell Josh. 'Yes.' Why should I keep this a secret? It's not me who's in the wrong. 'Tyler's been giving me a hard time, coming on to me, copping a feel whenever he can.' I say it lightly and try to shrug it off.

His face darkens. 'That's wrong, Louise. You shouldn't have to put up with that.'

'My thoughts exactly.'

'Have you spoken to anyone about it?'

I shake my head. 'It's my problem. I should be able to deal with it. The only upside of the SACKED programme is that I might not have to deal with it any longer.' I try to laugh but fail. This has affected me more than I'd like to admit, shaken my new-found confidence.

'In the new year – if we're both still here – we'll deal with it.'

'Thanks. I'd appreciate that. But what can we do?'

'I don't know,' he admits. 'But I'll think of something.'

'I never thought working for a renowned corporation would be like this.'

'Welcome to the cut-throat world of big business.'

I sigh. 'You sound very pragmatic about it all. I wish I could feel the same. You've given so much to this stupid company. You said it even cost you your marriage. Yet they don't give a second thought to dumping you, or any of us.'

'That's just the way it is. No jobs for life any more. It must be difficult if you're over fifty though. I reckon they'll be first on the list.'

'How awful.' It reminds me of my dad's situation and how heart-breaking that has been.

He'd worked for the same small engineering company in Milton Keynes for years and, then, at the age of fifty-seven, was made redundant. Try as he might, he couldn't find anything that used his skills. So he's ended up working in Marks & Spencer as a security guard. He makes the best of it, but he's not earning anything like he was. Though they do let the staff buy the food that's about to go out of date really cheaply, which Mum gets a kick out of.

I wonder if this is what some of my colleagues have in store for them. I feel so awful for the people who are older and have been working at Fossil Oil a long time. What will they do in the new year? Everyone is chasing so few jobs that some of them might not work again.

What an initiation to the Christmas party! I don't think this night could actually get any worse.

On the stage, Karen sings louder and we both look up. She's staring right at Josh again. 'Santa baby,' she croons. My colleague scoops up her blonde locks with one hand and piles them seductively on her head. She licks her lips and wiggles her hips.

'She definitely has the hots for you,' I point out. Karen's is not a subtle attempt at seduction.

'That's a very frightening thought,' he says.

'She is *so* going to regret this in the morning. Do you think I should get her down from there?' I feel quite protective of Karen as she's the only colleague I've become at all close to.

The song ends with a big flourish and, without warning, Karen launches herself off the stage as if she's leaping into a mosh pit.

'Good grief.' My heart is in my mouth. Now I'm worried for her safety.

She's held aloft on a sea of arms, Christmas-party crowd-surfing.

Next to me Josh laughs. 'I think she'll be OK.' Then, gently, he lays a hand on my arm. I turn to him and am surprised by the warmth, even tenderness in his eyes. 'I think you will be too, Louise.'

Chapter Twenty

Kirsten watched open-mouthed as Lance left the stage with Tyler and Melissa. She thought they'd come straight back to the table, but instead they disappeared into the depths of the manor. Perhaps Tyler had persuaded Lance to go straight home after his announcement. It was a wonder the staff hadn't turned into a lynch mob and strung him up to the glittery disco ball with some tinsel.

She was sure Tyler hadn't known anything about this; he must be reeling. This was the moment she needed to step up to the plate and support him, not just roll her eyes and think that it was so very typical of Fossil Oil.

Now she didn't really know what to do with herself, sitting here alone, just waiting. She fiddled with her glass, straightened the candelabra, ripped her *Merry Christmas to One and All* napkin into tiny shreds. Just as she was tempted to get out her Christmas cracker penknife and play with it, Simon reappeared in front of her.

'Can we find somewhere to have five minutes alone, Kirsten? There are too many flapping ears here and we need to talk.'

She scanned the marquee anxiously, looking for Tyler. 'I don't think it's a very sensible idea.'

'Since when has being sensible been any fun?' Before she

could protest, he took her hand and pulled her to her feet. 'I won't take no for an answer.'

'The past should stay in the past, Si.' She avoided his gaze. 'There's no point raking it up. I have nothing to say to you.'

'Then you can just listen.' A waiter passed them and Simon grabbed two empty glasses and a bottle of fizz from the tray he was carrying. 'I have plenty *I* want to say to *you*.'

He guided her through the crowd of revellers, still holding her hand tightly, and out of the marquee. Feeling both anxious and thrilled at the same time, she trailed in his wake as they made their way through the opulent rooms of the manor house. Many of them were in darkness now, some lit only by candles. Every sofa they came across appeared to be occupied by a couple in a passionate embrace. Kirsten didn't know all that many people at Fossil Oil, but even she realised that most of them weren't with their usual partners. There would be some sore heads and red faces in the office tomorrow, that was for sure.

Undeterred, Simon walked on, threading his way through the bodies.

'This is hopeless,' she said, looking for an excuse to turn back. 'All the quiet spots have been occupied. We should return to the marquee.'

'Oh, no,' Simon said. 'I don't give up that easily.'

It was a trait she remembered well about him.

'We'll be missed from the party.'

'That's the least of my worries,' he replied as he snatched up a throw from one of the sofas, threw open the French doors ahead of them and led her outside.

'It's freezing!' Kirsten protested as a wall of icy air hit her. She clutched her bare arms.

'Then we'll find somewhere warm.' He stopped to gently drape the throw he'd purloined around her shoulders, wrapping her as if she was something fragile and precious.

He'd always been so kind, so caring. She hadn't forgotten that either. With Tyler she could have frozen to death and he would have scarcely noticed. Oh yes, Simon was a different kettle of fish altogether. He was compassionate and thoughtful where Tyler was bullish and brash.

His fingers lightly brushed the sensitive skin on the back of Kirsten's arms, which made her shiver. Simon looked down into her face; his eyes were filled with tenderness and a river of emotions flowed over her. It was too much to be so close to him again. How could she possibly bear it?

The night had turned mind-numbingly cold. The mercury in the thermometer must be plummeting fast. A hard white frost sparkled on the trees and ground like icing sugar. A few flakes of snow drifted lazily in the air.

Simon took her hand again and, realising that resistance was futile, she let him guide her away from the house. Wide steps led them down towards the beautifully manicured gardens. Ahead was a broad parterre with a stunning fountain of a rearing horse as its centrepiece, the spraying water sparkling like crystals in the moonlight. Classical sculptures graced the four corners. Beyond that, the gardens fell away before melding seamlessly with the surrounding fields and woods of the estate.

Kirsten thought she might like to come back here in the summer to see it in its full and magnificent glory. Of course, she'd come by herself: she knew Tyler wouldn't be the slightest bit interested.

'My heels are sinking into the grass,' she said as they reached the vast expanse of lawn. Simon turned towards her and there was a mischievous glint in his eye. Kirsten held up a hand. 'Don't you even think about picking me up.'

He laughed. 'Let's stick to the path then. We'll head over there.'

A little way in the distance, tucked in among the shrubs, was a small lean-to building. The bottom half was ancient brick while the top was more like a greenhouse. When they reached it, Simon tried the door. He grinned back at her when it creaked open.

'We've left a hundred-roomed mansion and you've brought me to a potting shed?'

'It's not a potting shed,' he countered. 'It's a ... um ... Yes, it's a potting shed.'

They took in their surroundings.

'But it's a very nice one,' he insisted.

She smiled, despite not wanting to give him any encouragement.

'I feel really naughty sneaking in here.' But the feeling was much more than that. This was so wrong. She really should avoid being alone with her old lover. The man who she still thought of as the love of her life. The one that got away. There was really nothing he could say to her that could ever change that.

'It's warm,' he said. 'Come on in.'

'I shouldn't. Really. Someone might see us.'

Simon's eyes glittered in the darkness. 'Live dangerously!' He grasped her throw in his hands and gently tugged her inside.

Kirsten pulled back, but only half-heartedly, and they ended up giggling. They'd always laughed together so easily. Their whole relationship had been underpinned by laughter, fun and love. They'd had happy times, so many of them.

She couldn't think of that now. It was madness. Those times had long gone and she should keep that at the forefront of her mind.

The potting shed smelled musty, of earth and growth. It was still and calm and felt like a little oasis, cut off from the world. The raucous party in the main house felt a million miles away.

Workbenches ran along either side and on them were the

random tools of an absent gardener – trowels, forks, string, a myriad bits and bobs of horticultural detritus. It was a comforting place to be. She could imagine the people who'd worked here for hundreds of years.

'Look, there's a seat.' Simon urged her forward again.

At the far end was a sturdy wooden form that looked inviting. Above it was a heater fixed to the brick wall and Simon reached up to switch it on even though she didn't now feel cold at all. At one end of the bench there was a discarded newspaper and Kirsten wondered if this was where the gardeners took their tea break.

Simon swept the newspaper over the bench, sending dust motes in the air to be caught by the moonlight, and then indicated that she should sit. Which she did, suddenly careless of the white dress she was wearing.

The bottle of champagne was already open and Simon filled the glasses for them.

'Just one for me,' he said. 'I'm driving.'

'I'm supposed to be driving too,' she said, 'but I've already had my quota. Yet I don't think I can get through this night on only two drinks. I might as well go for broke.'

She and Tyler would have to make alternative arrangements about getting home, or maybe they could stay somewhere local, as he'd suggested. It was a shame this place wasn't a hotel. If the worst came to the worst, perhaps Tyler could pull rank and commandeer one of the sofas for them to spend the night on.

Simon sat down next to her and lifted his glass. 'A toast?'

'What to?'

'To us.'

She shook her head. 'There is no "us", Si. Not any more. All that was a long time ago and it doesn't do to rake up the past.' She couldn't even think about going there. It would be far too painful.

153

His face fell and she offered, 'A toast to Christmas, maybe?'

He nodded sadly. 'To Christmas then.'

They chinked glasses and sipped. The champagne was as chill as the night air. The bubbles danced on her tongue; it would have taken very little to persuade her to down the whole bottle.

He looked so handsome in his dinner suit. He always had. He was minus his bow tie now. Most of the men were, as there'd been a rather drunken young girl going round collecting them – something to do with a charity. Simon had clearly succumbed. The top button of his dress shirt was open and there was a strong pulse at the base of his throat. She wanted to place her fingertip on it to feel the life flowing inside him. There were so many nights when she'd wondered whether she'd ever see him again. Now he was here, right in front of her, and she felt like crying. Whether it was with relief, regret or what, she didn't know. Her emotions were running wild inside her. Kirsten tore her eyes away from him. She didn't think she could cope with any discussion about what had happened between them.

Keeping the conversation to more neutral matters and getting the hell out of here as quickly as she could would be very wise.

Chapter Twenty-one

'I don't suppose many of the staff will be having a merry Christmas now,' Kirsten noted. 'Not after Lance's speech.'

'I had no idea about that,' Simon confessed. 'It's not exactly an auspicious start to my career at Fossil Oil.'

'I despise this company now,' she said vehemently. 'And everything it stands for. They suck the life out of their employees, and for what? When they're bone-dry, with nothing left to give, they spit them out. I don't even work for them, yet I feel they own my soul. They're vile, Simon. Truly vile.'

'I didn't like what I saw this evening,' he admitted with a weary shake of his head. 'At this moment I'm wondering why I ever agreed to take the job.'

'So why did you?' It was out before she could stop it.

'I had to come back.' Simon laid his arm across the back of the bench, his body angled towards her. There was a slight draught from the expanse of windows above them and Kirsten pulled up her knees, wrapping the throw around her. They sat facing each other for a moment, both lost in their own thoughts. 'I tried not to,' he said, smiling wistfully at her. 'Believe me.'

He reached up and took a strand of her hair, twining it through his fingers. She didn't stop him. She wanted to lean against him, let him hold her in his arms, and it was taking every fibre of her being to fight it.

'You're the only woman I've ever loved,' he continued. 'We were the perfect couple. Everyone said so. I wanted to give you everything. I thought we'd take on the world together.'

'We were young and naïve.'

'We were in love, though?'

'Oh, yes.' Kirsten sighed. Being here, alone with Simon, she felt she should be honest with him. 'We were in love.' So much in love.

'I used to watch you sleeping sometimes,' Simon admitted. 'I couldn't believe you were mine. You were so beautiful. I missed you so much when I was away from you. Even when I slept I thought of you.'

It would sound ridiculous to her, if she hadn't felt exactly the same.

'I thought we'd have a wonderful life together. A big house, perhaps by the coast – or at least a weekend place there. Remember all our wonderful trips to Cornwall? We loved it there, didn't we?'

'Yes.' There were times, when she felt down or depressed, when she recalled those carefree trips with Simon. Walking on the beaches at St Ives and Penzance. Laughing as they tried to surf together. Having fish and chips sat on the seafront in Padstow. 'It's still my favourite place. I haven't been there in years though.' Too many memories.

'What about the weekend when we went down in Stu's battered old camper van? Him and that hippy girlfriend he had.'

'Melody.'

'That's the one. Mad but great fun. She used to do our tarot cards.'

'Yes, she did.' Mystic Melody had said they would grow old together. How very wrong she'd been.

156

'It was wonderful.' Simon was clearly relishing turning back the years. 'We rented surfboards. What a hoot.' He laughed. 'Then we all sat around the campfire at night, Stu with his guitar and too many bottles of cheap wine.'

'It was great.'

'Do you ever see Stu now?'

'No. Not for a long time.' So many friends had fallen by the wayside as she'd moved around with Tyler. 'We lost touch.'

'I loved it there. I've never been happier. Golden times. I thought we might live somewhere down there eventually.'

'We used to pick the houses we'd like,' Kirsten said. 'Ones we never thought we'd be able to afford, in the estate agents' windows.'

'There'd be a couple of kids – maybe more. With your looks, of course. I even knew what dogs we'd have: a black Labrador and a springer spaniel. They'd be called Dexter and Bounce.' He smiled again, but sadly now. 'I had it all planned out, you know.'

'We both did.' Kirsten's eyes brimmed with tears. 'Or so we thought.'

They were a year into their relationship when he'd been offered a job in Australia. Another step up on the corporate ladder. It was a great position, a huge salary. They'd been talking about getting married, when it came up. There'd even been a few conversations about starting a family. As Simon said, they'd been so in love. So very much in love. To this day, Kirsten didn't really know what had gone wrong.

'Did Australia lose its lustre?' Her throat was tight as she asked the question.

'Eventually. I've been in Texas for the last two years. Working for the Texan Oil Company,' he said. 'I tried to immerse myself in my job. For a few years, I think it even worked. I did a lot of charity work too, and that helped. I realised there were an awful lot of people worse-off than me. It still didn't make me forget you, though.' He stroked a finger tenderly over the back of her hand. 'But I'm getting older, Kirsten, and I didn't want to spend my life filled with regret. I just couldn't stay away any longer.'

'Is there a Mrs Conway?' A green-tinged pain nipped at the edge of her consciousness. Why did she have to blurt out a stupid question like that? She hadn't heard that he'd married, but then she'd deliberately tried not to take an interest in what Simon was doing after their relationship ended. Even now, it hurt to ask if Simon had a wife. Of course he would be married. Some gorgeous creature would have tempted him from his bachelor lifestyle by now. Probably someone the spitting image of Gwyneth Paltrow – all perfect teeth, blocked-blonde high-lights and perky breasts.

'Do you even need to ask that?'

Kirsten glanced at his hand. 'No wedding ring,' she observed. 'But that doesn't mean anything.' Tyler wore one, but it didn't seem to hinder any of his affairs. 'I thought you must have had a wife and at least two children by now.'

'No. I can't say that I didn't try to forget you. I did, Kirsten. God knows I did. But no one has ever come close to meaning what you did to me.' He sighed, and the intensity of his stare increased. 'There isn't a day that goes by that I don't regret that there isn't an "us".'

'You did what you did. There's no point in lamenting it. Life has moved on.'

'All these years have passed and I think of you every single day, without fail. You're always on my mind. We never fought, rarely argued. I still don't know what happened.'

She laughed, but it wasn't a laugh at all. 'Me neither.'

'The job was massive,' he said. 'I know that much. Huge. Much bigger than I'd ever imagined. I had no idea what I was walking into. The responsibility, the sheer volume of work was relentless. I was flattered that they thought I could do it, but it consumed me. Some nights I could barely crawl home to my bed before I had to start it all again the next day. I didn't even know which way up I was.'

The plan had been for Simon to establish himself and then she'd leave her job to follow him. For the first month they'd been on the phone regularly and had emailed at least once a day. She missed him desperately and couldn't wait to be there with him. It would be the start of a whole new exciting life for them.

But their conversations had become more infrequent and somehow less loving. With the time difference and their jobs, it became harder to speak every day. It pained her even now to think about it. She had felt the distance opening up between them and could do nothing about it.

'It was only meant to be for a short while,' she ventured. 'We should have been able to survive apart.'

'I thought so too,' Simon said. 'But you chose Tyler.'

'What else was I to do? I was young. I felt abandoned.'

'Why did you marry him? Of all the people in the world, why Tyler?'

'He was there,' she said, plainly. 'You weren't.'

'Are you happy with him?' A barely discernible crack in his voice gave away the depth of emotion behind the challenge.

'Happy?' Kirsten stared up through the glass of the potting shed and up to the moon. 'Ah. Isn't that the million-dollar question?' How could she begin to explain how she felt about her marriage when she wasn't entirely sure herself? 'Perhaps it depends on what your definition of happiness is.'

'You could have been divorced and remarried by now. But instead you've stayed with Tyler.'

'It doesn't sound like you approve of that.'

'I wish you'd come to Australia with me as planned.'

'It's all water under the bridge now.' But she, too, often wondered how different her life would have been if she'd joined Simon as they'd intended.

When it was clear that she wasn't going to follow Simon to the New World straight away, Tyler had swept in, so very eager to take his place. He was the one who provided a strong shoulder for her to cry on. There'd always been a fierce rivalry between the two men. In a rare moment of honesty, Tyler confessed that he'd envied their love. Then, like managing a delicate project, he'd proceeded to woo her. He bowled her over with a romantic onslaught – flowers, candlelit dinners, weekends in European cities in the best hotels. It was champagne all the way.

Kirsten threw herself into it, impatient to be loved again. She was determined that she wouldn't pine for Simon. He didn't deserve it. But she looked back now and was appalled at how needy she'd been. She hadn't wanted to be left alone. She'd wanted to be with someone, anyone. There were times when she questioned whether she had ever really loved Tyler. She thought she had, but in truth she'd never felt the same about her husband as she had about Simon.

That didn't stop her marrying him. Six months later she and Tyler had a hastily arranged but lavish wedding. Everyone assumed she was pregnant. The fact was, she was simply desperate to prove to Simon that someone else could love her as much as he had.

'We could have had a great life in Australia,' he said. 'I was devastated when I got your email saying you'd decided not to come. I could hardly believe it. You don't know what it did to me.'

Her head snapped up at that. 'What?'

'It was a cruel way to end it.' He turned his face away from her. 'It seemed so unlike you, but you obviously had your reasons. It was a great career move for me, but I'd done it for us.

Both of us. I can't blame you, I suppose,' Simon continued with a shake of his head. 'I handled it badly. I'd gone and Tyler was there to take my place. My heart just snapped in two.'

She frowned at him. 'Simon, I didn't end our relationship. What are you talking about? *You* were the one who sent an email ending it all.'

He gave a hollow laugh. 'Of course I didn't. I adored you.' His eyes met hers. 'I still do.'

She looked back, perplexed. 'What exactly did this email say?'

'You should know.'

'That's the very weird thing, Simon. I don't.'

Now it was his turn to look confused, but he shrugged and said, 'You told me that you'd fallen in love with Tyler. That he meant the world to you and you wouldn't be coming to Australia.'

'I hadn't fallen in love with Tyler. That's ridiculous. You were my life,' she said. 'I only started to see Tyler after we broke up. I needed him. He was the one who stepped into your shoes and helped to comfort me.'

Simon raised his eyebrows at that. 'I called Tyler the minute I got your email. He said it was true. That you were both sorry, but you hadn't been able to help your feelings. I was crushed. I thought we were soulmates.'

'We were,' she said. 'I couldn't believe you'd ended it so abruptly.'

'So . . .' he said, 'if I didn't send you an email and you didn't send me one, who could it have been?'

'Oh no!' Kirsten gasped.

'There could only be one person who did it.'

'Tyler,' they said together.

'That scheming bastard!' Kirsten raged. 'Wait till I get my hands on him. He did this?'

Simon's face was grey. 'He must have set up a fake account in my name, and yours too.'

'Why didn't you ring me?' she said.

'For the same reasons you didn't ring me, I expect. I was so stunned by the contents, it never occurred to me to check whether it really was from you. Who would dream of doing a thing like that?'

'Tyler,' they said again.

'I did call *him* to have it out with him. He'd stolen you from beneath my nose. He told me in no uncertain terms to stay away, that you didn't love me any more and didn't want to talk to me.'

'And you believed him?'

'Yes. He was my best friend. Why would I doubt him?'

'But you doubted me?'

'Tyler was so plausible. He said he was racked with guilt at how things had turned out.'

Kirsten sighed. 'I bet he did.'

'I thought I should just step away from the situation and, if you loved him, you should be free to do so.'

'Oh, God.' Kirsten put her head in her hands. 'He told me you didn't want to speak to me, that you wanted to move on with your new life.'

'Oh, Kirsten. You believed him?'

'I did.'

'So did I.'

'How could we have been so trusting?'

'He was our best friend,' Simon said. 'Or so I thought.'

'And yet he manipulated the end of our relationship for his own selfish ends. How could he do such a cruel, life-changing thing?'

Simon shook his head ruefully. 'The day you sent me an invitation to your wedding was the worst day of my life.'

'I didn't send you an invitation,' Kirsten countered. 'Of course I didn't. You were the last person I would have wanted there. As far as I was concerned, you'd dumped me from a great height. That must have been Tyler too.'

'It seems he's engineered our unhappiness.'

'I can hardly believe it. What a terrible thing to do to us both,' Kirsten said. 'I knew he was immoral, but I never knew he could stoop so low.'

Simon's expression was bleak. 'We should have had more faith in our relationship. How could we let him do that?'

'Would you have still gone through with it? Would you have still married Tyler if I'd come back to fight for you?'

'How can I answer that?' Tears were behind her eyes. She was struggling to process this latest revelation about her husband's deceitful nature. He had duped them both so easily and had changed the course of their lives in doing so. If she dwelt on that too much, she might just go insane. 'What's done is done.'

'Right until the last minute, I was going to jump on a plane. I swear to you. I was going to come right back and try to persuade you to change your mind.'

'But you didn't.'

'No.' Simon shook his head. 'I thought it was what you wanted. I didn't want to stand in the way of your happiness. Then it was too late. That was when it really hit me. You were gone and you were marrying my best friend.' He gave her a rueful smile. 'Some best friend, eh?'

She shook her head, part of her still unable to comprehend it.

'I got steaming drunk on the day of your wedding and picked up a nameless girl for the night. Afterwards, I thought I could find someone else. Surely the world was full of bright, beautiful women who could take your place? I thought I'd fall in love again easily when the time was right.' He reached up and stroked his thumb over the curve of her cheekbone. 'I was so terribly wrong.'

'There's no point to this, Simon.'

'There is. I've never stopped loving you and I don't think I ever will. I had to come back to see if you were deliriously happy with him.' Simon gently squeezed her hand and she suddenly felt achingly sad deep down inside. 'But you're not.'

'Tyler's my husband. That's all there is to it.'

'He did a terrible thing to us. It's even worse now I know that. He ruined our lives, Kirsten. Think of the future we could have had together. All I want to do is make that right.'

'You speak as if time has stood still.'

'Perhaps it has, for me.'

'I'm married to Tyler. For better, for worse.' A few short hours ago, she was vowing that next year everything would be different between her and Tyler. She'd been determined to work on their relationship. Even with this latest revelation to rock her world, could she turn her back on him? It was a dreadful situation. She'd thought Simon had left her and now it turned out that he'd never stopped loving her for one moment. It frightened her that she felt the same way. She looked at him, so handsome in the moonlight, and said bleakly, 'What can I do?'

'Leave him,' he said starkly. 'I still love you, Kirsten Benson. I always have. I want to hold you to me and cover your unhappy mouth with kisses. I want to bring the fire back to your sad, sad eyes. I want you more than I ever did. And I'm going to do everything possible in my power to take you away from him.'

Chapter Twenty-two

Melissa settled Lance in a quieter corner of the marquee, well away from the rest of the staff. She'd found a chair with arms so that he could stay upright in it rather than slide sideways on to the floor. He was talking loudly and incessantly about the success of his speech. Behind him, Tyler shook his head with disbelief.

She topped up her husband's glass with bourbon and handed it to him. 'Tyler and I have to sort out a little something, angel.'

'I love you,' Lance mumbled. 'Was I good, honey?'

'You were fabulous,' she said as she kissed his cheek.

'Was I good, Tyler?'

'Exceptional. Inspirational.' Tyler rolled his eyes.

She didn't bother to tell him that Lance would be too drunk to catch the sarcasm in his voice.

'Don't move.' She patted his shoulder. 'We'll be back shortly.'

As soon as she turned away, Tyler caught her by the elbow and hustled her along the corridor to the main house.

Melissa had a pang of anxiety. She was becoming more concerned about Lance as he got older. 'Do you think he'll be all right left alone?'

'He's fine,' Tyler muttered. 'One of the staff might club him to death while we're gone, but it's no more than he deserves.'

'I had no idea that was what he was going to say,' she promised Tyler. 'No idea at all.'

He tutted at her and then opened a grand door, pulling her inside. It was the library; on the couch in front of the fire, a couple were entwined in a passionate embrace.

'Out, out,' Tyler barked. 'I'm requisitioning this room for an important business meeting.'

The couple jumped up, startled.

'Oh, hi, Tyler.' Smirking, the girl straightened her clothes, patted her hair. 'How are things with you? It's been a long time.'

Tyler had the grace to look slightly discomfited. 'Fine,' he said. 'Now skedaddle, the pair of you. Get a room.'

She giggled at him. 'We should catch up sometime.'

'Yeah,' Tyler said. 'I'll text you.'

She grinned at him in a knowing way as she scuttled out with her partner.

'Who was that?' Melissa asked as the door closed behind them.

'Can't remember her name,' Tyler said. 'Works in Promotions. Very capable.'

Sure she is, Melissa thought.

When they'd gone, Tyler locked the door. 'At least we won't be disturbed now.'

She wondered if Tyler would want to make love. It was dangerous, but she was sure that was part of the thrill for him. Men like Tyler were always attracted by the forbidden, the risky. Strangely, for once it was the very last thing on her mind.

Melissa sat down on the sofa, smoothing her emerald-green sheath over her knees. The room was warm and it made her realise how very weary she was. All this subterfuge was exhausting. Tyler didn't sit next to her. Instead he stood by the fire, hand on the marble mantel like the lord of the manor.

'Come and sit with me, Tyler,' she said, patting the cushion next to her.

He shook his head and began pacing back and forth across the Chinese rug. 'Would you mind telling me what that was all about?'

'The first I heard about it was in the car on the way here,' Melissa told him in measured tones.

'Lance hadn't given me one inkling that this was coming,' Tyler fumed. 'I'm supposed to be his right-hand man.'

'He hadn't mentioned anything to me either, before tonight.'

'Lance talks to you about everything.'

'Not this. Bud Harman had only spoken to him today. This morning, I think. You know what it's like at Fossil. These hare-brained projects are plucked out of thin air and vanish again just as quickly. If I'd had any information, of course I would have told you instantly.'

Tyler tutted his displeasure again. She was normally so eager to please him. The thread that bound them together was as insubstantial as gossamer, she knew that, and she never wanted to do anything to risk severing their tenuous connection. Tonight, she couldn't care less. She'd done her very best for Tyler and it was never enough. She just felt old and drained.

'I'll have this out with him,' Tyler said. 'In the morning. When he's sober. I've seen him bad before, but I've never seen him so far gone.'

'Me neither.' She was worn out by Lance's drinking too. All the signs were that it was simply getting worse and worse as the years went by. Where would it all end?

'So, what was it that you *did* want to tell me?'

Melissa took a deep, shuddering breath. 'We're going back to the States,' she said. It was only voicing it out loud that actually made it seem real. 'To Washington DC. On Christmas Day.'

'Christ,' Tyler spat. 'Why don't I know about this either?'

167

'Lance is going to be heading up the SACKED project from there. It doesn't just affect the UK; Lance is going to be in charge of the global roll-out.'

'God help us.'

'What can I do?' Melissa asked. 'I'm leaving, Tyler. This ... us ... it will all be over.'

'What's my role in the project going to be?' He paced some more. It was clear that he hadn't fully understood what she'd said. 'Who's going to be running Fossil in Lance's absence? Will it be me? It better bloody had be. Has he said anything about that?'

'No. He hasn't. But I can tell you that's there's going to be a new international director.'

Tyler's head snapped up. 'Where does he fit in? I'm assuming he'll be working for me, so why haven't I been consulted on this?'

'I don't know.' She fiddled with one of her manicured nails. 'But I do know he's supposed to be here tonight.'

'Here?' Tyler looked perplexed. 'So why haven't I met him?'

'Perhaps the snow has delayed him.'

'Bloody hell.' Tyler snatched up the poker and stabbed angrily at the coals in the fireplace. Sparks flew up the chimney. One spat on to the Chinese rug and smouldered. Neither of them moved, and eventually it burned itself out. 'This is all I need. I'm being kept out of the loop on everything. Why? Lance normally leans on me.'

'He must have his reasons.'

'Well I wish I knew what they were.'

He was in danger of wearing a track in the rug.

'I'm leaving, Tyler,' Melissa stressed. 'I'm going back to America the day after tomorrow. Can we talk about this? What am I to do?'

He switched his attention back to her. Then he shrugged. 'What *can* we do? This has been great, Melissa. While it lasted. But we both knew it had to end sometime.'

168

The words almost wouldn't come, but she knew she had to say this. 'I don't have to go.' Melissa searched her lover's face. 'I could stay here.'

'And do what?' He jammed his hands in the pockets of his dinner jacket, his handsome face dark in the firelight. 'You need Lance. He needs you.'

'I could leave him,' she ventured. It was time to put her cards on the table. 'I could leave him and stay here with you.'

Tyler recoiled, which told her all she needed to know.

'Don't be ridiculous.'

'Is it?' She didn't want to beg, but she had to state her case. Had she really been nothing more than a fling for Tyler Benson? Did he have any feelings for her other than lust? She had to know once and for all. 'I'm good for you, Tyler. I know what it takes to be the partner of a man who lives for the company. Together we'd make a great team.'

He stared at her agog, which made her feel unsure of her footing.

'I was happy to continue as we were, but this announcement of Lance's has changed things. It's made me realise how much you mean to me.' Her mouth was going dry. There was a drink on the table next to her. She didn't know whose it was or what it was, but she downed it nevertheless. It was whisky and it burned her throat as she swallowed it.

Now there was no going back. Tyler had to know how she felt. There may not be another chance. 'We're good together. You said yourself that Kirsten doesn't understand the oil business. I do. I know what it takes to stay at your level. With me behind you, the sky's the limit. Leave her. Break free, Tyler. You don't love your wife any more.'

'I do love her,' he protested. 'You don't know what I had to do to win Kirsten. I can't let her go.'

'Then why do we spend afternoons in hotels together?' She

glanced at the door, towards where the couple had just left. The girl had made it clear that she was well acquainted with Tyler, and Melissa wondered how far that went too. 'It looks as if I might not be the only one to have enjoyed your attentions. Is that what you think love is?'

Tyler might think she was easily fooled, but he was a handsome man with power and she knew only too well where that could lead. There were always women who'd find that an attractive combination.

'This is over, Melissa. It has to be.'

'We could meet up if you come to Washington on business.'

He was non-committal. 'I'm rarely in the States these days.'

'Perhaps I could come back to London for weekends,' she suggested. Even to her own ears, she was sounding desperate.

'You know that's not possible. Lance needs you by his side.'

'Maybe that's why I feel like his nanny and not his wife.'

Finally Tyler came and sat next to her. He took her hands in his. Even this small contact with him made her long for him. She wanted to be in his arms again, to receive whatever crumb of comfort he had to offer.

'We've had a great time, Melissa,' he said softly. 'It's been fun.'

Fun. Was that all she meant to him? She hoped, against the odds, that it had been more.

'But now it has to end.' He moved away from her and lounged on the cushions at the other end of the sofa. 'You and Lance will have a blast in Washington. You'll love it.'

All Melissa could see was an endless round of corporate parties, Lance getting drunk at each and every one. Her taking him home, undressing him, cleaning up after him. Her life would be just the same as it was now. Except without Tyler.

'I don't love him,' she said, voicing that for the first time too. 'I haven't for a long time.'

Tyler's face said that that wasn't his problem.

'What am I to do?' Melissa could feel a deep panic gripping her. She was past her first flush of youth, but not old enough to be on the scrapheap. Was it wrong to still want someone who loved her?

Yet she'd seen Tyler looking at his young assistant, Louise. There was lust in his eyes. Had she ever *really* seen that when he looked at her? She didn't think so. The pain of realisation made her chest tight.

He might not admit it, but even Kirsten's days were numbered. Men like Tyler Benson always wanted the latest model, whether it was computers, cars or companions.

'Go back to Lance,' he said flatly. 'There was never going to be a future for us. Surely you realised that?'

She did now.

'Take him home, Melissa. Put him to bed. And, on Christmas Day, fly to Washington. What else can you do?'

So that was it.

'I look at you and Kirsten,' she said, 'and I see how Lance and I used to be. Don't turn into him, Tyler. It's not too late to change.'

'I'm going to,' he admitted. 'My new year's resolution is to look after Kirsten more. I've had a lot on this year and I've neglected her. I'm going to make a renewed effort. You may not think so, but our marriage *is* strong. Kirsten would never look at another man.' His expression said that he thought less of Melissa because she, foolishly, had. 'And I *do* love her.'

'Then you need to show her. Properly.' Melissa looked at him. He might protest his love for his wife, but he was just paying lip service to the notion of love and soon it wouldn't be enough for Kirsten to hang on to. She knew that only too well. 'If you don't turn things around, she'll end up like me, Tyler. Bitter, empty and despising her husband.'

171

'I should be getting back to the party, before I'm missed,' Tyler said.

He stood up, surreptitiously glancing at his watch, and she knew she'd been dismissed. After their time together, the clandestine afternoons spent blissfully in his arms, the deliciously secretive texts, this was how it was all to end.

'I've loved you, Tyler,' she said. 'I want you to know that.'

She stood too and kissed him, her lips, probably for the very last time, lingering on his cheek. She'd wanted someone to love her, to care for her, to make her his world. That was never going to be Tyler Benson. He was just like Lance. He'd always put himself and the company first. She should have known that.

'You'd never tell Lance about us?' he said, slightly nervously. 'It wouldn't do anyone any good.'

Least of all you, Tyler Benson, she thought. Melissa sighed. 'No, Tyler. I won't tell him.'

Her back was rigid with the effort of trying not to cry as she unlocked the library door. The precaution that hadn't been necessary at all. And, with as much dignity as she could muster, she left.

Chapter Twenty-three

I look around at my colleagues in dismay. The rate at which they're downing Jägerbombs is quite alarming. If only the company would stop dishing out all this free alcohol then they could save a dozen jobs. Mind you, I can't talk. I was only going to have a couple of drinks tonight, just to be sociable, but I'm filling my boots with free champagne while it's going. It could very well be my last chance.

The Christmas party is now starting to look like a bad night in the Wild West. All sense of decorum has been ditched and the dance floor is full of demented revellers. Karen is still going strong, though I have no idea how. That girl knows how to party. And some.

She seems, thankfully, to have abandoned all thought of getting off with Josh Wallace and currently has her legs wrapped round the waist of Ted Turner from Alternative Fuels, a man who wouldn't normally say boo to a goose. She's showing her knickers to the world. And I suppose I'm just grateful that she's actually wearing any. He's currently swinging her upside-down and she's gathering the remnants of party poppers from the floor with her long blonde hair. I'm feeling quite sick just watching her; I fear there will be many regrets in the morning. Part of me wants to move in and stop her, but I'm sure she wouldn't thank me for it. I'm hoping she'll forgive Josh for having paid more attention to me than her; I don't want to make an enemy of her.

Josh and I are standing on the sidelines, watching.

'Want to join the bun fight?' he asks.

'I'm not sure I do,' I admit. 'This is all a bit frenzied for me. At this time of night, I'm normally tucked up on the sofa in my jim-jams watching *News at Ten* with my parents. Some nights I even find that too exciting.'

'We should make an effort.'

'I guess so.' I throw down the rest of my champagne. Josh holds out his hand and takes me on to the dance floor.

'I should stand on the edge,' he says. 'No one should be allowed to see me dance.'

'They're all too drunk to notice,' I remind him.

The band are in full flow with 'Fairytale of New York'. The staff sing along raucously and we inch our way into the centre of the floor, which is pulsating with colour. Arms and legs are flying everywhere with a glorious lack of co-ordination. It's only a minute before I'm biffed by someone I recognise from Specialised Products.

Josh pulls me into his arms in a protective way. It's a casual movement, but I notice how my heart starts to race. Hmm. Then the tempo changes. He holds me tightly as we sway around, hardly moving to 'Baby, It's Cold Outside'. It's an intimate moment amid the madness, but even that doesn't last. A second later, Karen bounces into the woman next to Josh and then ricochets against me.

One of her false eyelashes is flapping loose and her lipstick is smeared round her mouth. Strands of pink, yellow and blue streamers litter her hair.

She pushes her face close to Josh's and shouts, 'Bloody great party, eh?'

'Great,' he agrees with slightly less enthusiasm.

'Dance with me,' she demands.

'Louise and I were just going to sit down,' he answers. 'Take the weight off our feet. We haven't got your admirable stamina. Maybe later.'

'I won't forget,' she says, wagging a finger in his general direction. Then she launches herself at Ted Turner again.

'Let's get out of here while the going's good,' he whispers in my ear. 'We can find somewhere quiet to put our feet up for half an hour.'

He's still holding my hand as we weave our way through the dancers and set off down the corridors of the main house in search of sanctuary. As we go, I see the chairman's wife heading towards us, her face as white as a sheet. A few metres behind her is Tyler Benson, expression grim. I wonder what's wrong now.

'Quick!' I tug Josh into an alcove and we press close together as they both pass without seeing us.

'What's the matter?' he whispers.

'I don't know why, but I just didn't want to bump into Tyler.' If he sees us heading away from the party together, he'll only make something of it, and that's the very last thing I want. 'He had a face like thunder.'

'Tyler likes to be in control,' Josh says. 'Something tells me he isn't at the moment.'

When we're sure they've gone, we emerge again. In the corridor we encounter a waiter and Josh stops him. 'Can we get some coffee served somewhere quiet?' He slips the man a tenner.

'Go into the library, sir.' The waiter indicates a huge door just down the corridor behind us. If I'm not mistaken, that's where Melissa Harvey and Tyler Benson just emerged from. 'I'll bring it to you in five minutes.'

'Thanks.'

So we head to the library. Josh opens the door for me and together we step inside.

'Wow.' I can't help but gasp. 'This place is fantastic.' As befitting a stately home, I guess, it's an incredible library, all dark wood and luxurious furnishings. This has been decked out for Christmas too and there's a large tree, trimmed in red, at one end. The lights twinkle invitingly. Baskets of poinsettia are dotted about, adding a festive splash of colour. Very sumptuous and tasteful. Clearly someone with a bit more festive restraint than my mum has done this. Self-consciously, I snap a few pics on my mobile for her.

Totally in awe, I wander along the mahogany shelving, running my fingers enviously across the endless rows of leather-bound books. It makes the little stack of paperbacks on my bedside table look slightly inadequate. 'I've never been in anywhere like this before.'

'Amazing, isn't it?'

'How can one family have all this?' I turn back to Josh. 'Would you fancy living somewhere like this?'

'I hope to one day. Well, maybe not quite so palatial. I have ambitions, Louise. I want to have a big house, my own land, ponies for the kids. That kind of thing.'

'At the moment, I'd just settle for a place of my own where I could pay the bills without going overdrawn.'

It seems strange to be alone in this majestic room with Josh, but I'm a bit tipsy and feeling slightly reckless. Besides, he's funny, handsome and ambitious. I haven't met anyone like him in a long time. On the very rare occasions I have, in the past, been dragged out with my friends to nightclubs, all the men there seem to be losers. Who wants a bloke that you can meet in a nightclub? Most of my mates pick up random men on the internet, but they don't seem to be without their issues either. Most of them are either weird and looking for casual sex, or married and looking for casual sex. Even I can see that Josh Wallace is quite a catch.

The lights are turned off in here, but there's a warm glow from the roaring fire and the Christmas-tree lights. Along the mantelpiece there's a garland of holly entwined with more poinsettia flowers. These ones are silk though, not real. Mum would definitely approve.

I flop into the cushions of the squishy sofa with a sigh of relief and kick off my shoes.

'Oh, this is bliss.' I rub some feeling back into my toes on the plush rug.

Josh goes to stoke the fire, and at the same time there's a knock at the door.

'Come in,' Josh says, and I giggle.

'You make it sound like it *is* your house,' I whisper, still feeling as if I have to speak in hushed tones.

'Just practising,' he says.

The waiter comes in and places the coffee down on the table. He nods to us before disappearing again.

The coffee set is fine china and there's a little plate of handmade chocolates for us. 'How exciting.'

'Shall I pour?' Josh asks.

'Thank you. White, no sugar, for me.'

He crouches and carefully pours the coffee, his hand steady and confident.

'This was a nice idea,' I say. 'Thanks.'

'My pleasure.'

When he hands me the cup he smiles, and it does very strange things to my insides. I move up on the sofa so that he can sit next to me, which feels a bit intimate.

Josh sinks back too, sipping at his coffee. 'This is more like it. I used to enjoy the Christmas party, but it's too manic out there for me. I'm obviously a lightweight now.'

177

'Me too. When I'm at home every night, night after night, I sometimes long to be out and partying. Then, when I get a chance to go out, all I want is to be at home with Mia.'

'She obviously means the world to you.'

I nod. 'Like any mum.'

'I know you split from her dad, but is he still in your lives?'

'No. Long gone. He left me not long after Mia was born, so he's never been around for her.'

'That must have been hard.'

'It was terrible at the time. But, if I'm honest, I'm glad it happened that way. Steve was an immature prick. I don't know what I saw in him now. Even when it was just the two of us, I never knew where he was. He was Jack the lad, there always seemed to be some dodgy deal going on.'

He was domineering too. Always wanted to know where I was, what I was doing. He hated me seeing my friends and, when we went out, liked to choose what I wore. I think that's another reason why I object to having to pick my clothing so as not to attract Tyler Benson's attention. I've been there before, and this feels every bit as controlling.

'The cracks were showing before I found out I was expecting. That was the final straw, really.' I purse my lips. Perhaps the champagne has loosened my tongue, or perhaps Josh Wallace is easy to talk to, I don't know, but I never normally open up like this. Before I think better of it I continue, 'Mia wasn't exactly planned and he just never wanted the responsibility. At least when she was born it was just me and her. I've never had to fight him for custody or anything like that. She doesn't remember him at all. Which, I guess, makes life easier.'

'He doesn't help to support her though?'

'No.' I shake my head. 'I've never had a penny from him. The day he walked out he stopped paying his share of the mortgage on our house. I'm up to my eyeballs in debt thanks to him. Still, he's very much out of my life. He lives in Spain now. Or, last I heard, he did. I haven't had so much as a text from him since he left.'

'What a tosser.'

I shrug. 'What doesn't kill you makes you stronger. Everything I've done, I've done by myself.'

'I can't imagine how that must feel as a father, never to see your own daughter.'

'It's his choice. And it might sound bad, but I don't want to share her with him. He might be her biological father, but there's nothing of him in Mia. She's all mine. Mia's a really great kid. She's as bright as a button.' I reach down to my bag for my phone. 'I've got a photo of her, if you'd like to see it.' Then I realise what I'm doing. 'How silly. Why would you?'

'No, I'd love to see her. I really like kids. Love them. I hoped that I'd have a couple by now, but it never worked out with me and Corrine.' He smiles sadly. 'She wasn't that keen, and besides, I've heard it's quite difficult to make babies if you're never actually in the same room together, let alone the same bed.'

'I've heard that too.'

'Travelodges prove to be an excellent contraceptive.'

'That's a shame.'

'One day,' he says wistfully.

So, even if he is humouring me, I pull out my phone and flick to the stash of photos of Mia. I scoot up next to him so that he can see them better in the low light. My daughter is posing this, that and the other way. In all of them she looks unbearably cute.

'Wow,' Josh says, cooing over them as I hoped he would. 'She's lovely. A stunner. Like her mum.'

'Well . . .' I'm embarrassed now and I put my phone away. 'I'm sure that's enough of that.'

He takes a strand of my hair and twines it gently around his finger. We're close, so close. Then, before I really know how it happens, our lips meet. A delicious warmth floods through me. It's so long since I've been kissed by a man, especially a man like Josh Wallace, and my head spins.

Then we're lying full-length on the sofa and I want him. I want him so badly.

Chapter Twenty-four

Kirsten stood up and wrapped the throw tightly around herself. It was time she left the warmth of this little sanctuary and went back out into the cold to find Tyler. And God help him when she did. Before she lost all reason, she should leave Simon.

'I can't do this, Si,' she said sadly. 'I might have loved you once, but our time has passed.'

'I don't believe you. We both know now that we've been cheated out of our love by Tyler. How can we simply ignore that? We've wasted too much precious time. I want to give you the future you deserve.' He stood too and took her in his arms. 'Don't walk away from me.'

The way he made her feel frightened her. The attraction she'd felt for him as a younger woman was every bit as strong now. He'd been the love of her life and part of her knew that he still was. Whatever she said, there was no denying that.

Things had gone wrong with Tyler over the years, but she had loved him. Once. However, she'd never felt that same intensity of passion that she had with Simon. He was right, they'd been soulmates. Maybe, given the chance, they could be once again. But she dared not risk it.

Her mind was racing, still flicking through snapshots of all the good times they'd had together. The times they curled up together on the sofa on rainy Sunday afternoons to read in contented silence. Simon would read one of the classics, she a trashy paperback. Whatever they did they'd been so at ease in each other's company. He had been the perfect lover too. That was all too easy to call to mind. He'd been tender, strong, caring. It made her shiver inside just to think of it. If she was brutally honest with herself, Tyler had never moved her the way Simon had. But it was so long ago, and they were different people now. And she, for one, had commitments.

'I'm Tyler's wife.' She'd been *his* bride, not the bride she was destined to be. Her voice was unsteady as she spoke. 'Tyler behaved despicably and told a terrible lie to break us up, but we did let each other go, Simon, and we both have to live with that decision. It's too late to do anything about it.' She could hardly bear to see the disappointment, the pain in Simon's loving eyes. 'You have to accept that.'

It would make her just as bad as Tyler if she even considered reviving her relationship with Simon. Where would that lead? It would cause pain to everyone concerned and she could never be responsible for that. She'd always believed absolutely in fidelity. She supposed one of them in their marriage should.

'I feel as if I let you down, Kirsten. Badly. In the worst possible way. I should never have trusted Tyler. I took his word as true and yet he deceived us both.' His fingers tightened on her arms. 'Don't let that stupid mistake blight the future. It's not too late. We could be happy again, together.'

'I'm married, Simon. I love someone else.'

'You don't,' he said starkly. 'I've seen the way you look at him, the way he looks at you. Whatever you might have had together is long gone. Even I can see that.'

'That doesn't mean I can just leave Tyler and trail along after you after all this time. You're asking too much of me.'

'We can take it slowly,' Simon said. 'Get to know each other again. Now I've seen you, I know you still have feelings for me. Whatever the obstacles, love like ours doesn't just die.'

'I'm sorry, Simon. This can't go any further. We can't even be friends. It's too difficult.' She didn't think she could be near him and not want to be with him. 'If you're going to work for Fossil – and I hope you reconsider that move – then we're going to bump into each other at these things. We'll smile and be polite, but that's as far as it will go.'

'That's a shame, Kirsten,' he said, 'because from where I'm standing it looks as if you could really do with a friend.'

That nearly had her undone. Simon could always read her like a book. It was so hard to turn away from this. All she wanted to do was reach up and stroke his cheek, to feel his mouth on hers once more, to be protected in his strong embrace. He'd always been so different from Tyler, but how could she be sure of him now? Perhaps ten years at the top of the corporate ladder had changed him too.

She stepped away from him. 'I must go back to Tyler.'

'You know where I am, Kirsten.' He reached into his jacket pocket, pulled out a card and gave it to her.

She gave a hollow laugh. 'A business card?'

'It's the best I can do.' He pressed it into her palm. 'We had something that comes around only once in a lifetime. I just didn't know that then, and I'd give anything to turn back the clock.'

Kirsten sighed shakily.

'If you ever need me, just call. Night or day. I'll be waiting. I love you. And I'm a patient man.'

She turned her face to him and kissed his lips. It was meant to be fleeting, a token of their friendship, but he caught her by the waist and held her close. The sensation was almost over-whelming. The feel of his mouth on hers was new and exciting, yet familiar and comforting, all at the same time. Oh, how she'd adored this man. She could feel herself drowning in the sensation, letting herself be drawn into his love. It took a great effort to pull away from him.

When she did, Simon was smiling sadly.

'That can never happen again.' She wrapped the throw tighter around her shoulders and prepared to make her escape. If she didn't do it now, she'd be lost. 'You'll find a lovely woman. Someone younger and more beautiful than I am. You'll have your 2.4 children and you'll be ecstatically happy.'

'You think so?' He gave her a doubtful smile. 'And what about you, Kirsten? What kind of future do you predict for yourself?'

'One where I'm still Tyler's wife,' she said flatly.

She slowly backed away, step by step. At the door of the potting shed she took one last look at him, to imprint this moment in her brain. 'Goodbye, Simon. Be happy.'

Then she fled back towards the party.

The snow was falling heavily now and the grounds of Wadestone Manor looked spectacular, but that didn't make up for the sadness in her heart. The pain was actually physical, like stomach cramps, and she wondered how long it would take to leave.

She still loved Simon Conway. God help her. It was even more difficult now that she knew the truth behind their break-up. Tyler had manipulated them both for his own ends. Simon hadn't left her, he hadn't stopped loving her. The thought made her feel nauseous.

Why couldn't Simon have found someone else to love? Stayed away? Remained on the other side of the world? It had been easier then. Now she ran the risk of bumping into him whenever she went to a Fossil Oil function. She ran the risk of having her heart torn apart all over again whenever she saw him. Also Tyler had yet to discover that Simon was to be his boss. She wouldn't want to be anywhere in the vicinity when he did. Then the shit would hit the fan. Well, perhaps he deserved it after what he'd done.

Kirsten picked her way along the now-snowy path, high heels the most inappropriate footwear. The snowflakes landed on her face, her hair, the dampness ruining her style. It was the least of her worries. How would she stop thinking about Simon? In moments of weakness, would she think of dialling his number? It was better to rip his card to shreds so that it was out of harm's way. One day, the temptation to call him, to hear his voice, would prove too great and she couldn't do that. She didn't dare. Kirsten still clutched it tightly in her hand. No good could possibly come of it.

So she took one last, longing look at the little white card in her palm. Simon Conway. She ran a finger lovingly over his name. Then she tore the card into tiny pieces and threw it into the air, where it mixed with the whirling snow and drifted slowly down to the ground.

Chapter Twenty-five

Tyler knew he had to get back to the party, and fast. Kirsten would be missing him and, knowing her, she'd start to wonder where Melissa had disappeared to as well. The only person he needed to stay away from was Lance, otherwise he might be tempted to lump him one. Even though he was older and, supposedly, wiser. He hoped Melissa would take him home straight away and that would be the last he'd see of either of them.

His fling with Melissa had been fun, and until now she'd been cool. It was probably just as well that they were leaving the country. He could see that it could have ended very badly.

Tyler meant what he'd said to her. He was going to try harder to make his marriage work. Kirsten wasn't an idiot; she knew when he was trying to pull the wool over her eyes, and he wondered how much longer she'd put up with it. Having gone all-out to snatch her from under the nose of Simon Conway, he hadn't been the best husband. But Kirsten was the ultimate trophy wife, and he should look after her better. It wouldn't be good for his CV if she walked out on him. From January, he was going to be like a new man. Swear to God.

As he approached the marquee, the cacophony of noise was mind-blowing. The band had upped the ante and modern hits belted out. Tyler could have done with earplugs. He liked to think he was still young and hip, but watching this lot he realised that he was getting too old for all of this. If he was promoted to chairman in Lance's place – and who else would there be to fit the bill? – then there'd be no Christmas party next year. He'd send an email round to the staff wishing them Merry Christmas etc., and take the managers across the road from the office for a pint, and that would be the job done. This was a ridiculous extravagance. There was a day when the oil business had been all about the entertainment, but that day was long past. This was the real world now and they had to cut their cloth accordingly. There'd still be the corporate sponsorship, obviously. And he'd never want to miss his annual trips to the Grand Prix. Monaco was his favourite venue. He'd make sure he and Kirsten were booked into one of the best hotels this year. Maybe the Hotel de Paris, or the Hermitage. She'd like that.

Tyler looked around, but he couldn't see his wife anywhere. He hoped she hadn't got into one of her sulks and gone home. She was a beautiful woman, if high-maintenance. But then, weren't they all?

From the corner of his eye, he saw Melissa rejoin Lance, so he swerved away from that side of the marquee. The band stopped playing and a magician took to the stage: The Magnificent Marvo, the large, fancy lettering down the side of his box of tricks proclaimed. Without further ado, the magician called up Karen from Customer Accounts on stage to assist him. The crowd were whooping and hollering.

She was a fine girl, Tyler thought. A bit too much of a blabbermouth for him to risk anything with her, but nevertheless quite a looker. If discretion had been one of the cards she was holding, he might have thought differently.

Now he was just wondering how she was currently staying upright. Whenever he'd seen her this evening she'd had a glass in her hand and she was weaving alarmingly. The magician was doing some sort of trick where he made her lie across two chairs, which gave the opportunity for everyone in the front few rows to look up her skirt. At the top, her breasts were barely contained. Two fluffy, marshmallow-like pillows with a life of their own bounced joyfully. Many a red-blooded man must be thinking about burying his head in those.

Tyler skirted around the back of the main body of staff, still looking for Kirsten. He grabbed a glass of wine from a passing waiter. At this stage in the evening, the drink was flowing like a river in flood. Then, without any warning, he pulled up short. Surely his eyes were deceiving him.

Straight ahead of him there was a bloke who looked suspiciously like Simon Conway. The ghost of Christmas past. Tyler shook his head. He must be more drunk than he thought. It couldn't be Conway. What would he be doing here?

Then, just as he'd convinced himself that he was imagining things, the man turned towards him and it was indeed Simon Conway. Tyler recoiled as if his old friend had punched him in the stomach.

The crowd cheered and Tyler snapped his attention back to the stage. The Magnificent Marvo had pulled the chairs out from beneath Karen from Customer Accounts, who now seemed to be floating on thin air. Tyler knew how she felt. It was as if his legs had been kicked from beneath him and he was no longer grounded in reality. The crowd roared their approval. Tyler was too frozen to do anything but stand and stare.

Conway walked up to him.

'What the hell are you doing here?' Tyler barked. This was no time for pleasantries.

'Hello, Tyler,' Conway replied.

As smooth as ever, Tyler seethed inwardly. Now he remembered why he'd hated him so much. When they were friends – and how long ago was that now? – everything had always gone

Simon's way. He had the best mates, the best jobs, the best cars and the best women. No struggling and striving for Conway. Oh no. He only had to blink and everything he wanted fell straight into his lap.

They'd been friends – good friends on the surface of it – but Tyler had never felt it was an equal relationship. When they played sport – squash or golf, whatever – Simon always won. He was the bright star to whom everyone gravitated. There were people in life who had an excess of charisma, and Conway was one of them. Tyler had tried to emulate it in his time. But he didn't think you could learn charisma; it was something that just oozed from your pores. If you were lucky enough.

Tyler had always been in Conway's orbit, yet felt as if he hung precariously on to his coat-tails. He picked up the scraps that his friend discarded along the way. Until it came to Kirsten. Tyler laughed to himself. God, Conway had fucked up big-time with that one. With a little help from his good self.

He'd seen his chance when Simon got the position in Australia with Petro Oz. He'd been headhunted, of course: no grubby job-chasing for Conway. No doubt it was a fantastic career move. He just made the slight mistake of leaving the cracking girl he was in love with behind and all alone. It was the first time Tyler had known Simon to take his eye off the ball. And Tyler had been waiting.

All it had taken in the end were a few well-aimed emails. A few late-night-heartbreak calls from Conway were easily swatted away. That was the end of it. So they couldn't really have loved each other that much, despite all their 'soulmate' shit.

Kirsten was devastated. Of course she was. She'd never have looked at Tyler otherwise. All the time she'd been Conway's girlfriend, she'd only ever had eyes for him. She looked at his rival with such love that it used to turn Tyler's insides to water with jealousy. He wanted her to look at *him* like that. Even after

189

all this time, after ten years of marriage, he still wasn't sure she ever had. Yet he, Tyler Benson, had taken the biggest prize. There was no man happier than him the day he'd walked down the aisle with Kirsten on his arm. He had won her away from Conway. If not necessarily fair and square, he had still won her.

Now, after all these years, his nemesis, the monkey on his back, Conway had returned. Here he was, as large as life. It made him want to claw his own eyes out.

Simon held out his hand and reluctantly Tyler grasped it. They went through the motions of a civil greeting, though it was clear that each of the men was sizing up the other. Tyler wondered if, in a pissing contest, he'd come out on top. It might be a close-run thing. He wondered if Kirsten had seen Simon. What would she think about her former lover being back in town?

'I'll ask the question again,' Tyler said, jaw clenched. 'What are you doing here?'

He glanced around to see if Conway had come as a guest of someone from another department. Perhaps Fossil was doing business with him. Though it seemed a strange idea to bring him to the Christmas party. He'd kept track of Conway's movements for a few years. His rise in Petro Oz had been meteoric. Why wouldn't it be? He'd bet a tenner that Conway didn't have a drunken sot of a chairman to deal with on a daily basis.

'I've joined Fossil Oil, Tyler,' Conway said.

That knocked the wind out of his sails. 'What?'

'I'd hoped that Lance would have spoken to you by now,' Conway continued.

'Well he hasn't.'

Conway tutted. Tyler didn't like the sound of this at all. Was this the man that Melissa had earlier this evening warned him about? If Conway was to be working for Tyler, then he should have appointed him. Not Lance. What was going on here? Was he losing his grip on the business? He'd always thought he had Lance under his thumb. It didn't bode well that all along the chairman had been capable of independent thought.

'I'm the international director.'

'I should have been consulted on this. I can't have you working for me.'

'I'm not going to be working *for* you,' Conway said. 'I'm your new boss, Tyler.'

Was that him who just gasped out loud? Surely this was a mistake? Conway was to be his boss? Who had decided that? Lance knew that he had history with him, that there was no love lost. Whatever made him, or anyone, think this was a good idea?

'Over my dead body,' Tyler said.

'I hope it doesn't come to that.' Conway gave him a sardonic smile.

On the stage, Karen from Customer Accounts was bowing, bigging up her part. As she left, The Magnificent Marvo was preparing for another trick.

'We need to clear the air between us, Tyler,' he said.

Simon looked as if he wanted to punch him. Well, just let him. That would be a good start to his career at Fossil Oil. 'From where I'm standing the air seems perfectly clear.'

'You couldn't be more wrong,' Simon said.

But before he could respond, the crowd started to chant, 'Tyler! Ty-ler! Ty-ler!'

With a smug smile, Tyler turned away from Conway to see what was happening.

Up on stage The Magnificent Marvo was beckoning to him and the staff were shouting *en masse* for him to go along.

'Ty-ler! Ty-ler! Ty-ler!' It rang in his ears. They wanted him.

This would show Simon Conway that he was one of the lads. It would mark him out as the most popular man in Fossil Oil.

That would give him something to think about. He wasn't just going to walk in here and kick Tyler Benson around. Oh, no. He had the support and respect of his staff.

Tyler buttoned his dinner jacket. 'Would you excuse me, Conway? My staff are calling for me.'

'Tyler, I really don't think you should.' Simon turned his gaze anxiously towards the stage.

The staff started to stamp their feet. They wanted him. Only him.

Tyler held up his hand. 'I know what I'm doing.' This would be a textbook lesson in how to handle the staff of Fossil Oil. 'Watch and learn.'

He marched away from Conway. He could hardly bring himself to even think 'new boss'. Well, fuck Conway. The staff wanted *him*. This would show Simon Conway what he was made of.

'Ty-ler! Ty-ler! Ty-ler!' The staff pressed against him, jostling as he fought to get to the stage. To a man – and woman – they were all tanked up now. This sounded more like a gladiatorial tournament than a magic routine. It was only as he got closer to the stage and the sound of the staff's applause was ringing loud in his ears that he realised what he'd done.

The grinning magician was slowly opening a black box. Then he kick-started a chainsaw and brandished it in the air. The crowd cheered louder. Tyler Benson's step halted. A gulp travelled down his throat. His blood went very, very cold. It would appear that he'd just volunteered to be sawn in half.

Chapter Twenty-six

Kirsten made her way through the corridors of Wadestone Manor. Everyone else was drunk, staggering about. Girls leaned on each other for support or on men who weaved just as much as they did. Yet there was a purposeful edge to Kirsten's stride. She was on a mission. A mission to find Tyler and take him home where she could give him a piece of her mind.

She'd had enough of this dreadful Christmas party. Even by Fossil Oil's usual standards, it had been exhausting and emotionally draining. Also, if she kept her feet moving firmly forward, then she wouldn't be tempted to turn tail and run back to Simon as fast as she possibly could.

It had flipped her world, seeing him again tonight and finding out that he still loved her, that he had loved her all along. It was going to take a while to regain her equilibrium after that revelation. Now she wanted to go back to her house, wipe the floor with Tyler and then snuggle into her pyjamas, sleep alone in the spare room and blot out this whole wretched evening. She'd never felt lonelier in all her life and just wanted someone to hold her. But not Tyler. She wanted Tyler to stay the hell away from her until she'd calmed down.

Passing through one of the rooms, she discarded her throw,

tossing it over a couple who looked like they needed a little more privacy. Oh, to be young and so carefree. To have the ability to lose yourself in another person's body without pause to consider the complications or consequences.

She didn't think she'd done that since Simon had left.

At the entrance to the marquee Kirsten pulled up short. There was something going on up on the stage, a magician doing a trick of some kind, but she was too far away to see what. The staff were certainly enjoying it. They were cheering in a boisterous manner, baying for someone's blood, it seemed. But everyone was crowded on to the dance floor and her view of the entertainment was blocked.

Kirsten scanned the room, looking for her husband in the middle of the fray. That's where he'd usually be. Melissa and Lance were in a far corner at the side of the dance floor. Lance was slumped sideways and it looked like Melissa was trying to cajole him to do something. They should go home too. Their very presence was now an insult to the staff.

She craned her neck to see if she could locate Louise too, but there was no sight of her either. A frisson of alarm prickled her neck. That didn't bode well. Why were she *and* Tyler both missing from the party?

The magician was whipping the crowd to a frenzy and, as he raised a chainsaw in the air, Kirsten realised that he must be cutting someone in half. An old trick, but a crowd pleaser none the less. Duly the crowd roared its approval. Well, she certainly didn't have the stomach to watch that. All she wanted to do was find Tyler and leave.

She turned and got out of there as quickly as she could. The rest of the manor was quiet now that the main attraction was in the marquee, and she made her way down the corridors. The last thing she wanted to do was bump into Simon again. She hoped he'd gone home too. She also hoped that tomorrow he'd tender his resignation from Fossil Oil and leave the country, go back to Texas, or Timbuktu – anywhere she didn't have to see him again and know that she could never, ever be with him.

She opened the doors to a few rooms, but they were mainly populated by members of staff lost in the throes of passion. In what was obviously the snooker room, in the dim light there was a couple on top of the table, getting very friendly with each other. Kirsten backed out swiftly.

By the time she reached the reception desk Kirsten still hadn't found her errant husband, but she decided to order a taxi anyway. She'd just go home. Tyler could do whatever he wanted. She asked the woman behind the desk to order one for her and texted Tyler to say she was leaving.

'There'll be a car here for you in about twenty minutes,' the receptionist said as she hung up.

'Is there somewhere quiet I can wait until then?'

The receptionist pointed to yet another corridor in this rabbit warren of a building, one Kirsten hadn't been down before. 'The library is just along there, madam. It's tucked out of the way a little. That should be quieter for you.'

'Thank you.' Kirsten went along to the cloakroom and retrieved her coat. She checked her mobile, but Tyler had yet to reply. And this was a man who was permanently welded to his iPhone. He even disappeared into the shower with it sometimes. Where could he possibly have got to?

Moments later, she found the library and ducked inside. It was a vast room, luxuriously furnished and lined with splendid oak bookcases. The long windows, which probably faced on to the front of the house, were draped with heavy burgundy curtains. It was in darkness apart from the welcoming glow of the roaring fire and lights twinkling from an opulent Christmas tree in the far corner. Kirsten felt frozen to her bones and she rubbed her arms hopefully. It would be good to spend a few moments in here thawing out. She wondered if any warmth would ever reach the chill that was settled deep in her heart.

But as she walked towards the fireplace, she heard a noise. It was clear she wasn't alone here. So much for a secluded retreat. Every single nook and cranny of this place was filled with copulating colleagues. It looked as if this room too was hosting a 'team bonding' session. Perhaps there'd be a boom in Fossil Oil babies in nine months' time, with lots of children called Holly, Ivy and Tinsel. Oh, well, she'd leave them to it.

As she went to tiptoe out, a head popped up from behind the sofa. Despite the gloom, Kirsten recognised Louise.

'Oh.' Her hand flew to cover her mouth, but the exclamation was already out.

'Mrs Benson,' Louise said, straightening her dishevelled clothing. 'I can explain.'

It was then that Kirsten noticed the man who lay full-length on the sofa beneath Louise. She backed away as quickly as she could. Kirsten didn't need to see this. To catch Tyler in the very act of betraying her. She could hardly see him in the dim glow of the firelight, even if Louise hadn't been shielding him, but she didn't need to look any further to identify who it was. Who else could it be? The sucker punch of emotion to her stomach told her all she needed to know. She saw him scrabble at his clothes.

'How could you, Tyler?' A sob caught in Kirsten's throat. 'Here of all places? How could you do this to me again?' She backed away, legs shaking. She'd known that Tyler was unfaithful to her. Of course she had. But this? How could he be so carelessly blatant? And at the office Christmas party? Kirsten felt nausea rising. All she wanted was to get out of here, and *now*.

'Please Mrs Benson,' Louise cried out. 'This is not what you think. Wait!'

But before Louise could say another traitorous word or Tyler could start to try and sweet-talk her as she knew he would, Kirsten turned on her heel and fled.

Chapter Twenty-seven

The Magnificent Marvo seemed to be much more drunk than was desirable in a magician who was about to cut him in half, and Tyler was sweating profusely. Clearly Marvo had also been enjoying the free bar.

Tyler was locked in a long black box on the stage. A box that looked way too much like a coffin for his liking. Marvo, in Tyler's mind less than magnificent, was lurching alarmingly, buzzing chainsaw still in hand. The box was tight all around him. Just his head stuck out at one end, his feet at the other. The edge of the hole for his head was pressing down on his Adam's apple and making it hard to even swallow. Yet every second, there was a nervous gulp travelling down his throat.

Tyler, terror mounting, wanted to shout out to someone to help him. But how could he lose face in front of the staff? They were all cheering and whistling at his discomfiture. He had to man up and act the good sport. He hoped he didn't piss himself.

This was probably the worst thing he'd had to do in the name of team bonding. There'd been that time in a restaurant in Hong Kong when he'd eaten live prawns that had just had some kind of alcohol poured on them, presumably to stun them enough to cope with their fate – much like the staff of Fossil Oil. But all that had resulted in was a night spent with his head down the loo of his five-star executive suite. A small price to pay for showing you had more bollocks than anyone else.

But this? This looked properly dangerous.

The Magnificent Marvo brandished his chainsaw with glee. The staff roared their approval.

'Don't struggle,' he said in a theatrical manner to Tyler. 'You won't feel a thing.'

His eyes look mad, Tyler thought. And not entirely pointed in the right direction.

'Well,' Marvo added with a cackle, 'not much.'

The magician slipped the whirring chainsaw into a groove in the box around Tyler's middle. Subconsciously, he sucked in his tummy. He wanted to stay as far away from the blade of that chainsaw as humanly possible. Even though it was a fake. It had to be, didn't it? It still looked far too bloody realistic for his liking.

Beads of cold sweat were running down his forehead and his armpits were uncomfortably sticky. He should have just said no, bowed out gracefully with a self-deprecating smile. More pertinently, it should be Lance who was in this box. Preferably with the chainsaw at his neck.

It was all the fault of that bloody Simon Conway. If he hadn't been here watching, Tyler would have made some excuse to stop this. But as it was, he couldn't. There was no way he could lose face with Conway here.

What was he doing back now, anyway? And working at Fossil? The thought irritated his brain, buzzing like a particularly persistent wasp.

It was bad. Ominously bad.

Kirsten would be furious when she saw him too. He wondered where she'd got to. He sincerely hoped she hadn't come across Simon yet. He couldn't bear it if, even after all this time, her eyes still lit up when she saw him, as they always used to.

He'd have to find a way to get rid of Conway. There was no way there was room in the Fossil Oil universe for both of them. Conway was kryptonite to Tyler's Superman.

Fretting about Conway, he hadn't realised that the chainsaw was now cutting deep into the box. His mouth was drying and his ears rang with the distressing whine of the saw.

The Magnificent Marvo lifted his free hand and gestured to the crowd. 'Do you really want me to cut him in half?' he shouted.

'Cut! Cut! Cut!' they brayed.

Tyler scowled. They could sound not *quite* so enthusiastic at his discomfort. There surely must be some trick way that this worked. But the Magnificent Marvo hadn't yet let him in on it.

Then, as the shouting became louder, Tyler was sure he felt a nick on his stomach. His eyes widened in fear. Surely he'd imagined it?

There was another. This time it was more than a mere nick, it was definitely a cut, which made him wince in pain.

'Aaaagh!' he cried out. 'You've cut me, mate!'

'What?' The Magnificent Marvo was clearly struggling to hear him above the noise of the chainsaw and the rowdy audience.

There it was again. This time it really hurt.

'You've fucking cut me!' Tyler called out at the top of his voice, just as Marvo killed the chainsaw.

All the staff fell quiet now.

'You've cut me,' Tyler repeated.

'It's impossible,' the magician said.

'You have!'

The Magnificent Marvo jerked back on the chainsaw. He grinned at the aghast crowd, but now there was sweat on his forehead too. Hastily he gave the chainsaw to his assistant.

Tyler couldn't wait to get out of the box. There was a disconcerting trickling of warm fluid round his waist.

200

One of the women in the front row gasped. 'There's blood!'

Tyler twisted his head, making the edge of the head-hole slice into his neck. When he looked, sure enough, spots of blood had dripped out and fallen on to the stage.

'Oh, Christ,' Tyler said. 'Get me out of here! Now!'

Hurriedly Marvo unclipped the hinges that held the box shut. He swung it open, his grin fixed firmly in place. The audience stood frozen with bated breath. With an air of reluctance, the magician looked down at Tyler.

'Oh, fuck,' he said.

Then, hitting the stage with a resounding thud, The Magnificent Marvo fell into a dead faint.

Chapter Twenty-eight

Now I'm panicking horribly. 'Quick, quick,' I say to Josh. 'We have to go after Tyler's wife.'

Honestly, I've never moved so fast in my entire life. Josh is still tucking his shirt back into his trousers. 'Why didn't you say anything?' I scold.

'I didn't really want her to know that it was me here,' he admitted. 'Imagine what Tyler would say?'

'But now she thinks that you were him.'

'It'll be fine,' he assures me. 'There's nothing to worry about. Really. As soon as she bumps into Tyler again, she'll realise her mistake.'

I'm doing my very best to rearrange my rumpled clothing. My dress was rucked up almost round my waist and one of my boobs was making a bid for freedom. I stop and look down at him. 'Do you think so?'

'I don't know what made her think it was her husband in the first place. If she'd have come and got a better eyeful, then she'd have realised it was me. We don't even look similar.

'I'm not sure she was in a fit state to be thinking rationally.'

'Probably been hitting the booze like everyone else.'

I give Josh a long, hard stare. 'Except you.'

'Can't afford to lose my licence. The price I have to pay is watching everyone around me get wasted.'

'Including me?'

'You're hardly wasted, Louise.'

But there's no denying that I've had far too much to drink to be thinking straight. 'This was stupid,' I say. 'I don't know what got into me. I never behave like this. Now look what's happened.' I put my head in my hands.

'Hey.' Josh sits up. 'We haven't done anything wrong. You got a bit tipsy and let a colleague kiss you. That's all.' He grins at me. 'And very nice it was too.'

I smile back when I don't want to. I want to be cross. Cross with myself. Cross with Josh. Cross with Tyler too.

'This isn't me,' I tell Josh. 'I have limits, barriers. I'm not the sort of woman who snogs a random man on the sofa.'

His face falls. 'I didn't realise I counted as a "random man".'

Now I've pissed him off too. 'You're not. Well, you are.' I let out an exasperated sigh. 'You know what I mean.'

Josh reaches out and takes my hand. 'It's the Christmas party, Louise. The entire point of it is for everyone to get lashed and behave inappropriately with their co-workers. It's the one time of year that everyone lets their hair down. If you haven't done that, then you've had no fun at all.'

'I feel as if I was having too *much* fun,' I confess as I scuffle round on the rug searching for my shoes, which seem to have disappeared under the sofa.

My mum always used to tell me that if you keep your shoes on and both feet on the floor, then you won't come to too much harm. I'm beginning to think she was absolutely right. It's excellent advice that I must pass on to Mia as soon as she hits puberty.

'I don't want you to think that this is who I am.'

'I don't. I promise you.' He makes a little gesture that might be crossing his heart.

I'm worried at how far this might have gone if Kirsten Benson hadn't interrupted us. I hate to admit this, even to myself, but I was quite happy getting all cosy with Josh Wallace. That was foolish of me.

'I'd hate to become the subject of a water-cooler discussion with Tyler,' I continue. 'I know what he's like. He's bad enough as it is. I don't want to be the butt of his sexist jokes.'

'I hope you know that I'm *not* like that.'

I turn to him. He's propped up on the cushions now, attractively tousled and looking for all the world as if he can't see why I'm making such a fuss.

'I don't though, do I?' I reason. 'This is the first time we've even met properly. We've just had passing chit-chat in the office, that's all. Until tonight we hadn't even had a proper conversation, and now look what we've done.'

He grins at me. There are little dimples in his cheeks which are irresistibly cute. But it's thinking like that which got me into this situation, and I must stop it at once.

'We haven't really done very much though, have we?'

'I'm the mother of a small child, Josh. I have to be responsible. I barely date, for fear of bringing someone unsuitable into her life.'

'Not a word of this will pass my lips. Particularly not to Tyler Benson,' he swears. 'And I won't even tell your daughter that you're a Bad Mother either.'

While he chuckles at my humiliation, I grab a cushion and swat him with it. 'I am *not* a bad mother!'

'Of course you're not.' Then he stops smiling and stares at me intently. 'Don't be so hard on yourself, Louise. When did you last have a night out? When did you last do something a little bit outrageous?'

I can't even remember. 'I think it was July the seventeenth.'

'Last year?'

'Two thousand and six.'

'Then it's probably time you did it again.'

He takes my hand and squeezes it. In the firelight, his eyes gleam. If you ignore the wild goings-on in the marquee outside, this is a very romantic setting. No wonder my head has been ever so slightly turned.

'I'm not looking for a quick fling,' Josh says. 'That's not who I am either. I'm a one-woman kind of man.'

'I don't know. This has gone too far, too fast.' I pull my hand away. I don't want to compromise my position at work. I don't want to get a reputation. This job is too important to me. If Tyler hears that I've been free and easy with Josh, then it might give him ideas too. 'Let's just pretend this never happened.'

His face is sad when he says, 'If that's what you want.'

'I do.' I make sure that my dress and its contents are jiggled back to where they should be. 'Now I'd better go after Kirsten Benson. I have to explain to her. All I want is to make sure she hasn't got the wrong end of the stick. I can't have her thinking you were Tyler.'

So, before Josh can say anything else, I dash out of the library and hurry to find Tyler's wife to tell her that – much like me – she's made a terrible mistake.

Chapter Twenty-nine

Tyler was bleeding. Everywhere. While the Less Than Bloody Magnificent Marvo was being revived, his lovely assistant helped Tyler out of the black box, which seemed to have taken on even more coffin-like proportions. His legs were shaking, unsteady, and he wasn't entirely convinced that he wouldn't soon be lying on the floor next to Marvo.

Across his stomach there was a thin red line which oozed blood. His favourite dinner shirt was shredded. Below that was another cut, underneath his belt, which had sliced through his trousers and boxer shorts. Any lower and his manhood would have been in serious danger. Tyler shuddered at the thought.

The crowd were still whistling and cheering even though there was blood – *real blood!* Perhaps they thought it was all part of Marvo's marvellous act. Well, Tyler knew better. And, the very first thing he'd do in the new year would be to sue the arse off the magician for trauma. You always assumed these things were totally foolproof. Not so, it seemed.

One of the half-naked firemen who'd been wandering round all night with Karen from Customer Accounts jumped on to the stage. He threw The Magnificent Marvo over his shoulder like a sack of spuds and unceremoniously carted him away.

No one seemed overly concerned that Tyler was mortally wounded.

'Do you do first aid?' he asked Marvo's assistant.

'No.' She looked at Tyler blankly. 'This has never happened before. There are some serviettes here.' She handed him a *Merry Christmas to One and All* napkin.

Tyler dabbed gingerly at his wounds with it.

Heads would roll for this, Tyler thought. He was making a note of the staff who were guffawing most loudly. They would go right to the top of Lance's SACKED list. Then we'd see who was laughing.

Of both Josh and Louise, there was no sign. He'd hoped that one or other of them might have come to his rescue. Kirsten was still missing too. Typical. She was never around when he needed her support. That was one thing he'd say for Melissa, she was always there for Lance, through thick and thin. If only Kirsten had been as loyal to him. He punched in her mobile phone number, but it went straight to voicemail. He stabbed in a text instead.

Dying! he wrote. *Need urgent medical assistance.*

That should bring her running. He wanted her to take him home. It had been a terrible Christmas party. This one certainly wouldn't go down in the annals of office-party history.

As he couldn't locate his wife, he called Louise instead. She picked up instantly.

'Tyler?'

'Where are you?' he hissed.

'Erm . . . ' Tyler thought she sounded cagey. 'I'm just in reception.'

'Did you not see what just happened on stage?'

'No. I was . . . er . . . a bit busy.'

'Where have you been all night?' Tyler complained. 'I've hardly seen you.'

'That doesn't matter,' Louise said. 'Your voice sounds really shaky. What's the problem?'

'The problem is,' he said, 'that I've been attacked by a madman wielding a chainsaw.'

'*What?*'

'I had an accident with The Magnificent Marvo. Or, more specifically, he had an accident with me.' Tyler sighed. 'Look, I need your help. I've had a traumatic experience. Meet me in the library in five minutes. I'll explain it all then.'

Tyler hung up. Louise would know what to do. Not only was she very easy on the eye, she was proving to be an excellent and dedicated assistant. Tucked under his wing, this girl could go a long way in Fossil Oil. She just had to play her cards right.

He headed to the bar. The staff, who were still busy necking Jägerbombs as if they were going out of fashion, self-consciously cleared a path for him.

'Brandy,' he said to the barman. 'Make it a double.'

The man handed it over without a word and Tyler downed it. He slammed the glass back on the bar. The barman raised an eyebrow in question and Tyler nodded. The glass was instantly refilled. That went the same way as the other. Now he was starting to feel better.

Still oozing blood and clutching his trousers to keep them up, he headed off towards reception. At the very least he'd need plasters, or a bandage. A clean shirt wouldn't go amiss. He knew that Louise would organise something. She'd recently been on a first-aid course, so he'd be in safe hands.

When everyone else deserted him, he knew he could count on her. That meant a lot. Well, her loyalty would be rewarded. He'd liked her the minute he laid eyes on her. There was more than a flicker of attraction there and he was pretty sure it was mutual.

Chapter Thirty

Kirsten didn't know what to do. Where could she go? Where could she hide? Tyler would come after her, she was sure.

Well, she didn't want to see him, didn't want to hear the honeyed words, the ridiculous explanation that would pour from his mouth. He was so well practised in the profuse apology that it meant nothing any more. She would get out of this place, and *now*.

This time he'd gone too far. After the last fling, with his assistant Debbie, he'd promised her *faithfully* that he wouldn't do this to her again. Well, he had, and she couldn't stand it any more. The deceit had torn her into little pieces and she was done with him.

It was only blind fury that was stopping the tears from rolling down Kirsten's cheeks. They hung precipitously balanced on the edge of her eyelashes while she dared them to fall. She felt like she'd been hit in the stomach by a bowling ball, and it had driven the sour taste of that tepid, mass-produced turkey dinner back to her throat.

Heaven knew, she hoped she'd been wrong this time. But she never was. Call it a woman's intuition if you like. Whatever you called it, her instincts were unfortunately infallible on the Tyler front. She'd known that he was a selfish and unfaithful bastard for years, she just wondered how many more times he would have to prove it to her before she plucked up the courage to leave him for good.

But why that little girl in her Primark dress? She was no different from the last one, and she was certainly no older. Kirsten doubted she was more than mid-twenties. Maybe younger. Beneath all that make-up and the strutting confidence of youth, it was hard to tell. How could she compete with that? She kept herself in good shape, but there was no denying that she was the wrong side of forty. Perhaps it was just that all men approaching middle age needed their menopausal egos massaged by a bimbo in a skirt that barely covered her bottom and whose IQ was never destined to keep pace with her age. But she was being bitchy and, worryingly, this girl looked a cut above that. She was bright and seemed as if she knew exactly what she was doing.

Also Kirsten was one to talk about stupidity. If she was that clever, why did she keep taking Tyler back, making excuses for him and insisting that underneath it all he loved her? Finding out that he'd engineered the downfall of her and Simon's relationship had been bad enough. This was the straw that broke the camel's back.

Tonight she'd finally woken up to Tyler Benson's ways. He was one leopard who'd never ever change his spots, and for her own sanity she had to get away from him. His days were not only numbered, they were filed in little boxes, ready to be put away once and for all. She wondered what Simon would think of this. He knew what Tyler was like, probably more accurately than she did. Instinctively her fingernails curled into the palms of her hands as she approached the reception desk, and she forced herself not to cry. Not yet. When she was at home and alone and no one could see her, then she would cry.

'Is my taxi here yet?' she asked at the desk.

The girl frowned. 'I'm really sorry. I'll ring them again for you. They should have been here by now. The snow's getting worse though. I wonder if they're able to drive up the hill to the manor. Let me get on to it for you.'

'I'll wait outside,' Kirsten said.

'It's really very cold,' the receptionist warned.

'I'll be fine.' Kirsten couldn't feel anything. If she sat out there and froze into a solid block of ice she couldn't have cared less. Her marriage was over and she wondered whether she'd ever have the capacity to feel again.

Leaving the girl to phone the cab company, she walked out of the front door and left the cloying warmth of Wadestone Manor. The night was very snowy now and it was settling on the ground. An inch or more must have fallen since she'd been out in the posh potting shed with Simon. The temperature was hovering around the wrong side of freezing and she felt the harsh elements of the crisp winter night trying to invade her inadequately clad body.

Kirsten wasn't sure if she was afraid. There was a tense numbness in her whole body, but she was almost certain it wasn't fear. There might even have been a sense of release, of closure somewhere in there. Whatever she felt, she knew there could be no looking back, no hesitation, no regrets. She would only go forward from now on, and that thought created a tiny spot of lightness in her heart.

Pulling her coat around her, she went to sit on the steps at the front of the house. As she looked round, she noticed a relatively sheltered spot in the lee of a stone pillar on the portico and headed towards it. It was in shadow, away from the revealing glare of the Hollywood-style lighting, and Kirsten huddled inside it, pulling her coat tightly around her. The night air was frosty and clear and it was as instantly sobering as being plunged into a bath full of iced water. All her senses felt sharpened, alive. The piercing cold penetrated Kirsten's lungs as she breathed in and out, but her breath was pleasingly steady, controlled. Tiny white vaporous clouds ballooned in front of her as she exhaled. She stared out at the snowy wonderland scene, the towering Christmas trees that flanked the house, the lights strung in the trees, and it soothed her. Soon it would be Christmas, and who knew what that would bring?

Her bottom was cold on the stone step and she regretted not wearing thermal underwear. But then it wasn't every day one went to a Christmas party and ended up wandering round outside in sub-zero temperatures instead. Even a pair of big pants from Marks & Spencer would have offered more protection than what she had on. Why was it that she persisted in wearing flimsy silk and lace underwear after ten years of marriage? Even if they didn't find them a huge turn-on, didn't most men eventually get used to their wives wearing practical underwear and tights?

Tyler never would. He was definitely a silk-and-stockings man. Some days she longed to slob around in a tatty tracksuit and sagging knickers whose elastic had gone through being washed too many times. But she had at least tried to bring his wandering gaze back to rest on her occasionally. When, briefly, it did, she hadn't wanted to be caught in a sports bra and big comfortable knickers that didn't match.

Would the lure of expensive frillies have ever been enough to keep him coming back over the years? What would have happened when it wasn't only the elastic that had sagged but the contents inside? Sometimes she'd felt she could prance round naked with a rose between her teeth and Tyler wouldn't have noticed. It was never going to be reliable as a long-term strategy for keeping one's husband, the Agent Provocateur approach to marital bliss, Kirsten concluded miserably. She'd known it in her heart all along and now she'd been proved right.

Why couldn't she be pink-faced and apple-cheeked like the women on all of those reality TV shows, who could keep their husbands through their culinary expertise and their ability to wave Cif Cream Cleaner like a magic wand? She'd tried everything. The way to Tyler's heart was not through his stomach, it wasn't even through his genitals. And now she'd run out of vital organs to try. She was beginning to wonder why she had ever made so much effort in the first place, as she doubted whether her husband even had a heart.

Now she'd be free of him and could wear whatever pants she liked. It was a small step towards independence, all things considered, but the thought cheered her greatly.

She stared at the stars, shimmering steadfastly in the blackness of the night. That was what Simon was. A bright pinprick of light in the darkness of her life. And now he'd dropped back so, so casually on to the scene. It was as if he'd never been away. Her heart seemed to have taken up exactly where it had left off a decade ago.

How would Tyler cope with Simon as his boss? No doubt he'd be even more unbearable to work for, and she pitied his poor staff. Even Louise. Despite their illicit relationship, she'd probably take the brunt of it. Well, good luck to her. That's what the girl had stupidly signed up for.

Kirsten sighed and hugged herself. It had been so wonderful to see Simon again. Her eyes filled with tears just thinking about him. She dared not even let herself dwell on it. Wasn't it supposed to be bad pennies that turned up again, not good ones? It was just as well she'd ripped up his business card, otherwise she'd be sorely tempted to call him. Simon would know what to say. Simon would know how to put everything right.

She scanned the immense driveway, but there was still no sign of her taxi. Surely it would be here soon?

Her phone rang and she saw from the display that it was

213

Tyler. There was nothing she wanted to say to her husband, so she let it go to voicemail. A moment later a text pinged in from him too. She didn't even look at it. Nothing Tyler could say or do would change her mind this time. From this day forward, the less she had to do with him the better.

And what of Simon? Where was he? Had he already left the party?

She'd loved him so much that her heart had been filled by him. But ten years on she wondered what love was. She wasn't sure she had a definition for it any more, or believed in its vain promises, invariably broken. It certainly wasn't the stuff romantic novelists churned out.

Love wasn't running hand-in-hand along a deserted beach, candlelit dinners for two, or rampant sex every night complete with multiple orgasms that required you to be peeled off the ceiling, faint with ecstasy, afterwards. Love was producing edible meals night after relentless night, and rowing about the children you'd borne together. It was struggling to pay the bills, keeping the paintwork on the windows from peeling, and mowing the lawn. It was squeezing lovemaking into the daily grind rather than spending all day in bed in a haze of sated delight. It was doing all those things and still, at the end of the day, being each other's best friend in life, each other's bedrock. That was the sort of love she could have had with Simon, she was certain. Their love was grounded, real, it would have deepened, developed into something solid and sure. It would have become the ordinary, day-in-day-out kind of love, the sort that makes marriages last for twenty, thirty, forty years. The kind of love that she and Tyler had never managed to achieve.

Kirsten was startled by the thought. Perhaps she'd been out of love with Tyler for a lot longer than she'd realised. Their marriage ended here and now. That was her vow and this time she'd keep it. She was leaving him and it felt as if a weight that she'd been carrying around for years had been lifted from her shoulders. Suddenly, she felt as light and free as one of the snowflakes that were falling all around her.

Kirsten felt as if she should cry, but bizarrely she wanted to laugh. Holding out a hand, she caught a snowflake and watched it melt on her open palm. That was what she felt for Tyler now. Somehow, just like the snowflake, he was melting away, disappearing to nothing in an instant.

There would be a painful aftermath. Of that she had no doubt. Tyler wouldn't let her go lightly. He'd make it as difficult as possible for her to divorce him. It might not be that he still wanted her, but he'd hate to feel as if he was losing anything.

It was ridiculous, but she actually felt like dancing in the snow. A giggle rose in her throat at the thought. Why shouldn't she? She didn't have to answer to anyone now. Feeling like a silly schoolgirl, she shrugged off her coat and left the shelter of the portico, going down the steps to the front of the house. In the chill night, Kirsten lifted her face to the snow and then her arms. The icy flakes tingled as they landed on her bare skin, which burned almost feverishly. They soaked into her dress and clung to her.

Within seconds her shoes were sodden, but she didn't care. She twirled and twirled, spinning amidst the snow. If she could stay like this for ever, then she might be happy.

A few moments later, when she was feeling dizzy and light-headed, a car pulled up next to her and she stopped whirling.

'You know you'll catch your death of cold?'

She'd assumed it was her taxi, finally arrived. But when she turned to look, it was Simon, in a low sports car with a softly purring engine. White smoke clouds billowed from the trembling exhaust. They cascaded upwards against the natural order of gravity, to float away into nothingness in the freezing, expectant sky.

215

He'd slid down his window and was leaning out. Snowflakes landed on his hair and the arm of his dinner suit. Kirsten found that she wanted to brush them away.

'Has anyone ever told you that you're crazy?' he said.

Kirsten let her arms fall to her sides. 'I've never felt more sane in my entire life.'

He laughed. 'That's quite a worrying thought.' Then, 'What exactly *are* you doing out here?'

'I'm having fun,' she said. 'For the first time in many years.'

'Well,' he said. 'In that case, I could join you. Maybe even whup you in a snowball fight. Or I could offer you a lift to somewhere.'

'I *am* getting cold,' Kirsten admitted. 'I'm heading for home. I'd ordered a taxi, but it hasn't turned up yet.'

'You could consider me Conway's Reliable Cars.'

It only took her a moment to consider it. 'I think that would be an excellent idea.'

'No Tyler?'

She shook her head. 'No Tyler.'

'Jump in.' He reached across to open the car door in anticipation.

Kirsten retrieved her coat and slipped it on to her shoulders, giving an involuntary shiver.

'The heater's on full blast,' Simon said as he took in her now-chattering teeth. 'We'll soon have you warm again.'

She slid into the car next to him. It was hot inside, comforting, and smelled of new leather. The upholstery was warm to the touch. She sank gratefully into the seat next to him.

'Kick off those wet shoes,' he instructed.

She did, and enjoyed rubbing her tingling feet on the plush carpet in the footwell.

'So. Where to?'

'I'm not sure.' She wanted to go home, but it seemed so safe a choice now that the whole world was her oyster. No longer would her place of residence be dictated by Tyler's career. It seemed like another small but important liberty.

'We could go to my place?'

Kirsten shook her head. 'I'd rather go home.' She couldn't think of anywhere better. It was unnerving enough being with Simon again; perhaps familiar surroundings would settle her. 'We live in Hampstead. Is that too far?'

'Not at all. Settle back. Enjoy the ride.'

He flicked on the sound system in his car and the soothing voice of Emilia Mitiku drifted out. It was like being cosseted in a cosy blanket and she smiled to herself. Simon always had liked his music mellow.

Their eyes locked briefly before Kirsten broke the contact and turned to stare out of the slightly misted window.

The car purred away, the gravel giving a protesting crunch in its wake. She turned in her seat to watch Wadestone Manor slowly recede into the background. The lights were all blazing out into the night. The huge Christmas trees sparkled with all their might. Inside, the party would still be in full swing for a good few hours yet. Tyler would no doubt find something to distract himself in her absence, and good luck to him. She turned back, keeping her eyes fixed to the road ahead.

This would be her very last Christmas party with Fossil Oil, with Tyler, and the truth of it was that she was so glad to be leaving it all behind.

'OK?' Simon asked.

She felt elated and wired. But also tired and maybe a little weary. 'Yes. I'm fine.'

And, despite everything, she knew that she would be.

Chapter Thirty-one

Since her meeting with Tyler in the library, Melissa had just wanted to cry. Eventually she could hold her emotions in check no longer and she'd stolen away from Lance for a few minutes. She'd gone and locked herself in one of the cubicles in the powder room. Now she let the tears flow untrammelled; they felt as if they were pouring straight from her heart.

Surely it was only teenagers who allowed themselves to get into such a terrible state over the opposite sex? How could she have reached half a century on this planet and not realised that they would all, eventually, let you down?

Melissa sat on the loo seat and hugged herself. Damn Tyler Benson for reducing her to this. Taking a tissue out of her diamanté clutch bag, she dabbed at her eyes. At the age of fifty-five she'd hoped that her life would be settled. That she and Lance would be growing old gracefully together. How had that plan gone so very dreadfully awry?

Melissa wondered whether it was too late to change things now. Was there any way that she could get Lance to address the problems his drinking caused? Fossil Oil would probably pay for him to go into a rehab programme. The first step, of course, was getting him to admit it. Lance was actually quite happy to be a drunk. It was only those around him who had to contend with the devastating consequences.

She knew that the answer to her problems wasn't to blot them out by having affairs. Until now, she'd managed to kid herself that they were meaningless to her. That was until she met Tyler Benson. He was cut of exactly the same cloth as Lance and yet she'd still fallen for him. Perhaps it was *because* he reminded her so much of Lance when he was younger and in his prime. It was heartbreaking for her to admit this, but Tyler had made this year worthwhile. Without their illicit trysts to look forward to, she didn't know how she would have managed her empty life. Lance hadn't made love to her in years and it was a horrible thing to know that she had to turn to strangers for affection, no matter how fleeting. Despite his not-so-hidden agenda, Tyler had made her feel attractive, wanted once more.

Well, this time, she'd been the one who got burned. That was the price you had to pay for playing outside the rules. And, God, the pain seared through her. It was enough to make her turn to drink herself.

Still, she couldn't sit here all night. Lance would be waiting for her. There was no doubt he needed her. In his own way, he adored her. It just wasn't in the way that she wanted him to.

Straightening her back, she held up her head and let herself out of the cubicle. In the powder room there were about six girls, all in their best party dresses, chattering away. They flicked blusher on cheeks that didn't need it and slicked layers of lip gloss on to their full, plump mouths. Melissa smiled to herself. They were all bright young things and she hoped they'd make better choices in their lives than she had. There was so much to play for at their age.

One girl smiled tentatively at her. 'Are you OK?' she asked. 'Is there anything I can do to help?'

She wanted a friend, someone to understand what she was

going through. This girl was probably talking about a drink of water or bringing her a chair. If only she knew.

'I could get you some tea or something?' she prompted.

It would be nice to have someone to sit quietly with for five minutes while she gathered her wits, perhaps have a soothing cup of tea as she suggested, but Melissa didn't want to be drawn into conversation. Not now when she couldn't trust her own voice. 'No, thank you. It's kind of you to ask, but I'm fine. Really.'

'Are you sure?'

Melissa nodded. 'Yes. It's just been a very long evening.'

The girl, not looking terribly convinced, smiled and turned away. Her thoughtfulness nearly had Melissa in tears again.

Instead, she turned away from the other women and fixed her own make-up, repairing the ravages of her tears. With a deep breath, she faced herself in the mirror. In the low, soft-focus lighting, she could make believe that she was ten years younger. As long as she ignored the dull ache deep in her bones that told her otherwise.

Back in the marquee, the music was blaring out, a pointless, relentless, pounding beat. They should go home now or it would give her a pounding headache to match. The mood for partying had long since gone.

Lance was still slumped on the chair where she'd left him. The detritus of the party surrounded him – spent crackers, party poppers, tatters of *Merry Christmas to One and All* napkins. In the midst of it all she spied the penknife that had been in Kirsten's cracker. She must, at some point, have dropped it on the floor. That could be dangerous. So Melissa bent and picked it up, popping it into her own purse.

'Hello, honey,' she said, slipping into the seat next to her husband. Had he even noticed she'd been gone? 'How are you feeling?'

His voice when he answered was slurred. 'Fine, angel.'

He was completely gone now. His eyes had entirely lost their focus and there was a bottle of bourbon at his elbow which was virtually empty.

'We should leave, honey,' she said. 'Shall I go and find Martin?'

'Everyone's still partying.' Lance waved a hand in the general direction of the dance floor.

It certainly was full. All the staff were crowded together, having clearly decided to make the best of what had surely been their most memorable Christmas party. She felt so very sorry for them. What would the new year bring for some of the people who'd simply done their best to do a good job? How would they all pick themselves up and start again?

'I should stay until the end,' Lance said.

Like a captain going down with his sinking ship, Melissa thought. Lance was lucky that the staff had chosen to drown their sorrows rather than lynch him.

'They can manage without you,' she cajoled. 'You stay here. I'll get the car.'

Lance caught her hand. 'I love you,' he said. For a flickering moment, his eyes were lucid. 'Do I tell you enough?'

This wasn't the time to raise her concerns, to tell him that her life was empty, that she was nothing but a bitter shell. But when was it?

She kissed his forehead. 'You tell me all the time, honey.'

Lance reached for the bourbon bottle and squeezed the last drop of it into his glass. If she brought him another bottle now, she was sure he'd drink that too.

'Good,' he said. 'Anything to keep my angel happy.'

Melissa pinned a smile on her face. 'I'll be back soon.' She kissed him again and went to look for Martin.

And fought the urge to just keep walking, walking, walking and never stop.

Chapter Thirty-two

'I couldn't find Mrs Benson anywhere,' I tell Josh when I return to the library. 'I don't know where she's gone.'

I've looked high and low, everywhere in Wadestone Manor, to try to find Tyler's wife to explain to her that it wasn't, in fact, her husband that she saw me kissing. But to no avail.

I shake my head, cross at myself. What a silly mistake that was.

Seriously, I tried every room I could think of, but couldn't see her anywhere. I heard someone crying in the ladies' loos and wondered if it might be Kirsten Benson. But before I could say anything, the chairman's wife came out. She was red-eyed, blotchy-faced and clearly very upset.

I wanted to say something to comfort her, but what can you say to someone like that? All I could do was offer her a cuppa and a bit of a sit-down. Sometimes that can do the trick, but she wasn't interested in my tea and sympathy.

We've never been introduced, so she doesn't have a clue who I am. I've previously only caught a few glimpses of her at the office, but she always looked so groomed, so in control. The cut of her clothes and the scent she wears both shout money. One day, I'd love to be like her. She's a woman who is obviously in charge of her destiny. She wouldn't put up with rubbish from the likes of Tyler Benson. Melissa Harvey is legendary at Fossil Oil for her coolness. I wonder what's happened to make her so awfully distressed?

I tried to see if she wanted to talk or needed any help, but she pretty much blanked me – and who could blame her? I'm only an office minion. She's so far above my station that I didn't really feel I could push it any further, but it was horrible to see her looking so miserable and alone.

Instead I decided to mind my own business and press on. I needed to find Kirsten Benson before she found Tyler. And, of course, failed. What a mess.

'Tyler has asked to meet me here,' I tell Josh.

'Why?'

'I don't know. He seemed to be all in a lather. Sounded like some kind of emergency.' It will only get worse when he realises what's happened. 'It's probably a good idea if you're not around.'

'You don't want me for back-up?'

'No. I can handle this.' If I'm honest, I don't want Tyler to see us closeted in here and put two and two together. He'd definitely make five out of it and that would seriously harm my credibility in his eyes. I should never have got myself into this situation with Josh. I need this job and, whatever happens, I've got to keep Tyler onside.

Josh touches my arm and, for one moment, I think that it would be nice to have him here, supporting me. In the little time I've known him, he seems like such a strong and reliable person. But then again, I don't want Tyler to think I'm weak. It's fair to say that I'm in a right quandary.

'Perhaps I'll catch up with you later,' I tell him.

He looks at me sadly. 'If that's what you want.'

I nod.

'You're a great woman, Louise,' he says. 'Really great. Don't let Tyler put you down.'

'I'll be fine, really.'

'Promise you'll call me if he steps out of line.'

'I will. But now you'd better go.'

So, with obvious reluctance, he leaves.

The fire has burned low and it's chillier in here, but the log basket on the hearth is empty. I rub my arms to keep me warm and pace up and down on the rug. How am I going to break the news to Tyler of his wife's mistaken identity? He's not going to be a happy bunny, to say the very least. I might be wrong, but I get the impression that their relationship is on a bit of a knife edge, and this isn't going to help.

A minute later Tyler bursts through the door like a whirlwind. The hushed, calm atmosphere of the library changes in an instant.

'Look!' he bellows. 'Look at the bloody state of me.'

Tyler briefly holds out his arms and I get a view of his abdomen.

He is, indeed, in a very bloody state. His dinner jacket is shredded across the middle, as is his shirt and the top of his trousers. His belt is still in place, but he's having to hold up his trousers with his hands and I can see his boxer shorts beneath them. Blood is oozing from a wound across his stomach and his hands are covered in it too, from where he's been clutching himself.

'Good grief! What's happened?'

'The Magnificent Bloody Marvo, that's what's happened!' Tyler looks as if he might like to hit something. His hands are balled into tight fists and his face is red with anger. 'A drunken magician. Veronica must have booked him. I'll have words with her about that too. The stupid bastard nearly cut me in half.'

'On stage?'

'I was a fraction away from death, Louise,' he says dramatically. 'He was as pissed as a parrot. Like everyone else here.'

'You need some medical assistance,' I tell him, trying to calm him down.

'I know that!' he screeches. 'That's why I called you. You're a trained first-aider. Give me some bloody first aid.'

He's stripping off his jacket and throws it, blood and all, on to the sofa. Hurriedly I try to scoop it up before it damages the antique furnishings.

Muttering all the while, Tyler is unbuttoning his shirt, which is also covered in blood. 'Look!' He points at his stomach. 'Look!'

He pulls that off too, tossing it to the rug. I make a lunge to try to rescue that from staining too.

Now Tyler is naked from the waist up. 'Have you seen this? Have you?'

Although I'm hesitant to get too close to my half-dressed boss, I inch forward. There's a long graze right across his tummy but, on closer examination, it's not actually too deep. The amount of blood that it's weeping exaggerates the extent of the wound.

'It looks worse than it is,' I offer, trying to reassure him.

'I'm bleeding to death here!' he yells. 'Do something!'

'Calm down, Tyler. Shouting isn't going to help.'

He's shaking with rage. I take his shirt and find a clean bit at the back. I kneel down in front of him and very gently wipe the blood away from the wound. Now I can get a closer look, it's definitely just a surface scratch, but I don't think anything is going to convince Tyler of that. He's determined to be mortally wounded.

'Hmm,' he says with a glint in his eyes. 'I would have paid good money to have you in that position.'

I straighten up immediately. There's nothing too much wrong with Tyler Benson.

'You need to find me some plasters or a dressing,' he says,

remembering his pain again. 'And quick. I could do with some new clothes too.'

Quite where I'm supposed to magic those from is beyond me.

'I need to get hold of Kirsten. I've phoned and texted her, but there's no reply,' he complains.

'I looked all over the house for her too,' I tell him. 'I couldn't find her.'

That pulls him up short and he stops whining to gape at me.

Now I realise what just came out of my mouth and I flush.

'What were you doing looking for my wife?'

I might as well come clean now, as he's going to know before long what happened earlier in the library.

Taking a deep breath, I say, 'Don't be cross.'

Which, of course, instantly starts him frothing at the mouth again.

'I was in here earlier.' This is the hard bit. 'With Josh Wallace.'

'Oh, really?' Tyler's eyes widen. 'So that's where you'd got to. What are you doing fawning over Wallace?'

'I wasn't "fawning" over him. We just came to get a bit of peace and quiet from the noise of the disco.'

'And?'

'Well ... er ... we got a little bit more friendly than we intended,' I confess. I'm struggling to take the higher ground on this one. Tyler Benson has me bang to rights. I shouldn't have been in here getting cosy with Josh. 'Mrs Benson came in and saw us together. I didn't mean it to happen.'

'Why would that bother my wife? It may be an astonishing lapse of good taste, but nothing more.'

'Unfortunately ...' the lump in my throat almost stops the words from coming out, 'she thought Josh Wallace was you.'

He waits for a moment, blinking rapidly as that news settles in.

'Oh, that's all I need.' Tyler slaps his hand to his forehead. 'She thought you were getting down and dirty with me?'

'We were only kissing. Nothing more.' I sound too defensive, even to my own ears.

'Well, thank goodness for small mercies,' Tyler snaps sarcastically. 'And you didn't manage to speak up and tell my wife that she was hideously mistaken.' My boss raises an eyebrow, giving me a lascivious look. 'Had your mouth full, did you?'

'No,' I say crisply. 'I certainly did not.'

'She'll kill me,' he says. 'She'll have my bollocks in a sandwich for breakfast.'

'I'm sure she'll understand once we find her and explain.'

'We? We?' Tyler storms. 'You're the one who has to do the explaining here, lady.'

'I will,' I promise in my most placating tone. 'I'll put it right with her.'

'Good luck with that,' Tyler says. 'She doesn't trust me as far as she can throw me as it is. You realise that this could irreparably damage our relationship, and it's all your fault.'

'I've said I'm sorry,' I plead. 'I'm sure she'll laugh when she realises it's a misunderstanding.'

'What does he have that I haven't got?'

'Sorry?'

'What do you see in him?'

'In Josh?'

Tyler postures in front of me.

'I don't see anything in him.' I don't see anything in you either, I want to add, but decide to keep my mouth shut. The less I say in this situation the better. I don't like to admit to myself that I'm quite taken with Josh Wallace and that it's probably a very good thing Kirsten Benson came in when she did. I'm certainly not going to tell Tyler that.

'Why would you go for the puppy when you could have the top dog?' Tyler kicks off his shoes. Then he starts to undo his belt and take off his tattered trousers.

227

I look at him aghast. 'What do you think you're doing?'

'Getting out of these wretched things,' he grumbles. Then he stops and leers at me. 'Why? Fancy joining me?'

Before I can say anything else, he whips off his trousers and stands there in his ripped boxer shorts and socks. He's a fit man for his age. Despite all the business lunches on his expense account, there's no denying he's in good shape. But it's still not a sight that I want to be beholding.

I had such hopes for this evening. I thought it was going to be glamorous and exciting. Now I wish I'd just stayed at home watching the *Strictly Come Dancing* Christmas special with Mum and Dad.

'You know,' Tyler says. 'I'm a man of the world and you're a woman who knows what it takes to get on in this business. I admire that in you.' His eyes flick up and down me in what he obviously thinks is an 'admiring' way. 'You do right by me and your career path in Fossil Oil will be a lot smoother. I'm going all the way to the top, Louise. Play your cards right and you could be there by my side.'

The thought makes me shudder. How can I possibly carry on working for a sexist bastard like this? Inside, I'm shaking with rage. Yet I feel so helpless. Tyler Benson has me exactly where he wants me.

Then a feeling of Zen-like calm descends on me and I know exactly what I must do. What Tyler says is true. I have to play him at his own game. There's nothing else for it.

'OK,' I say. 'I understand how it is.'

He grins at me smugly. 'Good. You're a great girl, Louise. You scratch my back and I'll scratch yours.'

He puckers up to kiss me, but I put a finger to his lips.

'Wait.' I step back from him. 'You're still bleeding,' I say softly. 'Let me go and find some first-aid supplies and some new clothes for you.' I hook my finger into the top of his boxer shorts and tug at them gently. 'Why don't you make yourself comfortable while I'm gone?'

Tyler doesn't need asking twice. In one swift move, he's out of his shorts and standing in front of me completely naked apart from his socks. This is more than I ever expected to see of my boss. He strikes a pose. His shoulders are squared, stomach sucked in – though the thin line of blood does him no favours whatsoever. Everything is ... well ... pumped. It looks like a move that has worked for him many times before.

'Wow!' I say.

He's clearly excited by my reaction.

Quickly, I scoop up all of his clothes. Bloodied jacket, shirt, trousers, shorts, the lot. I hand him his wallet, car keys and phone from the jacket pocket and reach behind me for the door key, which I slip out of the keyhole. 'I'll be back before you know it.'

'Don't be long,' he says. 'It's chilly in here.' He gives a mock shiver.

'Oh, you'll soon be hot under the collar,' I whisper. 'I can assure you.'

He grins at me, leering. 'Can't wait.'

Before I can think better of this, I quickly duck out of the door. As quietly as I can, I turn the key in the lock.

Chapter Thirty-three

Melissa made her way out of the marquee and through the end-less corridors of the manor house. Eventually she found the kitchens. She always knew where to find Martin. He'd be some-where out of the cold, with his feet up, trying to find a spare sandwich and a cup of tea.

Sure enough, when she pushed open a door marked 'Staff' only he was sitting in a well-worn armchair, fast asleep with a tattered copy of the *Daily Mail* folded on his chest. Melissa felt a sudden rush of affection for him.

Martin had been with them all the time they'd been in London. He was a kind man. A few years older than her, possibly. He was grey-haired, though it wasn't thinning, and a little soft round the middle. His black suit was rumpled and shiny with age. His tie was askew and Melissa resisted the urge to straighten it. He looked solid and dependable. Exactly the type of man he'd proved himself to be time and time again.

'Martin.' Gently she shook his arm.

Their driver jolted himself awake. 'Sorry, Mrs Harvey. Just having forty winks.'

She wondered when he ever slept, other than a catnap in the car or a convenient chair. He was at their house every weekday morning at seven o'clock to collect Lance and was invariably still on duty when he brought him home late at night. That didn't even include events like this, when he'd only be dismissed once they were ready for bed. Often he worked weekends. She was so wrapped up in her own issues that she didn't know about Martin's home life. Now she wondered if he had a family. If so, he must never see them.

'That's fine, Martin. I could do with a nap myself.'

'Are you ready to leave?'

'Could you bring the car around to the front of the manor, please? I'll go and get Lance.'

The chauffeur stood up. 'Is he all right, Mrs Harvey?'

She swallowed hard. 'He's in his usual state, Martin. I may need your help.'

Martin was accustomed to this and just nodded.

Melissa headed back to the marquee, collecting her coat from the cloakroom on the way. She slipped it on but the luxury of its sumptuous, soft folds failed to comfort her. She hated herself for it, but she needed Tyler now. Her heart ached for him. She needed his arms around her, his voice soothing her, whispering sweet nothings, telling her that he'd always be there for her and, for once in his life, actually meaning it.

However, when she got back to the party, her heart leapt to her mouth. Lance wasn't where she'd left him.

Then, as she scanned the room in a panic, she realised that some-how he'd found his way on to the dance floor. He was making a drunken fool of himself, lurching about. Since his announcement of the SACKED programme, all the staff were avoiding him like the plague so he was dancing in an empty circle by himself.

On the stage were the two half-naked 'firemen' who'd been wandering around with one of the employees collecting bow ties for charity. She'd done a good job and even Lance had given up his own neckwear. Now the three of them were doing a dance, something that even Melissa recognised had once been a big hit.

'Let's see Fossil Oil do it Gangnam style!' the DJ shouted. 'Whoop, whoop, whoop!'

The firemen started going through some dance moves and everyone on the floor copied them. Including Lance.

Melissa sighed to herself. This was all she needed. She'd never get him home at this rate. He loved to think of himself as a man of the people, even when the people made it blatantly obvious that they didn't want him. She'd just have to wait until he was ready to leave. Which would invariably mean poor Martin sitting outside in the car for an eternity when he could have carried on with his nap.

She found a chair away from the dizzying lights and sat down to wait. If there had been anything left in Lance's bottle of bourbon, she may have been tempted to drink it.

Lance was in full flow. He was jumping about as if he'd been electrocuted and was circling his arm above his head. He galloped across the floor and howled out, joining in with the other members of staff. 'Whoop, whoop, whoop!'

Then, before she knew what was happening, Lance staggered forward, clutching his arm. He fell to the floor, knocking into the Fossil Oil-logo ice sculpture as he did. The beautiful, frozen ammonite teetered gracefully and then tumbled from its plinth. It shattered on the dance floor in a thousand shards. All the staff jumped back.

Amidst the ice, her husband cried out in pain. In a heartbeat, Melissa was out of her chair and dashing forward to him. Everyone stared at him, unmoving.

She crouched on the floor next to him. Lance's face had gone grey. 'Are you all right, honey?'

He was sweating, his face contorted with agony. He gasped, his mouth working soundlessly.

'Help me,' Melissa turned to the people behind her. 'Help me, please.'

Thankfully, after a moment's hesitation, two burly men she didn't know stepped forward.

'Come on, Lance.' Melissa slipped her arm around his shoulders and, between them, the men hoisted him up. 'Let's get you home, sweetheart.'

With a heart-rending groan, he leaned on the men to support his weight.

'You can do this,' she said. 'Martin has the car waiting.'

'Let me catch my breath,' he finally wheezed.

So she and the two men guided him to the nearest chair and he slumped into it. 'Thank you,' she said. 'Thank you for helping me.'

'Can we do anything else?' one of them asked.

'I can manage from here,' she assured them and they faded back to the dance floor which, despite the emergency, had filled once more.

Lance held his body, rocking it.

'Are you in pain?'

'Indigestion. Overdoing it.' He drew in a sharp breath. 'Not as young as I used to be.'

'Can you get to the car? I could text Tyler, get him to help you.'

Lance shook his head. 'No, no. Don't call Tyler.' He looked up at her and his eyes were cloudy. 'I can do this myself.'

Part of her wanted to call the paramedics and the other part of her just wanted to get Lance out of here. The mood felt hostile now and it was clear that they'd overstayed their welcome.

She gathered a chunk of the ice into a *Merry Christmas One and All* napkin and held it to his forehead, which seemed to soothe him. When some of his colour had returned, she said, 'Shall we see if we can make it now?'

He nodded and, with her help, pushed himself out of his chair. He paused to steady himself.

'Martin's waiting for us,' she said. 'Soon we'll be home.'

233

'What would I do without you, angel?' he said.

He leaned heavily on her and she supported him as slowly, laboriously, they made their way out of the marquee and into the corridors of the manor. It was a beautiful place and, in different circumstances, this might have been a great Christmas party.

As she opened the front doors, the unwelcome chill of the night swept in. Swirling flakes of snow assailed them. The car was waiting at the bottom of the slippery steps and, when Martin saw them approaching, he jumped out in an instant and rushed to her aid.

'Everything all right, Mrs Harvey?'

Even Martin could see that Lance was worse than usual.

'He's not well, Martin. He collapsed on the dance floor.'

'Let me help.' The driver opened the car door and shouldered the bulk of Lance as they shoehorned him into the back of the car.

'Do you want me to drive you straight to the nearest hospital?' Martin asked. 'I can find it on the satnav.'

'Lance?' Melissa tried to rouse him. 'Shall we take you to the emergency room? Perhaps you should see a doctor?'

'No,' Lance said, his natural belligerence surfacing again. 'No doctor. Just need to sleep.'

She and Martin exchanged a worried glance.

'I'll do whatever you want me to, Mrs Harvey,' Martin said.

If they took Lance to a hospital against his wishes, he'd only cause a scene. What would a hospital say anyway? That he was a drunk. They both were painfully aware of that.

'Thank you, Martin,' she said. 'But we'll go straight home.' If he didn't improve she'd call a doctor or make him see one in the morning. They just had to get through the night.

'No problem, Mrs Harvey.'

Melissa got into the back of the car with Lance. She cradled his head on her lap and knew that in moments he'd be fast asleep and snoring. Panic over. Until the next time.

'Ready now?'

'Yes. Thank you, Martin,' she said. He looked at her in the rear-view mirror and their eyes met.

Martin pulled away down the snowy drive of Wadestone Manor. As they made their way through the overhanging canopy of trees, the line of coaches waiting to take what remained of the Fossil Oil staff back to their homes came into view. They were covered in a sharp, glittering sheen of frost. They all stood in darkness, showing that the drivers had at least had the sense to abandon their charges and seek refuge in the comforts of the manor. The car crunched past them until the headlights picked out the personal number plate of Tyler Benson's Mercedes parked at the very end of the row, furthest to the house.

'Could you possibly pull over please, Martin?'

He stopped the car at the edge of the drive and turned in his seat. 'Anything the matter, Mrs Harvey?'

'I'm going to do something that you shouldn't witness, Martin. Could you please oblige me by looking the other way for a moment?'

'Certainly, Mrs Harvey.'

As she'd predicted, her husband had already lapsed into a drunken sleep. She eased Lance's head from her lap and laid it on the leather seat. Lance grunted but didn't stir, so she slipped out of the car into the cold night. Her footsteps crunched unhappily on the frozen gravel as she walked away, each step of her delicate and totally impractical evening shoes sending a lonely ricochet of noise into the all-encompassing silence.

From her handbag she removed the penknife that Kirsten Benson had received as her present in the Christmas cracker. Didn't that feel like a lifetime ago? She flicked it open and gingerly ran her thumb over the blade. Surprisingly sharp for a novelty gift.

The car was Tyler's pride and joy. He certainly treated it better than he did his women. She'd miss him, and she hoped she wouldn't love him for long. The only thought that frightened her was the one that said unrequited love was often the only kind that endured. She wouldn't want to go through the rest of her life loving someone so undeserving as Tyler Benson.

She stepped forward to his car. The car park was dimly lit and there was no security that she could see. No CCTV. Perfect.

The sharp tip of the penknife pierced the sugar coating of frost and then the glossy paintwork as she dragged its tip over the door with the painful shrieking noise of a parrot being strangled. A bow wave of frost flakes showered to the ground. She carried on along the side of the car and up and over the boot, her hand never wavering in its steady progress, never needing to stop and retrace a fumbled line. The night was still, silent; there were no sounds to disturb the peace except for the steady bubbling exhaust of the patiently waiting Bentley, the uneasy screech of metal against metal, and the crunch of the hard, frosted grass beneath Melissa's feet.

When she reached the front of the car again, she defaced the bonnet with a deep and ugly scar – a scar just like their affair had etched into her heart. Then Melissa joined the line perfectly to where she had started her task. The act of doing it was pleasingly cathartic. She was purging herself of Tyler Benson, and that felt good.

The tyres were more difficult, but just as satisfying. Melissa pressed the penknife against black, unyielding rubber. She was slight and the Christmas-cracker penknife struggled to penetrate the hard material but she leaned all her body weight against it until she eventually felt it give. There was a small, satisfying gasp, which may have come from her mouth or from the tyre.

Moving round the car, she did the same to the others. This was for her and for Kirsten. She hoped this time Kirsten would realise what he was really like and leave him before it was too late.

She remembered complaining, at that frightful dinner – which already seemed a hundred years ago instead of a couple of hours – that there had been no joke in her cracker. It had taken her this long to realise that, all the time, she'd been the joke. No more though. Now Tyler Benson was the joke.

To finish, she put the tip of the penknife against the windscreen and dragged it down the glass with a pitiful screeching noise. She wondered if Martin would look round to see what she was doing. But when she glanced back at the car, he was staring resolutely in the opposite direction.

She continued scratching her message. However, she'd run out of windscreen before she'd finished. Melissa stood back and regarded it.

BASTAR

That would do. It was enough for Tyler to understand the gist of it.

Snapping the penknife shut, Melissa put it back into her hand-bag. It had certainly come in more useful than a plastic magnifying glass, toy whistle or any of the other frightful garbage one usually got in crackers. She smoothed her hair and then her dress. Despite her sadness, there was a triumphant elation in her heart.

Slightly breathless, she walked back to the Bentley and climbed in.

Lance hadn't even noticed she'd gone. His breathing was more even, less ragged, and he snored gently. It looked as if he'd recovered from his earlier wobble.

'Thank you, Martin. We can go now.'

The driver eased the car into gear and they moved away. She watched the snow whirl past the windows and fought down the tears.

Martin glanced back at her. 'Was it a good Christmas party, Mrs Harvey?'

'It was lovely, Martin,' she said. 'Just lovely.'

Chapter Thirty-four

Karen from Customer Accounts was drunk. And when she was drunk she became maudlin. It always happened. Perhaps it was because she mixed her drinks. Champagne, cherry brandy, vodka and Jägerbombs were, it appeared, a lethal combination.

She was sitting at a table by herself. How had that happened? Wasn't she usually Miss Popularity? Karen tried to scowl, but wasn't sure that her face was responding in the required manner. It was all that Louise Young's fault. She'd waltzed off with Josh Wallace and he was meant to be the one she got her hooks into tonight. Louise was the new girl. She thought she was her friend. What was she doing snaring the best-looking talent at Fossil? It wasn't fair. She'd thought that he was looking at Louise with puppy-dog eyes in the office earlier today, and had tried to dismiss the notion. But as soon as Josh had seen Louise all dolled up like that, he hadn't given Karen a second glance.

Tears were rolling down her cheeks and she bet her mascara was running. One of her false eyelashes had fallen off into her drink, which was tragic. It was too far down the glass to fish it out. Never mind. She swigged it anyway. You probably couldn't catch germs from false eyelashes. Or not many, anyway.

In front of her was the ice bucket full of the bow ties she'd

238

collected. It was supposed to be for charity and it was supposed to be great. That had all gone tits-up too.

She'd tried to do her very best and make it a fun evening. Normally she was the centre of attention, but that hadn't worked out this year. Lance's stupid speech had made everyone a bit weird. Then the bloody magician went and nearly sawed Tyler Benson in two. That had been fantastic, obviously. But she'd felt that a measly raffle for charity would have been a bit of an anticlimax after that. She remembered taking the bow ties, wresting or cajoling them from nearly all of the men with lavish promises. There'd been a plan. A good one. She knew that. Trouble was, she couldn't quite recall what it was.

She looked at the bow ties once more. Now what was she to do with them all?

There was a slow song playing but she had no one to dance with. When she couldn't cop off with Josh Wallace, she'd had high hopes for one of the firemen, but now they seemed to have disappeared too. She thought she'd last seen one of them with that Stella Swift from Production Planning on his lap. Typical. If she couldn't have Josh Wallace, she'd have settled for one of them. Either of them.

She scoured the room. Everyone had got someone. Except her. Even Josie Jones from Lubricants, who was WeightWatchers' biggest failure, was clamped in an embrace with Trevor Royston from Refinery Logistics. Alex Bercow from Group Performance Reporting had his tongue down the throat of Natalie Wilson from Distribution. And those two, Rose Collier and Rob Thomas, both married to other people, might be regretting this in the morning. There'd be plenty of red faces in Quality Assurance too.

'Thank you and goodnight, Fossil Oil!' the DJ shouted out. 'A very merry Christmas to you all!'

239

That was it. She was out of time and it looked as if she was going to go home alone. Merry bloody Christmas!

The music stopped and, after one last desperate snog, everyone left the dance floor. Her colleagues started to drift out of the marquee. The office party, it seemed, was over for another year. Karen sighed to herself. It hadn't been her best.

Still, perhaps there was time for one last drink. Everyone would be making their way out to the coaches, and that would take for ever.

Karen reached out for a bottle of wine, but misjudged it. The bottle toppled and she lurched to grab it. In doing so she knocked over the candelabra. She missed the wine but caught the candelabra by its base and righted it. What she didn't notice was one of the candles teeter and fall gracefully out of its holder and straight into the bucket of bow ties.

She staggered to her feet and mopped up the wine with a *Merry Christmas to One and All* napkin. Then she screwed it into a ball and tossed it into the champagne bucket on top of the now-smouldering bow ties.

There'd probably be some more abandoned wine on the other tables, she thought. She could even take a couple of bottles on the coach, which might liven up the journey home. There might be a spare bloke on there yet.

Left to its own devices, the napkin caught light and sparked into flame. That, in turn, helped the fire among the smouldering bow ties to take hold.

Karen tottered off in search of something else to drink. In doing so she knocked the table, and the ice bucket wobbled. So did Karen; she clutched the tablecloth to steady herself, which made the ice bucket crash to the floor. The flames licked out of it. Karen didn't see them and she couldn't be bothered to bend down to pick up the bucket. Instead she pulled the tablecloth down over it so that no one would notice it there.

The flames kissed the edge of the tablecloth and slowly licked along the length of it. Soon it was engulfed, and the flames jumped on to the gauzy folds of fabric festooning the marquee.

But Karen was oblivious. She'd found a bottle of wine and was appeased for the moment. She walked out of the marquee, muttering about the dullness of the Fossil Oil Christmas party to herself, and went in search of her ride home.

Chapter Thirty-five

I wonder how long it will take Tyler to realise that I'm not returning with a first-aid kit, or new clothes for him. Not much longer, is my guess.

I've decided that I can't stay at this party for a second more. I'll have to face Tyler's wrath tomorrow and will probably go to the very top of the SACKED list, but so be it. I couldn't stand by and let him bully or sexually harass me any more. No one should have to put up with that kind of behaviour in this day and age. And I've decided that I'm not going to.

I want to do a good job at Fossil Oil, not feel that my every move is being monitored by a sexist pig who thinks the only way for women to get on is to shag their way to the top. If that's what's expected of me, then I'll find another way to make a living. One where my business skills are appreciated more than the size of my boobs. So much for women's equality, eh?

Well, let Tyler Benson stew for a while. I can imagine him pacing up and down the Chinese rug in the nip and getting more and more irate. It's not a picture I want in my head.

Making my way towards the cloakroom, I note that some of the staff are streaming out of the manor now and it must be time for the coaches to leave. If I get a move on, then, perhaps

I could be on one of the first to go and be out of here before Tyler realises what I've done to him.

I come to a waste bin and dump Tyler's bloodied, shredded dinner suit and shirt into it. His underwear follows. It's all beyond redemption, anyway. For good measure, I toss in the key to the library door. That should hinder him from coming after me for a bit longer. Now I feel like going to scrub my hands with bleach, but that will have to wait.

At the cloakroom, I queue up to retrieve my coat. When I'm finally handed it, I turn to find Josh Wallace standing right there.

'How did it go with Tyler?' he asks me discreetly.

I pull him to one side, away from the wiggling ears and wagging tongues of our colleagues in the queue.

'Badly,' I tell him. I lower my voice to a whisper. 'There was a magician who got Tyler up on stage and he'd somehow managed to cut him across the stomach while trying to saw him in half.'

Josh laughs. 'You're making this up.'

'I wish.' I risk a smile. At some time in the future I'm sure I'll find this funny, but not now. I've probably just called a dead halt to my fledgling career. 'I've left him naked and locked in the library. I'm supposed to be in search of a first-aid kit and new clothes for him, but I've had enough of his bullying and innuendo. I've just dumped his clothes in that bin.'

Josh's eyes widen. 'Seriously?'

'Yep. I'm out of here.'

Now he guffaws. 'Remind me never to cross you, Louise Young.'

'I'm sure you're a wiser man than that.' Dad's words about people doing silly things when they've been drinking ring in my ears, but what's done is done. I'll have to suffer the consequences.

I see more of my colleagues leaving the manor. There's a steady stream now going out into the cold night air. 'I have to go. I want to be on the first coach out of here before Tyler realises I'm not coming back.'

My phone rings and I check the display. 'Talk of the devil.' I show it to Josh. It's Tyler calling. I turn it off.

'He's going to be apoplectic with rage.'

'Yes,' I agree. 'He is.'

Then we laugh together. Josh is such a handsome man and he looks younger and even cuter when he smiles. I should imagine he's under a lot of stress working for Tyler too.

'You realise people will be talking about this for years?' he says.

'I don't think I'll be around to hear it.'

His eyes meet mine. 'I hope you're wrong about that.'

I shrug. 'I'm sure I'll know by tomorrow.' Some of our colleagues start up a raucous chant, laughing as they leave. 'Look, I should go.' I want to get a seat at the back of a coach where I can sit and brood by myself.

Moving away from Josh, I think it's a shame that we work together, because I really do quite like him. He's a nice guy. Probably too nice for this company. If he thinks he's going to climb the ladder like Tyler, he'll probably get eaten alive; or he'll have to toughen up, turn into a corporate animal and lose himself in the process. But since I probably have no future at Fossil Oil now, perhaps it's OK if we do keep seeing each other.

I just want to set the record straight with him. 'Tonight, what we did before, it was ... well, it wasn't me. I don't do that kind of thing. But ... well ... it was fun.'

'I'm glad to hear it.'

'I didn't want you to think that's what I'd normally do.' I spend all my working week fighting off advances from Tyler Benson. Josh must know it was a one-off lapse.

244

'Don't go on the coach.' He catches my wrist. 'Let me take you home. The car's just outside and I could take you straight to your door.'

'Now you're asking me to break another of my own rules.' Yet I'm sure he can tell that I'm wavering.

'I won't tell anyone if you don't.'

I chew my lip indecisively.

'You'll be home much quicker that way.'

I smile. 'I can tell why you're Fossil's top sales executive.'

'Nice warm car with your own personal chauffeur, or a noisy coach with a load of pissed-up people from Chemical Processing?'

'That was the closer,' I tell him. 'Where do I sign?'

He takes my coat from me and holds it open while I slip my arms into the sleeves. Gently he envelops me in it.

'If we leave together, we'll be the talk of the office tomorrow,' I note.

Behind us is a couple in a passionate clinch. He has his hand up her skirt. I don't even know which departments they're from.

Josh grins. 'I think we might be a long way down the queue.'

So we make our way out of the manor house and into the snow. It's coming down thickly now. The tyre tracks of the cars that have already left are almost obliterated by fresh falls. As we head down the steps, they're becoming slippery with ice and Josh tucks his arm protectively under my elbow to help steady me.

Turning back towards the splendid house, I risk a glance at the library windows. Thank goodness there's no sign of Tyler in nothing but his socks. I wonder if he's huddled in front of the dying embers, trying to get a bit of warmth. I shouldn't laugh, but I do.

'What's funny?' Josh asks.

'Nothing,' I tell him. 'Just glad to be going home now.'

'So? How was your inaugural office Christmas party?'

'Not quite what I expected,' I admit.

He raises an eyebrow. 'I bet.'

I might be feeling smug with my ingenuity now, but already I'm wondering just how very cross Tyler's going to be in the morning.

Chapter Thirty-six

Tyler paced up and down in front of the dying embers of the fire. It was getting steadily colder in here and there was nothing to cover himself with. All he had was a cushion, which he was holding in a strategic position.

Louise wasn't coming back, he knew that now. She had duped him and he'd fallen for it. He'd texted her, he'd left abusive messages on her voicemail, but she hadn't responded.

He tried one more time. A more cajoling manner.

'Louise,' he cooed into his phone. 'Just call me. Come back. Bring me some clothes. I'm still bleeding and I'm worried.' He looked down at his stomach. There was a thin line of dried blood where the cut had been. Tyler gritted his teeth. 'This is a really funny joke and you got me. Ha, ha, ha. Now come back.'

He hung up. Ha bloody ha. He'd kill her when he saw her.

Tyler had tried Kirsten again too. And Melissa. None of them was answering her phone. Was there no one who would come to his aid when he needed them? He was so frustrated that he felt like hurling his iPhone into the remains of the flames.

Crossing to the windows, he looked out over the gardens in front of Wadestone Manor to where the snow was thickening now. There was a trail of revellers heading home, making their way towards the coaches that the company had laid on for them. It looked like the Christmas party was coming to a close and, if you asked him, it wasn't before time. This had quite probably been the longest night of his life.

Some of the staff were dancing across the snow, bunches of helium balloons collected from the marquee streaming from their hands. There was some raucous singing. Show some people a free bar and they turn into animals. Typical Christmas party. If it wasn't nailed down it would be nicked. And Wadestone Manor would be sending Fossil Oil a bill for a couple of grand for damages. It happened every year.

Tyler glowered at them. He'd noted their faces when he was being treated to a near-death experience at the hands of The Magnificent Marvo. There were some who were definitely grinning with glee. Well, come the new year, he'd make sure they were smiling on the other side of their faces. He'd chop them in half with his own brand of metaphorical chainsaw. Watch this space. There was absolutely no point being in a position of power if you couldn't abuse it every now and again.

He went back to the library door and tried it again. Definitely locked. Louise must have swiped the key and locked it from the outside. Damn that wretched woman. Tyler rattled the doorknob and banged on the solid, unyielding wood with his fist. Nothing.

Putting down the cushion, he tried to find the number for the hotel on Google but, of course, there was never a reliable mobile phone signal when you needed one. The spinning bar went round and round and round, but never connected him to the useful practicality of the world-wide web. Why had these places never heard of free Wi-Fi? All he could do was wait.

Then an alarm started up. A terrible, ear-piercing sound. He shot to the window again to see that the departing staff had turned round to stare back at the manor house. Some of them were pointing. All of them were agog. Tyler ducked behind the heavy brocade curtains in case one of them should see him in his current predicament.

Now there was a rush of people joining the leavers. They flooded out of the house and down the steps, and were herded by liveried staff from the manor on to the large expanse of lawn at the front.

Was this a fire alarm? What else could it be?

Someone had probably set it off as a prank. Hardly original. It had happened many times before.

Yet the look on the faces of the staff wasn't one of irritated boredom at having their party interrupted. They seemed genuinely worried. Could it be a real fire?

There was the sound of sirens and, seconds later, he saw two fire engines come screaming up the drive to the house and pull up by the steps to the entrance. The staff were all agog now. Karen from Customer Accounts was front-row, of course. Where else would that busybody be? He scanned the assembled audience to see if he could spot Louise, Kirsten or Melissa. But there was no sign of any of them. Damn them all to hell.

Two more fire engines swiftly followed. This couldn't be good news. The whole place could be ablaze. The amount of ancient, dried-out junk in this house would make it go up like a tinderbox. Tyler looked round, terrified. What if no one realised he was locked in here? Being nearly cut in half by a magician could soon pale into insignificance. He could be roasted alive in here and who would even realise? Panic set in and he ran to the door.

'Help me!' he shouted. 'Help me! I'm locked in!'

But the library was down a side corridor and it would, he realised, be impossible for anyone to hear him.

Back at the window he watched the firefighters as they spilled out of the fire engines and raced indoors.

'Oh, good God,' Tyler breathed. This could be really serious.

He tried to open one of the huge sash windows, but it was locked shut. Banging on the panes with the flat of his hands, he cried out again: 'Help! Help me! I'm trapped!'

Now he didn't care if they saw him naked, all pride was gone. He just wanted out of here. And fast. He was sure there was a faint smell of smoke drifting into the library, and he could imagine the blaze really taking hold, flames licking at his heels. A cold band of dread bound his lungs, making it hard to breathe. He hoped it was only that and not the start of the effects of smoke inhalation.

Outside, someone had purloined a case of beer and some bottles of wine. Happily they passed them round as if they were at a picnic. The staff had been moved back from the house and yet they'd pulled up the nearby benches, settling down to watch the show. All while he could be frying.

Yet another fire engine arrived and more firefighters rushed inside. This *was* serious. This was mega-bad. It had to be.

Tyler moved along the row of windows, trying all of them as he went. On each one he had a futile hammer with his fists and indulged in a bout of increasingly frantic shouting. His voice was becoming hoarse.

Now there really was a smell of acrid smoke, and – oh, no – was that a wisp of smoke under the door?

He ran back to get a better look.

It was. A delicate grey curl. As if someone was having a cigarette lying on the floor next to the door. But it was smoke nonetheless.

Tyler flew to the last window and heaved at it. To his blessed relief, it slid open. Reluctantly at first, after years of being untroubled with any kind of movement, but soon there was enough space for him to stick his head out. He forced the window further open with his shoulders and pushed himself as far out of the window as he could manage.

The cold air and falling snow slapped him in the face and chest. There was an orange glow to the pervading whiteness which was more than alarming.

'Help!' he cried, sounding more desperate than he would have liked. He waved his arms frantically. 'Help!'

Someone had to see him now!

Sure enough, all the heads swivelled in his direction. Some of them stopped with beer bottles poised at their lips. A few of them shielded their eyes as if against the sun.

Then, when their gaze finally fell on him, as one, all the staff burst out laughing.

Chapter Thirty-seven

'We're here,' Kirsten said, pointing at her house. 'The one with the black door.'

It had taken them a little over an hour to get back to Hampstead. Despite the increasing snowfall, it hadn't yet settled on the main roads and as they got past Watford and nearer to London it had petered out altogether.

They'd talked about little on the way home. She'd mostly kept her eyes closed, resting back against the seat, revelling in the warmth, listening to the music and letting her mind rove over the fact that she'd finally left Tyler. There was also a certain amount of marvelling that she was here with Simon once more. His solid strength next to her was comforting. He kept his hand on hers and neither of them seemed to mind the silence.

At this time of night, when everyone else was tucked up in bed, all the cars were lined up neatly in the street. 'Parking is always tricky,' she said, trying to keep the conversation at the level of the banal, uncertain of what might come next.

Simon drew in to the kerb as near to the house as he could. 'Nice.'

It *was* nice. This tall Georgian townhouse in a leafy side street had been home to her and Tyler since their return to

England. She'd thought they'd stay here until Fossil Oil decreed otherwise. Now it seemed to be her choice to be leaving.

'It's like your house, I expect: all chosen and paid for courtesy of Fossil Oil.'

'A perk of the job.'

'Or a golden handcuff.'

'Now what?' he asked softly. 'I don't want the night to end here. Now that I've found you, I can't bear to let you out of my sight again.'

She gazed at Simon. Even the air between them was charged. 'Then you'd better come in.'

He brushed his lips against hers. 'Are you sure?'

'Yes,' she said, her voice husky. 'I've never been more sure of anything in my life.'

Together they climbed out of the car and walked hand-in-hand back towards the house.

'What about Tyler?' Simon ventured as they reached the door.

'I don't think he'll be chasing after me, if that's what you're worried about. He'll be burning up the dance floor at the Christmas party for hours yet. He probably doesn't even realise I've left.'

'I don't want to cause trouble.'

She laughed, and her breath created a little cloud in the cold. 'I thought that was *exactly* what you came back to do.'

'Ah, yes,' he conceded with a grin. 'Maybe you're right.'

She let them both into the house. It was cold now that the heating had gone off and she flicked on the controls just inside the door.

This had been one of the better houses Fossil Oil had provided for them. The position was enviable. The garden was big but they had a gardener come in for a day every week to look after it. Their own furniture was still in storage somewhere as this one came fully furnished. It was done so tastefully that

Kirsten hadn't fought to change it as she had so often had to. Or perhaps the fight had simply gone out of her.

She went through to the kitchen, switching on lights as she did. Simon followed. Her skin tingled just because he was near.

The kitchen was one of the best spaces in the place. A few steps took you down from the end of the hall and then it opened out into a room that held every state-of-the-art appliance you could think of. There was a large range cooker fit for a hotel, a complicated coffee maker, a breakfast bar with a handful of tall stools around it, and full-length folding doors that looked out on to the garden.

If only she'd been a decent cook, then she could have fully embraced it.

'Coffee?'

Simon nodded. He sat on one of the stools as she went about making them both some espresso. While the machine hissed and burbled, she could feel him watching her movements, but they said very little. She was tired now and wanted something to enliven her while she considered how her future might unfold. It was all very well to have plans, have dreams, but you never knew what curve-balls life was going to throw at you.

Without asking Simon if he was hungry, she also put some bread in the toaster. There were times when only the comfort of carbs would do.

He'd stripped off his dinner jacket, which was slung over the stool next to him. The lighting in here was too harsh, but he still looked handsome under the glare. Tyler had to do everything in a frenzy of excitement and chaos, but there was a quiet energy about Simon. There always had been.

Turning, she saw him studying her intently. 'What?'

'I just like watching you,' he said. 'I can't believe I'm with you. Come here.'

She went to him and he pulled her into his arms. They held

each other tightly, so many words unspoken between them. Well, maybe there would be time for that now.

They stayed entwined, her head resting on his shoulder, until the toast popped out of the toaster and the coffee machine hissed that it was ready.

She pulled herself away from him to butter the toast and pour the coffee. 'We should go through to the living room. It'll be warmer in there.'

So Simon picked up the cups and she led the way, taking the plate of toast. In the living room she put the plate down on the coffee table and switched on the Christmas-tree lights. They sparkled out in the darkness. There was something so soothing, so welcoming about a Christmas tree. It instantly made the room feel homely.

'Very pretty.'

'Not my own work,' she admitted. 'I drafted in a company that Melissa Harvey recommended.'

Kirsten wondered how she would spend Christmas this year. She knew she couldn't face sitting across the table from Tyler for Christmas lunch, that was for sure.

She turned on the wall lights too and lit the gas fire while Simon settled himself on the sofa.

'It feels really strange being here,' he said. 'Surreal.'

Kirsten sat down next to him, curled into his side and relaxed into the cushions with a sigh. She tucked her legs beneath her so that she could snuggle in closer. 'For me too.'

'It's nice though.' He stroked her face lovingly. 'Who'd have thought the evening would turn out like this? It's just like old times.'

She nodded, choked by the flashback. It was, indeed, like old times. Her and Simon, easy in each other's company, snuggled down on the sofa. It was as if the past decade had simply been deleted.

255

She pushed the plate of toast towards him and took a piece herself.

'Thanks.' Simon bit into it gratefully. 'This is good.'

'My culinary skills haven't got any better, I warn you.'

He looked down at her. 'Is that something that might be concerning me in the future?'

Shrugging, she answered, 'That depends.'

He took another piece of toast and waited patiently for her to continue.

'I'm leaving Tyler,' she said when she was sure her voice was steady enough. 'I caught him tonight in a compromising position with his assistant, Louise. One in a long line of conquests.'

His look said, Typical Tyler.

It was true enough. Everyone knew what an unfaithful bastard he was. They couldn't go on like this. Or, more accurately, *she* couldn't go on like this. Tyler, on the other hand, seemed perfectly happy with the status quo. But it wasn't what she wanted any more. She wanted a partner, someone she could envisage being with as they were growing old. Someone she could share a life with in comfortable companionship. At the age of forty-two she didn't want to be still sparring like lovesick teenagers. She'd wanted them to work on their relationship, on trying to save their marriage – yet Tyler didn't seem able to see that his constant lying and deceit were slowly killing her inside.

She'd been sure, until tonight, that, deep down, she still loved Tyler. That they might overcome their difficulties. Now, with his latest infidelity, she was finding it hard to even like him. If she never clapped eyes on him again, it would be too soon.

'I'm done this time, Simon.' She let out a weary sigh. 'I can't cope with Tyler any more. The pressures of work and his obsessive need to be at the very top of the corporate tree have taken their toll on our marriage. It's exhausting. He leaves here at first light as he has to be first in the office in the morning, and the last to leave at night. Which means I rarely see him at his best. Mine has always been the bad-tempered, exhausted bit that's left over.' She sighed wearily as she poured her heart out. Maybe Simon didn't need to know all of this, but she felt it was better out in the open. 'Life was never going to be easy with Tyler. I accepted that the day I signed up, and you know him as well as I do. He's always been a challenge and, goodness knows why, that was probably some of the attraction.'

'Why *do* women like a bad boy?'

She shook her head. 'I don't know. It wasn't all dreadful though. Initially. I did love him, Simon. Not like I loved you. Never in that way. But we did have our moments. He was there for me – now we know why, of course. Yet I admired his single-minded ambition and urge to succeed. Now it's tainted with a selfish need to smash everyone else out of the way in the scramble. It's as undignified as it's unnecessary.' She sipped her coffee, enjoying the warm buzz it sent through her. 'In the beginning, Tyler's worst excesses were countered by a fun-loving nature and a desire to live life to the full. He can be great company when he wants to be.'

'I know only too well. Remember Toby's stag weekend?'

'I never did get the *full* details,' she said ruefully.

Simon raised an eyebrow. 'Probably just as well.'

'I can imagine it though,' she went on. 'It made for a roller-coaster relationship, but sometimes it was exhilarating to hang on for the ride and see where he would take me. Now the balance is gone. The highs are too far apart to be worth waiting for and there are way too many lows.' She looked up at Simon. 'I'm telling you all this, spilling the beans on my marriage, because I want you to know how my relationship with Tyler has been. If I'm going to break free, I never want to replicate that.'

'I understand.'

'Unfortunately, his quest for happiness, for fulfilment or

257

whatever it is that Tyler wants in his life, wasn't being sated by work. It wasn't long before he started turning to more and more forbidden fruit to get his kicks. Women, booze. I don't know what else. That's what's taken him further and further away from me. That's what hurts. Really hurts. I've tried to pretend it doesn't. But it does.' She let out an unsteady exhalation. 'Now it's going to be sorted out once and for all. There'll be no more rearranging the deckchairs as the *Titanic* slowly sinks.'

'I feel as if I came back just in time.'

'You probably did,' she acknowledged. 'I need a fresh start, Simon. I'm going to draw a line under all this. I want honesty. I want uncomplicated love. No more lies, no more deceit. I want someone who's going to be there purely for me.'

'I can fill that role,' he said.

It was her turn to glance at him. 'I know.'

'We *can* rebuild what we had, Kirsten. I promise you. I want to do that more than anything.'

'I'd like to say we should take it slowly. My head tells me that I shouldn't be going straight from one relationship into another.' Yet she had to admit to herself, her heart was urging her to do just that. 'There's so much that's happened to both of us in the last ten years. Are we still the same people that we were?'

'I guess there's only one way to find out. I, for one, hope that I'm not only older but considerably wiser.' He reached out and took her hand. 'As I told you before, there hasn't been a day in all this time that I haven't thought of you. Every night I've gone to sleep thinking of you, wondering where you are. I haven't forgotten a single thing about our time together. I just bitterly regret that, through my own foolishness, it ended. When I received your email all those years ago, I shouldn't have called Tyler. I shouldn't have listened to his side of the story. That was stupid of me. I should have got on a plane right away and headed straight back to change your mind.'

'My mind didn't need changing. I still loved you. Adored you. Perhaps I should have done the same when I got *your* email. But I was so devastated, I wasn't thinking straight.'

'Me neither.' Simon's handsome face darkened. 'I could kill him for doing this to us. We both let Tyler dictate the course of our lives. I'd like to think we've learned from that, at least.'

She nodded her agreement, still unable to grasp the extent of her husband's manipulation of them both. It was cruel and unforgivable.

'I'm so glad I came back, Kirsten. I wish I'd followed my instinct years ago instead of fighting it. Now I have a chance of putting it right. Until I did that, I was going to live for ever with "what if?"' He smiled at her sadly. 'Then I saw you tonight and nothing had changed. I was filled with such overwhelming feelings of desire, and love, and the need to take care of you, I don't want to let you go again.' He tilted her chin to make her look at him. 'I want nothing more than to make you happy.'

Her engagement ring and matching diamond-studded Tiffany wedding band sparkled in the overhead lights. She slid them both off and let them sit on the coffee table in front of them.

She was near to tears. 'I feel as if I've wasted so many of the good years of my life that I *do* want to throw caution to the wind and get on with living.'

'Me too.'

'Can I really trust you, Simon Conway?' she asked. 'I don't want my heart broken all over again.'

'Of course you can.'

'Do you swear you still love me as much as you did?'

'I do.'

His eyes met hers and the sincerity in their depths made her breath catch. 'Then take me to bed.'

Chapter Thirty-eight

I glance up at my parents' house. The lights are still on upstairs. That will be Dad, restless and wakeful until I'm home. Some things don't change. He was just the same when I was a teenager out on a date. He'd never go to bed until I was safely home.

The street my parents live in hasn't changed all that much since I was a child either. They bought their when they were first married and have lived here ever since. s been my rock throughout my life. They had uPVC windows put in a few years ago and the kitchen was upgraded shortly afterwards. There's a fancy water feature in the garden, but the front door is still the same colour it's always been. My parents aren't big on change.

I look up at the room that used to be mine as a girl, and picture Mia sleeping soundly there. My mum and dad put a brave face on it, but I know they sometimes find it hard for us to be back with them. There's no break from Mia's exuberance and occasionally I catch a glimpse of them both looking so tired and, I hate to say this, a bit old. I feel as if I've brought the responsibility of my failed relationship home with me. But now they can't simply pat my hand and tell me there are plenty more fish in the sea. Now there's Mia to consider. And the three adults in the household all scuttle round to work to her rhythm.

I hoped my new job would be my ticket out of here. Mia and I should have our own place. My parents should be enjoying the latter end of their working life in peace and comfort by themselves. Plus they're the sort of people who save up for years so that they can buy a new washing machine or something. They don't even have credit cards, so I know the amount of debt that I have is as terrifying for them as it is for me. I so wanted to relieve them of that worry.

Josh and I are sitting together in his car, parked up across the end of the drive, just talking. He's easy company and I'm glad he persuaded me to accept a lift with him rather than face the scrum of the Fossil Oil coaches.

We're bathed in the dim glow of the streetlamps and I'm comfortable and warm in the car. It's very plush and I realise that Fossil must be quite generous with their car allowance. I can hardly bring myself to leave and go out into the cold.

I'm exhausted after the party. What a night.

'If an angel flew across the room that frown will stay,' he notes.

'I'm thinking about tomorrow,' I admit to Josh. He's turned towards me in the driver's seat and the darkness picks out the line of his jaw, his cheekbones, making him look even more handsome. His eyes are dark with concern. 'With some trepidation, I'm wondering what will happen when Tyler sobers up.'

'Perhaps he'll see the funny side of things.'

'Is there one?' I sigh. 'Even if he doesn't sack me outright, can I still keep working for a man who I have absolutely no respect for?'

'Tyler's all bluster. A capable woman like you can keep him in his place.'

'His wife thinks he's having an affair with me. How do I handle that?'

Josh grimaces as he says, 'I'm not sure if you know this yet, but it's fairly common knowledge that Tyler is in a relationship with the chairman's wife.'

'Melissa Harvey?'

He nods.

'You're kidding me!'

'Karen is obviously slipping with her gossip.'

'Oh my God.' I can't get my head round this one. Why would someone like Melissa Harvey – someone who seems to have it all – get involved with a sleazebag like Tyler Benson? 'I assume Lance doesn't know.'

'I'm guessing not.'

As I'm still trying to process this, the lights in the hall flicker on and off. I laugh out loud.

'That's my dad,' I say to Josh. 'Obviously he thinks it's time for me to say goodnight.'

He strokes a finger across my cheek. 'That's a shame.'

'Yes.'

'I've enjoyed this evening, Louise. Can we do it again some-time?'

'I don't know. Could we really work together *and* be romantically involved?'

He raises an eyebrow. 'I think we should try.'

I laugh at that too. 'After tomorrow it might not be an issue.'

'Tomorrow is another day. Let's see what it brings.'

He tilts my chin and his warm lips gently brush mine. The sensation sends tingles all through me.

At that moment, my phone rings. We both roll our eyes but nevertheless I reach in my pocket for it and pull it out. I smile when I see the caller display.

He frowns. 'Tyler?'

'Worse.' I turn it to face him. 'Dad.' Punching to answer, I say, 'Won't be long, Dad.'

'I was starting to get a bit worried, Lou-Lou,' my father says at the other end of the line.

'Don't. I'm fine.' I hang up and tuck my phone away. If Dad rings again I'm not answering a second time. 'And they wonder why I want my own place again.'

'They're only concerned for you,' Josh says.

This time I kiss him properly and just hope Dad isn't watching out of the window. Then, reluctantly, I go to get out of the car.

'Thanks, Josh.'

'I'll see you at the office tomorrow.'

'I look forward to it,' I say.

'Louise,' he calls out as I'm about to shut the car door. 'We could make this work.'

'Maybe we could,' I agree. Then I skip down the path and catch my dear old dad peering through the letterbox.

Chapter Thirty-nine

Tyler looked for an escape route, but he was too high up to jump from the window. On top of all the humiliations he'd suffered tonight, he didn't want to add breaking a leg or even his neck to them. Plus there was the small matter of him being stark bollock naked.

'Help!' he shouted again, but the staff just stared at him. Was no one going to rush to his aid? Were all the Fossil staff totally lacking in compassion?

It looked as if the answer might be a resounding yes.

In a vain attempt to cover himself, Tyler tried to pull down one of the heavy brocade curtains, but to no avail. He was almost swinging on them but they weren't budging. Whoever had put these up had made sure they were going nowhere.

Now the smell of smoke was getting stronger and the fire alarm was still wailing away.

Where had Kirsten got to? Wasn't she worried about him? He could only hope she'd calmed down now after mistakenly believing she'd seen him with Louise. What was she thinking? Did she really think he was that careless?

Tyler sighed wearily as he listened to the whirling machinations of his own contorted brain. Why did he have to do this? And on a regular basis? Why put himself through all this anxiety? Wasn't his working life stressful enough without making his love life complicated too?

In spite of it all, he did love Kirsten. Truly. She was all a man could want. It was just that he needed something more. Something that would provide a rush of excitement. What did that say about him? Perhaps he was getting too old for all this philandering. After all, there's no lech quite as pathetic as an old lech. You only had to look at Lance Harvey to see that. It could well be that the day had come when he should think about settling down and embracing the hitherto unfamiliar concept of marital fidelity with open arms. He knew that was what Kirsten wanted. She deserved it too.

Now Simon Conway was back on the scene, and Tyler was sure she'd always carried a torch for him, no matter how much she might protest otherwise. Well, Conway would have to stand on the sidelines for this dance. There was no way he was going to worm his way back into Kirsten's affections. Oh, no. Not on Tyler Benson's watch.

Tyler breathed heavily. This little scare could well have provided a timely reminder of which side his connubial bread was buttered.

Chapter Forty

Together, Melissa and Martin manhandled Lance into the house. They struggled to get him up the stairs and tipped him on to the bed. Lance let out an inelegant 'Ouff'. One of his shoes fell off.

'Thank you, Martin.' Melissa straightened her hair. 'I can manage now.'

He looked as if he didn't want to leave her.

'Really, I'll be fine.'

'If you like, I could stay and make you some tea, Mrs Harvey?'

She thought about dismissing him for the night – no one should have to witness Lance in this state – but then Martin had already seen everything Lance had got to offer. He'd vomited in the back of the Bentley before now, had wet himself in his sleep. Martin was under no illusions. And she felt lonely, so very desperately lonely. It was comforting to have a friendly face here, someone who was always on her side.

'That would be lovely,' she said to him. 'You know where everything is?'

He nodded.

As soon as he left the room, she set about undressing Lance. He stirred as she tugged off his jacket.

'I love you, you know?' he slurred. 'I've always loved you.'

Lance being belligerent was bad enough, but Lance being maudlin was always a complete catastrophe.

'Of course you do, honey.' The words came automatically from her mouth now, bypassing her brain. She might have believed that once, a very long time ago.

'You're the only one who still loves me.'

She wrestled with the buttons on his shirt. 'Lots of people love you, angel.'

'No they don't!' He sounded tearful now. 'No one loves me. My boys don't love me. They never come to see me.'

'The boys are busy, darling. You know that. It's not that they don't love you.' Perhaps if Lance hadn't always been permanently pissed when they did come to stay, they wouldn't be in such a tearing hurry to get away again. They hardly knew Lance anyway. While their father had chased his corporate dream the boys had been sentenced to life in an expensive, loveless boarding school rather than a warm family home. Even in the holidays, which Melissa clung on to as precious time with her sons, he'd always been too busy to see them.

It was something she regretted bitterly. She should have left Lance to pursue his career and stayed in one place to give the boys the life they deserved. At the time she'd reasoned it away by convincing herself that she'd been protecting them from his drinking. Perhaps, in her own way, she had. But the boys weren't fools. They knew the score with their father. The only miracle was that she still had a good relationship with them, and she was thankful every day for that. Although they could never understand why she stayed with Lance. Frankly, neither could she any more.

'The company doesn't love me,' her husband continued. 'My entire working life I've slaved my guts out for them. Running round Europe at the drop of a beret.' He looked at her wistfully, his eyes cloudy with tears. 'You were right, Melissa. I'm being sidelined. Shunted into the buffers at the last-chance railway station. At sixty-six I'm over the hill. Pushed out of the way to make room for younger, brighter, hungrier men.'

The brightest and hungriest of them being Tyler Benson. Even now a pain nipped at her heart at the thought of his name. She could tell Lance that she'd been having an affair with his right-hand man, but what purpose would that serve? If she came clean, confessed all, it would only lower her to Tyler's level. She had to handle this with dignity. It was over, and the sooner she accepted that, the better. Tyler had used her, got what he wanted, and now he didn't need her any more. Well, more fool her. That was the price you had to pay for falling in love with someone unsuitable, and forbidden to boot.

Melissa went to undo Lance's trousers, but stilled her hands. He was fast asleep again, spreadeagled on the bed. He snored loudly, producing percolating bubbles of spit from the corner of his mouth which burst on the out-breath, considerately making room for the next watery eruption. She was used to it. Of course she was. But this time, something about the way Lance looked made her stomach turn. Was this what she had to look forward to for the rest of her life?

She thought back to a time when, after a night out, they would have tumbled together into the bed, craving each other, so passionate, so in love. It seemed like a very long time ago.

Wearily, she bent to pick up his fallen shoe and tugged the other one off his foot at the same time. Then she eased the throw at the bottom of the bed over him. Lance wouldn't know whether he was dressed or undressed, covered or not. Collecting his shirt and jacket, she put them over the dumb valet that stood in the corner. Perhaps she was every bit as dumb as it was.

Going downstairs, she found Martin in the kitchen. He'd taken off his suit jacket and was pouring two cups of tea.

He'd only switched on the lights that illuminated the work surface, so the kitchen was subtly lit. Just as she liked it. Martin turned when he heard her step on the stairs.

'I hope you don't mind, Mrs Harvey,' he said, nodding at his jacket. 'I took the liberty.'

'Of course not.' She slipped on to a stool at the breakfast bar and let Martin serve her the tea. 'I hate stools,' she said. 'What fool invented them?'

'You can't beat a good chair,' Martin agreed and that made her laugh, though she didn't know why.

'Do sit down, Martin. It's too late to be hovering. You must be exhausted. I know I am.'

He took the stool opposite her and they sat in the dim light, nursing their cups.

'I hope the tea's as you like it.'

'It's perfect,' she said and then took a moment to notice its soothing warmth. 'Just perfect.'

'Is Mr Harvey all right?' Martin eventually asked.

She shrugged. 'For now.'

'What will you do?'

She knew what he meant. He didn't have to spell it out for her. Martin knew as well as she did that this couldn't go on. 'I don't know.'

'I could take you somewhere,' he said, concentrating on his cup. 'Anywhere you wanted to go.'

Her mouth was dry. 'You'd do that for me?'

He nodded. 'I don't like to see you unhappy, Mrs Harvey.'

'But I am, Martin,' she admitted. 'Desperately.'

'He doesn't deserve you.'

She forced a smile. 'I think you're probably right.'

'I didn't mean to speak out of turn.' Martin stood up. 'I should go, Mrs Harvey.'

Melissa sighed. She couldn't do this any longer. Whatever

happened, she couldn't go to Washington DC with Lance. 'Will you wait for me?' she asked. 'I won't be very long.'

'Shall I go out to the car?'

'No, no. Sit here for a moment, Martin. I'd like you to be here.'

Something inside her had clicked. With blinding clarity, she knew she'd reached the end of the road with Lance. Melissa knew that if she didn't leave him now, then she never would.

Chapter Forty-one

Simon moved above her. Kirsten clung to the contours of his lean back and moulded her body to his. It was a long time since she'd known such all-encompassing ecstasy. Everything else that had happened tonight was obliterated as they moved together in a harmony of love.

Sex with Tyler had always been a marathon of athletics. He wasn't content unless they'd tried a dozen different acrobatic positions, and it had gone on for hours. It had become a performance, not a mutually shared pleasure. It felt as if he didn't want her, so much as his own ego-boosting gratification. She didn't have the stamina or the stomach for that now, so in recent months she'd tried to avoid it as much as possible.

Yet, with Simon, making love was just as she remembered. He'd loved her with strength and tenderness and without the need to resort to several chapters of the *Kama Sutra*. It was as refreshing as it was exciting. Making love to him had been like coming home, and she wanted more of it.

When they were sated, they lay beside each other, her body curled into Simon's, head rested on his chest. They fitted so well together. They always had.

'Are you sure you won't regret this in the morning?' Simon's voice was heavy with concern, his eyes dark under his fine fringe.

'It's nearly morning already,' she said softly. 'And there are a lot of things that I might well regret, Simon, but this won't be one of them.'

She'd always thought it would be difficult to be unfaithful, but it hadn't been so at all. Making love to Simon hadn't given her even a momentary pang of guilt. Perhaps Tyler's lack of morals had changed her own perspective over the years. She'd thought it would take away a little piece of her soul, when in fact she felt enriched.

Somehow, in the act of love, the years had melted away. They were back to where they had been before it had all gone so horribly wrong. The curtains were open and the dawn would be brightening. She loved the look of him in the orange-grey urban half-light, his strong body in silhouette.

Absently, he stroked her hair. 'What happens now?'

'I want to run away from it all,' Kirsten admitted. 'I'd like to pack a bag and just go. I fancy somewhere far away.' She grinned up at him. 'Preferably with a beach.'

'A beach?' He laughed softly. 'I could go for that.'

She was suddenly serious again. 'If we're going to be a couple—'

'And I sincerely hope that we are,' Simon interjected.

'—you'll never be able to work with Tyler. He simply won't tolerate it.'

'That may not be his choice.'

'Your job will become a daily battleground,' she said. 'It will permeate everything you do. Our relationship will be tainted by his presence. He'll make sure of it. Is that what you really want?'

'I'm sure we could work it out.'

She shivered despite the comforting warmth of his body against hers. Simon pulled up the duvet and tucked it round her.

'I think I'm done with this lifestyle,' she continued. 'I'm tired

272

of being nothing more than a corporate wife. It would be the same with you. Fossil Oil would dictate that you were needed somewhere else, and off we'd go on the same giddy roundabout.'

'I'm a different person to Tyler. I'd handle it better.'

'I'm sure you would, but it's still a rat race. The Fossil management programme is particularly destructive. Isn't there any way we can get off this dreadful corporate treadmill that just keeps going round and round to nowhere? It's like being a hamster on one of those little wheels – you pedal and pedal, faster and faster, until you drop off exhausted and call it early retirement.' She sighed with exasperation. 'I mean, what *is* the point of working for Fossil Oil? Is it helping world peace? Is it feeding starving children? Is it finding a cure for cancer?' Kirsten was beginning to feel impassioned. 'Can't we leave it all behind and do something worthwhile? I want to do something for myself again. I used to enjoy working. Now how do I spend my days? I hang around, go to the gym, visit the hairdresser. My life is empty, Simon. There must be more to it than this. I could *do* something.'

'Like what?'

'I've no idea, but I think I really would like to get right away from here. Go abroad. Anywhere. Have a completely new start. I must have skills that someone can use. Whatever happens, I know I don't want Tyler or Fossil Oil to be part of my life in the future.'

'If that's what it takes to keep you, then I'll do it,' Simon said. 'There's one thing you can be sure of: I won't ever let you slip through my fingers again. If it's what you want, I'll ring Lance and resign as soon as the office opens.'

'You'd do that for me?' It seemed so simple for Simon, so straightforward, but then he'd always been that way. There'd been a clarity to his vision that she'd admired. All these things that she'd tried to forget about him now came rushing back.

'Of course. He won't like it, but there it is. He'll have to accept it.' He took her hand. 'We've wasted too much time already.'

She was gripped by a fever of excitement. 'Let's just pack a bag and go somewhere. Now.'

'Don't we need to speak to Tyler?' Simon's dark eyes were troubled. 'We should face him together.'

She shook her head. 'We owe him nothing. He'll destroy us both if he can. He'll be coming back soon and I want to be gone before he does. The sooner I'm out of here the better.' Now she'd decided to go, there was nothing that could hold her back. 'He'll give me some whining excuse and lay guilt on me about it being the season of goodwill. He'll beg me to stay for a few more days and then he'll try to hold me here. I know what he's like. I'm not staying a moment longer, Simon.'

She couldn't sit through Christmas with him. It would be obscene. The pretence that they had a marriage was over. Kirsten wanted a clean break. They had no children to consider, there was nothing to hold her here. It wasn't even their house. Better that she should leave right away while her resolve was strong.

Simon shrugged. 'I'm not going to argue with that, if you're sure that's what you want. That it's *me* you want.'

'I do.' Kirsten turned to him and kissed him deeply. 'I love you,' she said. 'I've never stopped loving you.'

Chapter Forty-two

Dad, of course, is waiting in the hall. He's hopping about uncomfortably. 'You could have brought him in, you know.'

'I couldn't,' I tell my father. 'He's just someone I work with who was giving me a lift home.'

My dad harrumphs.

'You would have frightened him off in your tartan pyjamas.'

He looks down and realises that I'm probably right. I wonder what Josh would have thought of all the tinsel, garlands and festive tat that my mum has festooned in here as a welcome. There's a Santa on the windowsill with a glowing nose that flashes on and off. If I'd been in Josh's shoes I'd have high-tailed it out of here as fast as I could. I rub the Santa's portly stomach affectionately.

'Do you want me to make you a cup of tea?'

'Yeah,' I say. 'That'd be great, Dad.' Suddenly I feel weary down to my bones. My feet throb and I kick off my shoes to rub my toes on the carpet.

'Your mum always used to do that,' he says. 'When we used to go dancing.'

'You should go out more,' I tell him. 'I bet you could both still trip the light fantastic if you put your minds to it.'

'I think our dancing days are over,' he says. 'We like to stay in with you and Mia. The Christmas *Strictly* was brilliant tonight. I can't wait for the second part on Christmas Day. You missed a treat.'

While Dad tells me who got voted off and who stayed, who nailed the rumba and who didn't, we go through to the kitchen. He busies himself making tea. It reminds me of when I was a teenager and came back, usually heartbroken, from the school disco. Then Dad would ply me with tea and a mountain of hot buttered toast and tell me that I was the most beautiful girl in the world even though I had braces, spots and greasy hair.

On cue, Dad makes his offer. 'Any toast, love? I know you like a bit of toast when you come home late.'

I wonder if he remembers those times too. 'No thanks, Dad. I might just have a biscuit.' I don't have to ask if they've got any. The cupboards at my parents' house are always stacked out with tempting treats – chocolate digestives, bourbons, custard creams, Hobnobs, caramel wafers. When I move out, I'll be back to healthy fruits and nuts. I will, honestly.

Then my eyes prickle with tears. I watch Dad as he moves about the kitchen, humming as he does. He makes my tea with such loving care that my heart squeezes. I shouldn't be in a rush to leave them. I know how much they love having us here, despite the compromises, despite everything. It's lovely for Mia to have such a close relationship with her grandparents. I should enjoy this time with them.

'Here's me chattering on about *Strictly* and I haven't asked you about your lovely party. Did you have a nice time?'

I swallow down my tears as Dad delivers my tea and a plate piled high with a selection of biscuits. Comfort carbs.

'It was interesting,' I say, trying to sound non-committal. I nibble at a custard cream and gulp my tea gratefully. 'Not quite what I expected. Beautiful place.'

How can I tell him that I left my boss totally naked apart from his socks in the library?

Then I'm saved further explanation as Mum comes down in her dressing-gown. 'I heard you talking,' she says as she kisses my cheek. 'Was it wonderful?'

'Yeah. It was great.' Better a little white lie than a full-on description of a mad, mad night.

'We could go into the living room. I'll put the fire on.'

It would also mean her switching on the tree lights and all of the jigging, singing Santas that are lined up on the fireplace.

'I should go to bed. It's late and I've got work in the morning.' I don't add that it might be my very last day. 'I want to see Mia too.'

'She's in your bed.'

No surprise there.

I kiss them both. As I head for the door, I stop and take a deep breath. 'How would you feel if I invited someone to come for Christmas lunch?'

'Well,' Mum says, wide-eyed, 'there's a turn-up for the books.'

'Is that the boy that brought you home?'

I laugh. 'He's hardly a *boy*, Dad.' Then I feel myself flush. 'But, yes, that's him.'

'He'd be more than welcome,' Mum says. 'You know that.'

I can tell that they're both as pleased as Punch.

'He might not say yes,' I point out. 'But I'll ask.'

My mother is mentally choosing wedding hats already.

'Night, then,' I say. 'See you in the morning.' I kiss them both again. 'Love you both.'

'Night, night, Lou-Lou,' Dad says as he's done since I was a girl.

'Night, Dad.'

I climb the stairs and tiptoe into my bedroom. In the light

from her little pink Christmas tree across the hall, I can see that Mia is splayed out in the middle of the bed, thumb in her mouth.

As quietly as I can, I wriggle out of my dress. Then I pull the pins from my hair and let it fall loose. I run my fingers through it, massaging my scalp. I wonder briefly what it would feel like to have Josh Wallace's fingers run through my hair. Nice. I think it would feel very nice indeed. Slipping into my pyjamas, I slide into bed next to Mia and nudge her up until I can lie down too.

She stirs. 'Did you have a nice time, Mummy?' she murmurs sleepily.

'Yes,' I whisper, as I stroke her hair. 'It was lovely.'

'Did you dance with a prince?'

I smile to myself. 'Yes. Maybe I did.'

My daughter yawns. 'Shall I sing to you about King Wencas again?'

'Not now, sweet pea.'

'Is Santa coming tonight?'

'Tomorrow,' I tell her. 'Santa will be here tomorrow. Go to sleep.'

As I cuddle up into her, I can't help but wonder what else tomorrow might bring.

Chapter Forty-three

Tyler was still at the window shouting 'Help!' at the congregated staff of Fossil Oil, who remained motionless. No one, it seemed, was in a hurry to rush to his aid.

It was with great relief that he finally heard a noise at the library door. Seconds later there was some heavy banging, and next the shiny blade of an axe splintered the antique door. Not only had Louise locked him in here, but she must have pocketed the key too. He felt his jaw tighten.

A fireman broke through the wood and crashed unceremoniously into the library.

'You're all right now, mate!' the fireman shouted as he lifted his breathing apparatus and wiped a trace of sweat from his brow.

Tyler couldn't entirely agree with him. It may rate highly as one of his wife's fantasies – heaven knew she must have some – to be found stark naked by a strapping six-foot fireman, but unfortunately it wasn't one of his.

'Blimey, mate.' The fireman tilted his yellow hat back on his head as he gaped at Tyler. 'What have you been up to?'

'I was a little warm, so I thought I'd make myself comfortable,' Tyler answered tightly.

'I bet you did!' The fireman winked at him. 'It must have been one hell of a party.'

It certainly *has* been one hell of a Christmas party, Tyler's brain echoed bitterly. The repercussions could go on until doomsday.

'I'm Dale.' He shook Tyler's hand. 'Let's get you out of here then.'

'Can't you find me some clothes or something to cover myself with?'

'No time for that. The fire's spreading quickly. We've got to get a move on.'

Tyler felt the panic, which had so recently subsided, rise in him again. 'Where *is* the fire?'

'Oh very funny, mate.' Dale laughed as he walked towards the open window, kicking the matchstick remnants of the door out of his way. 'I've not heard that one before.'

At the window, there was now a waiting ladder. The staff had all moved towards the part of the lawn nearest to it, watching with great anticipation. At the bottom of the ladder two more firefighters stood waiting expectantly.

'At least let me take my socks off,' Tyler said.

But it was too late. Without further pleasantries, Dale grabbed Tyler by his waist and threw him, with all the elegance of a sack of King Edward potatoes, over his shoulder.

'What do you think you're doing?' Tyler screeched.

'Just my job,' the fireman answered calmly.

Tyler closed his eyes and battled with the rising anger that brought blood burning to his cheeks – both sets of cheeks. Louise had humiliated him enough tonight to last her a lifetime. He would not forget, or forgive, this easily. Someone would pay for this, and he knew exactly who it would be.

Dale staggered towards the window, Tyler dangling reluctantly down his back, his bottom bared to the world.

'I'm not going down there,' Tyler said. 'No way.'

'No choice. The corridor outside's filling with smoke.'

Tyler looked askance at the ladder. It might be the ground floor, but it was still a long way up and there were a lot of prickly shrubs between him and *terra firma*. 'I can manage myself.'

'No can do,' Dale said. 'Health and safety. I have to carry you.'

'Never.'

'It'll all be over in a minute.'

Yet Tyler knew that it would take him a lifetime to live this down.

Dale stepped up on to the windowsill. Tyler's heart went into overdrive, racing furiously. 'I could break my neck.'

'You're in safe hands.' With that he swung them both on to the ladder and started his slow descent.

When the staff realised what was happening, a massive cheer went up. Every jolting step down the ladder was agony and the cut across his waist was stinging with pain. He could feel his gentleman's tackle squashed against Dale's shoulder while a chill winter breeze played delicately over his bare arse. On top of that he could hear the fireman panting heavily beneath him. It was the most disconcerting and distressing experience he'd ever had.

Then, as he neared the ground, Dale handed him over to two of his waiting colleagues and the cheers morphed into wolf whistling. His shame was now complete and there was nothing to protect him.

The fireman placed him upright, went to brush him down, then thought better of it. Tyler stood stock still and bore it all stoically.

'There's a blanket in the engine, mate,' one said as he glanced down at Tyler. 'I'll get it for you.'

'Thank you,' Tyler said. 'I'm very grateful.' He hoped they understood sarcasm.

In so many ways, this had been the worst night of his life, and he suspected it wasn't over yet. He still had to find and placate Kirsten. His eyes scanned the sniggering crowd, but she was nowhere to be seen. It was a shame for her she wasn't here to witness this. How she would have enjoyed seeing him suffer.

Thank goodness there was only one day left in the office before the Christmas break. He normally hated this time of the year, but now he couldn't wait to get away from Fossil Oil for a few days of rest and recuperation. He just wanted to be at home with Kirsten, getting very, very drunk.

The sound of laughter and clinking glasses reverberated in his ears. They would pay. They would all pay.

Dale came over to him. 'That wasn't too bad, was it?'

'I guess it all depends on your perspective,' Tyler replied.

The fireman took off his yellow helmet and, with a glance down at Tyler's manhood, said, 'You might want to use this. It's a cold night.'

'No, thank you,' Tyler said.

With all the dignity he could muster Tyler held his head high, stood tall and, ignoring the childish titters and catcalls, strolled as casually as he could manage towards the waiting fire engine.

Chapter Forty-four

Upstairs again, Melissa tiptoed round the bedroom. Goodness knew why: it would have been possible to run the vacuum cleaner and play the radio at full blast in the same room and still not have woken Lance. She knew that, because in the past she'd tried it. But somehow, under the circumstances, it seemed appropriate to tiptoe. It would be difficult to have Lance awake while she packed her entire life into two reasonably sized suitcases and left him for ever. He was still in the same place, spreadeagled on the bed, half dressed. She stared down at him. Over thirty years with him and it had come to this.

Melissa wasn't sure what to do next. The speed and spontaneity of her decision had left her slightly light-headed. It wasn't that she hadn't thought about leaving Lance, of course she had. But she'd never really believed that she would.

Where could she go? What could she do? She might not intend to go to Washington, but she thought she'd take her airline ticket anyway. Perhaps she could exchange it, maybe fly back to New York and make a new life for herself. She still had a few friends there. Though how fair-weather they were, she didn't know. She had her credit card too, but she wondered how long it would be before Lance stopped her spending on it. He wouldn't take kindly to her leaving.

She tried to be as practical as possible. Sensible clothes rather than evening dresses, except for her favourite one. Racks of designer gowns in every hue faced her. There was a good chance that she might not need those again. After all, New York society might not be as welcoming without Lance attached to her arm. She didn't know what status – if any – the ex-wife of an ex-chairman would carry. At the moment, it didn't seem to matter. All that concerned her was that she should get away while she still had a modicum of sanity and self-respect left.

Melissa emptied the contents of her jewellery box on to the dressing table, the array of diamond-encrusted baubles clattering noisily across the glass surface. A quick glance at the bed told her that Lance slept on, blissfully unaware. Melissa surveyed the jewels dispassionately. There was one for every occasion – each anniversary, birthday, Christmas, the births of the children – each growing bigger and more glittering as the years passed. What would she have been given for her thirtieth anniversary, if she'd stayed that long?

Were they happier when they were just starting out together and had nothing but their love to sustain them? Is this what she'd ever envisaged for her future – a wealth of material goods, but a terrible emptiness at her core?

She pushed a ring on to each finger. Fingers that were showing a slight thickening of the knuckles due to the onset of arthritis and the telltale faint brown spots that speak of age as surely as grey hairs and wrinkles. They reflected perfectly what she'd been to Lance. A bauble. Bright, shiny and expensive, for decorative purposes only. An oversized pair of earrings followed, clipped to her ears to weigh them down with pain. They were too big, the proportions all wrong for her small face. She should have realised that years ago.

Spreading an array of gold chains over her hand, she selected three and fastened them round her neck, then draped two bracelets on each wrist. It looked vulgar, but she didn't care. Today she would wear as many gaudy, glittery things as she could to remind her of the years she'd been viewed as nothing but a convenient ornament. Now they might belong to her past, but they would help to pay for her future. She'd done so much for Fossil Oil. She'd been the one behind Lance, supporting him, helping to make his toughest decisions, giving him some of his best ideas. Left to their own devices, all he and Bud Harman had managed to cook up was this stupid SACKED programme. God help them both. If Lance had run that by her first, she'd never have given it breathing space. Yet what did she have to show for it? Well, these things could count as wages owed. She'd been at the coalface alongside Lance all along and she'd damn well earned them. She scooped the rest of her jewellery into a black velvet bag and tucked it securely into her vanity case.

Lance snuffled in his sleep like a hibernating hedgehog. How could she have stayed with him for so long, when all of his waking life was viewed through the bottom of a bourbon bottle? He was oblivious to everything else in his life. Even when he was stone-cold sober, which wasn't often these days, he didn't actually see her – really *see* her. It was probably just as well, considering. She'd never have been able to sleep with Tyler Benson if Lance had cared in the slightest where she was spending her time.

Melissa stacked her vanity case next to its matching siblings. She'd loved Tyler Benson, *really* loved him, in a way that she'd never loved Lance. She'd loved him hopelessly, obsessively. But he was a using bastard and she now hoped with every fibre of her being that he got all he deserved. She felt sorry for Kirsten too, who was innocent in all this mess. Melissa had the urge to ring Kirsten, to confess to her affair with Tyler and apologise for her appalling behaviour. Would it help if she could warn Kirsten that she was in grave danger of becoming an exact replica of herself in ten years' time if she didn't wise up and get rid of Tyler soon? She could call her and try to make it right between them. But then, who was she to dole out advice?

She put out a fresh suit and shirt for Lance to wear to the office tomorrow. Then she chose his neckwear, as she had done for the duration of their life together. After today, she'd do it no more and Lance would be left to choose his own ties.

The cases were heavy as she dragged them one at a time down the sweeping stairs of their London house. Martin came out of the kitchen when he heard her and took them from her hands.

They exchanged a glance.

'Is that all, Mrs Harvey?'

'Yes.'

'I'll put them straight in the car for you.'

'Thank you, Martin. I'll be out in a few moments.'

In the study, in the top drawer of the writing desk, Melissa found the two British Airways e-tickets that Veronica had printed out for Lance for the flight to Washington. Their passports were there too, and she tucked both of them into her handbag. If she couldn't change her flight, this would delay Lance long enough to ensure he wasn't on the same plane as her.

This was one room that she hadn't had decorated for Christmas. Lance wouldn't have liked the fuss. She searched through the plethora of tiny drawers in the walnut desk until she found some plain white paper. It didn't seem quite right to use their own elaborately headed vellum for such a letter. Melissa sat at the desk and composed the note several times in her head before she finally picked up the fountain pen beside her. It was hard to know what to say to Lance – she didn't think they'd had a conversation in the last few years. Not a real one, a conversation that was longer than 'How was your day at the office today, honey?' and the automatic reply 'Fine, thank you, angel.'

286

Come to think of it, she wasn't sure if she'd had a proper conversation with anyone since the boys had left. *They* talked to her all right. They begged, pleaded and cajoled her, trying to get her to leave Lance and find a life of her own. A life that would exist after them. Since the boys had flown the nest, her days had been made up of a series of drinks parties interspersed with bouts of needless shopping, empty of company except for mindless chatter over the champagne and canapés.

Would it be any different without Lance? It was a frightening thought. Her fear was that she was now so ingrained in the corporate lifestyle that she'd be unable to adapt to anything else. Did anyone out there value a person who was pushing the half-century from the wrong side? Maybe she could do some charity work, as she'd suggested earlier tonight. In a paid position, rather than as a volunteer. Heaven knew, she'd had enough experience at that too. Whatever happened, at least she was giving herself a chance to find out before it was too late. But perhaps it already was. That was something she might also have to face. Terror gripped her stomach. Life out in the cold wouldn't be easy. She held the banister and steadied herself, gasping hot air into her lungs. There was still time to get Martin to bring the cases back into the house and unpack them without Lance being any the wiser.

What would her husband do without her? Lance leaned heavily on her. How would he manage at Fossil without her counsel? Would he suddenly be exposed as wanting? Who would have his back? It certainly wasn't Tyler Benson as he'd believed.

The house would run itself, of course. That wasn't a problem. They already had someone in to clean, do the laundry and tend the garden. Melissa cooked for him, after a fashion, but he could replace those duties easily enough. It was the small things she did at home that he'd miss. Choosing his cufflinks, buying

his socks, covering up for him when he was completely inco-
herent.

The blank paper loomed before her, but she forced herself to
write, pushing down the feeling of fear, of foreboding.

My dear Lance, I'm so sorry to do this, she wrote in her fine,
elaborate hand. *I'd hoped we'd grow old together and be a
comfort to each other, but I can no longer stay.*

She paused to fight down the emotion that threatened to
overwhelm her. Perhaps she should just wait for a few more
days. It was Christmas, after all. Perhaps she could go to
Washington with Lance, get him settled, and then leave. It
wasn't too late to change her mind. She took some deep breaths
and forced herself on.

*I want to take the chance to make something of what's left of
my life before it's too late.*

She hesitated on the next part, but her decision was made.

I've been having an affair with Tyler Benson. Her pen shook
as she wrote his name. To hell to handling this with dignity. She
was taking Tyler Benson down. See how he liked being cast
aside.

*I know you'll find this a devastating blow. You have trusted
Tyler and you've been wrong to do so. I thought we were in
love with each other, but I realise that wasn't the case. He's been
using me to find out confidential information about Fossil Oil
and I've been using him for my own infinitely more complex
reasons. I wanted you to know this. Disloyalty in such trusted
staff is almost as unforgivable as it is in a wife.*

Lance would dismiss him immediately, and it was no more
than he deserved.

*I'm so very, very sorry to cause you pain. There's more to life
than Fossil Oil, my angel. I hope that somehow you're able to
work that out.*

Make your peace with the boys before it's too late. They

would love a chance to be your sons. Be happy, Lance. I hope you'll think kindly of me in the future when we've had time to make new lives for ourselves. I did love you so very much. I still do.

Melissa xx

She paused for the ink to dry and, before she could think better of it, folded the note and slipped it into a matching envelope. She wrote Lance's name on the front and underlined it.

Melissa took the note through to the kitchen. The sky was lightening now, dawn well on its way, and yet she hadn't been to bed at all. She felt wired, calm, shaky and still all at once.

Taking a bowl from the cupboard, Melissa poured some muesli into it and put it on the table, perfectly positioned in front of Lance's preferred seat. Alongside it went a jug of skimmed-milk from the fridge. She poured a glass of 'freshly squeezed' orange from the Sainsbury's container and set that down too. No one could say that she hadn't tried to keep Lance healthy over the years, and she suspected she'd continue to worry about him even though she was leaving. She propped the goodbye note against his glass, fixing it just so. Lance would be furious when he came down. There was nothing he hated more than warm milk.

Martin came back into the kitchen. He'd put his jacket on. 'Are you ready, Mrs Harvey?'

'I think I am,' she said.

She followed Martin into the hall. He lifted her coat from the chair where she'd discarded it and held it open for her while she slipped her arms inside.

Melissa picked up her handbag while Martin took her vanity case for her. He held open the front door.

Taking a good, long look around the hall, she wondered whether she'd ever have a home like this again in the future. Tears burned behind her eyes, but she wouldn't let them fall.

The Christmas decorations were quite spectacular. The lights shone out bravely.

She opened the door and a cold wind whipped through the hall, cutting them to the quick.

'The car's nice and warm,' Martin assured her. Then he escorted her to the Bentley, taking her hand as she negotiated the icy steps, opening the door for her.

'Where to, Mrs Harvey?'

It was a good question. Where to indeed? She hadn't thought beyond leaving this house and Lance and boarding a plane back to America, yet the flight wasn't until tomorrow evening. She had a day and a half to kill until then.

'Do you have any friends you could stay with?'

'No.' She didn't even need to think about that one, but it hurt her to say it nevertheless.

'A hotel then?'

'Yes. Of course. To the Ritz please, Martin.' If this was going to be her last two days in England, she might as well enjoy them in style. Even on Christmas Eve, surely the Ritz would be able to find a little suite for her.

'An excellent choice,' Martin said, and closed the door.

It was a cold, grey dawn that failed to show the country at anywhere near its best. At least it wasn't raining that terrible misty rain that the English optimistically called mizzle. The rain that permeated even the most content of souls and bled every semblance of joy from the bones.

The Bentley pulled away, moving down their avenue, until Martin turned on to the main road and joined the steadily growing drip of traffic. Eventually he stopped looking in the rear-view mirror and focused his attention on the route.

When he did, Melissa took a small, embroidered linen handkerchief from her handbag. It was only then that she allowed herself to cry.

Christmas
Eve

Chapter Forty-five

Someone exceedingly helpful from Wadestone Manor had gone down to the staff block behind the main house, away from the blaze, and found Tyler a waiter's uniform to wear. White shirt, black trousers, black tailcoat. If it hadn't been so bloody cold, he would have eschewed the tailcoat. It made him look stupid. Plus it was too short in the arms, as were the trousers, which flapped around his ankles. For all the shortcomings in the sartorial-elegance department of his outfit, at least he was fully clothed again. They'd also managed to find him some trainers; they were a good two sizes too big, but he'd done the laces up tightly. They'd been abandoned in an unused wardrobe – for some time, apparently – and Tyler had shuddered as he'd reluctantly inched his feet into them. Someone else's underwear would have been a step too far, so he was commando under his trousers. Normally he'd find it quite a turn-on. Today he didn't.

He stood alone now and watched as the flames over Wadestone Manor climbed higher. There were six fire engines at the scene, and the firefighters were battling bravely to hold back the blaze. It looked as if they were winning. The main fire seemed to have been contained in the marquee, which was pretty much destroyed. There would be smoke damage in the house – and of course a new library door would be required –

but with some luck it would all be salvageable. Tyler only hoped they'd got bloody good insurance and that some minion hadn't forgotten to pay it.

The Fossil staff had been ushered away and were, not before time, on their way home in the company coaches, the lure of their beds suddenly stronger than their morbid curiosity. Some had started up a rather tasteless rendition of 'Disco Inferno' as they went. Tyler noted who they were. Lance's PA, Veronica, had taken a head-count and the missing employees were hunted down by the firefighters. William Failsworth, an unassuming events co-ordinator, had fallen asleep on the snooker table, which was sporting a large and unsightly gash due to the over-enthusiasm of its previous occupants. One of the head-office receptionists, Celia Barnes, and Jeff Jamieson, a usually very staid business analyst, were found still having carnal knowledge of each other in a linen cupboard. Jeff had been blissfully unaware that the flames were nearly round his ankles along with his trousers.

Of Kirsten he could find neither hide nor hair. She must, at some point in the evening, have gone home.

There was nothing else for Tyler to do now but follow her. Despite the roaring bonfire in front of him, his fingers were turning blue with cold and his feet had already gone completely numb. He stuffed his hands deep into his tailcoat pockets, digging vainly for some warmth. He hunched the collar up against the cold. Saying a final farewell and a grudging thank-you to Dale the fireman, he headed off towards his car, shivering as he did. The settled snow flurried round his ankles as he walked, soaking through his lightweight, borrowed and rather shabby trainers. The quiet crunch of his footsteps on the gravel path contrasted with the angry noise that was raging in his head. He wanted to hurt someone. He wanted to hurt someone very badly.

His Mercedes was the last vehicle left in the car park. When he saw it his heart, if humanly possible, sank even further. The scratch that encircled it etched into his soul. That little piece of handiwork had Kirsten's name written all over it. He knew that penknife would come back to haunt him. Seems as if his wife wasn't in a conciliatory mood.

The tyres were flat and, having survived the inferno, he was now going nowhere in a hurry. The tyre sealer that came in lieu of a spare these days wouldn't begin to repair them – not even one, let alone four – so he'd have to call someone to come out and replace them all. Thankfully, there was a signal out here, but the battery on his phone was dying. There was still just about enough left to surf the internet and find a company to come out and change the tyres.

When he'd done that, Tyler used more of his precious battery life to ring Kirsten, but there was no reply from her phone. When it switched over to voicemail, he couldn't actually think of what he wanted to say, so he hung up. Instead, he blipped open the car and crawled into the back seat. He wished they'd been the sort of couple who'd had picnics, then there might be a nice warm tartan blanket in the boot. But they weren't and there wasn't. Lying down on the cold leather seats, he huddled into himself. Seconds later, sleep mercifully found him.

The rapping on the window roused him, and for a moment Tyler wondered where he was and why he was dressed as a waiter. Then it all came flooding back. The knocking grew louder and, rubbing his eyes, he opened the door. Dawn would soon be breaking, but for now it was still dark and a low mist clung to the snowy ground.

'Come to do your tyres, mate,' the man from Ezee-Tires said. He rubbed his hands briskly against the cold.

Tyler wondered how he hadn't died of hypothermia. Even

inside the car, he could see his breath. His body was stiff from the couple of hours' sleep he'd managed to grab in extreme circumstances. What he wanted now was hot coffee and an even hotter shower.

He clambered out of the car while the man waited patiently, stamping his feet on the gravel with his heavy boots. If he thought there was anything odd about Tyler being in an ill-fitting waiter's uniform, he didn't mention it.

'It'll be done in a jiffy.' The man jerked a thumb towards the cab of his van. 'There's a flask of coffee on the dash, if you want a drop. You look like you could do with some.'

At least one of Tyler's prayers had been answered. 'Thank you,' he said fervently.

'Sit in the van. No need for us both to be out here freezing our knackers off.'

Tyler could have wept at his kindness.

So while the Ezee-Tires man replaced his sabotaged tyres, Tyler sat in the fuggy cab of the van and availed himself of the man's coffee, enjoying the brief hit of caffeine it gave him. That would sustain him enough for the drive home.

He'd have to try to smooth things over with Kirsten as quickly as possible: he needed to be bright-eyed and bushy-tailed and in the office before Lance. The things he'd learned last night were vital to his future career with Fossil Oil and he'd have to find out how much Lance remembered of it when he was sober. Even by Lance's standards, he'd been well out of it last night.

It sounded pretty much to Tyler as if this was Lance's swan-song. It might seem like a plum job for Lance, but Tyler was also sure it would be a one-way ticket to early-retirement oblivion. There was no way Lance would be coming back from this kamikaze mission. On the other hand, it could be a crucial launch pad for Tyler. As the obvious replacement for the UK chairman of Fossil Oil, he'd need time to prepare his strategy, talk to the right people, buy a bit of support if necessary. If Lance was being forced to walk the corporate plank, then Tyler might need to be right behind him, giving him a hefty shove.

The chairman's job had his name all over it. He'd be a figurehead. Plenty of glad-handing and elaborate, calorie-laden business lunches with the right people. That's one of the reasons why Lance was like a walking wine vat. That was all the chairman's job was: walking round being happy-happy-smiley.

It was one of the reasons that Tyler most wanted the job too. No more headaches over sales figures, profit-and-loss and bloody net contributions. That would be someone else's problem. He'd had enough of that stress. If it hadn't been for Josh Wallace performing above and beyond the call of duty this year, then Tyler's arse could have been on the line too. It didn't bear thinking about. So long as Josh was still the golden boy, Tyler could bask in the glow. And that was all right by him. He could even pull Josh up the ladder with him, so his back was always covered. Much as Lance had done with him.

His thoughts turned to Melissa. Perhaps he'd been too harsh with her. Even though they were leaving England, Lance would still have a certain amount of clout in Fossil for the time being, and it always paid to have more friends than you did enemies. Maybe he'd send her some flowers to her new home. Louise could find out where that was for him. Right before he fired her. If Melissa came back to London for a visit, it might not hurt to meet up with her again. They'd had some fun while it lasted, and he could always trust her to be discreet.

The man had finished changing his tyres, so Tyler handed over his credit card, and with more thanks he palmed him a twenty. Who'd want to be out changing tyres before dawn on Christmas Eve, for goodness' sake? Though they'd added more than enough to the bill to compensate. Great Christmas spirit, eh? Still, it was done and the man jumped into his van and drove away, leaving Tyler standing alone in the car park once more.

Climbing into his car, he gunned the engine and turned the heater to full blast in the hope of stopping the chattering of his teeth. He checked his phone but there was still nothing but a resounding silence from Kirsten. The battery was almost dead, and anyway it was too early to call her. She'd be tired and deserved a lie-in. If she'd had a long time to sleep on the antics of last night, it might put her in a better mood when he did turn up. Then again, if she was awake, she'd be tearing her hair out by now. Well, let her.

He turned the car slowly down the sweeping drive towards Wadestone Manor. Driving slowly past, he noted the smouldering wreckage of the marquee. The ice ammonite would be nothing but a puddle. All those metres of chiffon and sparkly bits, the resplendent Christmas trees and the fake icicles, all snuffed out in a matter of moments, totally obliterated, forgotten for ever. It was just a shame that the rest of the Christmas party couldn't suffer the same fate.

The firefighters were still battling away, pouring torrents of water on to it, and he suspected they'd be here for the rest of the day. But there was an air of success about them now and it seemed as if they'd got it under control. Black smoke mixed with the mist, and the air was thick with the acrid smell. Tyler closed the air vents in the Merc, put his foot down and wheeled away. There was going to be some serious aftermath from this Christmas party. He could feel it in his chilled bones.

As he drove through the wrought-iron gates at the entrance and headed for home, it started to snow again. Fat, lacy flakes splattered on his windscreen. Tyler sighed. That was all he needed. A white fucking Christmas.

Chapter Forty-six

Simon twined his fingers through Kirsten's hair. Tiny beads of sweat slicked her skin and glistened between her breasts. She cried again with elation and arched against him.

Giving a shudder and a sigh of satisfaction, he let his weight sink on to her, his dark hair resting against the white swell of her breast. His skin was soft and smooth and felt like silk against hers. He was tanned, his muscles firm and defined. The watery grey winter sun was struggling to get up as it was still the wrong side of a civilised time. Half-heartedly it pushed through the fading darkness and cloud cover, failing miserably in its attempts to bring any warmth into the room. Kirsten pulled the duvet over them and snuggled into the heat of Simon's body. Despite the attempts of the weather outside, in here there was sunshine in her heart.

A few hours ago, the man lying next to her had been Simon the old flame, the one that got away. Now he was Simon her lover, her future, the old flame having been fanned into a brilliant, burning fire once again. A few hours ago she had been a faithful, unhappily married woman. Now she was an unfaithful and very happy one.

Flipping himself lazily on to his back and flinging his arm above him across the pillow, Simon eased her body against his.

Her lover's hair was tousled from sleep and stuck out at erratic angles, caused mainly by the bits in between the sleep.

'Good morning,' she said as he softly kissed the top of her head.

'You sound bright and breezy.' Simon looked down at her.

She felt it. Despite the lack of sleep and the hint of a hangover, there was a lightness in her soul that had been missing for too long.

'No second thoughts?' His voice was laced with concern.

'Not one.'

'That's good to know.'

'Now all we have to do is sort out the rest of our lives,' she said with a laugh. 'And I think that's better done after I've had a cup of tea.'

'I can take a hint.'

'You stay here.' She kissed him again. 'I think you've more than earned tea in bed.'

As Kirsten slid out from between the sheets, he caught her by the wrist.

'It was good, wasn't it?' His voice was thick with emotion. 'Just like old times. Exactly as I remembered.'

She turned his hand and planted a gentle kiss on the palm. 'It was like coming home.'

Kirsten reached for her dressing-gown, suddenly self-conscious in her nakedness. This had all moved way faster than she could ever have imagined. She brushed her hair with long, languorous strokes, watching herself in the mirror. Who was this strange, reckless creature that looked back at her? Kirsten wasn't sure, but she knew she liked her.

'I'd better think about making a move,' he said ruefully and with a wary glance at the alarm clock. 'I don't fancy facing Tyler's fury.'

'Tyler won't be home just yet,' Kirsten assured him. 'He'll

have found somewhere to spend the night.' Probably with Louise, if she knew anything about her errant husband. 'Nothing would get him up at this hour after the Christmas party. We're fine for a few hours, I'm sure.'

'I should at least call Lance,' he said. 'Let him know of my decision.'

'Are you sure about that?' That Simon would give up so much for her in an instant was a heady thought.

'Absolutely.'

'Then I'll leave you to it while I make us something to eat.' It was unlike her to be ravenous in the morning, but then so much about the last few hours had been unlike her.

'Mind if I hop in the shower too?'

'Help yourself,' she said. 'If there's anything you need, just shout.'

'Someone to scrub my back?'

Briefly she thought about joining him, and then realised that she'd been reckless enough for now. There was only so much you could do on an empty stomach.

'You're a big boy. You can manage.' She pulled her dressing-gown tighter and went down to the kitchen. 'I'll be back soon.'

In the kitchen, she made tea and found some bacon in the fridge. Simon had always loved bacon sandwiches for Sunday brunch – a time when they used to lie together on the sofa, feet entwined, sharing the newspapers, reading out titbits to each other, lazing the day away. Kirsten allowed herself a contented smile. She was looking forward to doing that with him again.

As she boiled the kettle for some tea and put the bacon on the grill pan, the doorbell rang. A glance at the clock told her that it was still before seven and, heart sinking, she knew the only person it could be.

She walked to the window by the front door and craned her neck to look. A rather dishevelled Tyler was standing on the pavement in what appeared to be a waiter's uniform. He didn't look very happy at all.

She hadn't expected him for hours, but if she had to face him now, so be it. Kirsten cracked the door open, blocking the way with her body.

'You'd deadlocked the door and left your key in the lock,' Tyler complained.

'Yes.'

'Why?'

'Because I'm leaving you,' she said. 'Or, more accurately, you're leaving me.'

'Don't be silly.'

'Why are you dressed as a waiter?'

'Long story. Let me in, Kirsten.'

'No. I'll get you a change of clothes, and after Christmas we can discuss divorce arrangements.'

He recoiled at that. 'Divorce? Have you lost your mind?'

'I think I've just found it, Tyler.' She looked at him with sadness. 'We can't go on like this. I know that. You know that. There are no children involved. We can have a clean break.'

'I don't want a clean break,' he insisted. 'I don't want a break at all.' He leaned against the doorframe, his face close to hers. 'I love you.'

'In your own way, I'm sure you do. But it's not enough anymore. I don't want to be beholden to you. I don't want to be beholden to Fossil Oil.'

'This is about what you thought you saw at the Christmas party, isn't it?' He sighed. 'You were mistaken. That wasn't me with Louise, it was Josh Wallace. She told me what happened.'

'Oh, Tyler. Listen to yourself. You don't think I'm going to believe that? I saw what I saw. Let's both live with that.'

'I will not have my marriage end because of a stupid mistake. *Your* mistake.'

302

She could tell him now all she knew about the emails he'd concocted all those years ago to break up her and Simon's relationship, but what was the point? Tyler would only deny it, and that would only mean more time spent arguing on the doorstep. He didn't need to know what had finally tipped her over the edge. She was leaving and that was the end of that. 'You don't actually have any choice. It's over.'

'Don't be like this, Kirsten. You're angry. I can understand that. But you've got it all wrong. I can explain if you just let me in,' Tyler wheedled. 'We can talk about it over a coffee. You know what the Christmas party's like. I've had a terrible night, Kirsten. First there was Lance's bombshell announcement, then I nearly got sawn in half by the fucking magician, then you thought I was shagging Louise when I wasn't and, to top it all, the marquee went up in flames and I had to be rescued bare-arsed by a burly fireman in front of the entire staff. I'm emotionally exhausted.'

'Oh, Tyler.' Kirsten folded her arms. 'Why is it always you in the middle of a drama?' Not that she believed half of his stupid sob story.

'It's Christmas Eve. Christmas Day tomorrow,' he pleaded. 'I'll tell you the full story later. I'll tell you why I'm wearing these stupid clothes. I'll open a bottle of fizz. Good stuff. And we'll be laughing all about it by Boxing Day.'

'I'll pack you a bag,' Kirsten said. 'You need to find somewhere else to stay.'

'On Christmas Eve?' He looked horrified. 'You can't be serious.'

'Perhaps Louise will accommodate you.'

'That's beneath you, Kirsten. There is nothing, *absolutely* nothing between me and Louise. I *love* you. You know I do.'

'Wait here,' she said. 'I'll be back in five minutes. Is there anything in particular you want?'

'No! Yes! I want you!'

'I'm afraid that's the one thing you can't have.' Kirsten closed the door, relocking it and once again blocking the lock by leaving the key in it. Despite her calm exterior, her heart was beating erratically.

Quickly she climbed the stairs. There was only so long that Tyler would remain outside. It would be just like him to try to kick the door in.

In the bedroom, she could still hear the shower running, and Simon was humming tunelessly beneath the torrent, blissfully unaware of the confrontation that was occurring at the front door. She closed the bathroom door so that it would stay that way. No need for Simon to be involved in this. It would only turn ugly if Tyler knew the truth, and she couldn't cope with any pistols-at-dawn stuff.

She grabbed Tyler's overnight bag from the wardrobe and filled it with clean underwear, socks, his favourite tie and a couple of shirts. Tyler's many suits hung in a tidy row, interspersed with equal gaps that smacked of military precision. Kirsten selected one, a mid-grey, mid-weight wool by Hugo Boss. She slotted it into a carry bag and draped that over her arm.

The doorbell rang again and Tyler let his finger stay on the buzzer longer than was strictly necessary. No matter. She was just about done.

Thankfully, he always left toiletries in the main bathroom too, so she was able to give him all he needed for a few days from there. She squeezed his sponge bag into the case, then closed the lid against the bulge of clothing and firmly shut the clasps.

Tyler rapped violently on the knocker. It was a brass lion's head and wasn't used to this sort of abuse.

She was already on her way downstairs when she heard him

shout, 'Kirsten, I know you can hear me!' He battered the door with his fists. 'Stop this silliness now, darling. Let me in!' He thumped again. He tried the bell and the knocker simultaneously. 'Open this door, Kirsten, or I'll kick the fucking thing in!'

Kirsten opened the door. Tyler was red in the face and foaming at the mouth. He was pacing up and down like a raging bull in his waiter's outfit. Mrs Hartley-Brown from number 42 was watching from behind the safety of her French shutters.

'You're waking the neighbours, Tyler.'

'It's Christmas Eve,' he roared. 'They've got a lot to do anyway.' He turned and gave Mrs Hartley-Brown the finger.

'I've packed you a bag,' Kirsten said. 'You can collect the rest of your belongings after Christmas.'

She put it at his feet and Tyler stared at it, all anger gone from him. 'You can't do this, Kirsten. This is me. Tyler. You love me. I'm your husband. For better, for worse. Remember that? What's brought this on all of a sudden? I thought we were happy.'

'I've been unhappy for years, Tyler.' She shook her head. 'You know that.'

'We can work it out. I promise. I said we would. We were going to spend Christmas talking.'

'I'm past that point.'

'I'll call you later,' he said. 'You'll feel differently then.'

She was wavering. She knew she was, and he knew it too. How *could* she do this to Tyler at Christmas? Yet she could hardly let him into the house now. Then he would know that her decision had been spurred by Simon's return. She didn't feel she owed Tyler any explanations at all.

'I have nowhere to go, Kirsten,' he said pathetically and, though she didn't want it to, it still tore at her insides.

Then he glanced at his watch and his mood changed. 'Look, I've got to get to work. I need to sort out the mess that Lance created last night. But I promise I'll come home early, as soon as I've finished, and we can sort this out.'

Kirsten smiled grimly to herself. And there was the rub. Whatever was going on in Tyler's life – his marriage could be crashing down around his ears – Fossil Oil would always come first.

He picked up his bag. 'Are there shoes in here?' he asked. 'I need shoes.'

She stared down at the garish trainers on his feet. 'Where did yours go?'

'I told you, it's a long story,' Tyler said. 'I'll fill you in on the details later when I come home.'

There was a pair on the stand in the hallway and she handed them to him.

Tyler moved away from the door. 'I *will* be back,' he said earnestly. 'I'm not letting you go without a fight.'

He threw the overnight bag, suit and shoes into the back of the car. The car that now seemed to have a deep, ugly scratch all round it. No doubt there would be a long story about that too. Well, she had no interest in it.

'Merry Christmas, Tyler,' she said. Her heart tightened with sadness, with regret. 'I hope you find happiness.'

'Some things are worth fighting for, Kirsten. You'll see.' He jumped into his car and wound down the window. 'This is *not* goodbye.'

But it was goodbye. Kirsten stood and watched him pull away. He waved at her hopefully as he drove down the street. Emotion closed her throat and she bit down on the tears that threatened. Perhaps if he'd noticed Simon's car parked a few doors down, he might have realised that he had a bigger problem on his hands than he imagined.

Chapter Forty-seven

Chubby fingers prise my eyelids apart until my eyes focus on a beaming face an inch away from my nose.

'Morning, Mia,' I say, yawning. Sometimes I wish I had a partner, just so he could take his turn with Mia's waking-up ritual.

'Wake up, Mummy,' she says, holding my eyes open. 'We've got things to do.'

I groan and cuddle her into me. 'Five more minutes.'

However, she's already in full fidget mode and any thought of sleep goes out of the window. I lift my head from the pillow and it throbs unhappily. I should have stuck to my most excellent plan of not drinking last night.

Even though Mia isn't at school today, she still wakes up at six o'clock to start her mission of getting me out of bed. While she sings to me – something so tuneless that I struggle to recognise it – the fog in my brain gradually starts to clear. It might not be a bad idea for me to get up straight away and head into the office. I want to be there long before Tyler so that I can compose my thoughts about last night, and without fail he gets in early. A little Christmas party isn't going to make the irrepressible Tyler Benson late for work.

I also need to type out my resignation letter. Though it pains me, I can't go on working for him. The man is a moral vacuum and serial groper. I'd like to think that I could stick it out until I found something else to go to – jobs are hard to come by these days – but after what happened last night, that really isn't a viable option.

'Come on, Mummy,' Mia urges again.

So, with heavy heart, I haul myself out of bed. I'm disappointed with myself as I don't want to be letting my daughter down. Or my parents. If I'm not working, then the burden of looking after us financially falls to them again. I can only hope it's not for too long.

'Is Gramps up yet?'

Mia nods. 'I heard him in the kitchen.'

'Be a good girl and ask him to make your breakfast while Mummy has a shower.'

Without argument for once, she takes her teddy, slips on her fluffy pink dressing-gown and toddles downstairs to see her adoring grandad. Dad makes the most perfect boiled egg, her favourite breakfast. One that she very rarely gets when I have to make it for her.

Making the most of my five minutes of peace, I stand in the shower and let the hot water work its magic on my hangover. The remnants of my expensive hairdo have morphed into a bird's nest this morning. So I wash and dry it straight, then, with a liberal application of make-up, I'm almost ready to face the world again.

In the hall, the dancing, glowing Santa Claus is already in operation. Mum is excelling herself. I daren't even open the living-room door as it won't help my pounding head one bit. But then, it is Christmas Eve. If Mum had her way, Christmas would start in August. At the latest.

When I join them in the kitchen, breakfast is in full flow and, of course, every single song on the radio is a Christmas tune. There's absolutely no putting it off now.

'Tea, love?' Dad asks. He looks as if he's been up and dressed for hours. No doubt Mum has organised him a long list of tasks for today, since he doesn't have to go in to work.

'Coffee,' I say. 'Strong. Very strong.'

'That bad?'

I nod my head, and instantly regret it.

'Will you be able to come home early today?' Mum says. She's still in her dressing-gown as the kitchen is very much Dad's domain in the morning.

'I don't know. I'll have to see how the day pans out.'

'But it's Christmas Eve. Surely there won't be much to do.'

This is the point at which I should tell them that my new, kick-ass career is already in tatters. I should tell them that I'm having to resign due to leaving my boss abandoned in the nude because he has done nothing but try to grope my boobs and bum for the last few months. But of course, total coward that I am, I don't. I can't tell them before Christmas and spoil their festive mood.

Instead I say, somewhat lamely, 'I don't know what the routine is at Fossil Oil as this is my first Christmas.' And last, it would seem.

Dad hands me a coffee that looks as if it would revive a corpse and I gulp it gratefully. The hit of caffeine sends a shudder through me. Then he passes me a slice of lightly buttered toast with words I've heard too many times in my life. 'This'll put a lining on your stomach, Lou-Lou.'

I lean against the work surface and dread the moment that I have to move.

'Don't eat standing up,' Mia says, proving that, on rare occasions, she does listen to me.

I'm probably going to have to face Josh Wallace this morning too, and that sends a rush through me that I can't decide is fear or elation. Perhaps things will look different this morning, as they so often do. He may have arrived home and wondered what he was doing thinking about getting entangled with an insolvent single mum. Whichever way, I hope he's realised that, if he's looking for a quick and uncomplicated shag, I'm not his woman.

Mum waggles her head to catch my attention. 'Dad and I were thinking of taking a certain someone into the shopping centre this afternoon to see . . .' and she mouths, 'S A N T A.'

'Santa!' Mia cries. 'Santa!' She's very good at spelling. 'We're going to see Santa!'

Mum looks at me apologetically, but she's the one who will now have to deal with Mia in hyperactive mode for most of the day.

'You come too, Mummy,' my daughter pleads. 'You can tell Santa that I'm the best little girl in the world.'

'I'll try,' I say. 'But I can't promise.'

Her face falls.

'I have to work, sweet pea, but I'll write a note for Granny to give him, just in case I'm not back in time.' I scribble on the bottom of Mum's shopping list.

I glance at my watch. 'I'd better head to the office.'

Mum touches my arm. 'Work isn't everything, Louise,' she says. 'Always remember that.'

'Yeah, yeah.' I wish. Again I fail to tell her that I'm going to have acres and acres of time on my hands in the very near future.

Scooping Mia into my arms, I give her a big, slobbery kiss and she squeals as she tries to wriggle away from me. 'Be good today, mini-monster.' Then, to Mum: 'I'll text you to let you know what time I'm coming home.'

The staff car park is empty as I swing into Fossil Oil. The roads were a bit slithery this morning, due to the snow that fell overnight, so it took longer than I'd anticipated to get here.

Why does everyone forget how to drive the minute a snowflake lands? The traffic was hell. I needn't have worried, though, as there's hardly anyone else in sight. They're probably afflicted with similar transport problems. Those who aren't too hungover to get out of bed, that is. It's with some relief that I notice Tyler's reserved space is also mercifully empty. A wave of nausea grips me when I think about facing him today. How bold, how vengeful I felt last night with a few glasses of champagne down my neck and my daring act of defiance. Not feeling quite so clever this morning, eh, Louise?

In reception, Celia Barnes, wearing dark glasses, is slumped over the desk, head on arms and, if the wet, snoring noises are any indication, fast asleep. She looks as if she still has the remnants of party poppers in her hair and there's a little dribble of saliva coming from the corner of her mouth. I wonder whether to wake her, but think better of it. She looks like she needs her beauty sleep.

Usually there's a little morning rush at the café in the atrium but today it's as dead as a doornail. I'm the only person around, so I order an Americano with an extra shot: I need something to get me through today.

Taking the lift to my floor, I walk through the open-plan outer office. Most of the desks are still empty, but the people who are here are in a similar state to Celia, slumped over their desks with not even a pretence of working. Normally there's the gentle babble of conversation, the hum of activity. But all is silent. At one of the stations, I can see a man stretched out asleep underneath the desk, still wearing his dinner suit from last night. As I tiptoe through, hoping not to disturb anyone, he gives the occasional rasping snore. Perhaps I should go back downstairs, get a tray of coffee for everyone and charge it to Tyler's expenses. Then I think that I've already done enough damage and should leave well alone.

I swing by Karen's office, but it's currently deserted and she's nowhere to be seen. I hope everything turned out well for her last night and that she managed to go home with someone, anyone. Maybe she had an encounter with one of the firemen models, or even a real firefighter, and is happily tucked up in bed somewhere. Fingers crossed she's OK and didn't get up to too much mischief. No doubt I'll hear all about it sometime. If this is to be my last day at Fossil Oil, I'll call Karen later and arrange to have a catch-up coffee with her in the new year. If she's still talking to me.

I scribble out a note wishing her a merry Christmas and leaving my phone number for her.

When I reach my office, the cheery explosion of Christmas decorations lifts my spirits. Amid the bleakly tasteful minimalism of Fossil Oil, it's an oasis of festive tat. I sit at my desk and switch on my computer.

I expect it won't be long before Tyler's here, and I brace myself to do what I have to do. Opening a new document, I type the words that I really don't want to. I'm letting myself down. I'm letting Mia down. I'm letting my parents down. But it has to be done.

Dear Mr Benson. I think formal rather than informal is more appropriate, given the circumstances. *Please accept my resignation.*

Chapter Forty-eight

It wasn't exactly the homecoming Tyler had expected. If he was truthful, he'd hoped Kirsten would be distraught, pacing the floor, torn between anger and relief when he eventually arrived, not knowing whether to condemn or capitulate, cry or crack him around the head with a karate chop.

Instead, there she was, *lounging* casually – very casually – against the doorframe, looking ... well, rather self-satisfied. There was something else about her too. A sort of disconcerting glow that he'd seen before, he was sure, but not for a long time.

He pulled on to the M1 to head to the office – the traffic even busier than usual as it was Christmas Eve. All those people headed home to see their loved ones, and here was he with an overnight bag on the back seat and a flea in his ear.

Then he smiled to himself. It was Christmas. Kirsten wouldn't stay mad at him for long. Of course she'd take him back. She always did.

The fact that he didn't come home – through no fault of his own, it should be stressed – obviously hadn't kept her from her beauty sleep as she was looking a little more than tousled. Perhaps she'd been in bed but hadn't been able to sleep through worrying about him. Not that Kirsten ever let on. His wife was a woman who liked to keep her cards close to her chest.

There were traces of make-up round her eyes, so she obviously hadn't bothered with her usual half-hour bedtime scrubbing-up routine in front of the mirror either. Tyler's mouth turned up at the corners. Of course, she was playing one of her silly little games. All this was her feeble attempt to show him that she didn't care. After ten years of marriage he ought to recognise her repertoire by now. Mind you, when Kirsten decided to play ice-cool, she could freeze water with just one stare. Well, this time he wasn't going to play by her rules.

He'd almost said to her that he wasn't going to beg. But of course he was going to beg. He was going to beg and cajole and vow to change permanently. And mean it this time. He *would* change. If it killed him, he'd be home by seven-thirty every night. First he'd let her stew a little longer. Kirsten obviously didn't realise just how close she came to losing him sometimes.

He'd been unfaithful too many times recently. Yet in ten years of marriage he'd only had about ten affairs. One a year on average. That wasn't bad going. If you thought about it, he'd only been 10 per cent unfaithful. Which meant, in effect, he'd been totally and utterly committed to Kirsten for 90 per cent of the time. How many husbands could say that? In the scheme of things it could have been a lot worse.

The annoying part was that she suspected him of playing away with Louise, and that was never going to be on the cards now. That woman was out as soon as he got to the office. That would make Kirsten happy. If he followed it up with a holiday in the Seychelles, and perhaps a new car, then he was home and dry. Job done, walk away.

When he stopped for the first traffic jam, Tyler sat and rubbed his hands over his weary face. This was different though. This had a nastier smell than his locker at the golf club. He just knew there was something awful lurking behind it, but he couldn't quite put his finger on it. Kirsten had always been so resilient. The harder you knocked her down, the faster she bounced back. Why was there no fight in her this time? How could she do this to him? Particularly now, when he was ready to transform them into Terry and June. And all over a stupid Christmas party.

Why on earth did she want to become independent at her time of life? He'd always provided well for her. She might well moan about him working all the hours God sent, but it didn't stop her taking the holidays, stuffing the wardrobes with designer gear and driving round in the top-of-the-range car that it paid for.

By the time he reached the office, he was already tired. Bloody bone-tired. He parked his car in his executive space, but even that failed to give him the usual thrill. It took a great effort for him to turn off the heater and get out of the door. Lance wasn't here yet, which was one small mercy. In fact, the whole executive car park looked like a ghost town. It would give Tyler time to get himself back into gear. The very first thing he would do was go to Lance's office, shower in his private bathroom and get rid of this ridiculous outfit.

The chill morning air made his waiter's uniform feel like a layer of tissue paper and the marble steps up to the revolving door were radiating toe-numbing cold through his feet. The whole office would be a total mess today, except for one person. And, in Tyler's view, that one person – his good self – had probably suffered the most.

Chapter Forty-nine

Kirsten clanked the cups as she set them out on the tray and then hugged herself as she waited for the kettle to boil. She'd felt a deep sense of sadness when she'd finally closed the door on Tyler. Unbelievably, her resolve had almost slipped. Almost.

He'd looked so pathetic standing there in his ill-fitting waiter's uniform, a look of dazed bewilderment marring his haggard but still-handsome face. She must have an incredibly strong nurturing instinct if she still had the urge to give Tyler hot sweet tea and Hedex and run a warm bath for him after all he'd put her through. It was hard to be the one causing the hurt, rather than the one getting hurt. But then there was a lurking satisfaction that eased itself to the forefront of her brain, combined with the sure and certain knowledge that she was doing the right thing, and the moment was gone.

It wasn't much of a goodbye after ten years of marriage and certainly not the scenario she'd envisaged, even in her blacker moments. Perhaps if Simon hadn't been waiting for her, keeping her bed and her heart warm, she would have taken Tyler back yet again and the whole jolly circus would have kept on rolling. Knowing that Simon loved her had given her the strength to move on, the final push to leave. Without him, would she have had the courage to see it through? She hoped she would.

No doubt Tyler would bombard her with flowers – ordered by his all-too-obliging assistant, Louise – when he realised that she really didn't intend to take him back this time. She wondered what Louise would think when she heard that Tyler was to have his freedom. There would be no wife providing a convenient excuse against commitment to hide behind. Tyler could be an emotional cripple all on his own. If Louise wanted him she was more than welcome to him. And jolly good luck to her. Heaven knew, the girl was going to need it. She looked so nice too, but Kirsten knew only too well that looks could be so deceptive. Perhaps Louise would see through Tyler's lies sooner than she had and would kick him into touch, but that was up to her. Love, as they so often say, is so often blind.

With a resounding ping, two slices of toast shot out of the toaster. Reaching for the butter, Kirsten applied it liberally. Today, the polyunsaturates could sod off. If she felt like clogging her arteries she would. The bacon smelled wonderful. She slipped it from the grill and the smoky, aromatic scent filled her nostrils. Her stomach rumbled in anticipation. It was going to taste wonderful, she knew it. Carelessly she flung it on to the toast with her fingers, licking the tasty remnants of fat from their scalded tips. She poured the water into the teapot and wondered whether old flames masquerading as oil-industry executives still liked Earl Grey tea for breakfast.

Hands laden with the tray, she kicked open the bedroom door. Simon was out of the shower, drying his hair, towel low on his hips. He wasn't a mirage. He was still here in the flesh, literally, and she could hardly believe it.

He smiled lazily at her. 'Did I hear someone at the door?'

'Hmm,' she said, nibbling a corner of the toast.

'Anyone important?'

Kirsten shook her head. 'No. Not really.'

The future, with nothing planned at all, opened up ahead of

her. It was hers, to make it all that she wanted. She could go where she liked, do what she liked. She was free to be loved as she'd always wanted to be. The thought was intoxicating. There'd be no corporate directives, no strategic postings, no Executive Development Programme. It wasn't only Tyler she was escaping from.

'So, what shall we do now, Kirsten Benson?'

'I think we should go back to bed. Eat breakfast. Make love.'

Simon nodded. 'Sounds like a plan.'

Slipping off her dressing-gown, she slid back into bed. Simon dispensed with his towel and joined her. His skin was warm, damp and delicious. Freshly showered, he looked young and firm. She wanted him again, but didn't want to appear too greedy for him. Kirsten smiled wickedly. Once upon a time, she'd thought Tyler was good in bed. It was funny how wrong you could be.

'We could skip the breakfast part,' Simon suggested.

'We can't live on lurve alone,' she countered.

He nuzzled into her neck. 'We could try.'

She laughed at that. 'You old romantic. Besides, there's no rush, we have all the time in the world.'

'We do,' he said. 'I very much like the sound of that.'

Nevertheless, in one smooth movement, he pushed the tray to one side and reached for her.

'I guess there's plenty of time for me to cook more bacon too,' Kirsten whispered as he pulled her close.

Chapter Fifty

Lance struggled to focus on the alarm clock through one open eye – the clock that had singularly failed to raise any alarm at six o'clock, when he usually rose. It told him that it was now nine o'clock and he would be desperately late for the office. Though it didn't really matter when you were the boss and it was Christmas Eve. He wouldn't be the only one who was tardy today. It must have been one hell of a party last night. He didn't remember a thing about it, which usually went to prove that he'd had a great time.

Still, Melissa would normally have woken him before now. She was failing in her duties, which was most unlike her. Perhaps she'd hit it hard last night too.

It was his last day at Fossil Oil in the UK and there was a river of red tape to wade through before he handed over. Bud 'the Hatchet' Harman had wanted to send in one of those high-flying young bucks to replace him, but he knew he could manage to talk him round. He needed someone he could trust inside Fossil in Europe to help him shake and make the corporate strategy for the future. He knew how the Brits liked to play it. Close to their chests. They didn't go in for flash, fast dealing.

It had taken him a good few of his many years at Fossil Oil to develop a loyal, caring team, and he knew who he wanted to

319

run the show from this end. Tyler Benson might be an arrogant son of a bitch on occasion, but he ran a tight ship. There was no denying that. He demanded the best from his team and he got it – by fair means or foul. When the line on everyone else's graphs was plummeting steadily earthwards, Tyler Benson's was still soaring to the skies. Most of it due to the superhuman contribution from his top sales manager, Josh Wallace. That young guy was impressive too. He was one of Fossil's rising stars. No doubt today's end-of-year sales figures would give him the ammunition he needed to fight his corner with Bud Harman.

Lance couldn't wait for this Conway chap to get on board too. There was someone who had oil flowing in his veins, with balls enough not to let Tyler get the better of him. Together they'd make a great team. He'd thought he was supposed to be at the Christmas party last night – a great opportunity for him to meet Tyler and the rest of the staff – but in the event he hadn't seen him. No matter. He'd be in harness soon enough. Lance checked the clock again. No more dilly-dallying. He needed to move himself and get into the office.

He turned over in bed to say good morning, but Melissa wasn't there. She must have slept in the spare room. Sometimes she did when she was restless.

Lance hauled himself out of bed, ignoring the dizziness that accompanied the move. In the shower, he let the soothing water revive his dull and aching body before slipping into his freshly laundered white shirt and business suit which were already laid out for him. Melissa was normally up and about with the lark. He popped his head round the door of the spare room, but the bed hadn't been slept in.

He went downstairs to the kitchen and was puzzled to find the table set for his breakfast. So Melissa *must* be up. Unless she did all this before she went to bed? The sight of muesli reclining drily in the bowl turned his stomach. It was bad enough the inside of his mouth feeling like a birdcage without adding to the effect by shoving seeds inside it. He would get the staff restaurant to send up a bacon-and-egg sandwich to his desk when he got to the office. There was nothing like a good dose of cholesterol to counteract the effects of a heavy drinking session. That was the key to it, and one that had served him well for many years. He just didn't tell Melissa. She had a morbid fear of cholesterol and spent her life trying to get him to eat udon noodles and couscous.

There was a note in Melissa's spidery handwriting propped against the glass of orange juice beside the bowl. He didn't have his reading glasses on, but it would probably tell him where she was. As he reached for it, the world span round a little. There was a tight pain gripping his chest, just like it had last night. He remembered that much. Lance lurched forward, clutching at the breakfast bar but instead knocking over the glass. The note, the glass and the bowl all tumbled to the floor, the latter two smashing against the slate tiling.

'God damn it,' Lance muttered. There was glass, muesli and juice everywhere. The note was swimming in it, the ink already blurred. There was no way he'd be able to read it now. Instead he punched Melissa's number into his phone and called her. It rang but, unusually, went straight to voicemail.

She'd probably gone to the gym or the shops or the hairdresser or somewhere else of national importance. Lance smiled to himself. She was a good woman, Melissa. Her business acumen had proved invaluable over the years too. No one had any inkling that she was the author of many of his best policies. That was their little secret. As was his love of alcohol. There weren't many who would have stood by him – not since the drinking became a regular habit – but she was his rock.

Oh, he knew about the other men in her life, but, well, she

321

was an attractive woman. Not just attractive – goddamn beautiful. And he knew she had needs. Needs that he couldn't fulfil – also not since the drinking became a regular habit. He may not be able to please her in the bedroom any more, but he tried to make up for it in other ways. He bought her diamonds, and ... and – well, mainly he bought her diamonds. At least she was discreet. There was no doubt about that. But he knew. He might get blind drunk, but he wasn't blind.

There was someone in the UK who she'd become attached to. He could tell that. Moving to Washington DC would be a new start for them. Melissa, despite her protests, would love it. She would be the belle of the ball. Even after all these years, he was proud to have her on his arm. She was the love of his life. From the moment he first set eyes on her, she always had been. Perhaps, with this new job, they could find time to be together more.

Time to go tie up the loose ends at Fossil UK. The cleaner would come in later and sort out this mess. Lance picked the *Financial Times* from the table and tucked it under his arm.

Pulling on his cashmere coat, he strode purposefully towards the Bentley, which was already waiting outside. Lance glanced at his watch. It was just before ten.

'Morning, Martin,' he said to his driver as he opened the door for him.

'Good morning, Mr Harvey,' Martin replied politely.

Lance settled himself in the back seat and shook open the newspaper. Shares up, shares down. Always doom and gloom.

'Martin, did you take Mrs Harvey anywhere this morning?'

'No,' Martin replied, 'I didn't, Mr Harvey.'

Martin, who had been waiting patiently for Lance outside the house since seven o'clock, and after only an hour's fitful sleep in the car, pulled into the steady stream of traffic and headed back towards the offices of Fossil Oil.

Chapter Fifty-one

I've just finished typing my resignation letter when Tyler slams into the office. He's like a bear with a sore head. He's also wearing an ill-fitting waiter's suit with a tailcoat and looks as if he hasn't been to bed.

'I don't know what you think you're doing here,' he barks by way of greeting.

'I'm only here to offer my resignation.'

'No need to offer your resignation,' Tyler says with a forced smile.

My heart lifts a little. Maybe he doesn't bear a grudge.

'Because you're fired,' he adds.

He does bear a grudge.

'I'm really sorry about last night,' I start. 'I shouldn't have left you like that, but it was the straw that broke the camel's back.' I take a deep breath. In for a penny, in for a pound. 'I've had enough of you touching me up whenever you think you can get away with it. You're always coming on to me, Tyler, and I don't like it. You treat me with no respect.'

He recoils at that, but soon he's biting back. '*I* treat *you* with no respect? Can I just remind you, *Ms* Young, that *you're* the one who left *me* stark bollock naked at the Christmas party?'

He has a point.

'I had to be rescued by firemen.'

'Firemen?' Now I'm confused. 'From what?'

'The fire.'

'What fire?'

'Another little matter from the aftermath of the delightful Christmas party is that there's nothing left of the marquee at Wadestone Manor,' Tyler informs me.

When I look aghast at him, he sighs. 'A fire started at the end of the party. It was a miracle it didn't spread to the rest of the building. No doubt you'd high-tailed it out of there by then. Or maybe you started it?'

'Don't be ridiculous.'

'I wouldn't put anything past you now, Louise. You'd locked me in the library, remember? *Locked!* When the fire started they had to smash the door to smithereens and lift me out of one of the windows, on a ladder. How does that make you feel, Ms Clever Clogs?'

Faintly nauseous.

'Thanks to you, the majority of Fossil Oil's employees are now intimately acquainted with my arsehole.'

I can see why he wouldn't be pleased with that. 'Was everyone else safe?'

'Yes. No casualties. The firemen got everyone out unharmed. Though I did hope that The Magnificent Marvo had burned to death in a horrible manner. No such luck.'

He looks at me in a way that says he hoped I might have too.

'Is that why you're wearing a waiter's outfit?'

'Yes. And the reason I'm carrying an overnight bag and sporting a suit over my arm is that my wife has seen fit to throw me out.'

I brace myself for this.

'It's Christmas,' he reminds me. 'I have nowhere to go. This is your fault too.'

'I can call her,' I suggest. 'Explain what happened.'

'She'd never believe you. It will be down to *me* to sort it out. But this will cost me dearly, Louise. I want you to know that.'

'I'm sorry.' It's safe to say that I'm now feeling like the worst person in the world.

'Get rid of all this tat.' He gestures at my Christmas decorations. 'Get the rest of your stuff and get out.'

I gulp. So this really is it.

'You're bright,' he says. 'You could have gone places with me behind you, but you had to go and fuck it up.'

Now I feel like lying on the floor and weeping.

'I'm going to go into Lance's private shower room before he arrives, get cleaned up and change into my business suit. By the time I return, I want you gone.' He holds up a hand and gives me a cheery wave. 'Bye. Have a nice life.'

I open my mouth to speak, but he says, 'Don't even think about asking me for a reference.'

Then he's gone.

I sit at my desk, stunned. What am I going to do now? I knew this would happen, but it still takes my breath away. As soon as Christmas is over, I'll be back to looking at the Situations Vacant pages in the newspaper and signing on.

Eventually, I stand up and go to stare out of the window. This is a great office and, despite everything, I'm going to miss it. Outside it's snowing again, and the view is of a city winter wonderland. Yet any Christmas spirit has suddenly gone from my heart.

I'd better get moving if I'm going to be out of here by the time Tyler comes back. Believe me, I'm in no rush to have another encounter with him. As requested, I clamber on to my desk and start to unpin the garlands that drape across the ceiling. Frankly, I'm tempted to leave it all here just to annoy him, but some of these are Mum's old faithfuls and I ought to take them home.

As I wind up the gaudy crêpe paper, there's a gentle tap on the door behind me and I whirl round. Josh Wallace is leaning on the doorframe, grinning at me.

'Just in time to help me,' I say, and lower a garland into his waiting hands. I climb down again and perch on my desk in front of him, looking and feeling very sheepish.

'How are we this morning?'

'I'm bearing up well considering that I've got a stonking hangover and Tyler has just fired me.' Before I can stop it a tear squeezes out of my eye.

'He hasn't?'

I nod.

Instantly Josh dumps the garland and comes to take me into his arms. I let him, not worrying for once who might see us. As he tenderly pats my back and whispers soft endearments, I sob into his shoulder.

'We'll sort this out,' he says. 'Don't worry. I'll have a word with Tyler.'

'I think it might fall on deaf ears.'

'It's Christmas. No one can be that heartless.'

'Kirsten has thrown him out.'

'Ouch.' He grimaces at that.

'I should call her, explain that it was a silly mistake.'

'It might help,' he agrees. 'Woman to woman she might listen.'

'I can only hope so.' Tyler might be a rat but this time he was certainly falsely accused. I can't stand by and let him bear the brunt of this error. I might never redeem myself in his eyes, but it's the least I can do to try to make this right.

I wipe away my tears and, when I've stopped snivelling, pick up the phone and dial Tyler's home number. It rings and rings, but no one answers. When it clicks to voicemail, I don't know what to say, so I hang up.

'She's not there.'

'Probably out giving Tyler's plastic a good battering.'

'I feel like a piece of low-life.'

'He deserved all he got,' Josh sympathises. 'You know that.'

'I don't know how I'm going to tell my parents. They thought I was going to end up running Fossil Oil, and I let them believe it. They'll be so upset for me.'

'All is not lost yet,' he says soothingly. 'You never know, if we appeal to his better nature, we might find that Tyler has a heart after all.'

Then Tyler appears behind him. His hair is freshly washed and he's in his more customary sharp suit. He adjusts the knot of his tie.

'If you're hoping for that,' he says with an evil glint in his eye, 'I think you're both going to be sorely disappointed.'

Chapter Fifty-two

'How long have we been lying here?' Kirsten asked, pulling the duvet round them.

'Absolutely ages.' Simon was dozing, drifting in and out of sleep.

'It's Christmas.' She traced a finger down his chest. 'We ought to think about what we're going to do.'

He planted a line of kisses along her throat. 'We don't have to *do* anything.'

'For once, I feel quite excited about the holiday. I want this Christmas to be a new start for us.'

'We should leave here, that's for sure,' Simon said. 'I'm not comfortable in Tyler's home, in Tyler's bed. It's not right. I might be stealing his wife, but there's no need to rub his nose in it.'

'We don't need to worry about that.'

'What if he decides to come back?'

'He already has,' she admitted. 'Actually, that was him at the door earlier.'

'You should have told me, Kirsten. We could have faced him together. There's no need to do this alone. I'm here for you.'

'I know.'

'You did tell him about us?'

'Not exactly.' She shook her head. 'I did tell him our marriage was over, though. I'm just not sure he believed me.'

'We should have been straight with him.'

'I couldn't face the confrontation. It's pointless with Tyler. You know what he's like. You would have ended up shouting or fighting.'

'Give me more credit than that.'

'I know Tyler. So do you. He won't take this well.'

'He blighted our lives, Kirsten, tore our love apart without any thought for either of us. He did it for his own selfish ends. I'm not going to have him put me on the back foot.'

'All I want is a quiet life,' Kirsten said. 'I've been unhappy for too long. We could shout and rage at Tyler for what he's done, but what's the point? That's all in the past. Now we have another chance to build our future together. Let's not think about Tyler at all.'

'I'd like to wring his lying neck,' Simon said.

'I know. Me too. But I don't want to expend any more energy on him. We're all that matters now. Us.'

'A few short hours ago you wouldn't even raise a toast to "us".'

'I was scared of my feelings, Si. How could I have possibly known the night would end like this?' She kissed his lips. 'Let's sneak away. Just me and you.'

'All right,' he agreed. 'We'll do it your way. You can still twist me round your little finger.'

'Good.' She grinned at him.

'We should pack a bag and go back to my place, though. Fossil have rented it for me. It's nice. I have some food, a king-size bed, a log-burning stove. I may even have logs.'

'I'm having trouble believing all this.' She reached up and tenderly touched his face. 'Am I dreaming this, Si? Here we are, making plans together. Is it true? Am I going to wake up and it's the day of the Fossil Oil Christmas party and I'll have to relive it all over again?'

'No.' He stroked the hair from her face. 'This is as real as it gets. The sooner we're out of here, the sooner we can begin our life together.'

She sighed as Simon pulled her into the crook of his arm and stroked the swell of her breast. 'Are you happy?' he asked.

'Blissfully. This is idyllic. The sun is streaming through the window, albeit rather pathetically, and we're lying here pretending that life is a bed of roses. The bubble has to burst. I want things to be different this time.' She propped herself up on her elbows and turned to him. 'Last night you promised me that we could stop the world and get off.'

'So I did.'

'Did you call Lance?'

'I tried but there was no answer. I didn't feel I could just leave a message. I need to speak to him in person.'

Kirsten hugged the sheet to her. 'It's going to ruin our relationship if we start again with the same emotional baggage. We won't last five minutes.'

'I promised you. I've waited ten long years for this, Kirsten, I'm not about to blow it. I'll call Lance again. Now.'

'Will you? If we're going to make this work, we need a complete change of lifestyle.' Kirsten stared at him determinedly. 'I won't be the neglected little corporate wife, sitting at home waiting for you.'

Simon lifted an eyebrow. 'Yet you would consider being my wife?'

Kirsten smiled. 'Of course. I love you. I should have been Mrs Conway all along.' She looked at him earnestly. 'But you have to swear to me that things won't be just the same this time.'

He pulled her against his body and stared wistfully at the ceiling. 'What do you want us to do instead?'

330

'I don't know. I can barely get my head round the fact that we're together again.'

'We could open a scuba-diving school in the Seychelles,' he mused.

'I've been there,' Kirsten admitted. 'It's very beautiful. One of Tyler's little conscience soothers. There are considerably worse places to live.'

'There's no doubt we'd leave the hamster wheel behind.'

'I can't scuba dive.' Kirsten hated to pour cold water on his plan – no pun intended – but it did seem pertinent to mention it.

'Neither can I. But we can learn. We can run the business end and get in experts to do the tuition.' Simon pushed himself up in bed. There was a flicker of excitement in his eyes. 'I've cashed in my share options from Petro Oz and Texan Oil. I had to when I left. Even as we speak, there's a heap of cash sitting in my bank account doing absolutely nothing but waiting for an opportunity like this. We can do whatever we want. If not scuba diving, we could buy a beach café, a restaurant, a small hotel, chalets for tourists.'

'Work together?'

'Why not? Or if you don't like the idea of that, maybe you could teach again, at a local school? We could even do something more community-based, if you want to. There are all kinds of opportunities that we could consider. I've been at the top of an international corporation. How hard could it be to run a small business of our own?' He raked his hair and his eyes held a look of steely determination. 'We could do this, Kirsten.'

She risked a half-smile. 'Are you serious?'

'Deadly.' He took her hands. 'I want to make you happy. I told you that. I'll do whatever it takes. If that means that we have to have sun, sand and sea as well as sex, then who am I to argue?'

Kirsten laughed.

'We need time to think this through and plan it properly,' he cautioned. 'I have enough money to start up a small venture and support us for a while.'

'I have nothing,' Kirsten admitted. 'I'm reliant on Tyler for everything. That needs to change too. I want my independence.' They had no money in this house, no equity. It wasn't theirs. Tyler, she was sure, would want to move away as soon as he could. He'd probably ask Fossil to find him a bachelor apartment right across the street from the office. 'There must be obstacles?'

'Of course there are, but we'll work through them together.' He cupped her face in his hands. 'I love you.'

Kirsten giggled excitedly. This might be the end of her marriage, but it felt very much like a new beginning for her. 'I love you too.'

He kissed her, his mouth firm, insistent, pressing against hers. 'Nothing can stop us now.'

'Nothing,' Kirsten agreed.

Chapter Fifty-three

Tyler folded his arms and stared at Josh. 'No,' he said. 'I will absolutely not reconsider. That woman is a menace.' He pointed in Louise's direction. 'She's not staying here a moment longer.'

'She's a great girl,' Josh said. 'You know that. With a bit of goodwill, you can both sort this out.'

Tyler stood up and paced his office. 'She's cost me my marriage and my dignity. Now she's paying the price.'

'You got yourself into this mess, Tyler. You can end it all now by playing fair.'

'When I want your opinion, I'll ask for it.' Tyler ground to an abrupt halt at the window and gazed out at the snow. He wanted nothing more than to get through this day unscathed and go home to Kirsten. That was a rare feeling. 'Push me too far and *you*'ll regret it too.'

'You need me, Tyler,' Josh said. 'We both know that.'

'Oh, do we?'

'My sales figures keep the department afloat and Lance off your back.'

Tyler sat down again and spread his hands on his desk. There was a malicious smile curling the corners of his mouth and showing the merest suggestion of his teeth. He looked like a pitbull terrier. Without a muzzle.

Tyler smiled sweetly. 'Are you sitting comfortably?'

Josh wasn't.

Tapping at his computer, Tyler turned the screen so that Josh could read it too. The smile widened to a cold grin. 'Shall we begin?'

Josh scanned the figures on the screen, which made for uncomfortable viewing.

'These aren't right,' Josh said. 'They show me as not hitting any of my targets in the last year.'

'These are my back-up figures,' Tyler said. 'For times such as these. I can make them as right as I want to. You're not out of the woods on this yet, Josh. You were the one on top of Louise when Kirsten thought it was me. In my eyes, that makes you complicit in this disaster.'

'You can't fiddle my figures,' Josh complained. 'That's just not ethical.'

Tyler laughed in his face. 'You should know me better than to think that would worry me. I always have these little beauties on standby. Just in case.'

'I've enjoyed working with you, Tyler. Even though some of your practices have been dubious. There are people in Fossil who don't like you, but I've always defended your corner. I've had your back, but this is beyond the pale. If you sack Louise, if you threaten me, then I'm done with you. You'll get your come-uppance.'

'Fine,' Tyler said. 'Sales managers like you are ten a penny. For every job we advertise there are hundreds of applicants. Someone will fill your shoes in five minutes. So, I'll accept your resignation too. Just get your little girlfriend to type it up on the way out.' He shooed at Josh as you would an irritating fly.

'You really are low-life, Tyler Benson.'

Tyler shrugged. 'Tell me something I don't know.'

Josh stood up and walked from the office, dazed.

Louise was at her desk, but it was clear that she'd been straining to hear what was being said behind the closed door.

'How did it go?' she stage-whispered.

Josh bit his lip. 'Hmm,' he said. 'Maybe not that well.'

Chapter Fifty-four

It was much later than usual when Lance eventually arrived at Fossil Oil's head office. The staff would be wondering where he was. Martin held open the door of the Bentley for him and he bounded up the steps to the entrance and into the airy atrium.

He must phone Bud Harman, Lance thought, and firm things up from this end. They'd been good staff here, dedicated, trustworthy, and he didn't want the whole shebang to collapse just because this was going to be his last day.

Instead of taking the executive lift straight to the top floor, he decided to take the stairs and walk up through the offices, giving him a chance to wish his faithful staff a merry Christmas. By the top of the first flight, his heart was banging in his chest. Could be that he'd overdone the dancing, unaccustomed as he was these days. Last night had been a heavy session, but wonderful fun, the few bits he could remember of it. You couldn't beat a good Christmas party.

His first port of call, the Customer Service Department, was deserted. Only half the staff were at their desks, and only half of those were still sitting upright; most were slumped against their computer terminals in a state of inertia. There was a deathly silence where there should have been ringing phones. Either someone had thoughtfully pulled out all the plugs, or similarly debilitating office parties had been taking place the night before throughout their customer network. A large number of the staff were wearing sunglasses indoors.

It was the same in Refinery Output. And no one at all had made it in to Alternative Fuels. He was terribly disappointed. These youngsters had no stamina these days. A few glasses of bubbly and they all went to pot. How were any of them going to make executive level if they succumbed at the first sight of corporate hospitality? No deals were going to be done today, that was patently clear. It wouldn't do him any harm to go home early either. It would be a pleasant change to be waiting for Melissa when she returned from her shopping trip or wherever she was. That was one of the dangers of becoming an old married couple – if you weren't careful all the surprises went right out of your life.

He needed to talk to Tyler about the hand-over. At least he knew that Tyler had more stamina. His right-hand man would be here come hell or high water. Fossil Oil was in his veins, just as it was in Lance's.

Veronica was at her desk when he reached his office, just as she always was.

'Morning,' Lance grunted at her.

'Morning, Mr Harvey.' She handed him the folder which contained his post. Each day she opened it, slotted it into place and made little notes as to how he should deal with each piece. The woman was invaluable; it was a shame she wasn't coming to DC with him.

He'd remember to ask her later what she'd bought Melissa for Christmas. It was sure to be beautiful. And expensive. She knew his wife only too well.

'The party went very well,' he said. 'Good work, Veronica. Make sure it goes on to Tyler's budget.'

'Yes, Mr Harvey.' She cleared her throat. 'I'm afraid there was a slight incident after you left.'

'Benson caught with his hand up a secretary's skirt?' Lance guffawed. It wouldn't be the first time.

'I'm afraid the marquee caught fire and was destroyed. Wadestone Manor has suffered some smoke and water damage.'

'Was it our fault?'

'It may have been. The fire investigators and insurance assessors are there this morning.'

'Keep me informed.' Every year someone landed them with a huge bill for damages. Why couldn't anyone party without trashing the place?

Lance headed to his desk via his drinks cabinet and poured himself a bourbon. He shuddered as the initial swig hit the spot. That was more like it. He sat down behind his desk, enjoying his first drink of the day.

The view out of his window on this side of the building was uninspiring. The city of Milton Keynes was growing at an alarming rate, changing rapidly from a scruffy, squalling infant into an attractive youth. Just as his own boys had. He looked at the photograph of his family on his desk. Melissa had been a wonderfully devoted mother and had more than made up for any lack of parental adoration he himself had felt. His job had been everything then. Whatever else came along took second place. Whatever crises occurred, Melissa dealt with them without bothering him. He'd always appreciated it, so that, luckily, he wasn't one of those sad cases who was left with nothing – money in the bank but no family, no friends, no future once the company had finished with them. He'd seen that scenario far too often to let it happen to him. He loved her and he would make this Christmas a great one for her before they went home to the States. He should text her, but at this moment he had more important things on his mind.

He glanced at his watch. It was one o'clock in the afternoon UK time, which would make it a fairly uncivilised hour of the morning in Washington. From his last conversation with Bud Harman, Fossil Oil International had also enjoyed, or endured, its Christmas party last night. He wondered if they'd managed to burn down the goddamn building too. But Bud would be in bright and early. He and Lance were both drawn from the same oil well. Lance picked up the phone.

'Hey, Bud,' Lance said when it was answered. 'How's it going?'

'Mornin', Lance.'

Bud, at least, sounded hale and hearty. It would be a brisk call. They always were. Harman wasn't the sort of man to indulge in social niceties during transatlantic telephone calls. He wasn't the sort of man to indulge in social niceties face to face, come to that.

'I know it's early but I'm calling about the SACKED programme. I want to get things firmed up before I leave for Christmas.'

'I wanted to speak to you too, Lance. You know how things move here. We had an emergency meeting last night before the Christmas party and the board decided that we won't implement SACKED just yet. There are global changes coming and we're going to put it on the back burner for now. Revisit it in six months or so.'

'Right.' Lance was pretty sure he'd already announced it at the party last night. He'd have to check with Veronica.

'That doesn't mean things won't change for you. I have good news, Lance. I'm promoting you to executive president. We had to let Don Fletcher go. The man just couldn't stand the pace.'

Lance was shaken to his very core. *Promoting.* The word reverberated in his brain. This wasn't a common word in Bud's vocabulary.

'It's a lot more travel, but you can do it based from London or New York, whichever suits you.'

He knew that. The executive president's role would see him going round the globe overseeing Fossil's interests. It was a very desirable position.

'You're on board?' Bud bellowed down the phone.

Lance puffed out his chest. 'I sure am.'

'I knew you would be. You're a company man through and through.' He could hear the metaphorical back-slap in Bud's voice. 'We thought Simon Conway could fit into the chairman's role,' he continued. 'He's a great asset to Fossil Oil and we should use him to his full potential. With Tyler Benson behind him, they'll make a great team.'

'Tyler will be disappointed. He's had his eye on my job for years.'

'We're not in this business to make everyone happy.'

'We could promote him to deputy chairman,' Lance suggested. 'New title, more money. It would smooth things over.'

'Do it then. We'll talk more in the new year.'

'Merry Christmas, Bud.'

'Merry Christmas to you too, executive president.'

Lance felt choked as he hung up. And proud. Much as he'd tried to tell himself otherwise, there'd been no doubt that he'd been teetering on the brink of corporate oblivion; now a saving hand, in the unlikely form of Bud Harman, had plucked him back to safety in the nick of time. There would be no global restructuring this week. The SACKED programme had itself, for the time being, been sacked.

Melissa would be pleased. If there was one thing she would like more than being a chairman's wife, it would be being an executive president's wife. It would probably entail a whole new wardrobe. Executive president of Fossil Oil – it sounded good. There would be no twilight exodus on Christmas Day. No grim

Washington winter. And plenty of time to finish off the turkey his wife had optimistically ordered.

He thought Melissa would choose to stay in England too, despite her continual moaning. She liked it here and she had things to keep her occupied. Some things that Lance wished didn't keep her *quite* so well occupied, but then that was life. In the dim and distant past, he hadn't exactly been as white as the driven snow himself. Still, her little affairs had never done them any harm and he could see no reason why that should change. They were both pretty content with their lot.

Tyler and the new recruit Conway would make a formidable team. Simon was honest, upright and straight-down-the-line. He would make a good chairman. His calm, direct style of management would temper the worst of Tyler's excesses and was the right choice to take Fossil Oil into the future. Tyler would like his promotion too. Another step up the corporate ladder. It was what he lived for. If they both played their cards right, the world was their oil well.

The telephone jangled next to him, shaking him from his pleasant reverie. Perhaps it was Melissa touching base. He massaged his shoulder, which still ached naggingly. He'd ask Veronica to get him some painkillers. That should see him right. With a contented smile to himself, he put the receiver to his ear. 'Lance Harvey,' he barked, 'executive president.'

He liked the sound of that.

Chapter Fifty-five

We go to the pub across the road from Fossil Oil, part of a massive chain of identikit venues but none the worse for it. I guess because it's Christmas Eve, the place is busy even at this early hour. It's always popular with the staff of the varied corporate offices around this part of the city, Fossil included. I recognise some of the faces that are already in here now, even though they should be at their desks. Us included, I suppose. The pub does a cheap all-day breakfast which is a major part of the appeal and, around us, dozens of bleary-eyed and clearly hungover people are tucking in. I find the canteen in the offices much nicer, but Josh wanted to be off the premises for the discussion we're about to have, and I had to agree with him. We definitely need some cooling-off space between us and Tyler Benson.

The hubbub of conversation is at such a level that Josh has to lean over when he asks me, 'What do you want to drink?'

'Just a cappuccino, please.'

'No breakfast?'

I shake my head. I'm too wobbly inside to want to eat and I'm grateful to my dad for the base layer of toast.

Josh queues to be served while I find an empty table. There's one by the window, overlooking the boulevard that leads right up to the city centre. It's fuggy in here so the glass is running with condensation and I resist the temptation to draw a sad face in it. Instead I pick up an abandoned napkin and wipe a clearing in the pane so that I can look through. There's nothing to see but cars easing their way through the slush on the roads and people hunched and hurrying into the nearest shelter from the falling snow.

Then, much to my relief, I see Karen arriving for work. She's wearing dark glasses and walking very gingerly. Though she is still wearing towering heels in the snow. It looks as if she's feeling a bit fragile this morning and I can certainly empathise with that. I think she's one of the few people who enjoyed the Christmas party. Not that she'll remember any of it. I'm just glad she's turned up unharmed. Then I realise that I'm starting to think like my dad, and stop.

A few moments later Josh comes back with coffees for both of us. He sets them down then pulls up a stool to sit on.

When we've both taken a sip, I say, 'So, we need to come up with a cunning plan.'

Josh grins at me. 'I only came into the office to find out how you were and give you some support. I didn't expect to find myself out of a job as well.'

'I'm so sorry,' I say. 'I didn't mean it to happen either. I don't know why you're smiling.'

'Me neither,' he admits. 'It just seems like a really absurd situation. I think Tyler's overstepped the mark this time. He's being totally unfair to you and he's falsified my sales figures to make me look bad. If it comes to it, I hope I can prove that to an employment tribunal. At the very least, my payslips show that I've been paid bonuses every month. You don't get that from underperforming.'

'That gives me some hope. Maybe we should go to Human Resources and tell them what's happened.'

'We could.' He looks hesitant. 'That would probably work

for my case, but they might not take kindly to what you did to Tyler.'

Ah. Of course, he's right. Tyler might have been in the wrong the way he treated me, but I haven't exactly helped matters. You know the old adage, two wrongs don't make a right? That.

'Maybe Tyler isn't being as clever as he thinks he is.' Josh looks at me over his coffee cup. 'We do have another bit of leverage. If we want to play dirty too, that is.'

'We do?'

'We could threaten to tell Lance and Kirsten that he's been having an affair with Melissa Harvey.'

'Do we know that for certain, or is it just office gossip?'

'I'm prepared to believe there's no smoke without fire.' Josh sighs. 'This isn't a route I want to go down, but what else can we do?'

I don't want to stoop to Tyler's level, but he's already proved that he's not a man to be reasoned with. 'Let's think about this very carefully. I'm anxious not to open a can of worms.'

'I don't want him to push you out,' Josh says. 'You're good at your job. I only wish you'd told me what he was doing earlier.'

I shrug. 'Tyler's the one with the power. He's holding all the cards. I'm the new girl. Who would have believed me?'

'I would have. Will you trust me now?'

'I think so.' Josh seems to be cut from a very different cloth from the men I've known before, and certainly from Tyler Benson.

'If that's the best you can do for now, then I'll take it.' He risks another smile. 'When you get to know me better, I hope you'll feel differently. You do still want to get to know me better?'

I nod. This is the moment I open up my heart to him. It's such a small step, but it feels like a mammoth leap into the unknown. I want to shield my daughter even more than I want to protect myself from harm, but I don't think it's good for her to go through life without a male role model apart from my dear dad. It's not good for me to be so self-sufficient that I end up old and lonely either. I'd like another child, someone to share our life, someone to love me. So, here I am willing to dive into the abyss of romance once more.

'You can come to my parents' house for Christmas Day, if you'd like,' I offer. I try to sound casual, as if it doesn't matter to me whether he comes or not, yet my heart is pounding in my chest and my palms are as damp as these windows. What if he turns me down? I'd feel like a fool. I rush on. 'It might be a trial. They'll both try to kill you with kindness.'

'There are worse ways to go,' Josh says. 'If you're sure it's OK, I'd really love to come.'

'Great.' I resist the urge to run round the pub, punching the air. 'I'll let you know what time and all that.'

'Can I bring something? Contribute to the meal? Buy some wine? I'd like to get Mia a gift too.'

Now we're both a bit awkward. 'Just bring yourself. That'll be enough.'

'Thanks, Louise. If I'm honest, I was dreading Christmas alone. I'll look forward to it.'

We exchange a shy and wary smile.

Josh drains the dregs of his coffee and puts his cup down in a very decisive manner. 'Now that we're fortified, let's go and get our jobs back.'

Chapter Fifty-six

Kirsten had just finished getting dressed when Simon came back into the bedroom after calling Lance Harvey. There was a sombre air about him and his face was pale and serious. It wasn't the happy, smiling countenance that had kissed her yet again before leaving the room not ten minutes earlier. She settled herself on the edge of the bed and waited. Simon sat next to her and took her hand in his. He fiddled with each of her fingers without speaking.

'You might as well spit it out,' she said when he didn't fill the silence. 'I gather Lance didn't take your resignation too kindly. Did he get all heavy and threaten legal action?' Kirsten studied his face, wishing she could read the veiled emotions. 'You have to remember that beneath that fading exterior beats a strong, litigious American heart.'

'No, he didn't threaten me with legal action,' Simon said with a ponderous puff of breath. 'He didn't threaten me with anything at all.'

'What then?'

Simon looked at her squarely. 'Before I could say anything, he offered me a promotion.'

'What?'

He gave a humourless half-laugh, shaking his head in disbelief. 'He offered me the chairman's job.'

'The *chairman's* job?' Kirsten rubbed her hand over her face. 'Does that mean Lance has been given the push? Is he not coming back from the SACKED programme?' She'd suspected as much.

'No.' He risked a wry glance. 'Quite the opposite. Lance has been promoted too. He's now executive president of Fossil Oil.'

'Oh my God,' she said, shuddering. 'The lunatics are finally in charge of the asylum.'

'That's pretty much what I thought.'

'Tyler will fling himself off the nearest cliff when he hears this.'

'I know.'

'So what did Lance say when you turned it down?' Kirsten grimaced. 'I bet he was livid.'

There was another uncomfortable silence, during which her heart started to beat louder and faster. Simon looked distinctly ill at ease, avoiding her gaze.

'You did turn it down?' she ventured quietly. 'Tell me that you did.'

Simon gazed at the wall, his eyes steady, unflinching. 'Not exactly.'

Kirsten buried her face in her hands. 'Please tell me I'm not hearing this.'

'I didn't say yes either.' Simon massaged his temples.

'But you didn't say no.'

He shook his head.

She took a deep breath. Already she could see all their silly, reckless plans floating away. She should have learned by now that when something sounded too good, then it generally was. 'So, what did you say?'

'I said I'd think about it.' He turned his face to her for the first time. 'He's going to keep the job open for me until the new year. I have to make a decision by then.'

Folding her arms around herself, she tried to ease the sinking feeling that had started inside her. 'I think the decision's already made, don't you?'

'It would be madness not to consider it, Kirsten.'

'And it would be madness to think that we could ever have a relationship if you decide to work for Fossil.'

The hangover Kirsten had forgotten she was due suddenly pushed itself to the front of her brain, making it throb violently. A churning nausea rushed to her stomach, she wanted to heave. This was Christmas Eve – she should be enjoying a bit of festive cheer, having a convivial glass of champagne while she made a ham-fisted attempt at mince pies and stuffed all the important little cavities of the turkey with pancetta or something. The thought of interfering with raw turkey gave her stomach another violent swish. She should be enjoying wrapping last-minute presents and wafting round the house lighting scented candles, filling it with the aroma of cinnamon and cloves, waiting, nerves shredded, for Tyler to come home. This wasn't the day to be having life-changing discussions, particularly not with a dehydrated brain. She should have known it. Wasn't it supposed to be Christmas Day that was the most stressful day of the year? Hers had come a day too early.

'What happened to escaping? To scuba diving, sun, sand, sea and sex?' Feelings of disappointment and rejection swept over her. Now that she'd finally plucked up the courage to leave Tyler, she didn't want her next relationship to turn out to be just as disastrous. She turned her attention back to Simon. 'We were going to run away together and start a carefree life of fun and freedom. We were going to grab back the years we've lost with both hands. How could you have forgotten that so soon?'

'I haven't forgotten,' Simon said steadily. 'I wanted to talk it through with you. That's what people in a relationship do.'

It wasn't what her and Tyler did. Fossil Oil said what they

wanted to happen, Tyler agreed, her opinion was ignored and she trailed along unhappily in the wake of everyone else's decisions. That's what had happened in her relationship. Now Simon was expecting it to be different all of a sudden. 'There's nothing to talk about.'

'I think there is.'

Kirsten closed her eyes and waited for her rolling stomach to still. 'I'm going to be sick unless I have a cup of camomile tea,' she said, getting up from the bed, her limbs leaden and reluctant.

Simon held her shoulders. 'I'll get dressed,' he said. 'Then I'll come downstairs and we can sit and talk it through rationally.'

It sounded perfectly sensible, perfectly reasonable, but she could feel him slipping away.

Kirsten was sitting at the kitchen table, elbows propping her up, nursing the insipid-looking tea, cherishing the burning sensation in her hands that, at least, contrasted with the sick numbness the rest of her body was experiencing. Simon, like Tyler, was going to let her down. It was inevitable.

Seconds later he appeared at the door and leaned on the frame, hands in pockets. He was wearing his crumpled dinner suit and equally crumpled shirt. His freshly washed dark fringe flopped forward on to his forehead. He pushed it back with his fingers and she resisted the urge to do the same. He looked absolutely terrible and she knew that she had never loved him more.

'You could have borrowed some of Tyler's clothes,' she said.

'Stealing his wife is one thing,' Simon replied, 'doing it while wearing his clothes is another.'

Kirsten smiled wearily. 'Do you want some tea?' she asked.

He strode across the kitchen and sank into the leather sofa by the French doors. Lounging back in it, he gazed out into the garden. Tyler never sat like that. He always sat upright, ready to pounce.

The snow had now reached this part of London. It fell in delicate swirls, landing softly in the garden, making it look as if someone had sprinkled icing sugar over everything. It was so pretty, it made her want to cry.

Simon turned his eyes to her. 'Come and sit with me.' He patted the seat next to him. 'I want to know what you're thinking, what you're feeling.'

'I'm feeling hungover,' Kirsten replied bleakly. 'Very hungover.' In all honesty, she didn't dare to begin examining her true feelings. Once that floodgate was open she felt as if she might never close it again.

She picked up her tea and crossed the kitchen to sit with him. If this was going to end badly, then she wanted to feel the comfort of his warmth one more time. She snuggled in next to him, laying her head on his shoulder.

'I could do it for a year, Kirsten,' Simon reasoned as he stroked her hair. 'While we're planning to set up another business. The salary is huge. We could bank a pile of cash that would cushion us for a long time. I have to consider it.'

She took a lingering sip of her tea and eventually shook her head. It seemed a perfectly acceptable argument, but she knew what Fossil Oil was like. It wasn't happy until it had drained all the life out of you. 'You'd be back on that treadmill, Simon. Trapped, unable to get off.'

'It doesn't have to be like that,' he assured her. 'It would buy us some time and it would look good on my CV.'

'You wouldn't need a CV for it to look good on if you were running your own scuba-diving centre or café.' She gave him a look that asked him to deny it.

'I need some fresh air, Kirsten.' Simon rubbed the back of his neck, strong smooth strokes with hands that had so skilfully seduced her body just a short while ago. 'This is a tough decision. I'd be walking away from a hell of a lot, from the top job, from what I've always wanted. I've got to get my head round it.'

Kirsten's hands started to tremble and she put her cup down before she spilled tea over both of them. 'If you walk out now, Simon, there'll be no going back.' Her voice sounded calm, but it belied the screaming that she was doing inside. 'You put a job before me once before. You left me alone because of your ambition, and look where that got us. I won't let you do it again.'

'That was different. Now we're older and wiser. This time we won't let Tyler drive us apart. I promise you.'

The telephone rang, making them both start, its shrill noise at odds with the subdued atmosphere in the glossy kitchen. Kirsten pushed herself up from the sofa and went to pick it up.

'Tyler?' she said, surprised to hear her husband at the other end. Normally when he was at work everything else was forgotten.

'I hated the way that we left things this morning,' he said. 'I just wanted to call to see that you were OK.'

Behind her she could hear Simon lever himself from the sofa and cross the room. She turned and held up her hand. Five minutes, she mouthed. Their eyes met and he shrugged sadly. A tight band squeezed Kirsten's heart and the words of endearment that Tyler was pouring down the phone blurred to an insignificant rush.

'I know I've got a lot of explaining to do,' Tyler continued. 'But we have too much to lose. We love each other.'

Simon was walking away and she was letting him. She watched him as he trudged down the hall, head hung low. He turned at the front door and waved, a tight unhappy movement that hurt like a knife being pushed under her ribs. Kirsten put her hand over the receiver, blanking Tyler out.

'Simon!' she called out. 'Don't go.'

Yet he was already out of the door. He closed it quietly behind him.

She stood like a statue, unable to move, as dead and as unfeeling as stone. He'd gone. Gone, gone, gone. She'd given him a choice and he had taken it. He was out of her life again as quickly as he had come back into it. Kirsten could feel her lip starting to quiver and she clamped it down, biting it with her teeth until she could taste blood.

Tyler's voice brought her back. He was shouting down the phone at her. 'Kirsten? Kirsten? Are you even listening to me?'

'I'm sorry, Tyler,' she said, speaking like a woman in a daze. Which she was. 'I didn't catch that.'

Her hands were shaking. It was going to take more than camomile tea, possibly even more than a gallon of Rescue Remedy, before she could start to make any sense of this.

'I'll leave work as soon as I can. The snow's getting quite bad here.'

'What?' she said automatically to her husband.

'I can make things right. I know I can. It'll be just me and you from now on. Hand on heart. I'll try to be the husband you want. You won't regret it.'

His voice was soothing, placating, wheedling, promising her all the things she had yearned for during ten long, lonely years. It ran over her like cool water. But it was as if it was all happening to someone else. Someone else who was capable of making rational decisions.

Then she paused, snapping back to listen to his final promise, letting it travel through her struggling brain, considering the implications, weighing the consequences one against the other. An exhausted sigh escaped Kirsten's lips.

'Yes,' she said without emotion. She didn't have the energy or the will to fight her husband any longer. 'Of course you can come home, Tyler.'

Chapter Fifty-seven

Josh and I appear at Tyler's office door just as he's hanging up the phone. He's reclining in his chair, feet crossed on his desk. There's a smugness about his face that I find nauseating. My resignation letter is still laid out in front of him. He looks up and scowls at us.

'I thought I'd given you two your marching orders. Did I not make myself clear enough?'

Josh ushers me into the room and then closes the door behind us.

'You've gone too far, Tyler,' Josh says reasonably. 'I know how you've been treating Louise. She should have put in a complaint to Human Resources about you sexually harassing her.'

'For goodness' sake,' Tyler says. 'Don't be dramatic. This isn't the Dark Ages. It's just a bit of office banter. She didn't mind.'

'I did.'

Tyler ignores me.

'She could still make a formal complaint against you,' Josh says.

Tyler sighs. 'They won't care. Look what happened to dear Debbie.' He holds up my resignation letter. 'Besides, I have paperwork. Louise is out of here of her own volition and, if you've got any sense, you'll be right behind her. Your careers are over here. I'll make sure of that.'

Now he turns his attention to me and I feel my knees quake. The shark eyes are colder and greyer than I've ever seen them.

'What's the matter with you, miss? Cat got your tongue? Or happy to have your little boyfriend do the talking for you?'

'You're going to apologise and you're going to give her back that letter,' Josh states.

Tyler makes a steeple of his fingers and rests it against his lips. 'And if I don't?'

Now it's my turn. I step forward. 'We don't want to do this, Tyler, but if you persist in being difficult then you leave us no choice.' I take a deep breath. 'You'll give us both our jobs back or I'll go and tell Lance that you've been having an affair with his wife.'

Tyler recoils and then springs out of his chair.

'Just waiting to deliver the killer blow then?' He shakes his head in disdain. 'I should have realised you were the one who'd be trouble. Now you're showing your true colours. You're the viper.'

He comes towards me and Josh blocks his path. The two men square up to each other: Tyler, hands on his hips, jaw tighter than Lance after a bottle of bourbon; Josh both relaxed and coiled at the same time.

I'm going clammy with fear. This is supposed to be the season of goodwill to all men.

'Lance would never believe you,' Tyler says.

'Are you sure about that?' Josh moves a step closer to him. 'Sure enough to risk everything?'

For a moment, it looks as if Tyler might relent. A look of wavering uncertainty crosses his face, but it's quickly replaced by steely determination.

'Lance will never get rid of me,' Tyler says. 'I'm his right-hand man. He couldn't function without me. You know that. My position here is rock-solid. You're the ones who are the losers. Accept it. Move on.'

'I'm so disappointed in you, Tyler. I've looked up to you. I've learned from you. When the staff here have bad-mouthed you, I've stood up for you. This is the thanks I get?'

'Boo-hoo,' Tyler says. 'I'm getting bored now.' He glances at his watch. 'It's Christmas Eve. I'm going home to try to make peace with my wife.' He turns his evil eyes on me again. 'Good luck to you both. See if she'll put out for you, Josh, because she never would for me.'

'That's it.' Josh shakes his head. 'You've gone too far.'

The tension in the room is palpable, but I'm still somewhat surprised when Josh pulls back his fist and hits Tyler right on the chin.

If this had been a cartoon, tweety birds would have circled round Tyler's head and he would have sunk slowly to the ground to a catchy little tune. As it is, his eyes close at the same time as he crashes backwards without pause or fanfare on to his office floor.

'Oh my goodness.' I drop to my knees next to him.

'Arrrgh,' Josh says. He nurses his knuckles to his chest. 'That hurt.'

'Not as much as it did Tyler.'

'Have I killed him?'

There's a groan from the prostrate Tyler and a flicker behind his eyelids.

'No.'

We look at each other in shock and then burst out laughing.

'I can't believe you did that.'

'Me neither.' Josh looks stunned. 'I haven't punched anyone since I was in the playground at primary school. I'd forgotten what a bad idea it is.' He rubs his knuckles again.

Another low moan escapes Tyler's lips.

'Come on, Josh. Let's get out of here. I think we should be long gone before he rejoins the land of the living.'

Josh grips my arms and turns me to him. 'I'm sorry, Louise. We definitely won't get our jobs back now, but I couldn't help myself. After what he said, I just really, *really* had to hit him.'

'What's done is done.' I normally hate any kind of violence but, if I was a bloke, I'd have been sorely tempted to do the same thing. Instead, my protest is less physical. I take my resignation letter from Tyler's desk and rip it into tiny shreds, then scatter it over his inert body.

'We're not going to tell Lance, are we?'

'No,' Josh says. 'Tyler's right. He probably won't believe us and he'll only come down on Tyler's side. He's too valuable to Fossil.'

'Shame.'

'It looks as if our position here is, as they say, untenable.'

'We tried,' I say. 'We could do no more than that. I really appreciate you backing me up.' My voice is clogged with emotion. Right now it feels as if Josh is my knight in shining armour. The one I've waited so long for. I put my hand on his chest and he covers it. 'Thank you. You've paid a high price.'

He shrugs. 'There are other jobs. It's not the end of the world. No one died.'

We both look down at Tyler, who is still out cold.

'Shame,' we chuckle in unison.

'I feel as if I need to go back to the pub and have a double brandy.' Josh does look quite shaken.

'We could do that,' I say. 'Or I could offer you a really wild option?'

Chapter Fifty-eight

Tyler was on all fours, shaking his head, still stunned, when Lance strode into his office.

'What are you doing down there, Tyler?' Lance observed jovially. 'If you're so goddamn tired after the Christmas party why don't you get the hell out of here now? Go home to that pretty little wife of yours.'

Tyler pushed himself up on his elbows, trying desperately to remember exactly where he was. He saw what he assumed was a confetti of resignation letter sprinkled all over him and the surrounding office floor, and the memory of Josh's fist connecting with his chin came rushing back. He tasted the blood on his lip and rubbed his jawbone, easing it back to its usual position. He would kill that bastard Wallace when he got hold of him.

'Sorry, Lance,' Tyler said, holding on to his desk and standing tentatively. He brushed scraps of paper from his suit. 'A little problem with interpersonal relationships. Nothing for you to worry about. There's always someone keen to take you down when you're trying to climb the greasy pole.'

Lance sat down in one of his chairs. 'I want to have a few words with you on that subject myself.'

'Ah.' So Josh and Louise had, indeed, spilled the beans. He'd hoped Wallace had been all mouth and no trousers. It seemed not. In truth, he'd been waiting for this. It was bound to come out. It was a miracle really that Melissa had honoured her agreement not to confess to Lance. He could only hope now that he could still keep it from Kirsten. Mind you, he wouldn't be surprised if Louise had phoned her too.

Tyler hovered behind his desk. Should he stand? Should he sit? Was he about to get hit again? He didn't think Lance seemed up to fisticuffs. His chairman was looking decidedly peaky after last night's excesses. There was an unusual pallor to his face. Still, just in case, Tyler did his best to disguise the burgeoning cut on his lip, so as not to present a good target for Lance to aim at.

'I don't suppose you've got any booze in here?' Lance asked hopefully.

Of course, every executive kept a bottle of bourbon handy in their office cupboard for Lance's sole consumption.

'I just happen to have a drop of your favourite, Lance. Let me pour you one.' Get him drunk, Tyler thought, utterly, utterly drunk, and get it all out in the open.

Tyler filled a crystal tumbler and handed it to his chairman.

'Cheers, Lance,' he said as lightly as he could. 'Merry Christmas.'

'Cheers,' Lance echoed.

Dusting off another glass from his drinks cabinet, he poured a nip of bourbon for himself. Not too much, as he had to drive back to Kirsten and he was probably still over the limit from last night. He perched on the edge of his desk and toasted Lance. The chairman's bourbon was already half gone, but other than that Lance was staying amazingly cool, Tyler thought.

Maybe he'd underestimated the man. Perhaps he would be able to forgive and forget and not think too closely about Tyler making love to his wife when it came to global restructuring.

Even though she'd agreed to him going home, Kirsten had

sounded worryingly distracted. The sooner he could get out of here, the better. He wanted to get Christmas over with as soon as possible and start next year with a clean sheet.

Tyler gulped his bourbon. 'Look, Lance, I'll come clean. We're both men of the world.' He spread his hands expansively. 'I know what you've come to say to me.'

'You do?' Lance was clearly taken aback. 'The Fossil Oil jungle drums must be in good working order, Christmas Eve or not.'

'I can't say that it makes me proud.' Tyler hung his head and shook it regretfully.

'Doesn't it?' Lance looked surprised.

Tyler paced the floor. 'It's not what I wanted to happen, Lance. I never did.'

Lance's mouth gaped. 'You didn't? I thought it was what you wanted all along?'

'No, no, no. I should never have let it go this far. I can only apologise.' He should just throw himself on Lance's mercy and get this over with. 'I feel it's only right that I offer you my resignation,' Tyler said.

'I hadn't expected that,' Lance said.

The chairman seemed to wipe a few beads of sweat from his brow.

'I'm sorry to have put you in this position.' Tyler hoped he looked suitably repentant. Was it really a shock? Surely Lance must have heard the rumours about him and Melissa before now? 'Can I ask you how you found out?'

'The usual way, I guess.' Lance shrugged. 'I've been busy on the phone this morning.'

'Who was it that told you?' He might as well hear it from the horse's mouth.

Lance took another swig of his bourbon. 'Bud Harman himself.'

'Bud *Harman*?' Tyler repeated. He was glad he hadn't taken a drink, otherwise he might have choked on it.

So it looked as if Louise and Josh had gone straight to the top, bypassing Lance completely in their attempts to discredit him. If he'd known they were going to tell Harman, that might have altered his negotiating stance considerably.

No wonder Lance could afford to sit there and look so cool. It was out of his hands now. Whatever action he took, no one could accuse him of being vengeful. He would have Bud Harman's blessing. It was game, set and match to Lance, and Tyler hadn't even had a chance to pick up his racquet.

Tyler laughed shortly and bitterly. 'So what's going to happen now?'

Lance shook his head. 'I need to speak to Bud again. I don't have to tell you, he'll be very disappointed, Tyler.'

'He has every right to be, Lance – and, of course, so do you.' Remorse, Tyler, think remorse. This could be rescued yet. He swallowed nervously. 'I don't *have* to go ...'

Lance drained his glass and put it down on Tyler's desk. 'You've resigned, Tyler. If you think that's the right thing, then you should stick with that decision.'

Tyler felt his mouth go dry. This wasn't what he'd expected.

'It might be a good thing,' Lance continued, sounding so very magnanimous. 'Fresh challenge and all that. We all need them from time to time. Perhaps I should have done the same when I was a younger man.'

It looked as if he'd walked straight into Lance's trap. He'd thought the old man would panic at the thought of him leaving. After all, what was he without Tyler Benson at his right hand? He'd thought he'd called Lance's bluff, but the wily old dog had played the trump card.

Lance stood to leave.

'I can stay if you want me to,' Tyler offered hastily, his voice coming out at a higher pitch than he would have liked. 'How will you manage?'

Lance shrugged. 'It's not the end of the world. Fossil Oil will roll on without you. Have a good Christmas, Tyler.' Lance patted his shoulder in a fatherly manner. 'I'd better be making tracks. Melissa will be waiting for me.'

Lance headed back down the empty corridor. There was virtually no one left in the offices now.

Tyler felt his blood run cold. Was that it? His career at Fossil Oil over with nothing more than a pat on the back and a cheery wave? There was something not right about this.

'Lance,' Tyler called out. 'Has this got something to do with Simon Conway's arrival? Did he want me out?'

'Conway? No need to worry about him,' Lance said. 'He just called me. He's not joining Fossil now. He's booked himself on a slow boat to corporate suicide. Said he's found something much more important than the oil business.' Lance laughed at that. 'You youngsters!' He shook his head. 'He's opening his own business somewhere. Abroad, I think. We've seen the last of him.'

Tyler was giddy with relief. Yes! Yes! Yes! Conway was gone! That was the best Christmas present he could possibly have. His nemesis was out of his hair. He could barely contain his ecstasy. He wanted to dance, sing, skip the light fandango and turn cartwheels across the floor. He restrained himself from punching the air and doing the conga along the corridor.

Then he remembered: it didn't matter whether Conway worked for Fossil Oil or not. He'd stupidly tendered his own resignation and Lance had grabbed it with both hands. That hadn't been his intention at all. How on earth was he going to explain it to Kirsten?

Chapter Fifty-nine

Josh Wallace was the obvious choice. Lance gnawed at the end of his pen. He should take Tyler's job after Christmas. There was no one else in a senior role who understood the system over here so well and he'd been propping up the whole of the sales team for some time now.

Someone new would come in as chairman. Perhaps this shake-up had been coming for a while and Tyler was getting out while the going was good. Yes, Lance thought, it would be good to have a new broom in. So be it. He should set things in motion now.

He got Veronica to call Wallace's number. It went to voicemail. No matter. That was the modern way.

'Josh, Lance Harvey here,' he said. 'Some good news that I thought you'd want to know before Christmas. I've been promoted to executive president and I'm offering you the position of sales director. Tyler Benson has tendered his resignation today and, as far as I'm concerned, you're the man for the job. When you pick up this message, call me and we can talk numbers.'

He dictated a note to Veronica. An offer letter needed to go to Wallace as soon as possible. She could sort out the contract for him in the new year.

Now that they probably weren't moving back to America, he was going to take a more relaxed attitude to his work, he decided. Between travels, he'd spend more time with Melissa. Perhaps even try to reconnect with the boys. When he had his feet under the table, they should take a vacation together. All of the family. The Florida Keys, maybe. Lance smiled to himself. It had all worked out very well indeed. It would be nice to bat out his days at Fossil Oil.

The snow was coming down heavily. Fat lacy flakes that whitened the sky and whirled hypnotically to the ground, whipped by the ever-present winds which hugged the slab-sided modern buildings that characterised the ever-burgeoning city. He wanted to be home now for Christmas. He wanted to tell Melissa of his promotion, of the change of plan. Yet again. But, as Melissa always did, she'd take it in her stride.

He poured the remains of the bourbon bottle into his waiting glass. One for the road. Sipping the amber liquid and for once savouring its taste, he watched the snow fall, softening as it did the sharp-edged man-made landscape. It almost looked pretty. He buzzed Veronica.

'Before you go, can you cancel my flights for Christmas Day?' he said. 'I'm not going to America now.'

'Certainly, Mr Harvey.'

Perhaps he'd take the week after Christmas off. Completely. That would be a first. Melissa would be surprised at her new, relaxed husband. Perhaps he'd even give up the booze. After Christmas. Mustn't be too hasty.

'When you've done that, you can go home.'

'Thank you, Mr Harvey.'

'Merry Christmas, Veronica,' he said.

'Merry Christmas, Mr Harvey.'

Lance drained his glass and placed it with exaggerated care on his desk. He called Martin to say that he was ready to leave, but the call went to voicemail. Unusual. He thought his driver would be out there waiting for him as he normally was. He punched the number in again, but there was still no response. Never mind: by the time he got downstairs Martin was sure to be there. He'd never failed him yet.

He called Melissa, but there was no reply from her phone either. Was no one picking up today? Goddamn Christmas. He hung up without leaving a message. He'd be home soon enough. If she'd told him she was going somewhere today, then he couldn't recall. Perhaps she'd simply got caught up in the frenzy of last-minute Christmas shopping. Lance smiled indulgently. It was just like her. He tutted to himself. He'd forgotten to ask Veronica what she'd bought for Melissa this year. But when he buzzed through to her office, his assistant had already left. Still, she always chose something wonderful and no doubt it had already been delivered and was waiting under the rather splendid Christmas tree in their living room. He was feeling in quite a festive mood.

Then he remembered he should have also told Veronica to send round an email to all of the staff to tell them that the SACKED programme had been shelved. Still, that could be done in the new year too. It would give the staff some good news to go forward with. Lance smiled to himself. Next year was shaping up to be a great one.

His eyes were beginning to feel heavy. It was time to call it a day. As he shrugged his coat on to his shoulders he felt a deep, dull pain shoot across his chest and down his arm, making him wince. Lance shook it away. It had dogged him all day – must be this damp British weather and the wretched snow. He could sleep in the car all the way back to London, rest up a little. That would be nice, as the traffic was probably going to be murder tonight. Still, Martin would look after him as he always did.

He retrieved his briefcase from under his desk. It was light, because it didn't have anything in it except for this morning's copy of the *Financial Times*, which he always failed to do more than flick through briefly. By the time he got home, Melissa would be back. She'd have a bourbon ready and waiting for him. After all these years it was nice that she still cared enough to do that for him. He ought to tell her more often. But she knew. After all this time, of course she knew. They'd have a good Christmas together. Melissa would like that.

As he turned to leave, the phone on his desk rang. The caller alert told him that it was Bud Harman again. Lance sighed. He'd just take this before he departed. As he reached for the handset, his arm went into spasm and he clutched the phone tightly, unable to release his grip. The telephone clattered from the desk, falling to the floor and cutting off the call. Following it, Lance sank to his knees on the carpet, a silent scream in his throat.

A searing hot pain shot through his chest. He thought of Melissa, he thought of his boys, he thought of how he should have done things so very differently. Then Lance Harvey, the newly appointed executive president of Fossil Oil, took his last breath.

Chapter Sixty

Melissa was having tea in the Long Gallery of the Ritz when Sebastian, her favourite concierge, came to speak to her.

'There's a gentleman at reception asking to speak to you, Mrs Harvey,' he said. 'A Mr Martin Sheffield.'

'Oh, Martin,' she said. 'Please ask him to come in.'

'I don't think he wants to. He said he'd rather stay in reception.'

'Tell him not to be so silly, Sebastian. Can you have another cup and some more tea sent too, please?'

'Certainly, Mrs Harvey.'

He turned and strode away.

The Ritz was bustling today and looking beautiful in its festive garb. Huge vases of seasonal flowers graced the long gallery and the pillars of the Palm Court were dressed with spirals of poinsettia and gold ribbon. A throng of chattering people enjoyed afternoon tea while the pianist was tinkling out a very agreeable selection of uplifting Christmas songs. She'd been ensconced here for a long time, watching everyone bustle to and fro, listening to the music. It was all so very lovely that it had quite taken her out of herself.

Melissa checked her phone. Lance had called her several times, but she'd let it go straight to voicemail. The last time was about an hour ago and there'd been nothing since then. The sad thing was that she had nothing to say to him. Their marriage was over and that was all there was to it. He'd be distraught, of course he would, but in time he'd surround himself with a horde of staff to cater for his needs and she was sure he'd barely notice that she'd gone.

She should be feeling panicked, cut adrift, but instead there was a quiet calm at the centre of her being. This had been long overdue and, now that it had happened, she felt she'd been given her life back.

The first thing she'd done on arrival at the Ritz was Skype the boys. She'd borrowed a laptop from the business centre and contacted them as soon as she could. When she'd told them she'd left their father, they'd been supportive, both of them. They'd also begged her to go out and see them. And she would, just as soon as she was able. There was talk that they might all meet up together in the new year and that would be nice. So nice. She missed them desperately.

When she looked towards reception again, Martin was coming through the glass doors. He was still wearing his work suit and seemed a little harried.

He walked up to her looking very ill at ease with his surroundings.

Melissa stood to greet him. 'Martin. How lovely to see you.'

Glancing round, he whispered, 'I'm more used to being round the back of these places, Mrs Harvey.'

'Not today, Martin. Today you're my guest.' She sat down again. 'What brings you here so soon? Is everything all right?'

'It's fine, Mrs Harvey.'

For a moment, she'd been worried that Lance had decided to send him to bring her home.

'Do sit down.' She patted the sofa next to her. 'I've sent for some more tea. I hope you'll join me.'

He was obviously feeling awkward, but he sat down beside her nevertheless. The tea arrived and Melissa poured him a cup. When she handed it to him, the delicate china looked ridiculously small in his hands.

'Are you settled in, Mrs Harvey?'

'Yes, yes,' she said. 'They gave me my usual suite. It's all lovely.'

'That's good to know.' Martin looked embarrassed. He sipped at his tea and she understood that he was a man who'd be happier with a mug in his hand. 'I've been worried about you.'

'That's very kind. I'm fine, Martin. Absolutely fine. Lance hasn't sent you, has he?'

'No, Mrs Harvey. Mr Harvey has no idea where you are. My lips are sealed. I just came to tell you that I've left Fossil Oil.' He took a deep breath. 'I dropped Mr Harvey at the office this morning and as I watched him go, something snapped inside me. I couldn't stay. I've had enough. So I took the Bentley back to the garage, left the keys on the desk and hopped on the train back to London.'

'Oh my goodness.' Melissa put a hand to her chest. 'This isn't because of me?'

'It's something I've been thinking about for a while.' He lowered his eyes. 'To be honest, Mrs Harvey, I've only stayed because of you.'

'Oh,' she said. 'That's very kind.'

He smiled at her shyly.

'How do you think Lance will get home?'

'He'll manage,' Martin said. 'He'll manage without us both.'

'You're right.' Though she knew he'd be furious when he found out that Martin had also absconded on Christmas Eve. 'If you've given up your job, what will you do now?'

'I'll think about that in the new year,' he said. 'I've got a lovely daughter, Julie, who lives out in Kent. She's always on at me to move down there, be closer to the grandkids. She's got three smashers. I might give up my council flat in town and do that. It would make her happy.'

'Do you know, Martin, in all the time you've been driving Lance – and me – I realise that I don't know anything about your life.'

She'd been so wrapped up in her own existence that she'd never taken the time to chat to him. That was a terrible thing. Perhaps she'd been blinded by her obsession with Tyler Benson. Or maybe it was because Martin had been there in the background, unobtrusive, ready to help. He was an attractive man too, and she'd never really noticed that before either. He was just Martin and always there. Now she noted that he was stocky, not overly tall. His face was ruddy; his eyes were kind and they were also a quite lovely shade of blue.

'There's nothing much to know, Mrs Harvey. I don't live an exciting life like you do. It's all very quiet.'

'I'm very glad to give up everything for a quiet life, Martin.' He knew only too well the things she'd had to endure in her marriage to Lance. He'd had an insight into parts of their lives that no one else knew about. She'd always valued his strength, his support and, most of all, his discretion. Martin was definitely a man you could rely on.

'I don't even know if you have a wife?'

'Widowed.' Martin cleared his throat. 'Pat died several years ago now.'

'I'm sorry.'

'It's hard on your own,' he continued. 'It's the little things you miss.'

'I think Pat was a very lucky woman.'

'I was recently retired from the police service, the Met. It was supposed to be our time together, to make up for all the time I

369

spent on shift work and hardly saw her.' He kept his eyes down as he spoke. 'You can never foresee these things, can you? That's why I took the driving job. I didn't want to be at home kicking my heels. It's been good for me. I've enjoyed it. You've been very easy to work for, Mrs Harvey.' He blushed at that. 'But, well, with everything that's happened, it's time to move on.'

'For you and me both,' she said.

'I'd better be going.' He finished his tea and became self-conscious as the cup rattled in its saucer when he put it down. 'It's tough out there, Mrs Harvey. I wish you all the luck in the world. If you need anything, you just let me know. Anything at all. You've got my number.'

'Thank you, Martin.' Tears rushed to her eyes and she dabbed them away. 'That's very thoughtful.'

He stood up. 'Well . . .'

Suddenly she didn't want to be alone tonight. No one should spend Christmas in a hotel by themselves, no matter how luxurious.

'What are you doing later, Martin?'

'Me? Nothing. Do you want me to drive you somewhere?'

'No,' she laughed. 'You're not my driver any more. Remember?'

'I still have my own car.'

'No, no. That's not what I meant at all. What I'm trying to ask is whether you'd like to come back and join me for dinner?'

He laughed softly and took in the opulence of the Ritz again. 'This is not my kind of place. I'm more at home in a transport café.'

'We can have dinner sent to my room. They do a lovely club sandwich and fries.'

He grinned at her. 'Now you're tempting me.'

'Don't let me be alone.' There was a catch in her voice as she said it.

'I'll come back at seven o'clock,' he said gruffly. 'If that suits you.'

'That would be perfect,' she said.

'I look forward to it, Mrs Harvey.'

'Melissa,' she said. 'Please, call me Melissa.'

Chapter Sixty-one

The doorbell rang and Kirsten was surprised. She hadn't expected Tyler for ages. He must have been driving at breakneck speed all down the M1 in spite of the snow. She hoped there wasn't going to be a tear-jerking scene. Her emotional bank account was on the verge of bankruptcy and Tyler always liked to do everything with high drama.

Peering out of the bedroom window, she was surprised that she couldn't see his car anywhere, nor him pacing up and down on the path like a madman. She slid the drawer of her dressing table closed and slipped into her outdoor shoes, turning to appraise the room. The bed sheets were still rumpled from her and Simon's lovemaking and she resisted the urge to cross the room and stroke the pillow where his head had lain for such a short, short time. She quelled the sour taste that came to her mouth and the feeling of utter desolation that gripped her insides like a vice. It looked as if she would be going out into the world, into her new life, alone. At least she was starting a new life. That was something to cling on to.

The doorbell rang again, impatiently. Car or not, that was definitely a Tyler-type ring. With one brief backward glance at the bedroom, she steeled herself, closed the door and clip-clopped down the stairs.

The strains of 'The Power of Love' drifted through the door. Was it carol singers? They hadn't had any visit their door for years, wherever they'd been living. Yet after a few bars she could tell that this was no fresh-faced, juvenile chorister that stood on her threshold. It certainly wasn't Tyler, because her husband couldn't sing a note. And this man was singing beautifully.

Kirsten opened the door.

Simon stood on the step in front of her. He was carrying two large plastic bags, one marked Henderson's family butchers in blood-red letters. It appeared to have the legs of a very large turkey sticking out of it. The other was from Sainsbury's and looked as if it was laden with vegetables of every conceivable shape and colour. He was still wearing his dinner suit and was also sporting a diving mask and snorkel perched on his head. The singing stopped mid-sentence.

Kirsten laughed at him. 'I thought for one minute you were Tyler.'

'Why?'

'He's on his way home.'

Simon let the carrier bags fall to the floor. 'Oh, Kirsten,' he said sadly, standing stock-still as if frozen to the spot. 'Don't do this,' he pleaded. 'Don't take him back. I had to go for a walk, I had to think. My brain was buzzing. This has all been a bit of a shock.'

'I thought you'd gone.' Her voice sounded small. 'I thought you'd walked out on me all over again. I couldn't stand it.'

'Never,' he said earnestly. 'I didn't leave you before and I'm planning never to leave your side for the rest of your life. Did what I said mean nothing?' His face was as bleak as the wintry sky above them. 'You've given me another chance and I'm going to make sure I grab that with both hands. We can go to the Seychelles, we can go to Spain or even Southend. Wherever you want.'

'You're too much of a realist to do this, Simon,' she said.

'I'm not,' he said passionately. 'I've called Lance and turned down the chairman's job. I'm not going to Fossil Oil.'

She stood there speechless.

'Kirsten Benson, I have just jacked in a very lucrative and esteemed career to chase some mad idea of opening a business doing goodness knows what, halfway round the world, in order to make the most beautiful woman I've ever known fall in love with me all over again. And I am standing in a very pleasant Hampstead side street on Christmas Eve wearing a snorkel.' He looked down forlornly. 'With a turkey for company.'

Kirsten laughed hesitantly.

'You can call me a lot of things, but a realist isn't one of them. Realist, no. Dreamer, yes.' He took her hands in his. 'I've dreamed for years that one day we'd be together again.' His eyes searched hers. 'Don't tell me I've blown it.'

'No, you haven't blown it.' She wound her arms round him and held him tightly. 'However, you *did* cut it a bit fine. A few minutes more and I'd have been gone.' Kirsten reached behind the door and produced her suitcase.

'You're leaving?'

Kirsten nodded. 'I told Tyler he could come home,' she said with a sad smile. 'I just didn't tell him I wouldn't be here waiting for him.'

'Where were you planning to go?'

'I don't know,' she said candidly. 'Maybe to the Seychelles. Alone.'

'Wherever we go, whatever we do,' Simon said, 'let's make sure it's together.'

'You really phoned Lance to turn him down?' Kirsten asked.

'Yes. When push came to shove, it wasn't half as difficult as I thought it was going to be. Fossil Oil or you? No contest.'

Simon folded her into his embrace and at that moment she

374

believed that he would never let her go again. Somewhere deep inside her she was still as dry and as crusty as week-old bread; she would need to soak in the milk of Simon's kindness for a long time to have any hope of rescuing that inner gentleness that had once been there. Gazing up at Simon, despite looking ridiculous with his diving-mask-and-snorkel attire, she could see the love for her shining in his eyes.

'I think we'd better make a move,' Kirsten advised, reluctant to leave the warmth of his arms. 'Tyler won't be far away, and I can't face another confrontation.'

'Where do you want to go?'

'I still don't know.' She gave an uncertain laugh.

'Well, at the risk of being called a realist again, I suggest we go back to my place in Milton Keynes and lie low for a few days.'

'You certainly know how to bring a girl back down to earth with a bump,' Kirsten replied wryly. 'Milton Keynes? Mind you, I do like the sound of the lying-low bit.'

Simon regarded the sleek black sports car balefully. 'There's just one snag,' he said. 'Either that turkey or this case will fit in my boot. Not both.'

Kirsten frowned.

'What do you want to do? Eat, or dress nicely?'

'I have an extensive range of designer lingerie in that suitcase,' she informed him.

'Sorry, old pal,' Simon said to the turkey as he left it on the pavement along with the carrier bag of vegetables.

He picked up the case and swung it into the boot of the two-seater. Then he turned to her, his face lit up. 'You know, if we're travelling light, we could just go straight to the airport and get the first flight out of here.'

Kirsten stared at him agog. 'Where to?'

'It doesn't matter. It would be a symbolic gesture to mark the start of our new, free-spirited life together.'

A shiver of fear and excitement went through her. 'Could we do it?'

'Why don't we try? I'm game if you are.'

'I am.'

It started to snow again. Heavy, lazy, lacy flakes that drifted serenely to the ground. So it was set to be a white Christmas after all.

'I wonder what the odds are on a white Christmas in London this year?' Kirsten said.

Simon pulled her to him and kissed her softly. 'I wonder what are the odds on you and me finding that we're still hopelessly in love after all these years?'

She stared at him thoughtfully. 'Will you still love me when I'm old and grey?'

He stared back at her. 'I will. Will you still love me when I'm bald and have dentures on the bedside table?'

'I still love you even though you're wearing a snorkel in Hampstead,' she said.

'That's good enough for me.' His warm mouth found hers again.

Kirsten closed her eyes and let Simon's arms fold round her, nestling into his body. She didn't think she'd ever felt such happiness.

It made her think of Tyler and whether he realised that this time it was over for good. A momentary cloud of sadness flitted over her brightness, and she wondered what the future would hold for him. An empty life of booze and broken relationships? She hoped not. Who knew, he may enjoy his life better now that he was free to dedicate himself fully to Fossil Oil without compromise. Maybe, for some people, that was what life was all about. Work, work and more work. She looked at Simon, a smile curling her lips and the love she felt for him rising to the surface like the bubbles in champagne. There was certainly more to life for her.

'Let's get going,' Simon urged. He pulled off his snorkel and tossed it carelessly into the boot next to the suitcase.

Kirsten took a last lingering look at the house. It was a beautiful house; she just wasn't sure that it had ever been a home. Tyler had worked hard for it, too hard, and perhaps ultimately that was what had caused their downfall. Too much time for work and too little time for each other. Well, he could have it all. With pleasure. All she would walk away with was this small suitcase and her sanity. What she had found was worth far more.

Propping the dejected-looking turkey and the bag of vegetables just inside the front door ready for Tyler's return – he might as well make use of them – Kirsten closed it behind her for the final time and ran to join Simon.

She slipped into the car next to him, happy to get out of the falling snow, which was clinging to the spindly trees along the pavement and starting to look alarmingly like the winter wonderland at the Fossil Oil Christmas party. Kirsten shuddered at the memory.

'Ready?' Simon asked.

She nodded silently, unable to speak, her eyes burning with tears of both happiness and regret.

'One thing's for certain,' Simon said lightly as he put the car into gear: 'I'll make sure that the parties are a lot tamer in the Seychelles or wherever we end up. All things considered, that was one hell of a Christmas party.'

Kirsten laughed tearfully. 'I suppose it was,' she agreed.

He squeezed her hand comfortingly and eased the car into the street.

As they turned the corner, neither of them looked back. If they had, they'd have seen Tyler pulling up behind them in his car and bounding up to the house with hope in his step.

Chapter Sixty-two

So, I lied to Josh about showing him a wild time. Though I have to say he doesn't seem to be minding too much.

We're currently at the shopping centre in the city, which is beautifully decked out for Christmas. When I say 'we', I mean all of us. There's Mum, Dad, Mia, me and Josh. I've decided not to go for the gentle introduction. If Josh thinks he wants to be involved in our lives, he might as well have it full-on.

On the very rare occasions I have seen other men, I took it gently – had at least a few dates before the subject of Mia even cropped up. It may have been the types I unwisely chose to date, but the minute most men realised I had a daughter in tow they went scuttling to the hills. So far, Josh hasn't done any scuttling at all. He's been treated to the unexpurgated Young Family Experience package and he hasn't flinched once. I admire that in a man. He currently has my daughter on his shoulders so that she can get a better view, and she doesn't seem to be fazed by that either. As I watch her giggling and wriggling, Josh holding tightly on to her sturdy legs, there's a little lump closing my throat that might be happiness, or it might be sadness that she hasn't had this before.

This year the shopping centre seems to have gone completely over the top with the decorations, and it's none the worse for it.

The place looks fantastic. Middleton Hall, the main square in front of John Lewis, is sparkling under a gossamer canopy of silver threads. Iridescent stars hang down, catching dazzling, twirling lights.

Santa's grotto is under the watch of a benign snow queen. She stands impeccable in white robes and silver crown, welcoming the children. Her attendant fairies fly on transparent wings above the magical scene that's been created to great effect. There are miniature castles with fancy turrets surrounded by sparkling moats and rivers of glitter.

Mia, of course, is speechless with awe.

Mum looks up at her. 'It's your turn now, little lady,' she says, checking her watch against the number printed on our timed ticket.

So Josh lowers her from his shoulders and we join the queue that snakes towards Santa's grotto.

As we get to the turnstile, Josh's phone rings and he pulls it out of his pocket. When he glances at it, his eyes widen. 'Lance Harvey,' he says to me with a puzzled frown. 'What can he want?'

'Take it,' I tell him. 'We can go and see Santa and meet you out here later. We won't be long.'

Mum hands over our tickets and they're clipped by a grinning elf.

'Why would Lance be ringing me?'

'It might be important.'

It also might be about him being sacked by Tyler, I think, but I obviously can't say that with my parents here. They're already fussing over Josh as if we've been together for years. Not only is my mother thinking about a hat, I suspect she's already mentally compiling a guest list. I don't want to tell them yet that all is not quite hunky-dory in Team Louise. I try to convey this message to Josh with my eyes and he winks back at me that he's understood.

'He might just be wishing me happy Christmas,' Josh says, laughing at how unlikely that is. 'Whatever it is, it can wait for a few minutes.'

'Are you sure?'

'Yes.' He lets his phone go to voicemail and pockets it again. 'I've never seen Santa in real life before. We can't wait, can we, Mia?'

He high-fives my daughter and I can tell she's already smitten by him. As I may well be too. Suddenly, I find myself hoping Josh Wallace is going to be in our lives on a permanent basis.

We're ushered into the grotto, which is a marvellous creation of a cave fashioned from fake snow and glitter. Mia slips her hand into mine while we walk through the twisty-turny corridor until we reach the man himself.

Santa's sitting on a silver chair and looks suitably rotund and ruddy, just as he should. I thought Mia might be shy, but I should have known my daughter better. As soon as she sees him she runs to hug him, squashing herself into his pillowy stomach.

'Now, Mia,' he says, checking the card that my mum has handed to him. 'What would you like for Christmas?'

Alarmingly, my daughter holds up her fingers to count. 'I'd like a micro-scooter in pink,' she starts. 'A Furby Party Rocker. A ballerina jewellery box.'

Even though she has no jewellery.

'An It's Teatime tea set. A ballerina Barbie. A KidiPet cat.'

'My, my,' Santa says, peering over his fake glasses. 'That's a long list.'

'I haven't finished,' Mia informs him.

Josh and I hide our giggles and he looks at me as if he can't believe what my daughter is coming out with. I feel much the same.

'A My Little Pony Crystal Empire. A trampoline.'

380

Over my dead body. I have no desire to spend every weekend in A&E.

'A Baby Born doll.' She takes a deep breath. Thankfully, she's running out of fingers. 'A Sleeping Beauty Glitter Dress.'

'My, my,' Santa says again. The poor man looks a bit shell-shocked now.

'Or a Cinderella Glitter Dress, if you can't get that one.'

I blame Mum for going through the Argos Christmas catalogue with her in September. I'm just glad there are a few of these things at home already, under the tree or stowed in the loft for tomorrow. Most of it has been bought by my indulgent parents, but I'm glad I was able to contribute. Without wanting to wish away Christmas, I do wonder what next year will hold.

'Have you been *very* good?' Santa asks my child.

'Yes. I am the bestest girl in the whole wide world,' she says proudly, quoting my parents.

Despite not having a father in her life, my child doesn't seem to suffer from self-esteem issues.

'Well, then,' Santa says. 'I can't promise that you'll get everything, but if you put out a little cake for me tonight and a carrot for Rudolph, I'll make sure that you get some lovely presents.'

'We put out whisky and one of Granny's mince pies,' Mia says. 'Do you like that?'

'Yes,' Santa says, trying to hide his grin. 'That's very thoughtful.'

'Last year Gramps drank the whisky,' she says, dobbing in my dad.

Gramps admits his guilt with an accepting shrug. Josh just shakes his head in amused bewilderment. Now he can be in absolutely no doubt what he's planning to take on. Brave man.

'I think I could get her a job in sales,' he whispers to me.

'Sometimes grown-ups do that,' Santa says, letting my dad

off the hook. 'But I don't mind. Now, Mia, would you like to choose a present?'

Mia grabs a prettily wrapped present from the pink pile. The biggest, of course.

Then we head outside with my beaming child and my parents, who both have tears in their eyes. I feel a little bit choked myself. It won't be long before she learns that Santa doesn't really exist and that everything she asks for won't automatically be delivered to her door.

When we're back out in the shopping centre, Josh says, 'Thanks so much for including me in that.'

'My pleasure.'

'Now I think I should treat us all to a twirl on the merry-go-round.'

'Yay!' Mia shouts and takes me by the hand to drag me there.

We all head over to the carousel with its pretty prancing horses. They're painted in pink, yellow and gold, suspended on twirling poles like candy canes.

'My Little Pony,' Mia says excitedly.

At the booth, Josh shells out a small fortune for tickets.

'Not for us,' Mum protests as he hands over a great wodge of cash.

'For all of us,' Josh insists, and my mother goes all girly. She's already his number-one fan. Poor Dad won't get a look-in tomorrow. Josh will get the juiciest cut of turkey, the crispest roast potatoes, the biggest bowl of Christmas pudding.

'I haven't been on a carousel in years,' she twitters. 'What do you think about that, Bernard?'

Dad just nods, but is clearly pleased to have the unique pleasure of some male company while undertaking these unseemly activities that are so often required of him. He's always the one stoically accompanying Mia into the swimming pool, ball-pit or bouncy castle as my mum doesn't like to mess up her hair.

While we wait for the carousel to stop so that we can get on, I say to Josh, 'You'd better check what Lance Harvey wants. Everyone will have disappeared for Christmas soon.'

'You're right,' he says, and pulls out his mobile.

He moves away from us slightly, clamping the phone tight to his head to try to block out the hurdy-gurdy music while he listens to the voicemail. As he does, I can see the colour of his face change. It goes from red to white and back again in seconds. Something is obviously very wrong.

When he hangs up, he turns to me. Now he's ashen.

'What?' My heart is in my mouth. Perhaps Tyler has decided to charge Josh with assault, or sue us both or something. What a great Christmas present *that* would be. Whatever it is, I'm frightened by the look on his face. Whatever Lance Harvey has said to him, it's clearly rocked Josh's world. 'Tell me. What's wrong?'

It's a moment or two before he can speak, and that worries me even more.

Eventually he blurts out, 'I've been promoted.'

I take a step back. 'What?'

Josh starts to laugh. He puts his hands to his head. 'Tyler's resigned and I'm now the new sales director of Fossil Oil.' His laugh slips towards hysterical.

'There must be some mistake.'

'I don't think so.' He holds out the phone to me and plays the message again.

Sure enough, it's Lance offering him the position of sales director, and he doesn't sound like he's joking. And why would he? Lance may be a lot of things, but I don't think he's a prankster. This does indeed sound deadly serious.

'Can this be true? I'm not doubting your ability,' I assure him, 'but why's Tyler resigned?'

'I've no idea,' Josh says. 'Something has clearly happened since we left the office.'

That's an understatement.

'I need to call Lance right away,' he says.

The merry-go-round slows as he presses to return Lance's call. It rings out as the current riders dismount. Mia is bouncing in her excitement, tugging on my hand. My mother is straightening her hair with her hand in preparation.

After a few seconds, Josh shrugs. 'No reply.'

'You'll have to sort it out in the new year,' I say.

'Yeah.' He still looks stunned.

'Until then' – I throw my arms around him and hug him tightly. He's deserving of this, I'm sure. Out of all the executives I've met at Fossil, he seems to be the only man who has some sense of integrity. He'll do a much better job than Tyler Benson any day – 'congratulations!'

'I guess so.' He's still perplexed by his good fortune.

'Mum, Dad, Josh has been given a promotion. He's going to be the new sales director of Fossil Oil.'

'Well done, lad,' Dad says, shaking his hand vigorously. 'Very well done.'

'How lovely,' Mum says, indulging in more hair-patting. She couldn't be more proud if she was his real mother. 'We should open a bottle of Buck's Fizz.' It's her celebration drink of choice as my dad gets it cheap with his staff discount in Marks & Spencer.

'That means I'm going to be your boss,' Simon points out.

'Oh, yeah.' That makes me frown.

'At least you can consider yourself unsacked,' he whispers to me.

'It will be a pleasure to work for you.'

He keeps his voice low so that my parents can't hear. 'I don't want it to affect our relationship.'

'We'll work something out,' I assure him.

His eyes shine. 'This is good news. More than I could have hoped for. The future looks bright for us, Louise.'

'I really hope so.' What a team we'll make!

Goodness only knows what's happened at Fossil in our wake, but I can't wait to find out. Looks like we'll have to be patient until after Christmas. Still, until then we'll have plenty to be cheerful about.

Who knew that all this would have happened at the Christmas party? I thank my lucky stars that Dad woke me and I went along, otherwise I might have missed it. I may never have had the chance to meet Josh and we could have continued to be nothing but colleagues who exchanged pleasantries. Now I hope I've found a man who will be in our lives for good. It's too soon to say, of course, but I have great hopes for this relationship. Together we could really go places. Someone with Josh's ambition and talent could provide both me and Mia with a stable, comfortable life. I like the sound of that.

The pretty painted horses are all empty now. It looks as if they're waiting just for us.

'It's our turn on the merry-go-round,' I say.

'Let's climb on board then.' Josh scoops Mia into his arms. He looks at us both with what I think is love in his eyes.

Josh takes my hand and helps me to step up as we take our places on the carousel.

Christmas
Day

Chapter Sixty-three

'Promise you'll hop on a plane and visit me soon, Mom.' The voice coming from the laptop screen didn't quite move in synchronisation with the mouth, but there were times when she was very grateful for Skype.

'Of course I will, darling,' Melissa said. She fought back a tear. 'As soon as things are sorted out here.'

Drew wanted her to go out and stay with him at the orphanage in Nepal that he managed. He was desperate to see her, he'd said, and goodness only knew she was desperate to see her boys too.

'We're always grateful for an extra pair of hands, you know, and you'd adore the kids. They're great. It's very rewarding.'

It sounded exactly like the sort of thing she'd love to do. Something she'd never previously dared to try, for fear of leaving Lance alone for a few weeks. Now she had left him for good and could do whatever she liked. If she thought about that too much, it made her feel dizzy.

She still had the laptop from the business centre, and from the comfort of her room had Skyped both Drew and Kyle on Christmas morning. It was lunchtime for Drew, and he didn't have long to talk. When he'd started there, a few years ago now, he'd introduced Christmas to the children of the orphanage and they celebrated it in the same way that they celebrated all the other Nepali festivals. She'd shipped an imitation Christmas tree and decorations to him that they put up every year.

Kyle was spending the winter season teaching snowboarding in Gstaad and hadn't yet been to bed. That was down to partying. It had been lovely to talk to him and she must see him soon too.

'I love you,' she said to Drew. 'I'll leave you to enjoy your Christmas celebrations.'

'You're not going to be alone, Mom?'

'No, no. You're not to worry about me. I'm fine, really.'

On the screen, Drew looked sceptical.

'I've been invited to have Christmas lunch with a friend.'

'Have fun.' He blew her a kiss and she returned it.

'Happy Christmas, darling.'

'You too, Mom. Love you.' The screen went blank.

She sat in her room quietly, tears still prickling behind her eyes. That would definitely be her new year's resolution, to see more of her boys.

Picking up her handbag and slipping on her coat, she left her room and caught the elevator down to the Long Gallery to wait.

She'd had a lovely dinner with Martin last night. True to her word, they'd ordered club sandwiches served in her suite, and it had been so nice. Despite her underlying sadness, they'd laughed so much together. He was very good company – funny and sharp-witted – and she wondered why it had taken her so long to realise that. He was an old-fashioned gentleman too, the type who opened doors and stood up until you were seated. Due to being a policeman and then doing a job that involved driving, he'd chosen not to drink alcohol either. It had been a refreshing change to eat dinner with someone who was still coherent by the end of it.

Today he was taking her to his daughter's house in Kent to

join the family for Christmas lunch. Although she was quite nervous about meeting them, she'd readily accepted his invitation as she had nowhere else to go, and no one should spend Christmas Day alone.

Yesterday afternoon she'd taken the decision not to return to America after all and had torn her e-ticket in half, throwing it into the waste bin. Now that she was on the verge of leaving, she realised how much she liked England. So much so that she thought she'd settle here permanently. A lot depended on Lance. She hoped he wouldn't be difficult with her divorce settlement and they could sort out their financial affairs without too much argument. She felt she'd put as much as he had into Fossil Oil over the years and deserved a decent payout, but he could be stubborn when he wanted to. She thought he would have rung her again by now, tried to persuade her to come home. Especially as it was Christmas morning. But she'd heard nothing from him.

She hoped that meant he'd accepted her decision. She also hoped he wasn't getting roaring drunk, but that was probably asking too much. The tears threatened again. Perhaps she should call him, see how he was faring. Thirty years together was a long time and Lance would no doubt be hurting. It had been a bad time to leave him, a terrible time. Yet if she hadn't gone yesterday, she might never have left at all. She toyed with her phone, fingers hovering over Lance's number. What would she say? 'Sorry' hardly seemed adequate.

The other person she wanted to call was Kirsten Benson. She wanted to confess to her about her affair with Tyler and apologise for all the hurt she'd caused. She felt sorry for Kirsten and that she should have been a friend to her. If only she'd reached out to Kirsten instead of Tyler, it could have saved them both a world of pain. However, that wasn't the kind of call you could make on Christmas Day. Perhaps she and Tyler could mend their marriage. Or maybe Kirsten too would find the strength to leave her destructive relationship. Whichever way the cookie crumbled, she hoped they'd find a way to enjoy Christmas together. With a bit of festive magic you never could tell what would happen. Melissa would let the dust settle and then she'd contact her in the new year and try to make amends somehow. For now, she put her phone away.

Moments later, Martin came into the gallery. He was dressed in the same smart light-grey suit that he'd worn last night and she thought again how very dapper he looked.

'Ready, Melissa? It'll take us about an hour to drive to Maidstone.'

'Are you absolutely sure your daughter doesn't mind me being foisted on her and her family?'

'Nonsense. She's looking forward to meeting you.'

'I don't have gifts for them.'

'That's not what matters,' he assured her.

'I hate to turn up empty-handed. I'll be sure to buy them a thank-you gift in the new year.'

Martin studied his shoes for a moment. 'You're still going to stay in England? I'm not going to have to rush to a plane later?'

She laughed. 'No. I'm definitely staying here.'

He smiled. 'That's good to know.'

'Though I did just promise Drew that I'd visit him out in Nepal. Maybe give him a hand for a couple of months at the orphanage he runs.'

'That sounds like an excellent idea,' he said with an approving nod. 'Wouldn't mind doing something like that myself.'

Taking her arm, Martin led her out of the Ritz and towards his car. It was a lovely car, a family saloon, not as ostentatious as the Bentley, which suited her just fine.

As he settled her in the front, fussing with her seatbelt, her phone rang. Lance. It must be. Her mouth went slightly dry as she fumbled her phone out of her handbag. She looked at the caller display. Tyler Benson. What could he possibly want?

She toyed with the idea of answering it, then changed her mind. Whatever Tyler was calling about, it wouldn't be to wish her a happy Christmas. Maybe Lance had challenged him after reading the note she'd left. Well, she didn't want Tyler to spoil her day now. He'd marred her happiness for long enough. She put her phone back in her handbag unanswered.

'Nothing important?' Martin asked.

'No,' she said. 'Nothing at all. Everything's fine.'

He climbed into the car and pulled away from the hotel. She hoped Lance didn't cancel her credit card, otherwise she wouldn't be able to pay the bill for her stay. Still, that was the least of her worries.

Martin was such a sure-footed driver, and always had been, that she relaxed back in her seat and stared out at the pretty snowy landscape.

An hour later they pulled up outside a modest semi-detached home on a housing estate. Christmas lights blinked on and off on the front of it even though it was daylight.

'Well,' Martin said. 'We're here.'

'I'm a little anxious.'

He took her hand and squeezed it. 'No need. They'll love you.'

They'd only just emerged from the car when the front door was flung open and two small children raced out.

'Grandad!'

As they barrelled into him, Martin scooped them into his arms and spun them round.

'Santa's been,' they told him breathlessly as he put them down again.

'Let's get inside and see what you've got then.' He ushered Melissa forward. 'This is my friend Melissa. She's come to see how good you are.'

'We've been told off already,' the little girl admitted as she slipped her hand in his.

'Come on in,' Martin said.

Inside the door, his daughter was waiting to greet them. She threw her arms around him. 'Happy Christmas, Dad.'

'And to you, love.' He turned to Melissa, who was hanging back. 'This is Mrs Harvey – Melissa.'

'I'm Julie,' she said. 'Happy Christmas, Melissa. It's lovely that you could come.'

And Melissa, who wasn't used to being hugged, relaxed into a warm embrace.

'Let's get you settled in and introduced to the rest of the gang,' Julie said, and led the way into the living room.

Before they followed her, Martin turned to Melissa. 'Merry Christmas,' he said.

She kissed him gently on the cheek. 'Merry Christmas, Martin.'

Chapter Sixty-four

'Christmas in St Lucia,' Kirsten sighed. She turned on her bar stool to look at Simon. 'Who'd have thought?'

'We didn't quite make it to the Seychelles, but at least we hit the same letter of the alphabet.'

'I'm liking this new spontaneous lifestyle.' One that isn't dictated by Fossil Oil, she added silently.

'We *are* only one day into it.'

'I know, but I like to think that, now we've broken free from the shackles of corporate slavery, we can do it.'

Simon laughed at her. 'We'll do whatever you want. I promise you that.'

She sipped her Dirty Banana cocktail – a drink of ripe banana, crushed ice, coffee liqueur and rum, all smooshed up with ice-cream. It was creamy and sweet, like a banana milkshake but loaded with alcohol. It was the perfect drink for Christmas Day.

The small hut – Crazy Larry's Lazy Bar – was open-air, thatched with palm leaves and facing on to a magnificent stretch of white sand. The Caribbean sky was cloudless, the turquoise sea sparkled invitingly. The bar was decked with fairly lights and there was a blow-up Santa hanging from the centre of the ceiling fan. Wham's 'Last Christmas' chimed out from tinny speakers. The temperature was way past eighty degrees.

'It doesn't feel much like Christmas at all,' she said.

'True.' Simon sighed. 'But it's great to be here.'

She thought of the sleet and snow they'd escaped from in London and felt as if that was another world. A world that she had no inclination to return to.

'I can't believe we've left our old lives behind so easily.' It had felt amazing to just turn up at Heathrow Airport and buy tickets for the first available flight to somewhere hot. As Simon had paid for the tickets, she'd felt reckless, free and liberated. She'd even left her suitcase behind – what was the point of lugging winter clothing with her? – and decanted all she'd need for a few days into a WH Smith carrier bag. As they'd raced laughing and breathless through the concourse to the departure gate, clutching each other tightly, scant luggage in hand, she'd felt loved for the first time in many years.

This was how she wanted to live her life now, according to her own wishes. Not bogged down by the demands of corporate life, by a husband whose deceit was becoming the stuff of legend, by insecurity and loneliness.

'I wonder where we'll end up?' she mused.

'Cornwall,' he said decisively.

Kirsten laughed. 'Sounds like you've been giving it some thought.'

'I have. When I woke up this morning it suddenly occurred to me: why don't we return to the place where we were at our happiest? We always loved it, and there's a lot we could do there.'

'Cornwall.' She nodded slowly, letting it sink in.

'We could buy one of those fabulous houses we used to look at. Have the kids. The dogs.'

'Dexter and Bounce?'

'Everything we once planned.' He took her hand and held it tightly. 'You could be the bride that you were destined to be.'

Tears rushed to her eyes. 'That sounds like a proposal.'

Simon smiled. 'I think it is.'

'Then, yes. I'd like that. I'd like that very much.'

Simon kissed her and she knew that she was where she should be. She was here, in the moment, with the man she'd always loved.

When they broke apart, he said, 'I don't want to rush you, though. For now, we can just rest, enjoy the sun and take time to get to know each other all over again.' Simon stroked her thigh. 'We've got a lot of catching up to do.'

She was very much enjoying the 'catching up' part. They'd arrived late last night, ragged, dishevelled and tired. But after a relaxing night's sleep and a lazy morning, she was beginning to feel human again. They'd booked into the hotel for two weeks and, after that, who knew? Perhaps they'd do what Simon suggested and head to Cornwall to settle. It sounded idyllic, and with Simon by her side she was sure it would be. Wherever she ended up, she wanted to do something fulfilling with her life, and this break would give her time to think what that might be.

Her phone rang and she reached into her beach bag. They'd bought a few essentials at the hotel shop this morning, since all she'd arrived with was underwear and toiletries. Now she had shorts, a bikini and suntan oil. As soon as Christmas was over they'd have to replenish their wardrobes a little, yet Kirsten didn't think she'd be needing her heavy coat and boots for a while. Perhaps never again.

She looked at the display on the phone. Tyler. She turned the screen and showed it to Simon.

'Take it if you need to,' he said.

'I have nothing to say to him.' She couldn't bear to hear his sob story. If he was alone for Christmas, then he had no one to blame but himself. Perhaps the lovely Louise would offer him some festive comfort. Kirsten couldn't care less. She was done with Tyler and her heart felt lighter for it.

She cut off the call and instead of returning the phone to her bag she dropped it into the rubbish bin at the end of the bar. Another thing she wouldn't miss.

Simon stroked her hair. 'I'll do everything I can to make you happy.'

'I'll hold you to that,' she teased.

She felt as if they had a bright future ahead of them, and could only hope she was right. This time there would be no three-strikes-and-you're-out, this time she'd have a zero-tolerance policy on infidelity. She looked at Simon and knew in her soul that he was a very different man from Tyler. He wouldn't cheat on her, he wouldn't let her down. Her only regret was that they'd wasted a decade without each other.

'Merry Christmas, Kirsten.'

The breeze lifted her hair, the sun warmed her skin and the man she loved kissed her softly on the lips.

Chapter Sixty-five

There are wonderful smells of roasting turkey and pigs-in-blankets coming from the kitchen. Dad, already wearing his Christmas paper hat, is setting the table. That should be my job, but I've been given leave to play with Mia, who is in a state of hyper-excitement after being lavished with toys by that generous old soul, Father Christmas.

I encouraged my parents to think modestly when it came to gifts this year, but they clearly haven't been able to stop themselves from spoiling their one and only granddaughter. As a result she's trying to play with every single one of her toys all at once. She has on her Disney Princess Sleeping Beauty Glitter Dress over her new Christmas outfit.

She got most of the things on her dreaded Christmas list. Except the trampoline. The trampoline was definitely a banned substance. I've been up with her since four o'clock this morning, when I gave up the battle to contain her in bed any longer. Mum and Dad, bleary-eyed and in their dressing-gowns, followed shortly afterwards. I bet you a pound that they'll both be fast asleep on the sofa by the time the Queen comes on the telly.

'What time is that young man of yours coming, Lou-Lou?' Dad asks.

'Dad,' I say shyly. 'He's not my "young man".'

'You know what I mean, love,' he says. 'He seems a nice sort.'

'He is.'

The doorbell rings. 'That'll be him,' I say. 'Whatever you do, don't smother him.'

Dad looks affronted. 'I don't know what you mean.'

'Don't start asking what his intentions towards me are before we get to the Christmas pudding.'

'Can I ask after that?' Dad teases.

'It might be the season of goodwill, but I will kill you with my bare hands if you do,' I counter.

'I hope he makes you happy, Lou-Lou.' Dad touches my arm, embarrassed. 'You deserve it. To see you settled is the best Christmas present I could have.'

'Will someone get that!' Mum shouts tetchily from the kitchen. She will be red-faced and flustered as she always is when she does Christmas dinner. That's mainly because she cooks for about twenty-five of us when there are in fact usually only four. An extra mouth to feed today will have sent her over the edge.

'I'll go.' I leave Mia, who pounces on her Gramps and tries to educate him in the dubious joys of My Little Pony. I smile as I see her place a tiny pink comb into his big, gnarled hands. Hands that have been treated to pink nail varnish more than once by said granddaughter.

When I open the door, Josh is standing there, almost hidden by a pile of beautifully wrapped presents.

'Wow,' I say. 'When on earth did you manage to go shopping for those? Did you do a ram raid?'

'The minute I left you last night, I raced round the shopping centre. Now I know why some of the shops stay open until midnight.'

'Thank goodness they do.'

'I couldn't come empty-handed,' Josh says. 'Not after you've been kind enough to invite me.'

'I just hope you've put some money in your patience meter,' I whisper. 'You're going to need it. I warn you, my parents are your biggest fans. They already have us married off.'

'Is that such a bad thing?'

Both of us flush.

Me and my big gob. To get us back on an even keel, I ask, 'How's Fossil Oil's new sales director feeling this morning?'

'Weird,' he says. 'Very weird. I still can't believe it's true.'

'Don't leave him standing at the door!' Mum again. 'You're letting all my heat out.'

'Come in.' I stand aside, letting Josh pass through into the living room. When he's there, I take the presents from him and pile them on the sofa.

My dad instantly abandons his little pony and stands up. 'Merry Christmas, son,' he says. 'Merry Christmas.'

Son. God, they are so embarrassing. I raise an eyebrow at that, but Dad is unabashed. He takes Josh's hand and shakes it until I think it might detach from his arm.

'Dad. Leave him alone.'

When Josh finally gets his hand back, he turns to Mia. 'Hey, you,' he says. 'What did Santa bring?'

'All this,' she says, wide-eyed. 'We can play with my It's Teatime tea set.' Another victim for her to monopolise.

'Let me take him through to Granny to say hello,' I tell Mia. 'Then you can have him.'

This boy is going to have to man up if he's going to be part of this family. Then I realise what I've said, if only in my mind, and feel a warm little squirming in my tummy. And it's not just because I've been on the Marks & Spencer Buck's Fizz since dawn.

I take Josh into the kitchen. There's a cloud of steam over the cooker and the windows are running with condensation. It's as hot as Hades as the turkey has already been in for hours. My mother likes everything Well Done. Dad has to restrain her from putting the sprouts on in November. My pink-cheeked mum is taking her apron off to greet him.

'Mum, you don't have to take your pinny off to say hello.'

'Of course I do.' She pats her hair. 'We don't stand on ceremony here.'

I don't point out that that's *exactly* what she's doing.

'Merry Christmas, Mrs Young.'

'Oh, do call me Audrey.'

At least she didn't say 'Call me Mum.' I should be thankful for small mercies.

'Lunch won't be long,' she says.

'Is there anything I can do to help?'

'Oh, no, no, no, no, no,' Mum says. 'Bernard will do it all. He's a very good sous-chef.'

Good luck with that, Dad.

'Louise, make sure your young man has a drink.'

'Orange juice?' I ask.

He nods.

'Get him something proper, Louise. We've got M&S Buck's Fizz.'

'I don't drink, Audrey,' he says. 'Have to keep my driving licence.'

'Sensible,' Mum says. 'Very sensible.'

Now she's fallen in love with him a little bit more. I fear this is going to be a long day. For poor Josh, not me. I for one am so glad to have him here and he seems to have slotted into my family seamlessly, which gives me a little glow.

As I pour Josh's drink, my phone rings and I retrieve it from the worktop. When I glance at the display, I'm shocked to see Tyler Benson's name. I move away from my mum and go into the hall, nodding to Josh that he should follow me.

'It's Tyler,' I whisper to Josh. 'What can he want?'

He shrugs. 'Perhaps he just wants to wish you merry Christmas.'

'And perhaps not.' I snap off the phone. 'Whatever it is, I don't want to talk to him now. It'll have to wait until the new year.' It can only be bad news. If he's resigned over something we've done, then he'll only want to harangue me some more. I don't need to hear that today. 'He's obviously a man with a lot on his plate. I wonder if he knows that you're going to fill his shoes?'

'I don't know. I would have thought he'd have been straight on the phone to me if he had, but I've heard nothing.'

'I wonder how things are on the domestic front. If he's made up with Kirsten yet.' I chew at my lip. 'I feel I should call her. Perhaps in the new year. I want her to know there was absolutely nothing going on between me and Tyler. Quite the opposite. I owe her that much.'

'I don't think you owe either Kirsten or Tyler Benson anything at all. It might not have been you he was sleeping with, but he was certainly no saint.'

'No,' I agree. 'I still hate to think of her having a miserable Christmas because of something I've done.'

'She'll be fine,' Josh assures me. 'People like that always come up roses. He's probably showering her with diamonds as we speak.' Josh raises his eyebrows. 'Speaking of which . . .'

'Don't tell me there's a diamond ring for me in that pile of presents?' Then, of course, I could bite off my own tongue.

He laughs. 'Not quite. But I do have something for you.'

So we go back to the living room. He hands a few of the boxes to Mia, who of course is delighted that her glut of presents hasn't yet ended. There's one for my dad and Josh puts aside a box for Mum.

'You didn't wrap all these yourself, did you?'

'No,' Josh admits. 'I availed myself of every gift-wrapping service on offer.'

'Wise man.'

He hands me a pretty little box. 'For you.'

I feel my heart pattering in my chest.

'Just a little something.' He's bashful now.

When I open it, there's a beautiful charm bracelet inside. The ones that are all the fashion at the moment. The expensive ones. One of the ones that I've lusted after in the shop window every time I've passed and yet never thought I'd ever have a chance of owning. It isn't 'a little something' at all.

I gape up at him. 'It's too much.'

'No,' he says. 'I want you to have it.' He clears his throat, lowering his voice so that Dad and Mia can't hear. 'I know we've only known each other a short while, but ... well, you already mean a lot to me. Sometimes it feels just right, doesn't it? I hope you feel the same.'

There are tears in my eyes when I say, 'I do.'

He takes the bracelet from the box and fastens the pretty glass hearts and charms around my wrist.

'I can buy you a new charm at every special occasion,' he says.

'That would be nice.'

Then, in one smooth move, I pull the piece of mistletoe from above the door that Dad so carefully positioned there under Mum's instruction. I hold it above Josh's head and kiss him deeply. His arms fold around me and I know that I want to be in this strong embrace for ever.

'Yuk,' I hear Mia say.

Josh and I break away from each other, laughing. When we look at her, she's got her eyes covered and blurts out the very same thing that I do whenever I see people kissing on television. 'Get a room!'

Josh scoops her up and the two of us hold her in a huddle.

His eyes, locked on mine, are filled with love. 'Happy Christmas, Louise,' he says.

And, do you know, I think it definitely will be.

Acknowledgements

My first book, *Let's Meet on Platform 8*, was published in 1997 and there are many people who've accompanied and helped me on my journey to this book, my twenty-fifth novel.

If it wasn't for Clare Foss, my editor at Headline, then I'd never have had my first book deal, so I will always owe her a tremendous debt of gratitude. We had some amazing years together, Clare; thank you so much for that.

In recent years it has been the fabulous team at Little, Brown who have taken over the mantle and have done wonderful things with my books. My eternal and heartfelt thanks to David Shelley, Cath Burke, Manpreet Grewal and Emma Williams. It is an absolute pleasure to work with you all. I love you for your dynamism, focus, spreadsheets and so much more.

Thanks also to my lovely agent, Lizzy Kremer, and the team at David Higham Associates. Lizzy, you have no idea just how good you are. The breadth of your skills as an agent is staggering: fabulous editorial eye, total empathy with your authors and a thoughtful negotiator. There are so many reasons why I adore you and am grateful for your ministrations. Agent of the Year, every year!

To my mum, who has always been my greatest supporter. No one is better at haranguing the bookstores and supermarkets if my books aren't on the shelves. Your love and strength of character have made me the person I am today.

To Lovely Kev, my love, my best friend, who many years ago, gave up a sensible job to run the office at Matthews' Towers. We've had much laughter and some tears along the way, but this ride has given us a great life and some wonderful memories. Love you to the moon and back. (P.S. my car needs petrol).

I'm also blessed with so many good friends who have always championed my books and who have been there for me over the years. I daren't even begin to list you all by name as it would take up pages, but you know who you are and you're very dear to me.

Last but certainly not least, I'd like to thank my dear readers. Without you buying my books and enjoying what I write, I wouldn't have had this fabulous career at all. Some of you have been with me since the very first book, some of you are new converts, but you're all very important to me. I love how you cheer up my day with comments and laughs on Facebook and Twitter. You give me the best feedback on my books. We've been lucky enough to have some great outings together and it's lovely to be able to class many of you as personal friends. Thanks for choosing to spend your time with me.

I owe so many people thanks for helping me to sustain a career in publishing for over eighteen years. I might write the words but that really is just one small part of being an author. So many other people have to come together to make up the rest of it. Without them, I couldn't possibly have done it. Thanks once again.

Right. Better crack on with the next book!

Love books? Love chatting? Love competitions . . ?

Join

Carole Matthews
and her fabulous fans online

[f] /CaroleMatthewsBooks

[t] /carolematthews

Or visit: www.carolematthews.com

To sign up for her newsletter and read the latest news, reviews, gossip and more